FOR YOU, THE READER...
A SPECIAL INVITATION

<u>Come journey with us to the
wildest frontiers of the heart...</u>

Diamond Wildflower Romance

<u>A breathtaking new line of
searing romance novels</u>

...where destiny meets desire
in the untamed fury of the
American West.

...where passionate men
and women dare to embrace their
boldest dreams.

...where the heated rapture
of love runs free and wild
as the wind!

DESIRE BECKONED

Noah sensed that the smoldering volcano within this woman would prove equal to the flames erupting inside his body. They were two rivers of molten lava on converging courses . . .

"Noah," she gasped.

Never had any man touched her so. Never had she known her body could exert such power. She wanted him . . .

"Isobel."

Breathing unsteadily, he traced a finger down the row of buttons on her bodice until he came to the gap where one had fallen away. He flicked apart the buttons on either side, widening the gap until his large warm hand found its way inside. His fingers ran lightly over her bare skin and caressed the taut, jutting peak of her breast.

"Tell me what you want, Isobel," he whispered . . .

This book also contains a preview
of the newest Diamond Wildflower Romance,
SUMMER ROSE by Bonnie K. Winn.

CATHERINE PALMER

DIAMOND BOOKS, NEW YORK

This book is a Diamond original edition, and has never
been previously published.

OUTLAW HEART

A Diamond Book/published by arrangement with
the author

PRINTING HISTORY
Diamond edition/July 1992

ISBN: 1-55773-735-5

Diamond Books are published by The Berkley Publishing Group,
200 Madison Avenue, New York, New York 10016.
The name "DIAMOND" and its logo are trademarks
belonging to Charter Communications, Inc.

PRINTED IN THE UNITED STATES OF AMERICA

10 9 8 7 6 5 4 3 2 1

For Sylvia Johnson

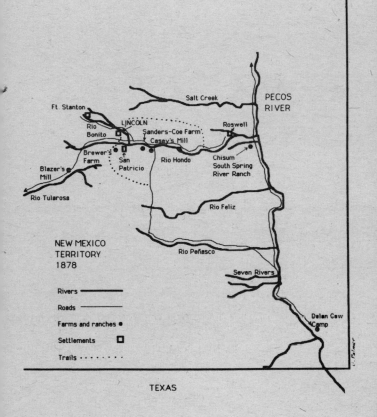

NEW MEXICO
TERRITORY
1878

Rivers ———
Roads ———
Farms and ranches •
Settlements ☐
Trails · · · · · ·

TEXAS

Prologue

February 18, 1878
Lincoln County, New Mexico Territory

The chill of winter hung in the canyon like the breath of a dying man. Damp snow muffled the tread of the horses' hooves. The three riders did not speak, preferring instead the warmth of the cotton bandannas over their mouths and noses. Their eyes moved, darting along the worn trail, up the ridge topped by scraggly pines, and through the shadowed forest on either side. At the sound of wet snow sliding from a branch, their shoulders stiffened, and their hands twitched involuntarily toward the six-shooters at their hips.

Dapper in a brown English tweed coat and tailored jodhpurs, one rider led the way. A second, slender and tall, with a face that bore the classic lines, clear skin, and curling hair of a marble Grecian statue, rode with a quiet dignity.

The third might have been hewn from granite. He was massively built, with broad shoulders and lean, hardened legs. His rugged face, skin the color of sunbaked adobe, was visible beneath the wide brim of his black hat. A mop of dark brown hair and a thick black beard framed eyes that matched the crystalline blue of a New Mexico summer sky.

A remuda of six riderless horses and two mules followed the three leaders. Behind the stock rode three more men. Two were nondescript in appearance. The third, a slight, scrappy boy with fine brown hair, sloping eyes, and prominent front teeth, was the only member interested in speaking. A running description of his exploits—interspersed with hoots of laughter—kept the youth occupied.

As the party began the descent toward the river, a frigid wind swept through the canyon. The lead rider turned, beckoning the other two to approach.

"Dick," he called over the hiss of wind, "we'll be in Lincoln by nightfall. Have you told Buchanan about the trouble?"

Dick Brewer frowned. His classic features darkened as he glanced at the third rider. "Noah doesn't need to get mixed up in this, Mr. Tunstall. He's a John Chisum man, and you know how reluctant Chisum is to get involved."

The three rode in silence, studying the orange fingers of sunset that stretched to grasp the slice of blue-gray sky above the canyon. Beneath the brim of his black hat, Noah Buchanan scrutinized the trail, studying the faint tracks he'd been aware of all day. A group of people—a party of seven horses, he calculated—rode not far ahead.

"You'd better tell me about the trouble." His voice was deep, almost too low to be heard above the rush of the wind.

"Since you've been gone," Tunstall began, his clipped English voice rising higher with tension, "two factions have formed. I assure you, Buchanan, it was nothing I intended when I moved to Lincoln County. On the one hand, I stand in partnership with the young lawyer, Alexander McSween. He's sorting through my business affairs and advising me. I've opened a store and a bank in town. On the other side—"

"Dolan." Noah spat out the name. The devious Irish landowner had gradually been eating up the territory, forcing out the small ranchers, terrorizing the Mexicans, and charging outlandish prices in his own store.

"Yes. Jimmie Dolan. Dolan is not pleased that I opened a store to compete with his. As you know, he controls Sheriff

Brady, and he's thought to be in league with the Santa Fe Ring."

Noah nodded, half listening to Tunstall's nasal voice and half studying the pattern of the tracks ahead. The party had stopped, had spent some time resting, then had gone on at a slower pace.

He was tiring already of talk of the tension that had been straining the territory's seams since Jimmie Dolan moved in. He scanned the brow of the ridge. Coyotes would be starting their evening hunt. The woods were filled with wild turkeys, deer, jackrabbits.

"Dolan has countered me at every turn. He's caused McSween a great deal of trouble. In fact"—Tunstall paused and gazed directly at his blue-eyed companion—"this December while on their way East to settle some business matters, McSween and John Chisum were jailed."

Noah tightened his grip on the reins, his attention now focused on the Englishman. "Jailed? John Chisum?"

"Dolan put out the word that your boss had bad debts. They've required him to reveal all his properties, and he won't do it. Chisum's still locked up in Las Vegas—and not likely to be out anytime soon."

Noah scowled at the tracks. Not far ahead they left the trail and disappeared into the woods. He didn't like it. Any of it. Tunstall and McSween squaring off against Dolan. Chisum in jail. It looked bad for Lincoln County.

Reaching up, he resettled his hat lower on his head and pulled his bandanna a little higher on the bridge of his nose. As he rode onward, his hand slipped to the leather holster on his leg. His fingers, strong and brown, rested lightly on the bone handle of his six-shooter.

Chapter

1

February 18, 1878
Lincoln County, New Mexico Territory

Isobel stood, her crimson boots side by side like drops of bright blood on the snow. She stared at her feet for a moment in silence, thinking how far they had come from the sprawling pasturelands of her beloved Spanish Catalonia to this slushy trail in the godforsaken New World. Weeks aboard a wave-tossed ship; days across the Texas prairie to Fort Belknap; miles along the Goodnight-Loving cattle trail toward Santa Fe . . . and for what?

Sighing, she pulled her lace *mantilla* closer around her face, then lifted her chin and walked on through the scrubby, wind-whipped trees. Her emerald hem swept across fallen brown pine needles, the ruffle on her skirt rippling along behind.

It had happened here, she thought, near this very place. A shiver of apprehension coursed through her as she looked through the twilight at the secluded forest. Five years earlier, her father—the powerful Don Albert Matas—had been jerked from his buckboard wagon and brutally gunned down.

Isobel tightened her knotted fingers inside her ermine muff

4

and squeezed her eyes shut against the sting of tears. As a child, she had believed her father strong, invincible, impervious to the whims of fate. Yet his death, when it came, had been no more glorious than that of a cur.

Forcing away the fear that haunted her—transforming it to the more comfortable heat of anger—she gritted her teeth. Why had the lawless Americans done nothing to find her father's murderer? And not only a murderer but a thief. The killer had stolen the packet of land-grant titles and jewels that had been her inheritance—the bride-price to secure her marriage to Don Guillermo Pascal of Santa Fe.

She inhaled a deep breath of crisp pine-scented air. The anger, the betrayal, burned brightly in her heart to this day. Five years had passed, yet the pain inside hadn't healed—it had grown rancorous instead, inflamed and aching to the touch.

Shaking her head, she willed the anger into determination. She reminded herself that the five years spent managing her father's vast estates in Spain had been good ones. She had overseen lands, governed workers, and carved a faith in herself that could not be shattered. And then she had traveled to America.

Though at twenty-three she knew her hopes of marriage might appear dim, she was legally betrothed to Don Guillermo. She would see to it that he married her. She would recover her stolen inheritance as well. Maria Isobel Matas was not one to cower when faced with a challenge.

Glancing behind, she scanned the scrub-oak and twisted-pine woods. The small party of travelers who had accompanied her from Texas to New Mexico—the itinerant priest, the missionary doctor and his family, the schoolteacher—rested from the journey. Their horses grazed, tethered in a clearing a safe distance from the trail.

The delay would put them in Lincoln Town after dark—too late for her to speak to the sheriff. She chose not to tarry and drink coffee. Instead she walked alone through the forest, back toward the trail, thinking.

If only her father hadn't come to the New Mexico Territory. He'd still be alive, his golden hair shining in the sunlight, his deep laughter echoing over the rolling hills of Catalonia.

Hoofbeats thudded across the damp snow, up the trail.

Highwaymen? *Bandidos*, such as the men who had murdered her father?

Her eyes darted to the trail. Alarm froze her breath. Her traveling companions were too far away to be of help, and she had left her pistol in her saddlebag.

With instinct born of terror, she melted into the gray shadows of a huge alligator juniper tree. She pulled the silk gathers of her skirt close against her thighs. Her heart beat with every thud of the horses' hooves. She leaned against the rough trunk and peered through the lacy folds of her *mantilla* down the light-dappled trail.

"Things are looking ugly indeed in Lincoln Town, Noah." A young voice. English—not American.

She cocked her head out. Three riders, faces half-hidden under red scarves. Several unmounted horses and mules behind. Other men at the rear of the party, barely visible.

"You should be glad you've been away on the trail, Noah. Mr. Chisum's a good man. You'll stay out of the worst of the trouble if you continue in his employ."

"Chisum keeps to himself, all right. Lets me run the cattle the way I see fit. But with Dolan stirring things up and conniving to land Chisum in jail, there may be a few changes around South Spring River Ranch."

The second man—the one called Noah—rode tall on his black horse. Dressed in dark leather from his muddy boots and heavy chaps to his long coat, he wore a thick beard and a black felt cowboy hat. His blue eyes darted back and forth . . . watchful, alert, missing nothing. This man—and not the other—knew of life.

"You don't suppose Mr. Chisum would take my side against Dolan, do you?" The Englishman's voice held a note of hope. "Assuming he's released soon?" Sandy hair, a porcelain-smooth face, and side whiskers lent an almost fragile appearance to the young man, who could not have been more than twenty-five years old. Isobel found herself wishing him the aid he desired.

Noah shrugged. "Chisum stays out of a fight until it touches his own back door."

He studied the trail as he rode. Isobel stared with alarm at the freshly trampled snow.

"Don't worry," the third rider put in—a slender man, with the classically handsome eyes and curly hair of picture books and statues. "Just some trumped-up charges, I reckon. John Chisum can't be pinned down for long, and it's my guess he'll come out fighting mad against Dolan."

"I expect so—" the Englishman began. A loud squawk just yards from Isobel shattered the stillness. She whirled, dropped her muff, and clutched the rugged tree trunk.

"Turkeys." Noah rose in his stirrups and searched the gathering dusk. "I had a feeling we'd run across some. How about it? You want to see if we can bag one?"

"Sure!" The slender man slid his rifle from his saddle scabbard and spurred his horse. "Coming, Tunstall?"

"No, thank you." The Englishman beckoned the three riders behind the stock. "But go on—all of you. Perhaps McSween's wife will cook it up for us when we get to Lincoln."

As the men set off through the trees toward the nearby ridge, Noah glanced aside. His gaze fell upon Isobel. He blinked once. Reining his horse, he let his unknowing companions ride on. His eyes narrowed. He raked them up and down the young woman. Emerald gown, red ruffles, lace *mantilla*, ermine cape. Then he focused on her face.

Her breath went shallow. His bright blue gaze memorized her hazel eyes, her nose, the high curve of her Spanish cheekbones, and her lips . . . he lingered on her lips.

"What have you there, Buchanan?" the Englishman's voice rang out.

Noah looked at Isobel an instant longer, as if to confirm the strange apparition in the woods. She straightened, trying to swallow the dry knot in her throat.

This rough man might do anything. Yet there was something in the way he looked at her. Or perhaps it was the way he held the reins in his hands . . . gently, expertly, as if he were an *artista* and not a cowboy. She had seen the hands of a poet, and this man's hands—though large and strong—showed no malice.

He turned in his saddle. "I thought I saw something in the brush," he called to the Englishman. "There's nothing here."

Glancing at her one more time, his eyes flashed with . . .

what was it—warning? Then he spurred his horse and thundered through the woods and was gone.

Isobel licked her wind-parched lips. Her eyes focused on the nearby ridgetop. At that moment she saw what the others had *not* seen. Armed horsemen—forty or fifty of them, she calculated quickly—guided their horses down onto the trail from the ridge.

"Tunstall!" A shout rang out to the lone Englishman not far from the tree where Isobel hid. "That you, Tunstall?"

"It is I." He reined his horse. "Who's there?"

"It's me, Jesse Evans, and Rattlesnake Jim Jackson—and a whole posse Jimmie Dolan sent to round you up. He's made us deputies." The riders advanced to within twenty yards of Tunstall, filing down the trail. Isobel saw they would meet directly in front of the big juniper tree.

"Come ahead, Tunstall," the man called Rattlesnake commanded. His heavy jaw and wide nose were coated with the blue light of the setting sun. "We ain't gonna hurt you."

"What is it you want, Snake?" Tunstall kept riding, even though the men facing him threw up their rifles so the stocks rested on their knees. Isobel shook her head, willing the Englishman to stop and draw his own rifle. Didn't he see that these men meant to harm him?

Snake urged his horse forward. "Not now," Isobel heard him mutter to Evans. "Let's wait until he gets nearer."

She clutched the tree trunk. Her *mantilla* buffeted her face. She must warn the Englishman! At that moment Tunstall's companions burst among the unmounted horses. They whinnied. Scattered.

"Take cover, Tunstall!" Noah shouted. "Head for the trees!"

"Now!" Snake swiftly raised his rifle-sight to his eye and fired. The bullet slammed into Tunstall's chest. He jerked backward and dropped from his horse to the frozen ground.

Evans leapt from his own horse and ran to where Tunstall lay in a heap. Men cheered. Evans jerked Tunstall's revolver from its holster and shot the Englishman in the back of the head. Then he turned the gun on the dead man's horse and pulled the trigger.

The other men in the posse crowded forward, a mixture of

triumph and horror written on their faces. Evans cocked back his head and looked from Snake to the men around him. "With the two empty chambers in Tunstall's gun, the judge'll think he fired first."

Snake smiled, his heavy jaw jutting forward. "Good idea, Evans."

"Let's go round up the rest of Tunstall's men and give them the same medicine!"

Trembling, Isobel watched as Evans remounted and rode away. Four men—including Snake—remained. They stretched out the Englishman's body and wrapped it in blankets. Chuckling as if it were a joke, Snake pillowed Tunstall's head on a folded overcoat. Then he laid the horse's head on the Englishman's hat.

"This is—" Isobel whispered, icy fear melting before crackling rage. "This is abominable." And suddenly she saw her father—lying just as Tunstall now lay—murdered. Golden hair matted with his own crimson blood. His laughing mouth transformed into a grimace of horror. Slain with no one to defend him.

As she raised her head, the wind caught her lace *mantilla*, tugged it from the comb, and whipped it across the trail like a dancing white butterfly. She caught her breath. Snake's pale eyes darted up, then narrowed. A frown creased his face. He straightened, spat, and stepped over the body of Tunstall.

"Don't move, señorita." His voice dripped with contempt. "Hey, fellers. Looks like we got us a Mexican. There—behind that juniper tree."

Isobel swallowed the last of her fear and touched again the raw, stabbing wound of her father's death. As if on cue, the familiar anger flowed through her. If she, too, must die, she would die bravely. Lifting her chin, she stepped from behind the tree and moved out onto the shadowed trail.

"Yo—" She stopped as the men turned to her, their eyes wide. Forcing herself to think in English, she opened her lips. "I have seen the murder. I curse you—*asesinos*—assassins!"

"I'll be damned!" Snake whisked his rifle to his shoulder. Before he could pull the trigger, a horse thundered across the trail. Its rider swept Isobel from the path of a bullet.

"You're dead, you Mexican bitch!" Snake's voice rang out. "I swear I'll kill you!"

"Get down, get down!" Noah Buchanan rode through the trees, his head low against raking pine branches. Isobel crouched in front, barely able to breathe for the steel band of his arm around her waist. "Keep your head down. We'll ride till we lose them."

She twisted in his arms. His mouth was hidden by the red scarf, but his blue eyes burned in the darkness. "Who was the Englishman?"

"Damn." The man's breath was hot against her ear. "They got Tunstall, didn't they?"

"Rattlesnake killed him," Isobel hissed over her shoulder, her anger returning.

"Quiet!" Noah's leather-gloved hand clamped across her mouth. "Didn't you see how many were in that posse? Are you crazy, ma'am? They're all over these woods now."

She shook her head free from his hand. She, crazy? This man was *loco* the way he rode his horse through the forest as though he were possessed of sight in the darkness.

"There were two who did it—Rattlesnake and Evans," she said. "Snake rode forward first and shot your Englishman. Give me your rifle and horse. I saw the man—I shall make him pay!"

"Whoa, there." Noah reined his horse to a halt in the shadow of an overhanging sandstone lip. He sat breathing heavily for a moment, then lowered the bandanna to his neck. "Give you what?"

"Your horse—your rifle." She turned in his arms and stared at the bearded face beneath the black hat. "For revenge."

His eyes went deep, searching her face, denying the final word from her mouth. She saw concern written across them—a gentleness that should have been embarrassing to a man of such immense size and power.

"Revenge," she repeated. "It is what I seek."

He didn't answer. But the softness in his eyes seemed to grow.

The man was a contradiction. Raw male strength and an undeniably ruthless self-confidence emanated from every pore. Yet his eyes held the tenderness of a child.

As if words were not necessary between them, she could feel a deep pain that rose out of him and mingled with her own. She sensed that he understood what witnessing the murder had done to her. Unspeaking, he beckoned the ache in her heart, called it out of hiding.

Around her all was suddenly calm—the wind, the horse, the trees, her pounding heart. And the man, gently summoning her hurt . . . the brutality she had witnessed, the blood, the utter emptiness in her heart . . . her father. She fought to keep her anger burning.

Without a word he stripped away the protective layers she had built so carefully. His blue eyes laid her anger to waste, and all he left her was the raw pain.

Covering her face with her hands, she folded inward. Tears ran down hot cheeks, ran between her fingers, soaked through her gloves. Her stomach muscles tightened. She pressed a knotted fist against trembling lips.

Then warm arms came around her, drawing her into a dark cocoon. A place with the scent of worn leather, dust . . . and the trace of something undefined . . . a muskiness that hinted of bare male skin beneath the rough flannel shirt against her cheek.

"Now there, little lady." His voice was low, murmuring against her ear. "Revenge never did a lick of good. Those men are going to pay for what they did one way or another. You put everything you saw right out of your head, hear?"

He stopped and lifted his head, listening. "The woods are clear. The posse's gone to Lincoln to tell Dolan they've done his dirty work. . . Listen, I rode past your people. I'll take you back. You'll be safe."

He turned his horse in the direction of the trail. The rhythmic gait eased the tension in his shoulders. Brushing fingertips across her eyes, she focused on the silhouettes above. Piñon, cedar, juniper. A hawk drifting overhead. The trace of cloud.

The horrors of the evening began to drain away. Her numbed senses came to life. There was a velvet silkiness about the darkness that enfolded the horse and its two riders. She drank in the stillness, the quiet.

Noah's arm shifted, still tight around her. His thumb

pressed just beneath her breast. A swift and unfamiliar sensation coursed through her. Instantly alert again, she saw herself draped against the warm man, this stranger. She was conscious of his thighs, lean and hard, against her own; his broad chest, solid as granite against her cheek; his heart, beating strong in her ear.

She recognized with a start this highly improper—highly dangerous—situation for a woman of her position. The man had rescued her and now—by all that was right for one of his lower station—he should remove his hand from her waist. He should stop . . .

She closed her eyes. His breath stirred the hair on her neck, where her *mantilla* normally would have lain. His hand . . . each individual finger . . . warmed the skin beneath her breast. . . .

Her head snapped forward. She straightened away from him. Clearing her mind of the unfamiliar thoughts that had usurped it, she forced logic to reassert itself. She must get back to her horse, her rifle. The lawmen of Lincoln County had failed to bring her father's killer to justice. Now she had seen some of them—men who claimed to be deputies of the law—ruthlessly murder another man.

Something must be done.

The horse picked its way up the hill. Noah watched the moon rise over the ridge above the pines. He had to take the woman back to her party and rejoin the men. No doubt they would have regrouped after Dolan's posse cleared out.

Damn Dolan and his lawless ways. John Henry Tunstall had been a good man. And young, barely over twenty. Now all hell would break loose. No doubt the lawyer Alexander McSween would go after Tunstall's killers.

He shifted in the saddle and let his arm relax around the woman's slender waist. She held herself on the horse pretty well, he thought with mild surprise. Her straight back and raised head indicated years of training. That strange accent . . . Spanish. But her hair was golden in the moonlight. It didn't fit with his image of a señorita.

Of course, she looked the part of a rich Spanish doña— shiny green dress all ruffled with red lace, red button-boots, jeweled tortoiseshell comb keeping her dark blond hair in place. Proud and noble.

There was something about the way her long neck curved into her shoulders. He gazed at the moonlight silvering the silken gold ringlet that curled down her back. If he took out her comb, the whole mass of hair would come tumbling down. Its mysterious, spicy scent would waft out into the air and—

"There is my party, *vaquero*," she spoke up, wondering why the cowboy had seemed to lose his way. "Beside that fire."

Noah cleared his throat and turned the horse. Well, he'd been on the trail with John Chisum's cattle for months now—what else could be expected of a man who found his arms wrapped around a fine-smelling lady?

He peered through the trees. Tunstall's men were gathering at the fire. There was Dick—Noah's own closest friend and Tunstall's foreman. And the others . . . Billy Bonney, Middleton, Widenmann.

"Miss Matas!" A young spectacled gentleman hurried toward the horse as Noah guided it into the clearing. "We've been so worried. Thank you, sir. I'm sure Miss Matas's uncle will reward you for risking your life—"

Noah held up his hand. "No problem."

Isobel glanced back at the bearded man. So calm his face was, always so controlled.

"Isobel, are you all right?" Susan Gates rushed to the horse's side, her pale face almost ashen in the moonlight. "When we heard the shots, I was scared to death you were down on the trail."

Isobel's expression softened at the schoolteacher's concern. "I was walking when the men came to kill the young Englishman."

"You saw the whole thing?" one of Tunstall's men asked. "You saw who shot Tunstall?"

Noah slid off his horse and lifted his hands. Isobel slipped into his arms, but when her feet touched the ground, she stepped aside. She had been close to the cowboy long enough.

The men gathered around. She lifted her head. "Rattlesnake shot first, then Evans. It is my opinion we must find the killers. Justice must be done."

"Whoa there, señorita." Noah touched her shoulder, but she shrugged his hand away. "You belong with this good man and his people. Leave avenging Tunstall to these fellows."

"But, Noah," one of the men cut in, "she's a witness. She could help us out. She could testify."

Noah bent to pour himself a cup of coffee. "Dolan's men saw her. Snake swore he'd kill her." The men looked at one another as he straightened. "The best thing she can do is get out of here. Where are you going, ma'am?"

"I travel to Lincoln Town to speak with the sheriff."

"Someone murdered Isobel's father near this place five years ago," Susan Gates explained in her soft voice. "She's come to find out who did it and to see that he pays."

Silence filled the clearing.

At last Noah took off his hat and rubbed the top of his head. Isobel was not surprised to see in the firelight that the man wore a frown of concern on his face. At least, she thought it might be a frown, somewhere beneath the thick black whiskers. His eyes reflected the blue of the fire's flame, and his brown hair was thick and full. He turned his gaze on her face, and for a moment neither spoke. Then he let out a deep breath.

"If you're going to Lincoln, you can bet Snake'll find you." He looked at the other men. "One of us is going to have to protect her. And maybe we can use her testimony. . . . How about you, Dick? Your place isn't far from here. She could stay there with you until the trouble blows over."

Dick Brewer looked away, his light gray eyes troubled. "They killed John, Noah." His voice was low. "It's not that I wouldn't protect a woman, you know that. But I was Tunstall's foreman and his friend. I'm going after them."

"We're all going after them!" A shorter young man—a boy with down-turned eyes and crooked teeth—elbowed forward. "Hell, Buchanan, you can't expect one of us to babysit the señorita! You're not a Tunstall man, and Chisum's in jail. Why don't *you* protect her?"

Noah coughed into his tin coffee cup. "Not me, Kid. I've got papers to deliver to Chisum and my own business to attend to. If you think I'm going to—"

"But that's just it." The boy jabbed Noah's broad chest with his finger.

"You told us John Chisum ain't gonna sell you no land unless you can prove you're willin' to settle down—and knock off that reputation you carry around. Now, say you come along with this señorita—hey, what say you *marry* her? Chisum would sell you the land double-quick at that. You know how sentimental he is about families and all."

"Marry her." Noah felt the blood siphon from his face. "Billy Bonney, you're a fool. There's no way—"

"Can you be serious?" Isobel interrupted. "Never would I marry this . . . this dusty *vaquero*! I am the betrothed of Don Guillermo Pascal of Santa Fe. Nor do I need a protector. I'm a better marksman than most of the men in Catalonia. I ride like the wind. I'll go with you on this journey of revenge."

"Hold on!" Billy stepped backward from Isobel as if she were possessed. "You can't go with us. The men who killed our boss have the law on their side. And the law in Lincoln County is as crooked as that trail down there. You'd best get on up to Santa Fe and marry your rich *muchacho*."

"Not until I find my father's murderer."

"Isobel," Susan broke in, "you must consider what these men are saying. Tunstall's murderers have threatened to kill you, and you have no protectors. Why not take on Mr.—"

"Buchanan," Billy put in. "Noah Buchanan."

"Wait a minute." Noah held up his hand again. "I never offered—"

"Isobel." Susan laid a hand on the other woman's arm and gently led her from the restless crowd. "We're friends. Please listen to me."

Isobel surveyed the serious dark gray eyes, the thick red hair, the thin hand placed upon the small bosom. Yes, she and Susan had become close friends on the journey. She hadn't planned to consort with the others. They were only peasants—a poor missionary doctor and his family. A skinny schoolteacher. A traveling Mexican priest. Yet they had won her with their simple ways and light spirits.

Susan especially had opened the frozen doors to her heart. For years she had kept people away for fear of losing them—just as she had lost her father. Susan had entered slowly and moved her to bare her painful past.

"Now, Isobel, I know the killing of the Tunstall man was a

disgrace. Terrible." Susan bit at her lower lip for a moment.
"But you can't afford to lose your *own* life. You must find
your father's killer and get your inheritance back. And you
must have protection. We all know how well you ride and
shoot—but you'll never survive against fifty armed men. You
need someone who knows the land and the people around
here. You need a man who can protect you while you go about
your business—he might even *help* you, Isobel. If you won't
go to Santa Fe right away and get married like you should,
take on this Buchanan fellow."

Isobel glanced at the huddled group of men. Billy Bonney
and Dick Brewer clearly were exhorting Noah to action. Sighing, she turned back. "Don Guillermo doesn't need me now
anyway," she whispered, admitting for the first time what
she didn't want to believe. "I have nothing to offer. Legally he
should marry me. But his family is powerful, and if I push the
marriage without the dowry—"

"Then you *must* have your land. Go to Buchanan and tell
him you'll do it."

The corners of Isobel's mouth lifted a fraction. Noah
Buchanan had not actually offered to let her take him on. Yet,
it was a wise decision. She lifted her head, gave her friend a
quick hug, and hurried across the damp snow to the men.

"Very well, Buchanan," she snapped. "I'll accept you as my
protector. We leave at once."

Noah looked around at the other men. "Sure, I'll take you
on—if you'll marry me."

She gasped. *"Borrachón!* What have you been drinking?
I'm telling you that I'll allow your protection—not become
your wife. If you protect me, I'll bear witness to the authori-
ties about the murder."

"If you want my protection, you'll have to marry me." He
hooked his thumbs into the black suspenders beneath his long
canvas coat and looked appraisingly at her. "These are
Tunstall men, but I'm a Chisum trail boss. That frees me to
take care of you without getting involved in the trouble."

"No."

"Sure. We'll get the *padre* over there to hitch us up. Or the
missionary. Take your pick. I'll tell folks you're the wife I've
brought from Arizona."

"No."

"Yeah. Chisum's ranch is three days' ride from here. We'll head for Dick's place tonight. Dolan's posse won't suspect us. With that blond hair and if we dress you right, you'll be safe."

She stared at the blue-eyed man. "I am already engaged."

He glanced at the priest, who had stood quietly in the background. Then he leaned down and spoke in a lower voice. "We'll get the church to—what do you call it—annul it after a while. You know, extreme circumstances . . . marriage without parents' consent. We'll think of something. Hell, the last thing in the world I want is to be *married*. We'll keep up appearances until I've convinced my boss to sell me the land I've been after—and until the trouble blows over. Then you can go to Santa Fe and marry your *don*. I won't lay a hand on you."

"Damn, Buchanan!" Billy laughed. "I wouldn't go that far."

He chuckled. "It'll be all on the up-and-up, señorita."

She folded her arms across her breast. Did she really need this man's protection? She thought of her father—murdered so easily, despite his heavily armed guard. She thought of her future with the unseen Don Guillermo, who had not even responded to her letter of intent to journey to America. She thought of the stolen land-grant titles.

The land. That was what she wanted more than anything—to own and manage her own holdings, her own cattle. Her dark eyes lifted.

"Can you shoot, Noah Buchanan?"

"He's better than any of us," Dick Brewer spoke up. "Noah's an excellent shot—lightning-quick on the trigger. That's why Chisum doesn't want to sell him any land. Figures he's too wild."

Noah shrugged, a crooked grin lighting his face. "Well, señorita?"

"A bargain. If you swear to protect me while I search for my father's killer and regain my stolen land titles"—she could hardly believe what she was saying—"then I'll marry you and prove to Mr. Chisum that you are very *settled*. And I'll be your witness in the law courts."

He nodded slowly. "I reckon so."

"Hot damn, we got us a weddin'!" Billy slapped his thighs and hooted loudly. The other men broke into awkward guffaws. "Yo, *Padre*—pull out your weddin' sermon."

"Kid," Dick broke in. "We've got to get to Lincoln. They'll be wanting John's body. . . ."

"Shucks." The young man kicked a pinecone. "Well, Buchanan—best of luck, old man. Tell us when the first little buckeye's on the way!"

Grinning, the men mounted their horses. Dick leaned over and clasped Noah's shoulder. "It'll work out. You're doing the right thing."

The riders headed for the trail, leaving the quiet party staring after them in the darkness. Noah was the first to move. He grabbed his horse's reins and nodded to Isobel.

"Well, let's get married."

The priest agreed to wed the pair, but only after dire warnings.

"It cannot be a holy bond," he murmured. "You've only met—and the bloodshed . . . ah, well. Perhaps it's God's will. A new union, a new life begins when another life passes away." He cleared his throat. "Dearly beloved, we are gathered here tonight . . ."

Isobel barely heard him. Instead she stared down at the pointed toes of her red boots. What had she done? Minutes ago she was planning to marry Don Guillermo of Santa Fe. And now this leather-clad, brawny trailman who owned nothing but his horse and gun would be at her side every moment.

The ceremony ended, and Susan clasped her. "God go with you!" She thrust a bundle of clothing into her friend's arms. "Take these, Isobel. Wear them—and stay out of your Spanish dresses. They'll recognize you right away if you look like that."

She nodded, numb. And then the party set off. With Isobel on her bay just behind, Noah guided them down the moonlit trail. He explained the circumstances to the frightened group that had cast its lot with Lincoln Town.

Jimmie Dolan—with his store and lands—reigned in the county. He had kept the small landowners financially strapped until the young Englishman, John Tunstall, moved to the area.

Looking for investments, Tunstall started his own store and ranch at the advice of his friend and partner, Alexander McSween. Now that Tunstall had been murdered, McSween and his men would seek revenge.

The young Presbyterian missionary, Dr. Taylor Ealy, explained in turn that he had been summoned to Lincoln—along with his wife, two young daughters, and Susan Gates—by McSween. The spectacled man shook his head as his group parted from Noah and Isobel. "Looks as if we're already in McSween's war," he said quietly, "and we haven't even gotten to Lincoln."

"Just keep quiet about tonight's business." Noah surveyed the little party. "None of Tunstall's men will ever mention having seen you—or me and the señorita, for that matter. Go straight to McSween's house tonight. And Doc—you're going to have your work cut out for you."

Isobel watched her companions ride down the trail north to Lincoln Town. Noah turned his horse and set off toward the east. She guided her bay gelding behind his black stallion for a few miles until they came to an old wooden cabin with a sagging front porch.

Totally alone for the first time in her life, she followed this man who was no more than a stranger up the steps into the cold, dark house.

Without speaking, he lit two oil lamps and began to build a fire in the fireplace. She watched him work. His forearms rippled as he placed heavy logs on the crackling kindling. His brown fingers hung a large iron pot of water on the hook over the blaze. Broad back. Shaggy brown hair. Muddy boots. Leather chaps. Black suspenders. Such a common man, this Buchanan, so rugged and brutish.

"Like to take a bath?" He said it so abruptly that she took a step backward.

He walked across the room, dusting his hands on his thighs, then he pushed open a door and carried her bag into a small bedroom. "Dick keeps the tub by the wall. Water's heating."

She stepped into the back room and surveyed the narrow iron bed, the washstand with its chipped white crockery, the window fitted with paper, and a tattered red curtain.

While she waited, Noah lit the hanging oil lamp, filled the tin washtub with hot water, and shut the door behind him.

Still hardly able to believe the turn of events, she walked to the door and listened to him whistling in the other room. Dare she trust the man? She slid her revolver from her bag of clothing and carried it across the room to the tub. After setting it on a wooden table, she disrobed and slipped into the water.

Closing her eyes, she laid her head back on the high, hard rim. Steaming water thawed frozen limbs and eased aching muscles. Movement rippled behind her eyelids. Horses cantering up a trail. Men shouting. Gunshots.

She turned in the water, her legs curled. Drifting, she felt strong arms around her waist . . . gentle breathing in her ear . . .

Noah sat on a three-legged wooden stool before the fire and warmed his hands. The second pot of water had just begun to boil. He thought of the woman in the next room. She'd probably crawled into bed by now. She had to be tired, no matter how wild and hotheaded she talked.

He smiled and shook his head as he poured a large basin full of hot water and set to shaving his whiskers off with Dick Brewer's straight razor.

Good old Dick. He hoped his friend could stay out of the worst of the trouble. Of course, being Tunstall's foreman, Dick was bound to get into the thick of things. Noah peered into the cracked mirror by the iron cookstove. If Dick got hurt, he couldn't stand by, no matter what promises he'd given the señorita.

Of course, the way she acted today, he'd probably have trouble keeping *her* out of it.

He dipped his head into a second bowl of fresh water and scrubbed his scalp. She'd said her father had been murdered in Lincoln County. Who could have killed him? She was crazy to come after the killer all by herself.

Of course, Noah thought, *he* was crazy to have done what he did. Marry her? John Chisum would take some fancy convincing to swallow that one. But it had seemed like a good idea at the time. Billy the Kid's idea, he remembered wryly . . . *loco*.

He took off his shirt and pants and soaped himself down. Trail dust was getting a little old. He'd be glad to settle down and fix up his own cabin. Then he could really begin to make his dream come true.

He toweled off and stared for a long time at the flames, thinking of the small packet he had brought in his saddlebag from Arizona. Pens, ink bottles, notebooks. Soon he'd start to put down the thoughts he'd been having for years. Stories— like the ones he had read as a boy. Only his would reflect the world he knew. Trail rides, roundups, cowboys. The life of the West was passing, and he wanted to capture it before it faded completely from memory.

Tossing the towel onto the back of the chair, he lifted his head. The thought of writing sent him searching Dick's cabin for paper. Maybe he'd start right now. He'd write about the incident today—the señorita and the Dolan gang.

Dick never kept paper . . . maybe in the bedroom. He hesitated at the door, then eased it open. He looked first to the bed, but it was empty. The thought struck him that she'd run off. He turned to the tub.

The sight made him suck in his breath and take an involuntary step forward. The woman lay curled in the water, asleep. Her pale lids were closed, and a fan of dark lashes lay on each cheek. Her chin was tucked into the pearl white hill of her shoulder. Long golden hair floated around her shoulders and lay against her slender arms.

His breath ragged, he took another step toward the tub and let his gaze roam down her. Soapy water half covered her breasts. They were full and round with dark tips erect in the chill air. One hip rose out of the water. Her long legs curled against her.

He was staring at her pink thigh when she turned just a little. A soft moan escaped her lips.

Isobel blinked twice, trying to focus. She felt light, serene. She looked up and turned her head. Where was she? At home . . . at her uncle's *casa* near the fort . . . on the trail?

A figure, outlined in light, stood above her. She stared at the stranger unabashed. His strong, clean jaw was squared with tension. Moisture glistened on his massive bare chest. His hair shone a damp blue-black. His sapphire gaze penetrated.

She shifted again and lifted her hand to her eyes, trying to clear the vision, but he was still there—this most stunning man she had ever seen—still standing before her. She shook her head.

"Who—who are you?" Her voice was husky in the night air.

"I'm Noah Buchanan," he answered. "I'm your husband."

Chapter 2

"Noah Buchanan?" Isobel involuntarily leaned forward, grasping the sides of the tub for support. The action brought her breasts into full view. Her long hair clung like a damp cape of golden silk to her bare shoulders.

Noah's breath caught in the back of his throat. Her hazel eyes widened, then flashed with indignation as she slid down until the water lapped at her chin.

"Buchanan," she snapped. "The towel. Please."

He looked at her a minute longer, then took his time sauntering to the bed.

As he fetched the length of white homespun, she tried to sort through the mental images she held of the man who had become her protector. Shaggy black beard, dusty denims, travel-worn leather.

His massive frame reappeared over the tub.

"You don't look the same, Buchanan," she said.

"I shaved. Makes a world of difference on a man."

Though he spoke in a slow drawl, his blue eyes sparkled as they flicked down her body when she lifted to jerk the towel from his hands. Fear parched her mouth. Her eyes darted to the pistol on the table near the tub. Its pearl handle beckoned.

"Turn around, Buchanan." Her voice was even, low.

He looked as if he were about to speak, then lifted his dark brows and did an about-face. A moment later he heard a single word in a deep throaty voice. "Now."

An invitation? He didn't think so. When he turned, his eyes met the business end of a pistol leveled at his heart. For a moment he couldn't reconcile the two images—the dripping, wild-eyed woman who'd leapt from the tub and now stood grim-lipped before him, and the feminine beauty in the water.

"Take your hungry eyes away from me, señor!" she hissed, cocking the gun for emphasis. "Stay away from Isobel Matas, or you'll taste hot lead for your supper."

"Whoa." He took a step backward and held up his hands. "Just calm down a minute. I didn't mean any harm by walking in on you. I was looking for some paper."

"Paper?" She cocked her head. "Why paper?"

He didn't answer.

"Why paper?" Her fingers tensed on the pistol handle.

"Damn it—I wanted to write something down." With a movement swifter than the strike of a rattlesnake, his hand shot out and knocked the pistol from her grip. A blast of flame and smoke erupted from the barrel. The hanging glass lamp shattered. The gun clattered across the wooden floor. As the light died, he grabbed her arm and jerked her against his chest.

"Don't ever pull a gun on me again, you hear?" he growled. "I don't take kindly to that sort of thing under most circumstances. But when I'm unarmed and someone I've taken an oath to protect draws on me, that's downright—"

"Let me go!" She tried to keep the note of hysteria from her voice, but the nearness of this rough man, the heat of his naked chest pressing hard against her damp breasts, the raw scent of his skin sent a fear plunging into the core of her stomach like the edge of a jagged knife. "I demand to be free!"

He stood rooted to the sagging plank floor. His heart thundered. His jaw felt rigid with tension. The vixen's face was shadowed, but the moonlight had slipped in through the ragged red curtain and lit her hair with a soft glow. Her body, trembling against his, suddenly felt frail, fragile.

The fingers that had clamped over her arm encircled the slender limb and overlapped his thumb. The hand that held her waist pressed tightly to him was damp with the moisture from her bath. Her small palms pushing at his bare chest had no more strength than the wind. Her breath, warm on his neck, was tremulous with fear . . . fear of him.

Relaxing his shoulders, he let out his breath and shook his head.

"I'm not going to hurt you, Isobel." He eased his grip on her waist and loosened the hold on her arm. "I told you that. I made a vow in front of Dick and Billy and the boys."

He stared into her eyes, wanting her to understand the importance he attached to his word.

"John Chisum says," he went on, "if you want to get to know a man, find out what makes him mad. You just got to know me pretty damned well."

She swallowed, searching his face for the meaning behind the words. She had never seen such anger in a man. Anger that flashed in his eyes like a blue flame, then melted into a gentle pool. Anger that made him jerk and shake her, then softened his voice almost to a whisper. Anger that lasted no more than a moment—and then vanished in a breath.

"As to wanting to be free," he was saying, "you're free as a bird, señorita. As far as I'm concerned, you can high-tail it to Santa Fe tonight, and no one will know the difference."

"I cannot do that. I must go to Lincoln Town."

"If you're going to Lincoln, you need a sharpshooter by your side. But I'll tell you something, lady. You draw a gun on me again, and you can say *adiós* to the best shot west of the Pecos."

"The best shot west of the Pecos?" She tossed her head. "I shall have to see that to believe it, señor."

The moon kindled a silver flame in his blue eyes. Aware she hadn't moved away from him, he sensed strength surging into her with the rise and fall of her breasts. Newfound resolution set her fine jaw.

"Stick around Lincoln County and you'll see it," he said. "I can outdraw any man in the territory—including the Kid. But that's not my occupation of choice. It's not what I aim to do with myself from here on."

She stepped aside and tightened the linen towel. "And what do you aim to do with yourself, Buchanan?"

He grinned at the odd way her Spanish tongue spoke the cowboy phrases he used so casually. She had tilted her head up a little, and the moonlight caught her cheekbone, defining the high curve and sparkling the dew on her lips.

"I aim to take you straight to John Chisum the minute he gets out of jail." He watched a drop of water make its way down a slender golden tendril and hang like a diamond against her forehead. "I'll introduce you as Isobel . . . no, Belle. Belle Buchanan—a slip of a lady I met and married in Tucson. How's that?"

"My name is Isobel Matas."

"You'd better be Belle Buchanan if you don't want Snake Jackson after your hide. You're an American from Arizona. And you're just the shyest, quietest little thing Lincoln Town has ever seen."

"If I'm to be Belle Buchanan, quiet and shy for your John Chisum, you had better be the fastest gun west of the Pecos—or your little *desposada* will change swiftly into Isobel Matas, the fastest gun in Catalonia."

Noah scratched his chin for a moment, suppressing a chuckle. He'd tangled with a few women in his time, but he'd never met one as sure-talking, high-strung, and mule-stubborn as this young Spanish gal. Nor had he run across any quite as pretty. Pretty but ornery, he thought. He'd have his work cut out breaking her in.

"You put on your shyest little smile," he said, tilting her chin up with the crook of a forefinger, "and I'll keep my trigger finger ready. We'll settle up the matter of my land and my cabin first, and then we'll check into this question of your father."

"My father first." She brushed his hand aside. "We'll find my father's murderers first. Then we may speak to your Chisum."

Noah felt his hackles rise again. Was he going to have to argue every tiny detail with her? "We'll ride for South Spring River Ranch *first* and see if Chisum's out of jail. I want to let this trouble over Tunstall's death die down a little before we hit Lincoln Town and start poking around."

"I've waited five years," she said evenly. "I've traveled

many miles. I'll wait no longer. Now, go, Buchanan. Leave
me to sleep. I must speak to the sheriff tomorrow."

"For your information, Sheriff Brady deputized the posse
that rode down on us today. Sheriff Brady gave a lawman's
badge to Snake Jackson—the man who shot Tunstall in cold
blood. Sheriff Brady's a Dolan man. You ride into Lincoln tomorrow and you'll be the one eating hot lead for supper."

He headed for the open door, but he paused with his hand
on the latch. "And it's Noah . . . *Noah* to you . . . not
Buchanan. I'm your husband, don't forget."

As he shut the door behind him, Isobel sagged against the
bed frame. No, she would not forget the man was her husband.
How could she? If she chose to stay in Lincoln, he'd be with
her every moment. Ordering her around, barreling into things,
insisting on his own way in every situation. He was a bull, she
thought. Rough and unrefined. Headstrong and stubborn.
Powerful.

Sliding onto the thin, lumpy mattress, she closed her eyes.
Instantly he filled her mind. The firm bronzed plane of his
bare chest, the brown flat circles of his male nipples, the solid
muscle of his shoulders. She shifted uncomfortably. Again she
felt the blood-stopping grip of his hand on her arm, again the
gentle curve of his finger beneath her chin.

He was a bull. Once more she forced the thought into her
mind. Brutish and forceful. So unlike the sleek portrait of her
betrothed, Don Guillermo Pascal of Santa Fe.

Her eyes opened. She slid off the bed, scampered around
the scattered shards of the broken glass lamp and rooted
through her saddlebag until her fingers closed on the jeweled
oval pendant. Lifting it high into the darkness, she dangled it
over her head.

Here was the *torero* who could easily defeat the bull! Here
was the nobleman of Spanish blood who could outwit the
roughshod cowboy of unknown heritage. Here was a true
man.

She made her way to the window and drew back the tattered
red curtain. Prying open the golden locket, she studied the familiar features. Strong jutting chin, firm lips, aquiline nose,
deep-set brooding eyes, a shock of black hair falling across his
forehead.

Guillermo. With his thrown-back shoulders and finely tailored frock coat, he was truly an excellent example of a Spanish don. For so many years now . . . ten, eleven? . . . she'd known this man would become her husband. She'd been prepared and educated for that life, for the grace and elegance that would be her lot.

Guillermo Pascal owned a sprawling hacienda, a stable of fine Arabian horses, ranchlands that stretched across many miles in the northern half of New Mexico Territory. He was wealthy; he was of noble breeding; he was Spanish; and he was hers.

After snapping the locket shut, she slipped the golden chain around her neck and padded across the floor to the bed. She glanced down at the fragments of shattered lamp, knowing she should sweep them up, but Isobel Matas had never touched a broom in her life.

Her father had had nobler plans for her. Her mother had brought her up to be served—not to be a servant. Someone else would have to sweep the glass, someone meant for menial tasks, for the base work of the common laborer. Shrugging, she found the fallen pistol, replaced the spent cartridge in the chamber, shoved the gun beneath her pillow, and climbed into bed.

The moon was sinking and the first rays of the sun were slipping over the tall pine trees when Isobel waded out of the shallows of slumber. She fought to catch the remnants of her dream—of that magnificent man who strode through the purple-ribboned depths, his chest so broad, his shoulders so strong, his eyes so blue. Blue! Her eyelids fluttered. Guillermo Pascal's eyes were not blue.

There was a faint sound in the room, a tinkling, scraping noise. She eased onto one elbow and peered into the gray light. For a moment she saw nothing. Then a tall form next to the wall slowly moved.

Noah Buchanan. He wore his high black hat again, tilted slightly toward the back of his head. The sleeves of his plaid shirt, its blues and greens muted with wear, had been rolled to his elbows. A thick leather belt buckled with a silver clasp held up his denim trousers. In his hand he held a long stick. She frowned. A gun? A rifle?

No . . . a broom.

Humming softly, he swept the pieces of broken glass. Unaware of her watchful eye, he raked them into a tin dustpan and headed out the door. She shook her head. This *vaquero* who could knock a loaded gun from her hand, who could guide his horse through darkness, who had walked through her dreams all night . . . this cowman of the plains was sweeping.

As she started to slide from the bed, he strode back into the room and heaved the washtub into his arms. Through the open door, she caught the evocative smell of frying bacon. He sweeps . . . he draws baths . . . he cooks! Mystified, she crept out of bed and peered around the doorframe.

Noah had just reentered the cabin and was hanging the tin tub on a nail beside the front door. Whistling softly, he stalked across the narrow room—every bit the bull Isobel had labeled him. His shoulder grazed a hanging copper pot, one knee knocked a rickety chair aside, and his worn brown boots thudded on the floor.

But as he leaned over the fire, he might have been a *cocinero* in the finest kitchen in the grandest castle in Spain.

"Come, let us join our cheerful songs with angels round the throne." He sang the barely audible words as he broke six eggs into sizzling grease in the frying pan. "Ten thousand thousand are their tongues, but all their joys are one."

Bemused, Isobel eased the bedroom door shut and propped a chair beneath the handle. She wanted no accidental intrusions this time from Señor Buchanan.

But as she sorted through the meager collection of petticoats and faded skirts Susan Gates had thrust into her arms, she found herself smiling. Noah Buchanan was indeed a strange man—on the one hand, roughshod and earthy; on the other, gentle and unpretentious. Perhaps they would do well together for the few days of their marriage.

A wash of unbidden guilt crept through Isobel as she slipped Susan's petticoats over her head one by one. She had married Noah Buchanan under God's eyes—and by the hand of a priest. She studied the shining gold crucifix that hung on her breast beside the locket of Don Guillermo.

For as long as she could remember, she had faithfully attended mass, observed the holy days, recited her rosary— done everything her mother had brought her up to do. She made a weekly confession, and when her sins seemed too scant and innocent, she invented one or two to tell the priest. But this marriage that was a sham and yet had been undertaken beneath the terrible eye of God was surely a sin worthy of the harshest penance.

How would she be forced to pay? she wondered as she fastened the row of mismatched buttons lining the bodice of the blue gingham gown. Would she lose her chance to wed Guillermo Pascal? Or perhaps never uncover the truth behind her father's death? Or something worse.

"Dios mio," she whispered, making the sign of the cross on her chest. She knew she was strong. Her heart was brave. But in her mind God was harsh, omnipotent, given to anger. His sacraments were not to be toyed with. Yet she had done just that.

Struggling with the foreboding shadow these thoughts cast across the morning's bright sunlight, she slipped a pair of black kidskin boots over her red silk stockings and laced them tightly. She would make the best of the situation, she decided. She would see to it that the false marriage lasted no longer than was necessary. Noah Buchanan would remain the stranger he had been from the beginning. For a few days only Isobel would become Belle Buchanan—a golden-haired bride from Arizona, a soft-spoken, gentle woman like Susan Gates the schoolteacher.

Setting her shoulders with this resolve, Isobel brushed her hair into a tight chignon and wistfully buried her tortoiseshell comb deep in the saddlebag. The thought of facing the world without her *mantilla* was uncomfortable. To be bareheaded in public had always been considered a disgrace.

Sighing, she thought of the trunks of gowns making their way by mule train to Lincoln Town for eventual transfer to Santa Fe. Gowns of red Chinese silk, black ribbed silk, fine ivory British linen, maroon chiffon, mulberry gauze, beige satin, blue serge, violet damask, scarlet velvet, green taffeta.

There were Chantilly lace *mantillas* and silk *mantillas*, fitted jackets, hooped skirts, cloaks, silk stockings of every hue, corselets, robes, capes, blouses, petticoats, and shawls. She had packed away combs of ivory, ebony, silver, and gold; filigree pendants, pearl-drop earrings, chains, brooches, and beads.

But Belle Buchanan must wear no finery. The uneven hem, the sagging petticoats, the patched shawl, the limp cotton dress were her lot. As she started for the door, Isobel found herself wishing for a mirror.

Drawing a white woolen shawl across her shoulders, she reflected on her brilliant *mantóns* embroidered in exotic birds and flowers. How many hours she and her mother had spent selecting their vast wardrobes, picking just the right combination for a *baile* or for an interview with visitors. How they had stood before long gilt-framed mirrors turning this way and that.

Now Isobel had no way to gauge the fit of the schoolteacher's faded gown or to judge the turn of her own loose chignon. What would Noah think? she wondered.

Snapping off all thoughts of the man in the front room, she set the chair aside and pulled open the door. He stood beside a rough-hewn pine table, setting out checkered napkins, tin forks, and chipped white plates. He'd brought in an odd assortment of pine and fir branches that he had arranged in a tall tin mug. Her heart warming to this strangely gentle bull of a man, she started across the floor.

"Good morning, Noah Buchanan," she said softly.

He glanced up, stiffened momentarily, and let his gaze trail down the slender figure approaching. Like some madonna of the prairie, the woman was dressed all in soft blue with a white cotton shawl about her shoulders. The sunlight from the front window framed her, backlighting her golden hair. Her neck, bare of adornment, was long and straight, her hazel eyes clear, her pink lips moist.

"I'll be damned." He shook his head to clear the surprise and let out a low chuckle at himself. "You sure have changed. You look regular now." He could see the line of her mouth turn down, the light dim in her eyes.

"Oh, yes." She glanced at the fire and shrugged. "Susan Gates gave me the dress. It's not my usual attire."

"But it looks fine on you." He wanted to rectify his careless comment, to make her somehow understand what he'd meant. Why did the words come so hard? "You look downright pretty, Isobel. Like you belong here."

"I do not belong here."

She marched across the room and seated herself grandly on a chair whose uneven legs nearly tossed her to the floor. Righting herself with studied grace, she cleared her throat, lifted her chin, and met Noah's gaze.

"I belong at the hacienda of the *familia* Pascal in Santa Fe. The daughter of Don Albert Matas has been brought up to wear the clothing of a *marquesa*. I'm trained to manage a vast number of servants, host officials of the government, conduct *fiestas*, and bring up the sons and daughters of my husband in the tradition of our Spanish heritage."

"Servants, government officials, *fiestas*—sounds like a great life. A real humdinger of a time." He sat down opposite her and lifted the skillet from the nearby fire. "Care for some scrambled eggs, *Marquesa*?"

She bristled, but glancing at his face, she read the curve of his lips. A shock of brown hair had fallen over his forehead, framing blue eyes that sparkled with life. The tension in his bronzed arms slackened as he held the frying pan under her nose. Despite her miff at his mockery, she relaxed.

"*Sí.* I am hungry."

The cowboy deposited a spoonful of fluffy yellow eggs on her battered tin plate and eased a slab of crisp fried bacon beside them. He reached into an iron kettle and with his bare fingers pulled two steaming biscuits into the chill morning air. Tossing them onto her plate, he reached back into the kettle for a second handful. Without asking, he poured her tin mug brim-full of dark coffee, knifed a pat of butter onto her biscuits, and salted her eggs.

"God, thanks for this new day and Dick Brewer's grub." Noah closed his eyes as he spoke. "Amen. . . . Good thing Dick had his chickens penned up tight. We'd have been scrounging for breakfast otherwise."

Isobel stared in confusion. Was this a prayer? Uncertain, she crossed herself and followed his actions by spearing a forkful of eggs.

"Dick's always been a good hand at managing things." He spread his biscuits thickly with butter as he spoke. "Tunstall was right to make him foreman, you know. Dick's had education—he can read some, and he keeps the figuring up to date."

"And you? Have you an education, Buchanan?"

"The name's Noah. And the answer is 'not much.' " He took a sip of coffee. "I can read, though. Mrs. Allison taught me a long time ago when I lived at their house in Texas. Jane Allison—you ever heard of her?"

She shook her head. Her stomach had warmed with the intake of food, and her interest in his background was piqued despite her intention to keep him at a distance. He looked calm, his long body set casually in his chair, one hand waving a buttery knife as he spoke. His smile was easy and his deep laugh ready. He appeared comfortable with life, as if he had chosen this common man's lot.

"I know only my uncle who lives at Fort Belknap," she answered. "Who is this Mrs. Allison?"

"Richard and Jane Allison. He owns land around Fort Worth. They're English folks." He smiled, remembering those mist-enshrouded early days, and later the sun-filled afternoons. "They had the finest library you ever saw. Books from floor to ceiling. Mrs. Allison took a liking to me. Couldn't have any children of her own, she told me once. Anyway, she liked to take me into the library and feed me tea and little biscuits. Then she'd start reading me stories. When I got old enough, she taught me to read the books myself. I'd go in nearly every afternoon after I'd washed up, and I'd sit down in that great big leather chair she had—and I'd read. I reckon I read nearly every book in that library."

"But how old were you when you lived with Señora Allison?" Isobel could hardly imagine that his parents had turned him over to strangers. In Spain there was always family to step in and care for young ones.

"Oh, I didn't *live* with them. Mr. Allison took me in with the other hired hands when I was about six or seven. Put me to work in the stables shoveling—" He paused and cleared his throat. "Shoveling out the stalls. I didn't mind. Got to be near the horses. It was a pretty good life. I didn't leave till I was fifteen—guess that says something for the Allison family. What about you? Are you educated?"

Isobel smiled as she scraped up the last of her eggs and popped the forkful into her mouth. "Very," she said. "I attended a convent boarding school for many years in Spain. When I was quite young, my father sent me to a finishing school in France. I speak six languages—Spanish, English, French, German, Portuguese, and Latin. I'm trained in every fine art from painting to embroidery. Arranging homes is my great love."

"Arranging homes?" Noah looked up from his plate, and his eyes darted around the narrow cabin with its row of hanging tin utensils, its rickety table and chairs, its worn rag rug. "What's to arrange?"

"But furniture, of course! I have a fine collection of my own furniture arriving shortly—along with my trunks of clothing. I enjoy decorating a home, giving it a touch of refinement and gentility. But I'm certain you could never understand that, Buchanan. Yet you and I are alike in some ways."

"And how's that?" He found it hard to imagine that he and this fancy señorita with her highfalutin education could have anything in common.

"Fine books. Horses." She sat back in the chair and studied the fire. "I was away at school when the news came of my father's murder. At first I was determined to go to America immediately and avenge his death. But my mother was devastated and she knew nothing of my father's businesses. So I stayed with her—organizing the books, paying the debts, running the estate. Five years passed, and I learned that my greatest love was the land. The cattle. The horses . . ."

"Then you're a _vaquero_ yourself."

"Oh, no!" She laughed at the image of herself in dusty leather chaps and a flopping sombrero. "Not a cowboy. I'm a lady. But now my mother has remarried, and my brother is grown. My stepfather and brother fight between them for control of the estates. In Catalonia, you see, we follow the tradition of the _hereu-pubilla_. Only one child—the firstborn son—can inherit the father's property. My brother is called the _hereu_, the property owner's heir. He'll win the legal battle against my mother's new husband eventually. It's our way."

"But what about you, Isobel? What about all that work you did while your little brother was growing up? You ought to get something out of it."

A soft line of bitterness formed at the corners of her mouth. "I'm not considered worthy to hold the land in my own right—even though I brought my family through the worst years. Nothing is left for me in Spain. I can't marry—I'm already betrothed to Don Guillermo of Santa Fe. Besides, I'm too old. I'm considered a *soltera*, a spinster. So I've come to avenge my father's death and to find the man who stole my land titles."

"That's it, then." Noah shoved his chair back and poured himself another mugful of coffee. "The *land*. You want your land back a hell of a lot more than you want to marry that greenhorn don in Santa Fe."

She shifted uncomfortably. "I wish to marry Guillermo Pascal, of course. But the lands are mine—and I want them back."

"You aren't going to have them long if you turn around and marry your Pascal fellow. The Pascals are a pretty ruthless bunch. He'll just absorb your property into his own, and that'll be that. Then your job'll be to start planning *fiestas* and turning out *bambinos*."

"That's not how it will be!" She pushed back from the table and stood up. "I'll manage my own properties—land grants that have belonged to the *familia* Matas from the earliest days of Spanish exploration in the New World. And I'll not be dissuaded from that dream. Don't presume to predict my future, Buchanan. You are nothing more than a common *vaquero* who knows precious little about the life of the nobility. Now, saddle my horse, and I'll ready myself for the journey to Lincoln Town."

"Hold on a minute there." Noah leapt to his feet, reached across the table, and caught her arm. He could hear her sharp intake of breath. She trembled as she had the night before. This time he didn't relax.

"First off, a cowboy's no less worthy of respect than some land-grubbing don. You'd better get that straight right now. Second, I didn't take any oath to be a servant to the grand *marquesa*. So you can quit ordering me around. I'll saddle your horse while you wash up these dishes, but you might as well accept that we're not going to Lincoln today. We're heading for Chisum's South Spring River Ranch until the trouble dies down."

She peeled his hand from her arm. She wasn't used to having anyone talk back to her. This insubordinate cowboy seemed intent upon grabbing her at every opportunity. He was towering over her even now, his blue eyes hot and his fists knotted . . . too close.

"You may go to the Chisum ranch, Buchanan," she snapped, "but I shall not. I'm riding to Lincoln Town to speak with Sheriff Brady." Starting for the door, she paused and looked back. "And *you* may as well accept that Isobel Matas does not wash dishes."

Without looking back, she stormed into the bedroom and gathered up her saddlebags. It had been a grave mistake to take on the *vaquero*, she realized. He was trouble. His tongue was too quick, his head too stubborn, and his hands too swift. When he had come into her room the night before, she had found him easy enough to look at. In fact, his thick brown hair and blue eyes were somewhat pleasing . . . more pleasing than she cared to acknowledge. And certainly he was strong and quick.

He might have made a decent companion—a protector, as she had contracted him to be. But Noah Buchanan did not seem to have the ability to behave as a normal hired man should. His willingness to sweep and cook and arrange pine branches belied his unfortunate propensity for demanding obedience and respect. The man was no servant.

She must take immediate action to sever their ties.

Hurrying out of the bedroom, she saw that the ramshackle living area was deserted. The fire had been banked and the dishes set in a pot of steaming, soapy water. Her mind made up, she marched out of the cabin and shut the wooden door behind her. From the blue shadow of the porch roof she could see Noah working with the horses. He smoothed out his stallion's Indian-weave blanket and looked up toward the house.

"You get those dishes washed yet?" he called. "There's a drying towel on a hook by the fire."

She drew herself up. "I am *not* a servant, Señor Buchanan!"

He was silent a moment, his jaw rigid. Then he strode around the horse and stalked up to the porch. Leaning his well-muscled shoulder against a post, he stuck out one finger and pressed it into the soft fabric covering Isobel's breastbone.

"We have a little rule out here in the West. Very simple. It's called 'I cook, you clean.' Now, Dick has let us use his cabin, and we're leaving it the way we found it. That's another rule we have out here. You got that?"

"And in Spain we have a rule also. 'A woman of property does not wash dishes.' "

"As I recall from what you told me, Miss Matas, you don't *have* any property. And you'd better get it into your head that you're not in Spain anymore. This is the American West and it's—"

He stopped. The haughtiness had drained out of her face, leaving an expression of defeat. Her brow furrowed as she focused on the distant ridge. A tendril of hair had slipped from her bun and lay curled on the shoulder of the faded blue dress.

At that moment he saw her as she saw herself: fallen from heritage, power, and wealth. Linked with a mule-headed cowboy who sassed her and ordered her around. Threatened by a man who was a cold-blooded killer. Uncertain of the future she had been so carefully trained for.

"I . . . I don't know how to wash dishes." Her voice was low, soft. "It was never taught to me."

"Damn." He took off his hat and tossed it onto a stool. "Come on, Isobel. I'm an old hand at this. I'll teach you how to wash dishes."

Chapter
3

The sun had painted the New Mexico sky in brilliant oranges and reds when Noah Buchanan and his little bride, Belle, rode into Lincoln Town. The ride had been long—and mostly silent after their initial discussion over which direction to take.

Up to her elbows in soapy water, Isobel had explained how urgent it was that she begin her search for her father's killers and regain her land-grant titles. Whoever had stolen them, she told Noah, had begun proceedings of transfer in Santa Fe. The news had come not a week before Isobel decided she must hurry to America and settle the matter.

Her uncle had searched for the name of the man who possessed the papers—but his search proved fruitless. Even Samuel Axtell, the powerful governor of the territory, had been unable to discover the perpetrator of the crime. If she didn't hurry, she told him, it might be too late for her ever to reclaim her land.

Drying dishes with a red-checkered towel, Noah had finally agreed, though it was against his better judgment that they go into Lincoln. The town would be up in arms over Tunstall's murder. Rattlesnake Jackson, Jesse Evans, and the rest of the posse would be there, along with Alexander McSween and

Tunstall's men. It would be a powder keg waiting for a lighted match.

Isobel had enjoyed the ride, and she began to sense that this part of the vast, untamed territory might easily claim her heart. She and Noah had forded the Rio Hondo, a rushing river that joined the meandering Pecos some miles distant. Though winter still lingered, she could see the area was fertile. The highlands wore shaggy pines and junipers, a carpet of dried needles, and here and there a jutting tumble of bare, lichen-covered gray rocks. As they crossed the Hondo Valley with its red and purple cliffs and tall, bare-branched poplars, they began to descend to a grassland.

"You'd better get to know New Mexico if you want to run cattle out here," Noah said during their break for a quick lunch of jerky and icy-cold river water. "That plant with the spiky leaves is a yucca, and the cactus over there with the round flat sections is called a prickly pear."

Isobel nodded, intent on absorbing his knowledge. Spain looked so different from this. The cowboy was right—there would be much to learn if the territory was to be her home. "And the trees we are sitting beneath?"

"Cottonwoods." He set his water bag in the niche between two stones. "Close your eyes and listen."

She shut her eyes and leaned against the gnarled trunk. "I don't hear anything."

"Come summer, when the leaves are thick and green, there's such a loud rushing sound you'd almost swear you were near a stream."

And so they had wound their way through grasslands covered with mesquite, kochia, and tumbleweed. They rode beneath the spidery shade of naked mulberry trees and over patches thick with dried blueweed and purple thistle. Birds seemed to feel it was high time for spring, for the mockingbirds and whippoorwills, and red-winged blackbirds and meadowlarks set up a chorus that accompanied the travelers down every long mile.

"Now, you see that?" Noah pointed to a twisted vine that lay just at the edge of the widening road into Lincoln.

Isobel studied the scattered houses, her attention drawn to the utter stillness of the town. She glanced down at the vine, suddenly impatient with the lessons of nature. "It's a *sandía*, of course—a watermelon."

Noah shook his head. "We call that a *mala mujer*."

"A bad woman?"

"It looks like a watermelon vine. Pretends like it's going to offer a man a little refreshment, a little relief from the hard life on the trail. But the *mala mujer* grows only cockleburrs three inches long."

"And so it's a bad woman—promising much but delivering only pain?"

He glanced at her out of the corner of his eye but didn't respond. "There's Sheriff Brady's house on your left. Appears he's out for the evening. His next-door neighbor's a friend of mine—Mexican fellow by the name of Juan Patrón. We'll stay with him."

A tightness constricted Isobel's throat. She was here now, in the little town of her father's burial—and no doubt the home of his killer. Somehow she felt a disappointment that it was not more imposing. There were only a dozen houses or so, most of them built flat-roofed of whitewashed adobe—*jacals*, Noah called them. The road curved a little, and she could just make out a central area of finer homes and a store or two. Corrals stood near several of the houses. Most had fallow garden plots stretching out behind.

"Isobel." Noah slowed his horse and caught her mount's reins. "I agreed to bring you to Lincoln—but while we're here, you'll do as I tell you. Got that?"

"As far as I can, I'll do what you suggest." She jerked the reins out of his hands. Her horse gave a skittering jump. "But when we disagree—you're free to go on your way. Isobel Matas makes her own decisions."

"You're not Isobel Matas anymore, sweetheart. You're Belle Buchanan—and you'd better not forget it."

He guided his horse to the small adobe home. It had two front doors beneath a wide overhanging porch, a *portal*. One door had been shut and locked. It bore a handwritten sign reading *"Cerrado."*

"This house is closed," Isobel said as Noah dismounted and looped his reins over the porch rail. "The sign says so."

"That's Patrón's store. He's been a schoolteacher here and a clerk of the probate court. But when his father was killed back in seventy-three, he took over the family business."

"Seventy-three?" She slid from her horse into his arms. "But *my* father was killed in seventy-three."

He held her for a moment, studying the wide hazel eyes. Once again he was impressed with how slender she felt, how almost fragile her young body was. With all her big talk and fearlessness, Isobel clearly thought herself the equal of any man. Yet here she was, her gently sloped shoulders wrapped in a shawl, her narrow waist beneath his hands, her fine, full bosom rising and falling with every breath.

"Noah!" She caught his wrists and gripped them. "Did you hear me? My father was killed near here that same year. What happened to Señor Patrón's father? How did he die?"

As her words penetrated his thoughts, Noah began to piece together the fragments of an idea. He slipped her hand into his own and squeezed. "I've only heard the story secondhand," he said in a hushed voice, "but we may have something here. Old Patrón was murdered by a gang. Horrell, I think their name was. They hightailed it to Texas a long time ago. But if I remember right, the Horrell Gang went on a rampage killing Mexicans."

"Mexicans? But my father was from Spain."

"It wouldn't have mattered. If you speak Spanish around here, you're considered a Mexican."

"But what's wrong with Mexicans? Why would anyone kill a man for speaking Spanish?"

He shook his head. She sure was naive for one so willing to jump into the thick of trouble. He brushed a strand of loose hair from her cheek.

"Don't worry your pretty head about it, Isobel. It's just one of the ugly facts of life around here. The main thing to remember right now is that *you* are an American. You don't speak Spanish—you don't understand anything anyone at the Patrón house says. Your name is Belle Buchanan. And you're my wife."

She nodded, suddenly aware of his warm hand holding hers, his fingertips resting lightly on her shoulder. His face had grown gentle again with that soft blue glow shining in his eyes, that subtle curve to his mouth. The scent of his leather coat stirred something to life in the pit of her stomach, and she wondered at the unfamiliar pleasure of this curling sensation. He stood close to her now, his great shoulders a fortress against trouble, his warm breath on her cheek a promise of . . .

Her eyes flicked to his. She opened her mouth to speak, but before she could form words, he bent his head and pressed his lips to hers. Soft, tender, his mouth moved over the moist curves as if searching, seeking something long buried.

She caught her breath. This male kiss, the first of her life, held a heat and a pleasure she had never imagined from the perfunctory salutations of mothers and cousins and aunts. Like a tiny spark on a bed of withered, dried brown leaves, a dormant feeling burst to life with a flame that coursed through her core.

It was over as quickly as it had begun. Noah lifted his head and focused somewhere behind her. His eyes went soft with recognition, and he smiled.

"Juan!" His voice held a note of relaxed cheer. *"Buenas tardes,* old buddy. Put down your six-shooter. It's me."

"Noah? Noah Buchanan!" The young man, not much older than herself, Isobel guessed, hurried across the darkened porch and down the steps. He moved with a pronounced limp. He was a large man, stout and well-dressed in a finely tailored Prince Albert coat. "Welcome. You've been away a long time. Come in, come in."

"Juan, I want you to meet someone." Noah turned and eased Isobel under his arm. "Juan Patrón, this is Belle Buchanan. Belle, meet Mr. Patrón."

"Buchanan?" The snapping black eyes darted from Noah to Isobel. "She is . . . your sister?"

"She's my wife, Juan. My wife. We married in Tucson just before I left."

Juan shook his head, as if unable to believe the sight before his eyes. "So pleased to meet you, Señora Buchanan."

"Thank you," Isobel said softly. "It's my pleasure."

"Noah, you are the last man on earth I would have guessed to take a wife." He paused and shook his head again. "Well, I'm happy for you both. Come in, come in. You must meet my wife and family."

As they started up the steps, Isobel caught Noah's hand and

raised on tiptoe to his ear. "The murder! You must ask him about the murder."

He nodded and gave her a little squeeze. She forced her thoughts to the coming events. This man at her side was only pretending after all. The kiss had been nothing more than a signal of the role each must play as man and wife.

She brushed at her dusty skirts and tucked the strand of hair into her chignon. But the burning on her lips remained, and that strange, unbidden life within her stirred again as she watched Noah's shoulders disappear into the shadows of the porch.

"Come, come!" Smiling, Juan held the door wide. "Please meet my wife, Beatriz. She comes from the French family Labadie, who have lived in New Mexico for many generations. *Querida*, this is Noah Buchanan, back from Arizona with his new bride, the Señora Buchanan."

The bright-eyed woman tipped her head in greeting. It was all Isobel could do to keep from throwing her arms around the tiny creature. Despite her French extraction, Beatriz wore a flowered *manton* and a lace *mantilla*—to Isobel, poignant reminders of home. Tucked in her ample skirts hung a pair of lovely young children. They hid their faces and giggled shyly when Isobel bent to tousle their heads.

"Sit—Noah, señora." Juan gestured to the gathering of leather-covered, straight-backed wooden chairs. "Beatriz will prepare a meal. How many days will you stay with us? Three, four? A week or two?"

Noah chuckled and folded his long frame into one of the chairs. Like an obedient wife, Isobel hurried to his side and silently perched on a stool. "We're just passing through, Juan. I need to settle up the details of the trail ride with John and then—"

"But you do not know? Señor Chisum is in jail!" Juan sat forward on the edge of his chair. "Many things have passed since you left, Noah. Lincoln is in a terrible state. I believe there will soon be war!"

"War?" Noah frowned and took Isobel's hand. "Don't worry, Belle, honey. We'll get to the bottom of this. What's going on, Juan? And you'd better start at the beginning."

The young Mexican spread his hands wide, as if to convey

his own bewilderment. His young daughter took this as an invitation to crawl into her father's generous lap. Juan stroked the child's hair and gazed pensively at his daughter's shining braids.

"It is difficult to speak of," he said in a quiet voice. "The Englishman, John Tunstall, was ambushed and killed yesterday."

"Killed?" Noah feigned surprise.

"Many stories fly in the wind about how it happened. Most believe he was shot down in cold blood by the posse sent by Jimmie Dolan. I saw for myself that he had been shot twice—once in the chest and once in the back of the head. It's a terrible shame. The Englishman was a good man. Honest, kind."

"Dolan. That figures."

"They brought in Tunstall's body. The judge has taken affidavits from Dick Brewer and Billy Bonney. And he's issued warrants for the arrest of the men in the posse. The constable is off looking for them. A coroner's jury is taking testimony right now down at the courthouse."

"Who's named in the warrants?"

"Jim Jackson—the one they call Rattlesnake. Jesse Evans. Others. They're saying at least forty men were in the posse."

"How's Alexander McSween taking all of this?"

Juan shook his head. "You know how he is. A lawyer! So mild . . . always thinking of the law, of justice and right. He can hardly believe it. He has a houseful of guests who arrived last night not long after Brewer and his men rode into town with the news. A missionary doctor and his wife—Ealy is their name. Two young children. A female schoolteacher, Miss Susan Gates."

Isobel bit her lip to keep from asking about Susan. How had her young friend survived the trip? What was this bloodshed and terror doing to her? She could imagine the gentle creature watching with soft gray eyes the arrival and departure of angry men, the bloody body, judges, and constables.

"Tell me about Chisum." With his eyes Noah acknowledged the arrival of a painted pottery bowl filled with steaming *atole* on the long table near the company of chairs. "I need to know what to expect."

"Chisum will not get involved unless he has to—you know that." Juan watched his wife dip a gourd into the cornmeal gruel and pour it into pottery bowls. As she began ladling boiled, salted milk over the dish, he turned and winked at Noah. "You are like Chisum in that way, my friend. Stay out of the thick of trouble as long as you can, *no*? Come—we eat. I shall tell of Chisum's troubles at dinner."

Isobel followed Noah to the table, hoping she was creating the right impression. She might as well be invisible for all the attention paid her. In this family the men were treated with honor and respect. Juan blessed the food and presided over the entire meal like some grand emperor. Yet there was a blanket of warmth, a quiet love that surrounded the little home and its inhabitants.

"I shall tell you the story of Chisum's jailing as it was told to me by Alexander McSween." Juan ate as he spoke, clearly relishing the opportunity to pass along a spicy tale. Isobel wondered how he had come to obtain such facility with the English language. She dared not ask.

"This past Christmas," the portly Mexican began, "John Chisum started on a trip to St. Louis accompanied by Alexander and Sue McSween. McSween wanted to settle some legal problems concerning the inheritance of an insurance policy he had been working on for some clients. Chisum had other business to tend to—he has health problems, do I understand?"

Noah nodded but said nothing.

"When the party reached the town of Las Vegas, the sheriff took them in and held the two men without any legal papers. When he finally let them go and they were on their way again, he returned for them with a gang of ruffians. In the confusion Chisum was knocked to the ground, and Sue McSween was left crying in the buggy. The men were taken back to jail, and Sue was driven to the hotel."

"But what was the reason for their arrest?" Noah felt his ire rising at this outrage.

"McSween was charged with trying to escape with the very money from the insurance policy case he was handling! Chisum was charged with debt. I cannot imagine how they could believe John Chisum might be in debt. The truth is, you see, they wanted your boss to make a statement of all his properties. And this is the law concerning debtors."

Noah grunted and shoved his chair back from the table. "Dolan's behind all of this. I'd bet anything he set up those arrests."

"It is bigger than that, my friend." Juan gave a glowering stare to his two children, as if to warn against any repetition of the words spoken. "There is the ring in Santa Fe, you know."

"What ring in Santa Fe?" Isobel could not keep quiet. What could such an organization mean to the Pascal family and her future?

Juan leaned dramatically across the table. "The men in high places have joined together in a ring of corruption, Señora. They are taking bribes, arresting innocent men, stealing land titles."

"Who's in the ring, Juan?" Noah caught Isobel's hand and pressed it to keep her silent. "Do you have their names?"

Juan shrugged. "But it is the governor, of course. Axtell is one of the main members. Even more dangerous perhaps is the United States District Attorney, Thomas Catron. Catron is a personal friend of Jimmie Dolan. The two men are working together to take over the territory. Your John Chisum will be lucky to get out of jail."

"But McSween's in Lincoln," Noah said. "How did he get out of jail?"

"Neither of the men was allowed to post bond. Santa Fe was behind that, you can be sure. Finally McSween was taken before the judge and set free to settle his matters in the East. But Chisum refused to reveal his properties, and so he's still in jail."

"It's worse than I thought." Noah looked at Isobel. "It wouldn't hurt you to go on up to Santa Fe, honey."

"Santa Fe?" Juan's voice was tinged with surprise. "But why would your wife go to Santa Fe?"

"She's got relatives up there. A . . . a cousin." Noah glanced at Isobel long enough to catch the flash of shock and anger that suffused her face. "Would you do us a favor now, Juan, and wire a telegram letting them know that Belle is here in the territory? I may need to send her up there right away if things go from bad to worse."

"But of course." Juan stood up from the table. "I was planning to walk over to McSween's house and see what has developed this evening. I'm sure we can rouse Mr. Paxton to open his telegraph office. Will you come with me?"

"Glad to. I need to stretch my legs anyway." Noah rose and patted Isobel's shoulder. "You stay here and visit with Señora Patrón and the kids, honey. I'll send off that telegram and be right back."

She leapt to her feet, nearly upsetting her chair. "I'll go with you."

Tension tightened her shoulders. Hot anger radiated from the place where Noah had patted her as if she were no more than a dog. Such a fine husband he would make—treating his wife like that.

"I'll not be left alone, *honey*," she hissed just beneath her breath. "And if you intend to send a telegram on my behalf, I'll know what it says."

Juan chuckled. "For one so quiet, your Belle has a strong will. I'm afraid you'll have to mend your stubborn ways, Noah Buchanan—or break your wife's spirit as you break the wild horses."

Noah stood in silence, hearing the wisdom in the Mexican's words. But this arrangement was only for a few days. A week or two at the most. The woman would have to bend to his will or lose his protection. He didn't have the time or the patience to work out a compromise on everything. With Tunstall dead, Chisum in jail, and the Santa Fe ring—with Dolan at the local helm—increasing pressure in the area by the day, he was going to have his hands full.

"Stay here, Belle," he said firmly. "I'll take care of everything."

She clenched her jaw as she watched the two men leave the table and walk to the door. Like servants, the señora and her children were already scampering to clear the table and put away the food. They eyed her as she followed the men and stood silently beside the open window.

"You did the right thing, Buchanan." Juan Patrón's voice drifted across the night. "A woman is best at home with her children and her cooking and her needlework. If your new wife is not happy with that now, she will be soon. You'll see."

"I hope you're right, Patrón." Noah turned and studied the black silhouette standing against the yellow light in the window—chin lifted high, shoulders set, back straight and stiff. "I sure hope you're right."

Isobel shifted her attention from the diminishing figures to the bustling family in the Patrón's little house. The table was already spotless, its rough pine top scrubbed clean and its rows of mismatched chairs pushed beneath. A clamor of giggles and pleas arose from the kitchen. Isobel wandered across the room to the narrow door.

Beatriz Patrón, surrounded by reaching arms and grasping hands, was doling out spoon-sized portions of yellow custard. Spotting her guest, she scolded the children into silence and smiled at Isobel.

"Flan?" she asked, holding out the dish. "Is good! You like?"

Isobel shook her head. "Where is Alexander McSween's house?"

The woman shrugged in confusion. "Not speaking English."

"Señora Patrón," she said softly, weighing the consequences and wondering whether she should speak to the woman in Spanish or French. *"Donde queda la casa* McSween?"

"No, señora—*por favor!*" The woman's eyes were wide with pleading. "No! *Quedarse aquí*. You stay here . . . stay! My husband say much trouble. Trouble! *Violencia!"*

Isobel sighed as the children's patience wore thin and they swarmed their mother again. The señora gave a wan smile as Isobel made her way out of the kitchen. A cramped home, tumbledown furniture, a pair of hungry children, corn to grind, clothes to mend, dishes to wash. This was the sort of life a woman could expect in such a town as Lincoln. And, no doubt, it was the sort of life Noah Buchanan would provide for his wife.

How fortunate she would be leaving the man soon.

But again the reality of her situation fell in upon her. She sank into a chair. Even now Noah was sending a telegram to

Guillermo Pascal. It was clear that the cowboy had chosen this action to alert her betrothed in case she needed a quick shelter.

But there was more behind this sudden move. If Guillermo came to Lincoln, he could take Noah's place as her protector, as the one to help her solve her father's murder. Noah would be free of her. Free to go his own way.

But what would Guillermo's reaction be when he read the telegram? Would he come to Lincoln? And if so, what would he offer her? A chance to back out of the arrangement? Help in regaining her stolen land titles? Perhaps a life as his wife? She closed her eyes, imagining the life she had always dreamed of. A huge estate upon which to ride. Strong, sturdy cattle. A long, rambling home filled with her beautiful furniture. Gracious parties attended by local dignitaries.

Her eyes snapped open. There would be no visits by members of the evil Santa Fe Ring if she had any say. And there would be no long rides across her miles of ranchland if Guillermo had his say. Noah had been right—the Pascal family would simply swallow her lands into their own vast properties, and she would be left the mistress of a house. A house not small and shabby perhaps, but a prison all the same. There would be small mouths to feed, meals to plan, stitching to fill her days. How different would the life awaiting her really be from the pitiful struggle of the Señora Patrón?

"Señora!" A gentle tugging at her skirt caught her attention, and she sat up. Curled at Isobel's feet was a glossy-eyed little girl, her shiny black braids tumbling down her back. This was the cuddly child who had crawled into her father's lap and gazed into his face as he spoke. Seeing the visitor's eyes studying her, the child giggled and tugged at Isobel's skirt again. "*La casa* McSween *es muy cerca. Por el lado del almacén* Tunstall."

So Noah had not gone far—just beyond Tunstall's store. Isobel grinned and stroked the shiny head. "*Gracias, mi hijita.*"

The child scampered away as swiftly as she had appeared. Isobel watched the little girl join her brother in a chasing game. Their mother had come to the kitchen door and was leaning against the frame, the skirt of her apron still in her hands as she dried them.

As the mother watched her children, her eyes softened and went moist. Her lips, still full and young, parted in a gentle smile. In a moment the tiny boy came running on chubby legs, a wail welling up from his breast at some injustice his older sister had committed against him. His mother swept him into her arms, her gentle mouth ready with a big kiss, her soothing words relaxing his tense body as she nestled his tumble of damp curls onto her ample bosom.

Before she could draw the attention of mother and child, Isobel slipped up from her chair and hurried to the door. Bending to her saddlebag, she slid her pistol into her palm. She straightened, drew her shawl around her shoulders, and crept into the night. Breathing in a deep gulp of fresh air, she hurried onto the moonlit roadway leading between the town's few buildings.

A glance back at the flat-roofed house revealed a subtle transformation in what she had been so ready to term a prison. In the glow from the window, the mother and child stood holding one another, a picture of warmth and security. Home. The thick adobe walls she had thought of as a barrier seemed now almost translucent as they glowed with moonlight, their caliche whitewash gleaming. The home was clean, swept and scrubbed, the children well fed and cheerful. The mother seemed content with her lot.

Turning into the darkness, she shook her head. Would she ever find such peace with Guillermo Pascal, his noble heritage and exalted position in the Spanish community of Santa Fe? Her thoughts refused to focus and instead rambled to the face of another man. How good it had been to ride with Noah across the hills. To feel the horse moving beneath her, responding to her commands. To learn of the new land she had vowed to make her own. To drink from the fresh water of a swift stream. To lift her face to the sunlight and fill her breast with clean mountain air.

She started through the darkness, shaking off a shiver in the chill night. As she passed a building containing a store and a saloon, she peered into the smoky depths. Men leaned at a crude wooden bar, swilling liquor, men little different from Noah Buchanan. He was such a commoner, so stubborn, thoughtless.

Then why did her lips still burn from his kiss? Why did her breath catch in her throat at the memory of his hard chest pressed tightly against her breasts? Why did that live thing curl and shiver in the pit of her stomach at yesterday's image of his hand hard against her waist, his thumb locked beneath her breast, his thighs like granite against hers while he carried her on his horse away from the path of the bullet?

Worse, far worse, was that persistent picture of his face. That gentle smile he wore had somehow lodged in her brain. She could see that smile even now as she hurried down the road, her leather boots stumbling over frozen wagon ruts. There it was as he poured steaming water into her bathtub . . . and there, as he offered her a spoonful of scrambled eggs . . . and again, when he plunged his arms into the pan of dishwater and began to teach his new wife the mysteries of housekeeping. . . .

But men were not supposed to be gentle. They were *matadors, torreros*—fighting life as if it were the bull who might rip open their hearts.

She hurried on, passing the courthouse, a corral, a small home . . . fighting the sense that somehow Noah Buchanan was all these things as well. Brave, strong as the strongest bull, keen of wit, quick-tempered, bold.

She pulled her shawl over her head, as if this might somehow block the thoughts that kept forming like fluttering butterflies over a bowl of honey. She had begun to follow the curve of the road when the thunder of hoofbeats sent a shiver of apprehension down her spine. Whirling on the frost-rimmed road, she scanned the hazy horizon.

There! At the edge of town they rode, a band of men— perhaps five or six—galloping like the wind. Fear clawed at her heart. She gripped the icy pistol in her skirt pocket as she willed her numbed legs across the road.

A tumble of stones, cemented together with mud to form a rough tower, rose into the night sky like a thick, knobby finger. She ran toward it, hopeful of finding protection in its shadow.

The tower was enclosed by a low rock wall and a gate. Isobel lifted the latch and slipped around the wall into the spiky, ice-crusted grass. She peered through a narrow chink to watch the riders approaching down the narrow road. As they reached the stone tower, the lead rider reined in his horse.

He held up one hand and turned to the others. "You see that, Evans?" His breath was a cloud of white vapor.

"See what?" The other rider edged forward. "We got an ambush?"

"No, not that." The man was silent for a moment, listening. Isobel studied the familiar low-slung jaw, the wide flat nose, the yellow eyes searching the darkness. "I seen a shadow run across this road just as we rounded the curve. It was her."

"Damn you, Snake! You had us scareder than a jackrabbit in tall grass. If you don't stop seein' that Mexican gal in every crick and holler, one of us is gonna have to give you what fer."

"I ain't seein' things this time, Evans." Snake drew his gun and leveled it at the tower. "There's somebody over near the *torreón*, I'm tellin' you. It was a woman runnin' across the road—and she wore somethin' white over her head, just like that Mexican gal that seen us level Tunstall."

"You fire that gun and you're gonna have more to worry about than some Mexican. And what if she is here, anyway? Who's gonna believe some no-account Mexican over us? We're deputies of the law, don't forget. And Dolan's behind us."

Snake reached into his saddlebag and jerked out a handful of delicate white fabric. Isobel caught her breath—her *mantilla*! He draped the torn Chantilly lace over the barrel of his gun and waved it in the air.

"You hear me, señorita," he called. "I got your veil—and I'm gonna get you."

"Aw, come on, Snake." Evans spat onto the road and dug his spurs into his horse. "What is it with you and Mexicans anyway? They ain't worth half the heed you pay 'em."

Snake flipped the *mantilla* into his open hand and shoved it into his bag. "Let's go, boys. Dolan's waitin'."

But when the other men spurred their horses into the night, Snake drove his own mount hard against the wall. Isobel shrank into the shadow, huddling in the tangle of dried weeds. Suddenly her gun felt useless, frozen in her palm. This was more than shooting targets at a match, more than hunting rabbits or deer. This was real. And she was afraid.

"I know you're there, *chiquita*," he growled. "I can't see you, but you can see me. You hear my words and don't forget 'em now. I'll find you, and I'll make you wish you had never laid eyes on Jim Jackson."

She swallowed, her aching finger trembling on the trigger of her pistol as she worked to turn her unbearable fear into anger. "You'll wish you had never laid eyes on Isobel Matas," she muttered as the horse's hooves clattered across the frozen land. Clambering out of the icy ball she had formed of her body, she came around the wall and shook her gun at the retreating form.

"You just try to kill me, *maldito*!" she shouted into the night. *"Asesino!* Murderer!"

A light came on in the small house near the tower. She stalked down the roadway, her blood pulsing in her temples and her nostrils flared in rage. A rifle-toting, grizzle-bearded man burst onto his porch.

"Hey!" he shouted. "Hey—what's goin' on out here? Who you yellin' at, girl? Nobody wakes up a Huff without reason. Hey, gal!"

Without answering, she lifted her skirts and began running, her heels pounding out her anger. Her shawl fell from her head and drifted to her elbows, catching the frigid wind in its billows. Her numb toes felt as if they were rattling inside her boots. The tip of her nose stung, and her eyes watered. She passed a narrow, empty lot and then came upon the long porch of a large, low-slung building. A painted sign creaked as it swung in the crisp air.

Tunstall Mercantile, she read, stopping to catch her breath. *Dry Goods. Bank.*

The image of the man who had worn the name Tunstall seemed to rise up like a specter. She saw his young face, the blue eyes wide with an innocence rarely found in men. His voice, soft with the lilt of the English tongue. The hat, the tweed coat, the brown kidskin gloves. And then, with the shattering crash of reality, the face of Snake Jackson blotted out the other visage . . . sneering, laughing as he pulled the trigger, shouting into the wind, "I'll get you! I'll get you!"

She shivered and drew back from the sloping porch. She

must find Noah. He must be alerted that Snake and Evans and
the others had returned to Lincoln.

Grabbing up her skirts, she set off again, this time toward
the call of the yellow lights in the large adobe house a few
yards beyond the Tunstall store. A rough wood fence rimmed
the large enclosure, and horses stood in a row in front of the
house. Porchless, the building was composed of two long
wings. Several small outbuildings—sheds and a small stable
area—were scattered behind it.

Settling her shoulders, Isobel marched onto the front step
and knocked hard on the door. She waited a moment. No one
answered. She turned the handle and walked in.

The room was crowded with men, all talking at once. Their
fingers rested on holstered guns. A fire crackled in one corner,
but the men had gathered around a central table. They leaned
across it, shouting to be heard.

Isobel picked out Dick Brewer, Tunstall's foreman and Noah's friend. He was bent over a sheaf of papers on the table.
Billy Bonney had pointed his gun to the ceiling and looked as
if he might fire it at any moment to silence the crowd. Juan
Patrón, his portly frame wedged among the others, was shouting, red-faced, at Dr. Ealy, who was arguing back from his
perch on a finely carved chair at the table.

But where was Noah? She scanned the room again. Perhaps
he had gone to send the telegram. But Patrón was here in the
house. Perhaps . . . a movement near a far window that faced
the road caught her attention.

From the wide sill Noah sat watching her. His blue gaze
was soft. His black hat crowned the crook of one knee.

As she approached, her shawl sliding unnoticed to the floor,
Isobel studied the patch of bronzed chest where Noah's plaid
shirt came together. There was a trace of dark hair she had
never noticed before. Why hadn't she seen the way his jaw an-
gled up, hard and square? Had his brown hair always had the
sun-paled streaks she now saw? Had his denim trousers always hugged his thighs so tightly?

Her tongue darted out to moisten her dry lips. Her mouth
felt parched. Her heart thundered in her breast with a quicker
beat than it had in the presence of danger.

He was wearing that gentle grin, a little higher at one corner than the other. She stopped at his side, but he did not move from the sill. Fingering a loose button on her bodice, she shrugged.

"I came." Her voice was low.

He nodded. "I was waiting for you."

Chapter
❧ *4* ❧

"You knew I would come?" Isobel leaned against the wall, aware for the first time of her damp hem, her muddy boots, her fallen shawl, aware that the arguing men on the other side of the room had not taken note of her arrival, aware that Noah's eyes had never left her face. "Then why did you tell me to stay at Patrón's house?"

"I'm supposed to protect you, remember?" Noah saw the color slowly returning to her face. She was breathing as if she had seen a ghost. "Did Snake Jackson and his boys pass you?"

She nodded. "Do the others know they're in town?"

"Not yet." He jutted his chin at the boisterous group around the desk. "They're too busy arguing over how to counter Dolan's latest move. Sheriff Brady has appointed Dr. Appel from Fort Stanton to perform a postmortem on Tunstall's body. The doctor's a Dolan man, and he's sure to support the posse's claim that Tunstall fired first."

She frowned. "I should go forward with my testimony right now."

"No." He sat up and caught her wrist. "Don't say anything, Isobel. Keep out of it for now. You'll do your part later on."

"Have you sent the telegram to Santa Fe?"

"Yes."

"Why? Tell me why you did that. I'm not ready to go."

"If things blow up here, you'll need a place to run to. I won't be able to protect you if this situation gets out of hand. These men have murder in their hearts. And Dolan's gang of ruffians will do anything for their boss. Did they see you?"

Her eyes shot to the tightening knot of angry men on the other side of the room. "Snake Jackson saw me as I ran to hide near the tower."

He lowered her beside him onto the sill. He swung his legs to the floor, his boots thudding on the bare pine slats, his palms resting on his knees. "Tell me what happened."

"I was hidden in the grass behind the wall when Snake stopped his horse. The others mocked him for thinking he'd seen me. They rode ahead, but again he swore to kill me."

Noah scowled and ran his fingers through the thick hair that had fallen across his forehead. It struck him that the woman was more exhilarated than terrified by her second brush with danger in the past two days. Her hazel eyes had gone green in the firelit room, and they studied him as if he were a strange, unworkable puzzle. Wavy strands of dark blond hair had escaped her bun to brush the arch of her brows. That button she had been fooling with had dropped off, and he could see the dark shadow where her breasts came together.

Damn. He ran the brim of his hat between his thumb and forefinger. Isobel was probably going to get herself shot by Snake Jackson one of these days. The man had a reputation for killing—him and Billy the Kid over there. Noah glanced up in time to see the Kid elbow his way to the forefront of the crowd, his gun waving in his hand as if it were an extension of his fingers.

Noah shook his head and focused again on the señorita. She was staring at her knotted fingers. They were long and slender, and he remembered how they felt sliding tentatively up his back when he was kissing her. The kiss . . . now, *that* had been a real mistake. A bigger mistake than agreeing to take her with him. A bigger mistake than treating her like some ignorant greenhorn at Patrón's house and thinking she'd obey. A bigger mistake than teaching her to wash dishes.

He shut his eyes, remembering the transformation of her

face from anger to hesitation to pleasure as she rolled up her sleeves and dipped her arms into the steaming soapy water. She'd chatted away the whole time she was washing. Something about a horse she'd had back in Spain—about how it had won a bunch of awards for jumping, about how she'd ridden it all over her father's estates, about how it could herd cattle and swim rivers and find its own way back home. She'd talked on and on, unaware of the effect her lilting voice had on him. Unaware of the way her full bosom, barely contained in the dress of a smaller woman, mesmerized him. Unaware of the tingle that shot up his arm every time she handed him a dish to dry and her wet fingers touched his.

The kiss had come from that: the touching, the story about her horse, the way she'd gotten inside his mind. Every mile of the long road to Lincoln had burned a picture in his thoughts. It was a picture of him holding Isobel in his arms, savoring the press of those luscious breasts, drinking in the honey of her ripe lips.

And now here she was beside him, her thigh curved against his, her lips still beckoning as if that one kiss had not been more than enough to get him into trouble.

She'd come to McSween's house—as he knew she would the minute Patrón got quiet enough for him to think about it. Snake Jackson had seen her and was crazy enough to try to kill her for seeing him murder Tunstall. Worst of all, he realized as he lifted his eyes and found her staring at him . . . worst of all, he was beginning to care what happened to the señorita.

It wasn't just the agreement he'd made in the woods; it wasn't just the witness she had been to Tunstall's death; it wasn't even the memory of her lying naked in that tub the night before. There was just something about Isobel.

"Salir de Málaga y entrar en Malagón," she said suddenly, breaking into a grin. "It means the same thing as when you say, 'Out of the frying pan and into the fire.' My father used to shake his finger at me and tell me that. I've always been *la alborotadora*, the troublemaker of my family."

"Now you tell me." Noah shook his head. "Well, Miss Troublemaker, if Snake Jackson's in town, that means the constable hasn't been able to serve the warrant on him. It also means he's over at Jimmie Dolan's house right now cooking up a plan. If we're smart, we'll keep playing the innocents— the young bride and groom new in town, just here for a brief visit. The fact that Chisum's in jail puts me on McSween's side in Dolan's eyes. But I've never been a joiner, and Chisum's bound to keep out of this mess as long as he can. If we play our cards right, we can probably lie low the next few days and then head for Chisum's place."

"What did you tell Guillermo Pascal in the telegram?"

"That you're here visiting some friends of your father's. That you may be up to Santa Fe any day."

Isobel frowned. How her betrothed would react to this news was anyone's guess. If he still cared to seal the marriage, he would probably come to Lincoln to find her. If not, he would remain silent. Neither response pleased her. The most important thing Noah was telling her was that they had precious little time to sort through the mystery of her father's death.

"Will you question Señor Patrón about his father's murder?" she asked.

Noah stood and took her arm. "Come on. If we head back to the house, Patrón will go with us. I'll work it into the conversation."

She rose and started across the room, conscious of his warm hand at her waist. He bent and lifted her shawl from the floor where she had dropped it, then drew it over her shoulders. But the warmth of his breath, the fire in his eyes, the heat of his fingers did more to quell the shiver inside her than any shawl could do.

As they passed the throng of arguing men, she spotted Patrón. The young Mexican was in the thick of the debate, his face red above his collar and his Prince Albert coat uncharacteristically disheveled. Noah called the man's name, but his deep voice was lost amid the shouts. Seeing the futility of attracting their host's eye, Isobel slipped away and pushed into the crowd. She elbowed Billy the Kid's ribs and pushed at Dick Brewer's firm stomach until she was at the table.

When the green-eyed young woman appeared as if by magic among them, the men suddenly fell silent.

"Excuse me," she said, trying to make her voice demure.

"My husband and I wish to return to the home of our host. Mr. Patrón, what seems to be the trouble here?"

Juan cleared his throat and wiped his brow with a folded white handkerchief. "Mrs. Buchanan—please forgive my rudeness. As I told you and your husband at dinner, there has been a murder. Mac—that is, Alexander McSween—has been so kind as to let us gather in his home to discuss the matter."

Isobel glanced around the crowd to the pale, long-faced gentleman who cleared his throat. She hadn't noticed him among the throng of shouting men, but now she saw that McSween was indeed different.

No older than thirty-five, his face was smooth, clean-shaven except for a drooping, bristly mustache that hung even with his chin. He wore a finely tailored suit and tie, polished boots, a pocket watch. His hands were clean and smooth, not calloused and embedded with dirt like those of the roughshod cowboys around him. The smooth line of his jacket revealed that he was unarmed.

"A doctor has been bribed to perform the postmortem on John Tunstall," Juan went on. "We're discussing ways to combat this injustice. Mr. Dick Brewer wishes to see Jimmie Dolan brought before a court of law. Mr. Billy Bonney wishes to bring justice to the murderers with the end of a gun. Dr. Ealy—"

"Dr. Ealy?" Isobel lifted her eyebrows as if she had never seen the man who had ridden across half of Texas and a great stretch of the New Mexico Territory with her. "Are you a medical doctor, sir?"

"Yes," Dr. Ealy answered, coughing uncomfortably at the ruse he was forced to take part in. "I'm a physician."

"Then why not have *two* doctors perform the postmortem?" she asked. "The other doctor will be countered by the truth of Dr. Ealy's observation. You must offer to help with the embalming, Doctor, or get a judge to rule for your assistance in the matter. It shouldn't be such a difficult matter to record the truth."

The men stared, their eyes fixed on the golden-haired woman in their midst as if she were an angel of light. Dick Brewer's handsome face softened into a smile as he stepped toward the table. "She's right, fellers. Buchanan's wife has the answer. We'll see to it that you're right there at the postmortem, Doc. It's a good idea—and it'll work. Thanks, Mrs. Buchanan."

Isobel tilted her head. "You may call me Belle."

The sea of men parted as she walked back toward Noah. He stood by the door, an amused grin on his lips. As she passed Billy Bonney, he stuck his elbow into her side and leaned toward her.

"How's married life, señorita?" he whispered, his breath heavy with whisky. "I see you and Noah there are thickern' calf splatter."

She paused, surprise widening her eyes. What was this gangly youth speaking of? Surely a casual observer had seen nothing untoward between her and her protector. Before she could think of a response, Billy chuckled.

"You're blushin' reddern' a greenhorn's butt after a day in the saddle," he whispered. "Rumor has it a purty woman can get ol' Buchanan's tail over the dashboard and rarin' to go fastern' he can draw his six-gun."

Isobel scowled into the light gray eyes, uncertain as to the Kid's exact meaning, but fairly sure she knew what he was getting at. "And what other rumors do you hear about Noah Buchanan?" she snapped. "I've heard he can draw faster than Billy the Kid."

The young man grinned. "They say"—the Kid leaned to her ear again—"a man who's fast on the draw is the slowest sort of feller when it comes to workin' the trigger of a woman."

Elbowing her, Billy guffawed as she brushed past him, her cheeks flushed and hot. "Hey, Buchanan," he shouted as the cowboy straightened from the door frame, "you bringin' yore wife to McSween's fandango Saturday night? You know he's tryin' to ease the tension in town. Why don't y'all come?"

Noah eyed Isobel's scarlet cheeks as she approached. "We'll see. I'm thinking of getting on over to South Spring River Ranch pretty soon now."

"Come on, Buchanan! You know I deserve at least one dance with the lovely lady. You may be faster on the draw than me, but I guarantee I'm the best dancer in town."

"You've got the biggest mouth in Lincoln County, that's for

sure." Noah grinned as Juan and Isobel joined him at the door. "Hey, Dick. Come here a minute."

The handsome young foreman detached himself from the group and walked toward them. As he approached, Susan Gates suddenly emerged from the shadows of a back room. Clutching her skirts in her hands, she rushed toward Isobel.

"Susan!" Isobel caught her friend. Thin shoulders trembled beneath her hands. "Susan—"

"You know this woman?" Patrón demanded, his brow drawn into a furrow.

Isobel glanced up at Noah.

"It's okay. Trust me, Juan. I'll explain it to you later." Noah winked at Isobel, as if to reassure her. Then he turned to Susan. "Miss Gates, this is our host, Juan Patrón, and I believe you've met Dick Brewer."

Isobel watched her friend nod politely at Juan, but when Susan looked into Dick Brewer's eyes, a pink flush spread across her face from her neck up to her cheeks. Though the two had seen each other previously in the forest, it seemed to Isobel as though they were meeting for the first time. For one moment the two gazed at each other as if there were no one else in the room.

Isobel glanced at Billy Bonney, wondering if the Kid had seen something like this in her behavior with Noah. Surely not. Noah was merely her protector, her companion. She had no more feeling for the man than she might have for a reliable stable hand or a loyal servant at her hacienda. Growing uncomfortable with the thought that anything untoward had passed between her and Noah, she caught Susan's arm.

"Tell me how you've been, Susan," she said, drawing her friend away from the group of men. "Are you well?"

Listening to Susan's lengthy response with one ear, she focused part of her attention on Noah, who was relating the arrival of Snake Jackson and the posse. Juan scowled. Dick nodded, his eyes darting from a studied concentration on Noah's words to a swift survey of the slender, red-haired schoolteacher.

"Do you need any more dresses, Isobel?" Susan was asking. "This one doesn't fit very well. You've lost a button. Why don't I come over tomorrow, and we'll shop at the Tunstall store for fabric. I'm quite a hand with a needle. Isobel?"

"That cowboy is looking at you, Susan." She maneuvered her friend away from Dick Brewer's line of focus so she wouldn't be tempted to turn and stare. "Keep clear of the man. He's in the thick of the trouble. He won't be any good for you."

Susan glanced over her shoulder. "Don't you think he's terribly handsome?"

Isobel nodded and shrugged. She preferred a man with a stronger frame, with massive shoulders and hands that could bring down a steer. She preferred a man whose face bore the weathering of life, whose eyes had seen good and evil—and whose mind was sharp enough to know how to choose the good. She preferred—

"Belle." Noah's deep voice ran through her body like a flood of liquid flame. She started visibly as the towering figure strode across the room.

"Don't allow any man to get near you, Susan," she whispered, squeezing the teacher's hands until her knuckles turned white. "It's a mistake to be drawn away from your dreams. A mistake, do you hear me?"

"Of course, Isobel. . . . Are you all right? You look awfully pale."

"I'll come tomorrow before noon. We'll go to the shops. We'll sew a dress, okay?"

Susan nodded, bewilderment veiling her dark gray eyes. "Take care."

Isobel turned before Noah reached her. Striding past him, she avoided his eyes and instead smiled at Juan Patrón. "Shall we go?"

As the three walked down the moonlit road, Noah hummed. He'd seen the immediate fancy Dick Brewer had taken to the skinny, redheaded schoolteacher, and he wanted to ponder this curious change in his old friend. Dick hadn't been a man to take after women. He'd often told Noah he preferred the solitude of the range and the company of a few good cowboys around a campfire to the meaningless chatter of women. It was commonly believed around Lincoln Town that Dick—like John Chisum—had once been broken by love.

Chisum had told Noah the story of the young woman he'd wanted to marry years ago. He had proposed, but the girl had been too eager to carry on being the belle of the ball to want to settle down. Chisum—being the impatient and stubborn man he was—insisted that the marriage take place at once or never. The girl had chosen the latter, and John Chisum had been a bachelor ever since.

Stealing a glance at Isobel, Noah took in the set of her mouth and the tight grip she had on her white shawl. She was detached, distant from him, as if nothing had happened between them. He stopped humming. Nothing *had* happened between them—and he'd damn well better remember that.

Like Chisum and Brewer, Noah had a reputation as a man to leave alone. Women had come after him plenty in the past, and he'd found their pleasures agreeable to warm a chilly night, but the thought of settling down with a wife was the farthest thing from his thoughts.

How could a man get up when he wanted, go to bed when he wanted, eat what he wanted, ride where he wanted—and write when he wanted—with a houseful of family?

The only woman he'd ever gotten close enough to admire was the Englishwoman who had taught him to read. But, by and large, Jane Allison had been miserable. Her main joy was the two or three hours she spent with a little stableboy each day. What kind of a life was that?

Now, take Isobel there—marching along in her damp skirt and muddy boots. Isobel would make a man the worst sort of wife. Permanent wife, he corrected himself, remembering that for the moment she *was* his wife.

He started humming again. He decided he didn't want to think about her. She was slipping into his thoughts too often. She was damn fine looking, of course. Any man would have to admire the tilt of her chin and the flash of fire in her eyes. She was smart and sassy and brave.

But it was clear enough that she wanted nothing to do with a *vaquero*, as she called Noah, and he wanted nothing to do with a grand *marquesa*. She'd already proven herself to be more than a handful. He'd begun to feel downright chipper at the thought of sending her off to her Spanish don in a few days. The only way to accomplish that, however, was to find out who had killed her father. And the sooner the better.

"How's your leg these days, Juan?" he asked, breaking the silence and startling Isobel out of her reverie. "Looks like you're walking better on it than the last time I saw you."

Patrón patted his leg. "It is not the leg, my friend. It is my back. You don't know the story of the shooting?"

"Did it happen the night of the wedding, when the Horrells got your father?"

Patrón's face took on a gravity that made Noah wish he hadn't brought up the subject. "No, no. My father was killed in seventy-three. John Riley shot me almost two years later. But it was a continuation of the anger against my people. Riley and a neighbor had accused some Mexicans of stealing from them. They shot them dead, and I demanded an investigation. When we went to arrest Riley, he shot me in the back."

"In the back?" Isobel stopped on the frozen road. "But wasn't this Riley brought to court for such an act?"

Juan shrugged. "Riley is allied with Jimmie Dolan, Señora Buchanan. He was never arrested for the shooting."

Isobel was beginning to piece together a picture of the type of men this Jimmie Dolan had working for him. The man held great power—and he used it for evil.

"Did Dolan have something to do with your father's murder, Juan?" Noah asked. "Your dad had a lot of influence with the Mexicans."

"No, Dolan had nothing to do with that as far as I can tell." Patrón's voice held a note of bitterness. "The Horrell Gang was simply a group of worthless men. Some of them were brothers in the Horrell family, others were just hangers-on. Mostly outlaws, renegades. In early December of seventy-three the gang rode into Lincoln for a spree. They shot up the town and got into a tangle with the Mexican constable. He was killed, but so were several of their gang. On the twentieth of December they returned to Lincoln for *revancha*—revenge. The Mexican community was having a Christmas dance at Squire Wilson's hall. The Horrells rode into the midst of the celebration and began shooting at us randomly. My father was killed."

Isobel walked in silence, imagining the horror of the festivity that had been transformed from celebration into bloodbath. Why was there so much killing here? Why so much hatred? She couldn't understand it. These *americanos* were barbarians, outlaws with bloodlust in their hearts.

"Didn't you go after the killers?" she asked. "The men who destroyed your father should have been destroyed in return."

"Killing and more killing." Patrón shook his head. "That is the futile way, Señora Buchanan. My father was dead. No other death could bring him back. You understand?"

She nodded, but she didn't truly understand. Where was the *venganza*—a man's proud avenging of his father's spilled blood? By all that was right, Patrón should have gone after the killers.

"The Horrells went on a rampage for about a month after that," Patrón was saying. "They rode through the countryside slaughtering Mexicans. In fact, they made a pact to kill every Mexican in Lincoln County. They killed one man—Joe Haskins—because he had a Mexican wife. Finally they went to Texas, stealing mules and horses, and murdering both Mexicans and gringos along the way. Some of the Horrells were ambushed and killed by the Seven Rivers Gang down south, but the rest made it safely into Texas. Of course they were indicted, but none was ever taken into custody." He paused. "Some of the gang—not the Horrell brothers, of course, but others who rode with them—even returned to Lincoln, I've heard. I don't pursue it now. It's better left alone."

Isobel studied the tower of stones as they passed it in the moonlight. If this Horrell Gang had ridden through the countryside in 1873 killing every Mexican in sight, might they have been the ones who murdered her father?

His golden hair would have distinguished him from the black-haired Mexicans of the territory—but his native tongues were Spanish and Catalan. Albert Matas had never learned a foreign language. He relied on translators in his business dealings. Perhaps he'd encountered the Horrell Gang on their journey to Texas, perhaps they had heard him speak and had gunned him down. It was a thin thread, a weak clue, but it was something.

"These Horrells," she said softly. "Which of them returned to Lincoln? What are the names of the men?"

Patrón frowned at her. "Señora, this event is none of your affair."

"Juan, there are some things you need to know about my wife," Noah cut in. The Mexican's face grew still, his eyes alert. "My wife's father was killed near Lincoln about the same time your father was shot down. We're looking for his murderer."

Juan studied Isobel for a moment. "I see. And you wonder if the Horrells may be involved. What else? Surely there is more. I am not so new to this world that I cannot see when a woman knows more than she is telling."

"I saw Tunstall's murder with my own eyes," Isobel said softly. "I was on the trail, traveling to Lincoln at the same time Dolan's posse murdered the Englishman. Snake Jackson has vowed to kill me."

"Stop." Juan held up his hand. "I do not want to hear more. You are deeply involved in the trouble, and if I hear your story, then I will become a part of it. Tell me nothing, and I will know nothing. Noah, your wife is in danger. I advise you to take her far from here to some safe place. If the Horrell Gang played any part in her father's death, she will learn nothing by staying in Lincoln. The Horrell War—as it is called—is seldom talked about now. Those who participated keep to themselves. Here in Lincoln County a man is free of his past. Look at Billy Bonney. Tunstall gave him a clean slate, taught him some reading, paid him well. But now I fear the boy's past will catch up with his present. He's hot for blood, isn't he?"

Noah shrugged. "Billy's always hot for blood. He's not strong on brains, but he's not short on guts either. Trouble is, he'd rather pull the trigger than talk things over. Tunstall was helping him change that. But now it looks like the Kid may start making good his reputation."

Patrón chuckled as if he had forgotten everything Isobel had told him, as if her story meant nothing. "How many men is Billy claiming to have killed now?" he asked as he climbed the steps to the portal. "Seventeen? Or is it twenty-one? *Ai*, Señora Buchanan—the men of the West will tell you many things. Do not believe one tenth of what they say, and you will have no trouble here."

Glancing at Noah, Isobel lifted her damp skirts and stepped into the warm house. If Juan was right, should she trust Noah? Could she even believe that the Tunstall-McSween faction was the more noble of the two? Perhaps this Jimmie Dolan was struggling against all odds for what was honorable and right. He did have the law on his side, they said, and he was closely allied with the powers in Santa Fe.

Doubt slinking through her stomach, she drew her shawl tightly over her shoulders and stood silently while Juan placated his distraught wife. Every word they spoke, she understood. Juan told Beatriz that Noah's bride was "too attached to him to be left alone" and therefore had run after her husband in the darkness. He told her that Noah was clearly "in love and too swept away" to discipline the girl.

Assuring the señora that she was not to blame for Isobel's escape from her care, he told her he would have a talk with Noah in the morning—and he would see to it that the man began to take seriously his position as head of the Buchanan family.

Juan's wife led Noah and Isobel across the front room and down a hall to a narrow wooden door. Unlocking it with one of the handful of keys at her waist, she slipped into the room and lit a pair of candles on an ornately carved bureau.

Awash in a yellow glow the guest room was spotlessly clean and set with simple furnishings—a wooden bed, a washstand, a chair. A small crucifix hung over the bed. A cross of woven dried palm leaves topped the washstand. The señora indicated the stack of logs and kindling by the corner fireplace, then tipped her head and left.

As the door shut, Noah headed for the fireplace. "What did Juan tell Beatriz to calm her down?"

Isobel stared at the single, narrow bed. "That I'm too attached to you to stay away. That you're in love with me." His broad shoulders stiffened for a moment. "Juan is going to talk to you tomorrow about the correct way to treat your wife."

Noah began building a fire against the chill in the room. "Well, Juan's a smart man, and he's going to stay out of the trouble any way he can. But if we've got him fooled about the marriage, that's a good sign."

Billy the Kid's words drifted through Isobel's mind as she

watched Noah stacking logs on his fire. Juan Patrón had spoken of love, too. Did they see something she couldn't?

She gazed at Noah's strong back, at the angle of his bent knee, at the tight curve of his buttocks. Without warning, the warm, unfamiliar heat spread across her stomach, curled down her legs, and settled into a throbbing nest somewhere deep within her. Her lips parted. She remembered his kiss. She lifted one hand to her bosom.

His head turned, and he smiled. "Good fire. Patrón keeps a nice *casita*."

She took in the tiny room, its closeness, the growing warmth of the fire, the single door, the narrow bed. She looked at Noah. He was prodding the fire, his arm golden in the light. His hair had fallen across his forehead. She had an impulse to go to him, to smooth back the hair, to feel its softness in her fingers, but something held her, a hidden dread, a faded, ragged memory.

She looked at the bed, and the memory came clear. She saw her parents' two bedrooms at the hacienda in Catalonia. There had been a bed in each room. A single door connected the chambers. Isobel's father, and not her mother, had explained the significance of the door.

"I visit your mother at night," he had explained, taking his inquisitive young daughter on his knee. She could still see her father's face, calm, careful. "I go through the door and lie in the bed with her. And there we play. This sporting is the way of men with women, *hija*. One day you will know this with your husband, Don Guillermo, to whom I have betrothed you from the year of your birth. It's a good thing, this playing of men and women. You'll like it."

But her father hadn't spoken the truth.

Some years after his death she'd seen her brother chasing one of the farm girls. Following at a distance on her horse, Isobel had watched her brother catch the youngster—who could not have been more than twelve—and toss her to the ground among some leafy trees.

Unable to keep away, drawn out of fear for the girl and confusion over her brother's behavior, she had slipped down from her horse and hidden behind a tree. There she had seen her brother tear away the sobbing girl's clothing. Grunting, he hadn't bothered to remove his own clothing, but had hurled himself onto the girl and forced her legs apart. He had grappled the small mounds of the girl's breasts while she screamed.

Isobel had turned away, unable to meld the image of the suffering girl and her groaning brother with the picture of her father and mother playing in bed.

Later, when the summer had turned to autumn and the girl had grown ripe with child, Isobel had spoken to her brother of what she had seen. He'd laughed in his seventeen-year-old manner and told her it had been nothing. Merely the way of men with women.

"Come over by the fire." Noah's voice made her jump. He was kneeling on the floor, his face half-golden and half-shadowed. He held a poker in one hand and beckoned with the other.

She surveyed the face she had come to know with the honest blue eyes, the straight nose, the strong lips. Those lips had been warm on hers. But the image of her brother in the woods sent an icy stab into her stomach.

"Where will you sleep?" she asked.

His eyes darted up, scanned her face. He looked at the bed, then his eyes softened. "Come here and get warm, Isobel. I told you I wouldn't touch you."

"Juan Patrón said I should not trust any man in the West. I think—"

"I think you had better just calm down and get warm. I want to talk about your father."

She sat on the edge of the chair, still wary of him. "What about my father?"

He jabbed the poker into a log. A spray of sparks shot into the air. "I think there may be something to this Horrell Gang thing. Do you know the exact day your father was killed?"

She shook her head. "Only that it was in late December of that year. He'd spent Christmas with my uncle at Fort Belknap and then had followed the Goodnight Trail north."

"Is your father buried here . . . in Lincoln?"

"At the cemetery. I promised my mother I'd go there." She stopped speaking. She'd dreaded the visit for so long. To see the visible sign of her father's death would make it all too real, too ugly. To see his name carved on the granite marker would confirm what she still didn't want to believe.

Noah reached out and covered her hand with his own. She was cold, rigid, trembling. Her dark gold hair had spilled out of the bun and now brushed her shoulders and drifted to her waist. She held the ragged shawl closed over her chest in one white-knuckled fist.

Again he had a sense of how vulnerable she was—how alone, at the mercy of fate. She was poor and scared, too, though she would never admit it. Without her land titles, Isobel had nothing but her clothes and furniture. And even though she insisted she could shoot well enough to protect herself, there was a cold-blooded murderer out looking to gun her down. That would leave anybody in his right mind a little shaky.

"We'll go to the courthouse tomorrow," he said. Her eyes lifted to his. "They'll have the record of your father's burial. We'll check out the date and see what we can come up with. Maybe we can find someone who remembers where the Horrell Gang was that day. But, Isobel, if it was the gang, you'll never be able track them down. I've heard there were more than twenty in the bunch. The best thing you can do is head up to Santa Fe and try to stop the transfer of your land titles."

She watched the flames lick at the adobe walls in the beehive-shaped fireplace. "You're asking me to forget my father's murder, to try to stop a land transfer that even my uncle could not penetrate. It all seems impossible. Without my lands I cannot marry Don Guillermo."

Noah stood up and slapped the wood dust from his thighs. "Hell, you've got *me*, Isobel. I mean, what more could a lady want?" He grinned as her eyes shot up, wide with surprise. "There's a good many women who'd gladly trade places with you. Why, I know of a gal right here in Lincoln who'd be mad as a peeled rattler if she knew about this arrangement."

"What arrangement?" Isobel stood. "There is nothing for any woman to feel jealous over. We have a *contrato*, a contract."

Edging past Noah, she walked to the washstand, drew her shawl from her shoulders, and draped it on the bed. She poured the porcelain bowl with chilly water, then splashed her face and rinsed her hands. Dabbing the embroidered linen towel on her cheek, she turned back toward Noah, who stood watching her by the fire.

"For that matter," she said softly, "there are many men who would gladly trade places with you, señor."

Noah took a step toward her. "I don't doubt that. For a woman who's fretting over lost land titles and some Spanish dandy she's supposed to marry, you have a lot of assets. Of course, you've hidden most of them from yourself."

"What are you saying? What assets do I have? My father left me nothing but great tracts of empty land in this horrible, bloodthirsty country where no man can be trusted. My brother and stepfather are feuding over the estates in Spain. I have only the jewels I brought with me—a few emeralds, some rubies. Don Guillermo—"

"Don Guillermo doesn't know what he's missing, Isobel." He caught her arm and pulled her closer. "You've got everything you'll ever need right now. Land and money—you can take care of those in time. But right now you have what counts. You're smart as a whip. You're gritty. You'll take on Snake Jackson and the whole Dolan gang if that's what it comes to. I've seen that in you, Isobel. You know how to ride, and you can use a gun. And you're pretty. Damned pretty."

She caught her breath. His hand burned on her wrist. She fought the unfolding heat in her stomach.

"What use is that to me now? Yes, I know how to wear the clothing of my country—the *mantilla*, the *manton*, the comb. I have the gowns and jewels to turn a hundred men's heads. But here I am, dressed like a peasant girl, without mirrors or combs or jewels."

"You don't need fancy gowns and jewels, Isobel." He lifted one hand and brushed a lock of hair from her shoulder. "You've got those eyes—green, yellow, brown. What color are they?"

"My brother used to say they matched the mud in a pig's pond."

"Well, that just shows your brother didn't know diddly-squat." He placed one finger under her chin and lifted her head toward the candlelight. "There's a wild cat that hangs around the bunkhouse. We call her Diablo. She's a devil, all right. Always in trouble, always slinking around and getting into things she shouldn't. If you can catch her long enough to get a good look at her, you'll see that there's fire in her eyes. It's a yellow-green fire that burns right through the brown and makes them glow like emeralds. Your eyes are like that, Isobel."

For a moment she couldn't move. Transfixed by the movement of Noah's lips, mesmerized by the warmth of his breath on her cheek, she gazed at his face. He was so close . . . so near she could almost feel his knee grazing her skirt, almost smell the dusty leather of his jacket. His eyes, locked on hers, held her, drew her, imprisoned her.

Trying to breathe, she touched her breast, felt her heart pounding as if it had lost all rhythm. The curling heat inside her slipped its bonds again, coursing through her body with a fire that made her weak and hungry and dizzy with an untested desire. She knew if she didn't speak, she'd lose herself, lose the precious control she had always held.

"You—you should write a book, Buchanan," she said. Her voice sounded oddly low and husky. "Any man who sees fiery emeralds in these mud-pond eyes of mine has lost his senses."

"My senses have never once let me down." Noah traced the line of her jaw with his fingertip. He could feel what she was doing to him, how unaware she was of the effect her full, damp lips had. His throat had tightened, and his breath had grown ragged with just one stroke of her skin.

She was soft, silky, dangerous. Like the cat, she was elusive. He shouldn't try to catch her. One look in those fire-lit eyes, and her spell threatened all that he held uppermost in his life. Freedom. Independence. Self-sufficiency.

He'd made up his mind to stay detached from women. They tangled a man's feet, tied him down, tightened the knots of their control over him. He didn't want that—ever. About as close as a night—maybe two—in a warm bed was all he planned to spend of himself on any woman. And this one was no different.

"I trust my senses, also," she was saying, those almond eyes poring over his face, coming to rest on his lips, then darting upward, sliding away to the window as if she might find an escape there. "And I sense that you aren't keeping the contract we made."

"I'll keep the contract as long as you want it kept, Isobel. But your words are telling me one thing, while your eyes and lips are telling me something else."

"No." She tried to step aside, but he caught her shoulders and drew her against him.

"Don't be afraid to trust your senses now." His hands slipped up and cupped her head. His strong brown fingers wove through the golden strands of her hair. His eyes caressing her face, he lowered his head and brushed his lips against hers.

Her breath was sweet, fragrant, coming in shallow gasps as she stood unmoving in his arms. She was young, fragile. All her bravado had evaporated in a mist.

The reaction puzzled him. Surely this gun-toting, haughty, gutsy woman had known the pleasure of a man before. Surely this head-tossing Spanish *marquesa* hadn't denied herself what most of the women he knew were all too eager to claim. But she trembled against him, and her eyes had deepened to pools, and her mouth was blossoming like the untouched petals of a new rose.

"Isobel," he whispered, suddenly uncertain. Uncertain she was what he had thought, uncertain his own dreams were as important as he had always believed.

"Kiss me one more time," she murmured, her eyes closed and her face lifted to his. "Just once, and then never again."

Chapter
❧ *5* ❧

The moonlight drifted through the iron fretwork on the window to paint a lacy shadow over the room. Unaware, seeing nothing but Isobel's full lips, Noah bent his head.

Softly, as if he might bruise the unfolding bloom, he stroked her lips. She held her breath, drawn into the warm haven of his arms. But when the tip of his tongue caressed the moist arc where her two lips met, a mew of pleasure escaped her mouth. Parting them, she felt him enter her, tease her hesitant tongue, then touch her there, as if inviting her to explore his mouth with her own kiss.

Unwilling—unable—to let the moment end, she rose onto her toes and slipped her arms beneath his coat and around his chest. Reveling in the heady taste of his tongue, in the rich scent of leather and soft flannel, in the rough graze of his chin against her skin, she ran her fingers down the corded muscle of his back. Solid, as hard as steel. Yet he had a pliant feel to his body that gave him a touch of vulnerability. As if she might somehow memorize the ecstasy of this briefly captured instant, she shut her eyes and allowed the feel of him to drift through and over her.

Growing in urgency, the kiss intensified. He absorbed the

touch of her fingers on his back, the press of her slender legs against his, the firm curve of her bosom on his chest. The sense that she was someone apart from him—someone he wanted to keep at a distance—evaporated in the crush of her heated lips and the almost inaudible moan rising from somewhere deep inside her. The spirit within Isobel—what gave her the fire that drew him—had burgeoned in a new form. In the undeniable passion of woman.

"Isobel." He heard the murmured word slip from his lips as they moved across her face, caressing her downy cheek, testing the fragile curve of her ear.

Shivering against him, she tilted her head to one side. Her heavy hair swung free of her shoulder and neck. She was lost in him, lost and aching for everything he had to give. Suddenly he wanted to draw out the deepest fire inside her. Desire beckoned. He sensed that the smoldering volcano within this woman would prove equal to the flames erupting inside his body. They were two rivers of molten lava on converging courses.

Running the tip of his tongue down the bare curve of her neck, he tasted the subtle fragrance she wore. A scent of flowers—violets and tea roses and gardenias—wove through him, heating the back of his throat, flaring his nostrils.

Her head rolled back in pleasure. His lips teased her throat, and his tongue tasted the hollow at its base. Lolling in his arms, she clung to his back, her fingers hot and tight. As his head dropped lower, his mouth seeking her, she raised on tiptoe and her back arched.

"Noah," she gasped. He pulled her close against the length of his body, his firm legs parting to either side of hers. Where they joined, she felt a rock-hard burning swell that jutted into her belly and rode the tender bone of her pelvis. As if he had lit a thousand candles within her, a sudden melting, a liquid throbbing, coursed through her.

His hands curled around her waist. His palms swept up to cup her breasts, lifting their heaviness and drawing them together, and then apart. She couldn't catch her breath. His thumbs slid over the thin cotton fabric of her dress to circle, but never graze, the swollen crests.

Never had any man touched her so. Never had she known

her body could exert such power. She wanted him—his gentle fingers plying her, his breath moist on her neck, his teeth nicking her earlobe, his hardness firm and compelling against her. Even more, she wanted the delicious ache that throbbed inside her, the tingle of her breasts, and the wanton weakness in her knees.

His fingers drew fiery circles around the peak of her bosom. She buried her face in the warm skin beneath his collar. He was soft there, almost tender. Feeling her own woman's power, she touched his bare skin with the tip of her tongue. The sharp intake of his breath nearly stopped her, but she tested him again, probing, tasting, savoring the man-smell of his body.

"Isobel." Moaning her name, he did as she had inwardly commanded. His thumb slipped from its entrancing circles and swept over the hardened bead of her breast. She caught her breath at the unbearable flames that shot through her, burning her thighs, melting her knees.

Breathing unsteadily, he traced a finger down the row of buttons on her bodice until he came to the gap where one had fallen away. He flicked apart the buttons on either side, widening the gap until his large warm hand found its way inside. The trappings of her sex, the petticoat and chemise and corset he expected to find, were all but absent on this woman who wore her own body as others wore their purchased finery.

Her moist lips left a wet trail along his neck. Her tongue darted through the crisp chest hair where his collar joined. He caught her breast fully in his hand. His fingers ran lightly over her bare skin and caressed the taut, jutting peak of her nipple.

"Tell me what you want, Isobel," he whispered. Unbuttoning the top of her dress, he eased the fabric aside until her bare shoulders glowed in the golden candlelight. Drawing away, he drank in her beauty. "You wanted my kiss, my lips on yours." As he spoke the words, he bent and brushed her flushed red lips with his. "You wanted my touch on your breasts." He placed a finger on her lips as she drew a breath to speak. "Don't deny it, Isobel. And now, now, what is it you want? Tell me."

His blue eyes had gone inky in the low flicker of the candles. She fought to steady herself, unable to lower her eyes from his for fear of seeing what—even now—his steady, magic fingers were doing to her breasts. She could feel him rolling their tips between his thumbs and forefingers, stroking her, lifting her, caressing her. But what was he asking? What did she want of him? How could she know?

"I want," she began, aware that the ache within her breasts had set her hips writhing slowly, hesitantly against him as if there she might find some release. "I want . . . I don't know, Noah. I don't want to—"

"I promised not to touch you, Isobel." He caught the small of her back with one hand and his fingers spread over the curve of her swaying buttocks. "I made a vow. But, Isobel— you have the power to release me from that promise. Tell me what you want. Tell me."

Tell him? Tell him what she did not know herself? Flashes of her brother tearing the clothing from his screaming victim darted through her mind. Memories of her father speaking of the nights of play with her mother twined through that horror. Somewhere . . . somewhere within these two pictures there was the answer to this need he had provoked so unbearably inside her.

But who was he, this man she had allowed to touch her as no one ever had? She'd been thrown into his unfamiliar world, swept away by a mere acquaintance, an American with none of the blood of her proud heritage, a common cattleman.

Why then did his words sound like poetry in her ears and his hands feel like music on her body? Why couldn't she pull away as she knew—somewhere in her mind—she should?

"Noah," she said softly. "I cannot tell you. I am . . . I—"

"Tell me, Isobel." He caught her arms in his hands and saw her eyes dart upward, suddenly afraid again. But why should she fear him? He couldn't believe she had never played her dangerous dance on the hips of other men. She was wanton, aflame, bewitching. Her breasts had overflowed her dress, taunting him with their ripe, dusky crests. Her full red lips had run their fire over him with such expertise that he had hardly been able to contain his desire for her.

"Isobel . . ."

Every emotion, every sense within her was tuned to this mystical magic flowing through her veins. Her body had become new, alive, possessed. Still captured in his arms, she lowered her eyes and gazed at her full breasts, golden and taut in the candlelight. Running her fingers gently over her own dark pink nipples, she felt their pebbled crests in wonder.

"I don't know what you've done to me," she whispered. "I don't know what I want. Except to ease this feeling inside me. Show me how, Noah Buchanan."

"Here's what you want," he murmured, inflamed at the sight of her slender fingers touching her own body. "Your lips are hungry for mine. Your breasts are hot and begging for my caress. You can hardly wait for my hands to stroke your thighs. You've gone all creamy between your legs for wanting me. Am I right?"

"Yes."

Her word was a gasp as he caught a handful of her skirt, brushed it to one side and slipped his fingers up the inner silk of her leg. She sucked in a breath, and her eyes went wide as his palm cupped the mound of dark golden curls between her thighs. His blue gaze trapping hers, he eased two fingers into her.

"This is what you want, Isobel," he murmured, fondling the moist folds of her womanhood.

She could hardly breathe.

"Do you like that?" He drew his fingers forward over the center of her pleasure until she cried aloud. "Are you ready to release me from my vow?"

Perhaps it was the moonlight or the crackling fire. Perhaps it was the turmoil that spun through her heart. Or perhaps it was simply the magic of a man's touch. But Isobel nodded. "Please," she whispered.

Holding her upright with one hand, he continued to stroke her with the other, reveling in the milky petals of her body. She had tossed her head back, her hair atumble around her shoulders and her round breasts swollen with need. Lips parted, she breathed heavily with mingling cries of pleasure. Her long neck curved up from her chest into her chin and he plied his tongue along it.

"Now," he said.

He lowered her onto the bed, her cotton skirt crumpling around her hips. His own body raged with need. He worked apart the buttons on his denim trousers while he continued to play with her. She sighed and danced on the bed, her hands woven through his hair and her mouth kissing his with a depth of passion he'd never known in a woman. She was a vixen, uncontrollable.

He felt his own body come free of the tight binding of his denims and surge toward her. At the touch of his shaft on her thigh, she stiffened. Her breath barely audible, she slid her fingers from his hair, down his chest, onto his naked throbbing skin.

"Ah, Isobel," he murmured, "let me come inside you and explore your secret places."

She stroked him for a moment, pondering the significance of his request. How thrilling it was to know that she had transformed this bear of a man . . . that her own body had brought him to such need. Smiling, she thought of the little boys she had seen passing water at the sides of the road in Spain. They had been so small and limp. But look at this man. She craved the hardened curve of the arrow that strained to fly toward the damp places between her legs.

"Come, then, Noah Buchanan," she beckoned. "Come and make my pleasure complete. Come and play with me as my father played with my mother when he walked through the door that joined their bedrooms."

"Play with you? Darlin', you haven't left me much time for that."

"Please, Noah."

Gritting his teeth, he tore down the scrap of underwear still clinging to her hips and used himself to heighten her pleasure. Kneeling above her, he gazed at the tangle of dark gold hair spread across the white pillow. Her breasts tilted upward, their peaks damp from his mouth. She bit her lower lip as he stroked and stroked her tiny pearl, knowing that its need was equal to his own.

Legs spread, she sighed aloud with pleasure. Her hands stroked his still-buttoned shirt and roamed down to his hard bare buttocks. With her feet, she caressed the wrinkled denims at his knees and felt his thighs pumping against hers.

"Isobel, honey, I need you," he groaned. Driven almost to the brink of his own constraint, he poised at her melting entrance and began to probe. He pushed against the sweet tightness and felt her barrier.

"Oh, lordy." The words were hushed. "I didn't expect this."

"What? Is something wrong with me?"

"Not wrong, Isobel . . . but you're untouched. You're a maiden."

"Yes," she concurred. "And a bride. Even God would have to agree with that."

He slid his shaft against her folds again, savoring the pleasure, yet knowing his next move would hurt her. "Isobel," he said, "if I'd known, I'd have taken it slower. Undressed you and all. Taken our time."

"Noah . . ." She writhed against him, wondering at his sudden withdrawal and hesitancy. How could he leave her this way—she felt so unsatisfied, craving so for more of his touch.

"Isobel, this part of loving is going to hurt you," he said. "Just this once. Never again, I promise."

She heard, but she couldn't imagine it. Her fingers moved onto his shaft and slid up and down. Then she lifted her hips toward him, aching for a continuation of the strokes that made her heart beat so fast and her body feel as if it were on fire.

"Isobel . . . darlin' . . . believe me, I don't want to hurt you," he groaned.

Cupping her hips in his palms, he positioned himself and drove through her maidenhead. She arched upward. Her fist flew to her mouth, stifling a scream. Eyes wide, she stared at him in fear and pain.

"Now, then." He kissed the tear that trickled from the corner of one eye. "Now it's all over. I'm inside you. Feel me. Feel how good it is for both of us, Isobel."

"It hurts," she whispered, thinking of her brother and the screaming girl he had wounded in this same way.

Never in all his born days had Noah Buchanan done what he did next. Even though his body sang with the need for release, he drew out of her and began to stroke her gently. He could feel her blood mingling with her dew on his fingertips and it tore through his heart to know he had caused such a strong woman such pain. But as he teased her again, she shut her eyes, relaxed, and began to sway with the rhythm of his touch.

"Noah?" she whispered. "It gives you this kind of pleasure to enter me?"

"Yes. And you'll like it, too—the feel of a man inside you—once the hurt goes away."

"I want to please you, Noah Buchanan. Come to me again."

"Isobel . . ."

"Please."

Realizing that he wanted her more than he'd wanted anything in a long time, he rose again and slowly slipped into her. Though she bit her lower lip, she made no sound. And as he began to thrust, a smile spread slowly across her face.

"Yes," she said. "Now I see."

He rose and fell, gripped with the most incredible need for release, yet forcing himself to wait until she was ready, too. He knew the intensity of his own climax would halt hers—and he wanted her to understand what lovemaking was all about.

Lowering his head, he suckled her breasts and rolled his tongue across her hardened nipples. She sighed and panted, lifting them toward him with her hands. Lost in a whirl of lights and stars, she moved against and with him, seeking a primal release. He whispered in her ear, words she couldn't understand through the fog in her mind. His breath heated her neck; his body dampened her breasts; his hands worked magic.

She rose and swirled, all memory of pain and heartache and confusion gone. Then she cried aloud as her body stiffened, shivered, and began to shudder, wracked with the ecstasy of surrender. Her thighs gripped his, and her fingers dug into his back, seeking a stronghold as the waves tore through her.

"Noah," she gasped. "Noah, Noah . . ."

Knowing she was free at last, he pushed deeply within her and held his breath as her velvet pulsations grew in intensity. Then he pounded into her, seeking to ease his own need, and finally tumbled over the brink. Trail dust, lowing cattle, a hard saddle, months without a woman all vanished in the utter heaven of Isobel's body. His face buried in her large breasts, his lips against one nipple, his fingers cupping her bottom, he groaned and pumped until he had given her everything inside him.

And then he lay, breath ragged in his throat, aware of her fingers trailing through his hair.

"Noah," she whispered.

He lifted his head and gazed into golden eyes lit by the glow of candle stubs. "Isobel . . ."

She stroked one fingertip over the crest of his dark eyebrow. "Now, Noah Buchanan," she said, a smile creeping over her lips. "Now I understand."

"Isobel." A cool hand rested lightly on her arm as the word drifted through her dream. "Isobel. Wake up. The morning's passing, and you've got work to do."

Her eyes flicked open. She stared at the serious face. "Susan? . . . Where is . . . what time is it?"

"Late. Nine o'clock or so. Noah sent me to look in on you."

Isobel struggled to her elbows. "Where is he?"

"He's over at Alexander McSween's place. He's been talking with Dick Brewer since before sunup."

"Were you there with them?"

Susan looked away, uncomfortable. "I was in the kitchen helping Mrs. McSween put breakfast on, and I heard the two of them. Not what they were saying, but that they were talking. They're best friends, you know."

Isobel nodded. The blanket had fallen to her lap, and she struggled to rebutton the edges of the small shirtwaist Susan had given her. "And you?" she asked. "Did you speak with Noah?"

"No, of course not. I mean, I hardly know the man." Susan took in the missing button, the tangled golden hair, the tightly laced shoes. "Isobel, what happened here last night? You're in your shoes, for heaven's sake."

Isobel stared down at her feet, feeling the pain that throbbed between her legs and aware of the tenderness in her breasts. "I fell asleep," she said finally. "I was tired after the long trip."

"Did you and Noah have a fight or something? Did he—he didn't try to—"

Isobel waved a hand across her eyes. "No, it's nothing, nothing. He wants to send me to Santa Fe. To Don Guillermo. We had a few words. Noah is . . . he's disturbing to me. A problem. I wish I hadn't agreed to our arrangement."

She tried to make the words sound true, but in her own ears they sounded hollow and empty. In fact, she realized the truth was that she wished Noah had not left the room that morning. She wished she had woken to find his big warm body pressed against her, his hair tangled from a night's sleep, and his hands eager to touch her again.

But for all she knew, Noah regularly slept with women in such a way. He probably thought nothing of it—and was ready to continue his life unchanged. She must do the same. She must focus on her future.

"Isobel," Susan was saying, her voice low, "if that man is bothering you, just tell me. We can figure out some way to get you up to Santa Fe. I know your don will take you in and protect you."

Isobel fiddled with a scrap of loose blanket edging. She knew nothing of the sort. And the more she thought about the man who had never written her, who was reputedly in league with the Santa Fe Ring, and who didn't even bother to stay in touch with her mother about the betrothal, the less she wanted to do with Guillermo Pascal.

On the other hand Noah Buchanan had made it clear that he wanted neither wife nor family to tangle his feet and clutter his life. Besides, the *vaquero* was not of her social class. Such a relationship was impossible even to think about.

She tried to laugh it off as she slid out of bed and hurried to the washstand to begin scrubbing her face. "Noah thinks he's the king of the world," she said. "He makes me wash dishes. He sends telegrams without my permission. He likes to give orders."

Susan giggled. "He gives *you* orders?"

"I know, I know," Isobel said as she stood in front of the small square mirror. "I'm the one who usually commands and makes decisions. Yes?"

"Well, you do have a natural inclination to make up your mind and expect everyone to go along with it, Isobel. I don't think that's any secret. But Noah won't let you get away with it?"

"He refuses to take his proper station in life seriously. He fancies himself my equal, even though he has nothing."

"He has a good mind and a good job and a quick draw. Out

West that can make a man a king. Look at Dick Brewer. He works for the Tunstall organization, but he owns his own land and he's really a boss in his own right."

"Yes, and what of Dick Brewer?" Isobel asked, turning. "Did you speak with him last night?"

Susan's pale cheeks flushed. "I did go out on the portal for some fresh air. Later on, Dick came out, too. We talked."

"Talked."

"Yes. Oh, Isobel—I think he's just wonderful! He's handsome and good and strong. I can't believe I'm just barely in Lincoln and I've met someone so perfect. I think I love him, Isobel."

"Love, Susan? You spoke with Dick Brewer for the first time only a few hours ago and now you're in love? Love isn't for the strong, Susan. In Spain we have poetry and songs of love. *Amor.* In Spain we say, *'Lo que el agua trae el agua lleva.'* It means what comes easily can also go easily. Don't place your life on such a fickle thing as love. You should work to arrange a profitable marriage for yourself, Susan. Tell your parents to find you a well-to-do man who can support you and give you a fine home. I've stayed in Dick Brewer's cabin. It's clean but very small and sagging. His land is nothing but rocky mountains with a tiny river nearby. Keep your thoughts from love, and you'll be much happier."

Susan shook her head, her eyes bright. "In Texas we also have a saying, Isobel. My Mexican friends used to tell me, *'Más vale atole con risas que chocolate con lágrimas.'* "

"Better to have gruel with laughter than chocolate with tears?" Isobel turned to the mirror again, a frown darkening her features. Susan was teasing her now, and she didn't like it. It was bad enough that she'd hardly had any sleep, that all night her mind and body had been possessed with the memory of Noah Buchanan, and that now she could hardly focus on her plans.

"Why are you telling me about *atole* and chocolate, Susan? I'm talking to you about men and love and the future."

"The proverb means that it's better to live in poverty but be happy than to live like the rich *marquesa* you want to be, yet have no inner joy. Why, I'd rather marry a cowboy like Dick Brewer and live in his sagging cabin and bear him twelve little

roly-poly Brewers than go up to Santa Fe and marry somebody like your wealthy Don Guillermo. Somebody I didn't
even know. Somebody who might not care a fig about me.
Somebody who might give me a grand house and lots of parties but couldn't give me his heart."

"What do you know about that sort of life, Susan?" Isobel
snapped, whirling on her friend. "It's always done this way in
the great families of Spain. It's been done this way for centu-
ries. No one sits about moaning for love. We marry and carry
on our bloodlines. It's our tradition. It's our obligation. It's *my*
obligation."

Susan stretched out her arms. "Don't be angry, Isobel. We
come from two different worlds. In my world it's okay to fall
in love and marry someone who isn't rich and doesn't have a
long pedigree. It's hard for me to understand doing it any
other way. And right now Dick Brewer just seems like he
stepped out of a dream."

"A dream? But dreams vanish, *pffft*"—she clicked her
fingers—"like that!"

"Maybe so." Susan walked to the iron-grated window and
knotted her fingers around the bars. "It's just that I always
wanted to know what it felt like to be in love. I wanted to
dance on top of the clouds. I wanted to know how it was to be
kissed and held and touched. Oh, I've bedded down with men
before, understand. Back when I was just a girl in Texas. And
sure, it was exciting and naughty and all. But I've never
known what it meant to really love someone. Really care
about them. I know it's quick, but I feel it. I really do feel it
with Dick."

Fumbling with the unruly buttons of her wrinkled bodice,
Isobel studied her friend. "Bedding down with men?" she
whispered, wanting to hear more about the pleasures she had
shared with Noah Buchanan in the night, wanting to know if
what she felt was typical, ordinary. Or if it was as magical to
others as it felt to her. "What do you mean, 'bedding down
with men'?"

Susan's solemn face suddenly split into a grin. "Come on,
Isobel! Sleeping with them. You know—taking off your
clothes and letting them touch you and everything. I know you
must do *that* in Spain!"

"Oh, yes." Isobel nodded. "Of course we do."

"Come, let's go for a walk down to the mercantile. I hear they've got hot coffee and fresh doughnuts for breakfast. Besides, we just have to get you out of that dress and into something that fits. I swear, girl, you look like you're about to burst right through. And that would never do in front of Noah Buchanan, now would it?"

Aware that she was blushing, Isobel jerked the white cotton shawl to her shoulders and wrapped it tightly around her bosom as she set off into the morning with Susan. The two women walked through the Patrón house, across the courtyard, and out onto the main street.

The day was warmer, sunny. The frozen road had begun to thaw. Bony dogs, rail-thin mules, rooting pigs made their way through the mud in the strange and empty silence of the morning. No people were out, yet wisps of piñon smoke floated from beehive *hornos* beside the squat adobe houses that lined the road. The smell of baking bread hung in the morning air, mingled with the scent of bacon and strong coffee.

Isobel lifted her skirts and strode alongside her friend, her tall form and long legs an easy match to the smaller woman's pace.

"Are you coming to the fandango Saturday night? The *baile*?" Susan picked her way through a scattering of puddles. "Everyone's saying it should help to ease the tension in town. I'm going. It'll be my last free weekend before I start teaching."

Isobel recalled Billy the Kid's taunting words. "I don't think I'll go. I've spent too much time already in the company of these rough American men."

"Dick asked me to go with him. He said I'd be his partner."

"And the bedding? Will you do the bedding with Dick Brewer?"

"The bedding!" Susan elbowed her friend. "For heaven's sake, Isobel. If you mean would I let him make love to me, I haven't thought that far ahead. No . . . I don't suppose I would. I'm too smart to take the risk of having his baby without us being married. I was lucky before, you know. Fooling around and not having to pay the price. But now . . . no, I wouldn't do it. I want to teach school until I find a decent man to marry me. And then, well, you know . . ."

Isobel wanted to shout that she did not know. Why didn't people speak more freely about such things? Why had her father told her only about adjoining bedrooms and playing? Why hadn't he explained the pleasures of it all, and the pain? And babies. No wonder her brother's young conquest had become swollen with child.

Isobel swallowed. What if she were pregnant now with Noah's child? What would happen to her then? The marriage to Don Guillermo would be impossible—not that she particularly cared, she was beginning to admit. But what would Noah's reaction be? And could she ever return to Spain bearing the bastard child of a poor American *vaquero*?

Noah was hardly the man to which his station had committed him. As she walked, Isobel pictured him as he'd been the night before. Hard and swollen against her. His body so strong and smelling of leather and fresh air. Kisses burning like fire on her lips. And how he had touched her.

"Susan," she began again. "Did you hear Noah Buchanan speak of me with Dick? Did he say my name?"

Susan eyed her friend. "Well, no . . . I didn't hear much of what they were talking about. But last night Dick told me a few things about Noah."

"Yes?"

"He said Noah had always been his friend—but that in the past day or so it seemed like something was bothering him. Eating at him. Dick said Noah wouldn't talk about it, but that they had always been able to talk about almost anything. And—"

"And what?" Isobel's fingers tightened on the white shawl. "What, Susan?"

"Dick said Noah . . . well, I'm not supposed to say. Dick made me promise not to tell."

Isobel stopped in the middle of the street, her sodden hem swaying against her boots caked with mud. "Susan, you must tell me. Noah Buchanan is bound to me. We made a vow—a silly, reckless vow. But it was a vow. He's going to stay with me until I've repaired my life. You must tell me everything you know about him."

Susan heaved a sigh and shoved her hands into the wide pockets on her green muslin skirt. She shrugged, as if resolving the inner struggle. "Well . . . Noah writes."

"Writes? Writes what?"

"Books, I think. No, I'm sure that's it. Dick said Noah writes books. Or maybe it's that he wants to start writing books. Anyway, with you to look after, he figures he's going to have a lot of trouble, Dick said. Noah's afraid he's not going to get started writing these books because he's having to haul you around. I guess he's pretty frustrated. Dick thinks he wishes he'd never agreed to the deal of protecting you so that you'd testify."

Isobel stared at the clots of mud on her fine leather shoes. Books? Noah Buchanan wrote books? She tried to visualize his tall form bent over a sheaf of papers, a pen gripped in his powerful brown fingers more suited for wrestling a steer than forming letters into words.

Noah was not the sort of person she could imagine ever sitting down at a desk. He was poorly educated and so very plain-spoken. And yet . . . he'd been read to by that woman in Texas, and he was just strange enough to want to do something like that. But what would he have to write about—dusty cattle trails, shooting sprees, herds of longhorn cattle?

And to think that he resented her for keeping him from his cow stories! Well, there was only one solution. She must put all thoughts of Noah out of her head and get to work solving the puzzle of her father's murder. She must forget the wild flame of his touch and the hunger of his lips on hers. The best thing she could do for herself—and for him—was to finish her business in Lincoln Town and leave.

Chapter

6

"I must stop at the courthouse," Isobel announced. Setting off in the direction of the single-story building across from the stone and adobe *torreón*, she heard Susan give a cry of exasperation behind her.

"The courthouse? But, Isobel! We were going shopping. Breakfast. Dresses."

"I must find out about my father, Susan."

The whitewashed caliche walls beneath the courthouse portal were cool and shadowed with blue. Isobel blinked to adjust her eyes as she started through the open doorway. She must learn where the public records were kept. She must ask for information. She must find out if the church kept records. Striding into the large dusky room, her head full of plans and her eyes still blinded by sunlight, she almost bumped into Noah Buchanan.

"Isobel." He caught her arms as she attempted to move past him.

"Noah." Their eyes met and held for a heartbeat. As her vision adjusted to the dim interior light, his body transformed from a massive dark shadow into the man she had come to know so intimately. She tried to make herself smile, but her mouth had gone dry. He took off his hat, his hair lifting and then settling against his head.

"Mornin', Isobel."

"Good morning, Noah."

In that brief moment it occurred to her that she had never seen as handsome a man in all her life. Nothing at all like the *guapo* Spanish dons who once had come to court her, Noah seemed to have settled comfortably into his own powerful body. He wore his musculature, his broad shoulders, his warm browned skin as another man might wear a relaxed and easy-fitting coat.

Clean-shaven and smelling like fresh rainwater, Noah had on a sky-blue shirt that matched his eyes. A battered black leather vest hung unbuttoned to the gunbelt and holster at his waist. Denim trousers skimmed his thighs. His fingers cupped the brim of his hat as gently as they had cupped her breast.

"I've got some information—" he began.

"I need to find out about my father," she said simultaneously.

"Here, Isobel. Here's the date and everything." He took her hand and set a sheaf of papers in her open palm. His voice was low, almost a whisper. "Your father was killed on January eighteenth, 1874. I don't know why you were told he died in seventy-three. He was buried on the nineteenth. There's a report here. It's sketchy, and I scribbled out a copy of it pretty fast, but I think you'll be interested in what it has to say."

Shoes cemented with mud to the wooden plank floor, Isobel stared at the papers. Susan edged up behind her, peering over her shoulder. "What does the report say, Mr. Buchanan?"

"We'll go over it outside." He took Isobel's arm. As he drew her to his side, she saw a middle-aged man peering at her through a pair of foggy spectacles. He was seated behind a rickety oak desk at the far end of the wide, single-room building. A score of rough pine benches had been pushed haphazardly against one wall. The plank floor was caked and blotched with fresh mud.

"Squire Wilson," Noah said, "I'd like you to meet my wife, Belle Buchanan, and her friend Miss Susan Gates. Belle, Miss Gates, meet Green Wilson, Lincoln's justice of the peace. This is the squire's place, the courthouse where Lincoln holds district court once a year. The rest of the year this is the town meeting room and the dance hall."

The heavyset man rubbed his eyes beneath his spectacles as he rose. "Pleased to meet you, ladies. You'll have to forgive me for not being more sociable. We've had a little trouble in Lincoln lately, and I've been up most of the night hearing affidavits, issuing warrants, empaneling a jury, and whatnot."

"Do sit down, sir." Isobel dipped her best curtsy.

"Belle, honey," Noah said and gave Isobel a husbandly smile, "the squire looked up that information on your friend's uncle for us. Now you'll be able to write to her back in Arizona and tell her how he died."

Isobel glanced at Noah's impassive face. "Oh, thank you so much, your honor," she said to the squire in a humble voice. "My dear friend will be greatly relieved."

"Not at all." The man fell heavily into his chair and began fumbling through some papers. "Fact is, I'm mighty glad to be of service. I keep all these damnable records, and nobody ever takes a second look at 'em. 'Course, now with all the trouble, you can bet the bigwigs up in Santa Fe will come snooping around."

"Thanks, Squire." Noah caught Isobel's waist and turned her toward the door. Susan followed the couple out into the brilliant sunshine. As they began walking in the direction of the Tunstall store, he spoke quickly.

"I just found out that the squire empaneled a coroner's jury last night to take testimony about the murder. They decided Tunstall was killed by Jimmie Dolan's posse. Several of the leaders, including Evans and Snake Jackson, have been identified. Nobody's said anything about our being there. None of Tunstall's men mentioned you."

"Has the constable caught Dolan's posse?" Isobel asked. "The murderers are probably still here in Lincoln."

"No one's been arrested yet, but things are in one hell of a mess. Some of the cavalry troops from Fort Stanton came to town late yesterday because the captain heard about the trouble. Sheriff Brady made the tactical mistake of ordering the Tunstall store to provide hay for the soldiers' horses. Now Alexander McSween is accusing Brady of larceny—of appropriating the hay from Tunstall's estate. So, in addition to issuing warrants for the arrest of Dolan's posse, Squire Wilson issued warrants for Sheriff Brady and his men. With the help of the Fort Stanton soldiers, the constable arrested Brady this morning. The squire just released the sheriff on two hundred dollars' bond."

"Everyone is arresting everyone else," Isobel said. Suddenly she understood why the town seemed so silent, watching, wary.

"The factions are dividing up quickly. The most important thing about all this is that tempers are hot and getting hotter by the minute. Alexander McSween has drawn sides and is going after Sheriff Brady and Jimmie Dolan. Mac's going to use all the legal know-how he's got to bring Dolan and his side to justice for the murder of John Tunstall."

"Was Dr. Ealy allowed to assist in the postmortem on that poor man's body?"

"Both doctors performed the postmortem."

"And?" Isobel's anger was diminishing as she strode through the mud alongside the strapping cowboy. Somehow she was coming to feel united with him—a partner in weaving through the political tangle they'd been trapped in. Susan slogged along behind the pair, puffing as she strained to keep up.

"Dr. Ealy recorded the truth," Noah said. "Tunstall's body was not only shot but abused. The report confirms what you said about Evans shooting the Englishman in the head after he was already dead."

A sense of relief washed over Isobel. "I must testify immediately," she said, determination flooding in its wake. "Let's go back to the squire, and I'll tell him everything. I'll relate what I saw in the forest, and I'll tell him that Evans and Snake and the others are in town. With Alexander McSween having the upper hand right now, my testimony will be all it takes to throw Dolan and Snake and the others straight into jail. The squire can send the constable—"

"Whoa, now." Noah slowed his stride. "We have to take our time with this, Isobel. You march into the courthouse with that story, and you're dead if Snake has half a chance to get at you. Besides, I want to make sure that the men you saw murder Tunstall really are Snake Jackson and Jesse Evans."

"Hey, we were going shopping for dress material!" Susan said, catching up. Out of breath, she had missed most of the hushed words between Noah and Isobel. "You stop running Isobel into the thick of trouble, Mr. Buchanan. You just tell her about what happened to her father this minute. Then we're going to get her into some decent clothes and send her off to Santa Fe."

Noah paused, his eyes narrowing as they raked down Isobel. Santa Fe? Was that what she wanted after all? After the night that had held such passion, after the kisses that had left him tangled and bemused and happy as hell all night long? She wanted to go to Santa Fe now?

"Tell me about my father," she said softly.

Her eyes were golden in the morning light. Her cheeks, flushed with the vigorous walk and the chill February air, gave her a radiant glow. She hadn't bothered to tie up her hair. Its dark wheat-colored waves floated at her shoulders—shoulders he had kissed.

He started walking again, more slowly this time. "It's all in the report." He studied her from the corner of his eye as she moved at his side, one hand clamped on the sheaf of papers, the other holding her white shawl at her breast. "Your father was shot once, in the chest. He died instantly, I'd guess. One of the guards was still alive when Dick Brewer found the carnage on the trail."

"Dick Brewer!" Susan lurched forward. "Dick found Isobel's father?"

Noah nodded. "He was coming to Lincoln for supplies. The report says that one of your father's guards told Dick a gang of about twenty had attacked the travelers. The man who killed your father wasn't the leader, but he was the biggest talker. The guard told Dick the men had robbed the group. The poor fellow died before Dick got him into Lincoln. There wasn't enough evidence to bring anyone in, so the law just dropped the matter."

Absorbing everything, Isobel stared down at the ink scribbled across the crumpled pages in Noah's bold handwriting. A gang of thieves was responsible for her father's murder. A gang who had ridden down the trail in late January. But who—would could it have been?

"The Horrells?" she asked. "Do you think they did it?"

Her face had gone pale. Her lower lip trembled slightly. He wanted to touch her but didn't. "We'll have to ask Dick, Isobel. I was out on the trail when all that mess was going on. I heard the tail end of it, but I don't have any of the facts. Dick will know."

"Let's go find him." Susan said the words so matter-of-factly that Isobel almost turned on her heel and started in the opposite direction. But there was more to this than just her father's death. She couldn't ignore the murder she'd witnessed. It was her responsibility now. Her duty.

"Before we find Dick," she said, drawing the shawl more tightly around her shoulders, "I must settle the murder of John Tunstall."

"Isobel!" Susan caught her hand. "Don't be a fool. You should stay out of this. You'll get killed!"

"Susan." Isobel directed her gaze to a tall building surrounded by soldiers sent from Fort Stanton to keep order. "Let's resume shopping for my new dress fabric. Our first stop will be the store of Mr. Jimmie Dolan."

A growing haze of piñon smoke had filtered over Lincoln Town when Belle Buchanan, her husband, Noah, and the new schoolteacher stepped onto the porch of the two-story Dolan Mercantile—better known as the House.

Four white posts supported the porch roof, which was also a balcony. Unlike most of the flat-roofed adobe *jacals* lining the single muddy street of Lincoln, Jimmie Dolan's store had a sloping, shingled hip roof with three chimneys. Eight windows on the lower floor and eight above assured the arriving shoppers that Dolan and his men were aware of their arrival long before they opened the front door.

"When I see the man who murdered Mr. Tunstall," Isobel said to Noah under her breath, "I'll say the word *yellow*. You'll know he's the one called Rattlesnake. *Blue* is for the man who shot second—Evans."

"Isobel." He caught her hand in his. "You be careful. Don't lose your head in there."

"But of course not. Belle Buchanan never loses her head."

* * *

"Silk is my favorite fabric," Isobel was telling Susan as they stepped into the cool shadows of the store. "The folds drape so nicely."

"Buchanan," a gruff voice called out from a crowd of men gathered around an iron potbellied stove near the back of the store. The scrape of chairs across the wood floor stretched the tension in Isobel's muscles. "Buchanan, don't you know better'n to come in here? Gawd, man, ain't you heard the trouble?"

Isobel glanced at Noah as the approaching men touched the six-shooters on their hips. He took off his hat. "Don't get testy now, fellows. I've just come into town off the trail. Whatever kind of trouble's going on, I have no part in it. My bride, here, is looking to make herself a dress to wear until her trunks come in."

"A dress to wear." Snake Jackson pushed his way out of the group. "Get your saddle-sore butt outa here, Buchanan. Jimmie Dolan don't want no Chisum men—"

"There!" Isobel interrupted the harangue by stepping forward and taking Snake's arm. "Do you see that yellow fabric just there? Near the ladder? That's exactly what I'm looking for. Will you get it for me, sir?"

For an instant Snake's slanted eyes slid across the room and combed down the rows of brightly colored fabric bolts. Then, catching himself, he jerked his arm away and spat a thick, arcing stream of brown-red tobacco juice into the brass spittoon near the door.

"Hell, no, I won't get you no cloth. Get her outa here, Buchanan, before I blast the three of you to kingdom come!"

"For going on a shopping trip, Snake?" Noah stuffed his hat back on his head. "That would look real good on the squire's books. Now, Belle, honey, exactly which bolt did you want Mr. Jackson to get down for you?"

"The *yellow*. That bright yellow near the ladder."

"Mr. Buchanan." A short, slender man entered from a side door. He was dressed in a fine black broadcloth tailcoat and trousers, a red silk brocade vest, and a stiff white shirt with a knotted black bow tie and scarfpin. He stood staring at the opposing groups for a moment, his small nose flaring with distaste. A mass of dark hair parted on one side framed his beardless, slightly puffy jaws. But it was his eyes—his narrow, beadlike black eyes—that sent a shiver down Isobel's spine.

"Mr. Buchanan, I'm afraid this is not an opportune day for shopping."

"Well, hello there, Jimmie. I'd like you to meet my new wife, Belle." Noah gave Isobel a little push forward. "And this is her friend, Susan Gates—a schoolteacher. Ladies, meet Jimmie Dolan."

"Such a fine store you have, Mr. Dolan." Isobel dropped the barest of curtsies. "Why, we've found a yellow silk right away that looks as if it will do just perfectly."

"Didn't you hear the man?" Evans elbowed to the forefront. "We don't want any Chisum man in our territory."

"I do like that *blue*." Her heart thudding heavily, Isobel addressed the red-faced Evans. "Would you, sir, be so good as to fetch down that blue calico?"

"Don't you hear too good, lady?" Snake started toward her, his eyes narrowing and his heavy, low-slung jaw gritted with distaste. "Jimmie Dolan ain't gonna serve no Chisum—"

"It's all right, Snake, Evans." Dolan's voice carried an Irish lilt that might have sounded pleasant on another man. As it was, the accent gave a sinister—yet oddly effeminate—hiss to his speech. "Mrs. Buchanan, I'm afraid we've had a little trouble in Lincoln. Perhaps you'd better do your shopping another day."

Isobel turned to Susan, whose fragile face had faded from pale to the white of bleached bones. Her dark gray eyes were as round as a pair of olives. The schoolteacher looked more ready to faint than to bolt. Isobel was almost set to back down when she caught a glimpse of her own tightly clutched shawl. Thinking of the gaping bodice beneath it, she squared her shoulders and gave Jimmie Dolan a demure smile.

"Dear Mr. Dolan," she said in her softest, butteriest speech. "I am in the uncomfortable situation of having almost nothing to wear. May I please see that adorable yellow silk? . . . Please?"

The dark Irishman glanced at the row of armed men looming behind him. One of their number, slightly better dressed than the rest—and wearing a battered brass badge on his chest—took a stump of cigar from his mouth.

"I'll get rid of 'em for you, Dolan," he said. "Just say the word."

"Why, Sheriff Brady, what are you doing here?" Noah drawled. "If there's trouble in Lincoln, hadn't you better be down at the courthouse? I mean, it just wouldn't look too good if someone knew the sheriff of Lincoln was hiding out at the House."

"Hiding out!"

"Sheriff. Buchanan." Jimmie Dolan put up his small, ring-bedecked hand. "Men, why don't you take your seats by the fire? I'll see that Mrs. Buchanan gets her cloth, and then these ladies can be sent on their way."

"Why, thank you, Mr. Dolan." Isobel gave him a radiant smile. "How thoughtful of you."

Reddening a little at the roots of his hair, Dolan made his way around the counter and hooked the bolt of blue calico down into his arms. "It's fifty cents a yard, ma'am." He tossed the fabric on the glass-topped counter. "That yellow silk is five dollars a yard."

Isobel could feel Snake Jackson eyeing her from his position against a wooden post. It was as if he were peeling away her mask . . . placing a lace *mantilla* on her head . . . remembering the flight of a white-shawled woman across the road to the *torreón*.

"Five dollars for silk. My, my." She fingered the yellow silk and then the cheap, coarse cotton printed with tiny white sprigs on a cornflower-blue field. "And the width?"

"Twenty-two inches for the calico. Eighteen for the silk."

"Hmm . . . I'll need at least twenty yards of this to make a dress, won't I, Mr. Dolan?"

She turned the dull fabric this way and that. Then, with studied grace, she pivoted until she was facing Snake. "Is there something wrong, sir?" she asked. "You have been staring at me."

Without taking his eyes from her, he straightened. "You always wear that shawl?"

She felt her knees fill with water. "I wear this white shawl for shopping in town. Normally I wear a dark green one. May I ask why you are interested in my clothing, sir?"

"I'm looking for a woman I seen in a shawl just like that one. A woman about your size—"

"Snake!" Evans bellowed the name from his position by the fire. "Damn it. Get over here!"

"You have a mighty unusual accent, ma'am," Snake went on, oblivious to the approaching Evans.

"My parents are from . . ." Isobel touched her dark-gold hair. "Norway. It's in Scandinavia. Europe."

"Like around where Spain is, maybe?"

She tried to smile. "Not anywhere near Spain."

"Get your snake-eyed mug back here." Evans stomped into the foreground, a half-empty bottle of whiskey dangling from one hand. " 'Scuse ol' Snake, here, ma'am. He thinks he's seein' ghosties ever'where."

"I am seein' ghosties. Spanish ghosties with little lace veils."

"Let's get out of here, honcy," Noah said, laying a hand on her shoulder. "We'll take twenty yards of the blue stuff, Dolan. Mark it down for me, and I'll send you the money when Chisum pays me for the cattle I ran over to Arizona."

A slow smile spread over the Irishman's face. "You'll have a long wait for John Chisum to be paying you, Mr. Buchanan. I'm afraid he's in jail."

"So I hear. They tell me some stinking coyote of a man is behind it."

Dolan measured the yards of fabric, his face impassive. "The coyote is a smart animal, I'm told."

"Feeds on carrion," Noah shot back.

Isobel placed her hand over Noah's to calm him. It moved her to see the depth of devotion he felt for this Chisum. She pictured the wealthy rancher as a fine man, as an equal with whom she might speak freely, as someone who would truly understand her—and might even help her. But if Noah lost his head now, all plans for the future might be blasted away in a flurry of bullets.

"How about buttons?" she asked Dolan, tucking the fabric under her arm.

"We don't have any. Most folks cut the buttons off their old clothes and sew them on their new ones."

"Hooks?"

"Those we have. And I guess you'll be wanting thread."

"Blue, of course."

"I'm assuming you own a sewing machine, Mrs. Buchanan."

"Oh, Mrs. McSween has a Wheeler and Wilson—" Susan blurted, then caught herself. "That is . . . she's in St. Louis and I imagine she wouldn't care if Mrs. Buchanan were to borrow it for a time."

"McSween, eh?" Dolan squinted at her. "So you're working for Mac, are you, Miss Gates?"

"She's a schoolteacher," Noah cut in. "She's just here to teach kids to read and write. And to be left alone."

Snake sidled along the counter. With one dirty finger he prodded Noah's arm. "What I want to know is why the hell you didn't do yore shoppin' at Tunstall's store, Buchanan. Him and Chisum are good buddies, we hear. Why don't you shop over at Tunstall's place?"

"I reckon you'd know the answer to that one, Jackson."

"And what's that supposed to mean, huh? You tryin' to say I done the Britisher in?"

A wry look crossed Noah's face. "All I said was, I reckon you'd know we couldn't shop at Tunstall's because it's shut down this morning. *I* didn't say you killed the Englishman. *You* did."

"Why, you—"

"All right, hold it there now!" The voice of young Billy Bonney drowned the sounds of argument in the mercantile.

Noah glanced over the top of Snake's dirty red hair to see the Kid striding through the front door. He was followed closely by Fred Waite and Atanacio Martínez, the town constable.

"We've come with a warrant," Martínez began.

In the next instant the store erupted into chaos. Guns drawn, men on either side of the room rushed toward the fray. Susan screamed. Isobel grabbed her friend and was making for the counter when Noah bundled both of them in the protection of his arms and drew them against his chest.

"Down! Get down," he growled. Barreling between two Dolan men, he kicked wide the counter's swinging door. He huddled Isobel and Susan against the side of a three-foot-high black iron safe. "Stay here. Don't move till I come back for you, hear?"

And then he was gone. Isobel buried Susan's head in her lap and cradled the sobbing young woman. Wishing she had a gun, Isobel scanned the rows of dry goods on the shelves behind her head. Black Leaf sheep dip. Tobacco paste. Pride of Denver soap. Glass lamp globes. Scoops and tongs. Tins from the National Biscuit Company. Red Cross cough drops. Chase and Sanborn's package teas. She noted cinnamon, guitar strings, corsets, union suits, ledgers, gloves, fans, and shoes. But no guns.

In the store not three yards from where the two women crouched, the arguing escalated.

"Hold on, now!" a voice bellowed over the rest. "I got a warrant here, and you boys better calm down and listen to it."

Isobel straightened on her knees and peered over the countertop. The constable whipped out a long white paper and began to read. "This here warrant is signed by Squire Wilson for the arrest of James J. Dolan, Jesse Evans, Jim Jackson, Frank Baker, Thomas Hill, George Hindman, William Morton—"

"What fer?" someone shouted.

"For the murder of John Henry Tunstall."

"The hell you say!" The arguing erupted a second time. Isobel searched for Noah among the mob of unruly men. He was nowhere in sight. If only she had her pistol, she would settle the matter as swiftly as a bullet shot through the heart of a man. The death of James Dolan and a few of his cronies would end this ugly matter. And Isobel would simply claim self-defense. Who could blame her? A lone Spanish woman, trapped against her will in a room full of madmen . . .

"As sheriff of Lincoln, I arrest *you* bastards!" Sheriff Brady suddenly announced. "Yeah, you there—Constable Martínez, Waite, and Bonney. You're under arrest."

"Hold on, now," the Kid protested. "You can't do that! We came in here to arrest these fellers. You can't turn around and arrest *us*, Brady."

"I sure as hell can and do."

"On what charges?"

"Disturbing the peace."

The momentary burst of laughter was followed by a sudden scuffle. A gun went off. Susan shrieked. Isobel squeezed her eyes shut and cupped Susan's head in her lap. But when the room quieted momentarily, she spotted a wooden ironing board leaning against a sign that read "Old Virginia Cheroots—4 for 10 cents." Propping the ironing board against the safe to form a makeshift barrier that would shelter Susan in her absence, Isobel whispered in the young teacher's ear.

"A gun, Susan. I must have a gun."

Crawling across the dusty floor on hands and knees, she at last located a derringer hidden in a crevice between two adjoining counters. No doubt secreted there for Jimmie Dolan's protection, she thought. She reached for the gun. A hand clamped over her wrist.

"Isobel," Noah hissed. "What in tarnation do you think you're doing?"

"I'll show how a woman of honor can finish such a *lucha* between cowards like these filthy *vaqueros*!"

"You're crazier than a locoed bedbug, lady. Let go of that thing." He pried Isobel's fingers from the pistol and tossed the weapon into an open drawer filled with packets of Putnam's fabric dyes. "Where's Susan? I've got to get the two of you out of this place before it blows."

"Here I am, Mr. Buchanan!" Susan whimpered.

Grabbing Isobel's wrist, Noah marched her toward the safe. "It's okay, Miss Gates," he said in a tender voice. "You can come out. We'll head out the back way."

Isobel crossed her arms over her chest, watching in distaste as Noah escorted the frail red-haired schoolteacher from behind the safe and the ironing board. Tears streaming, Susan buried her head against his chest.

"Oh, Mr. Buchanan, I just don't know how I'd have lived through all this if you hadn't come back for me. When Isobel left me here all alone and went off looking for that gun—"

"It's all right now, Miss Gates. Come on." Noah cast a black look Isobel's way, jerked on her arm, and hurried the two women toward the back door.

He could hear the hubbub growing behind him as Dolan's men swarmed Martínez and the others to make the arrest. He fully expected the Fort Stanton soldiers to trample in and join the fray. The last thing he needed was to get himself labeled a Tunstall sympathizer and sent off to jail. Especially when he had this hot-blooded Spaniard to look after. Imagine . . . rooting around for a derringer and thinking she could solve the whole mess!

"Let me go!" she was bellowing, twisting against his grip as he hurried her and Susan Gates down the muddy road. "Where are you taking me?"

"I'm seriously thinking of packing you off to Santa Fe and letting that don of yours try to keep his eye on you."

"He's not my don!" she snapped. "*You* are the man who married me, Noah Buchanan, and I demand that you start treating me with respect!"

Noah stopped dead still on the road. He dropped the arms of both women. "If I'm the man you married, Isobel, then you'd better by gum do as I tell you to. And from here on out, that means no pistols, no shooting, no taking matters into your own hotheaded little hands and scheming up notions that are sure to get somebody killed. If I'm the husband, that means I'm the boss. You hear me?"

Isobel tossed her head and gave a sniff of displeasure. "What you want is a weak little nobody for a wife, yes?"

"Damn right."

"Then you have married the wrong woman."

"Well, you're right about that, too."

"Oh, Jimminy," Susan whispered, cutting in. "Here comes that Dolan mob with the constable and Billy Bonney and Fred Waite under arrest."

"All right—the pair of you head over to Alexander McSween's house and set to sewing up a dress for Isobel. And I don't want to see hide nor hair of either of you around Lincoln Town today."

Simmering, Isobel stared at the towering cowboy who presumed to rule over her by his bartered title of "husband." His blue eyes fairly crackled as he met her gaze.

"You got a problem with that plan, Isobel?" he asked.

"Excuse me," Susan interrupted. Taking quick leave of

them, she headed down the far side of the road, past the Wortley Hotel and the Mills house on her way to the relative haven of the McSween home. The Fort Stanton soldiers who had been sent to keep an eye on things in Lincoln swarmed the approaching Dolan mob.

"My only problem here is with you, Noah," Isobel said, oblivious to the advancing melee. "You seem to forget that we made an agreement. You will protect me, and I will testify for you on the murder of John Tunstall. You have no right to behave as some king—"

"I think you left out part of the bargain, darlin'," Noah said, drawing her protectively against his chest as the throng of men surged past. "We got married, remember? And your job is to be my good little wife until Chisum sells me some land."

Isobel struggled to resist the pleasure of his finger stroking up and down her arm. She drew her shawl around herself and hugged the packet of calico fabric as if it might insulate her from him.

"A good wife," she said, "knows how to protect herself."

"I was ready to protect you. I put you and Susan in a safe place."

"*Susan.* Yes, poor Susan who weeps at the sound of a pistol. How happy she was to be taken under your wing like a helpless chicken—"

"You're jealous."

"Hah!"

"If you want me to treat you like a gentleman should, Isobel, you ought to try acting ladylike instead of as touchy as a teased snake."

"And allow myself to be shot through the heart by some worthless, filthy man like the one who killed my father? Never. I protect myself." She lifted her chin. "Where were you anyway? I looked for you in that mob. You were nowhere to be found."

"I was standing behind the coffee grinder ready to pepper anybody who came near you ladies. Then I looked down and saw you crawling across the floor in hot pursuit of that derringer."

The hint of a smile crossed Isobel's lips. "I'm good with a gun."

"You're good with a lot of things."

Her eyes darted up, and she read the twinkle in his. Her mouth twitched, and she shrugged her shoulders. "You know very little about me, señor."

"I reckon we can take care of that tonight, don't you?" He watched the color slip up her cheeks and enjoyed the fact that for once Isobel was showing every sign of being the blushing little lady. "Now, I'm going to head you over to Mac's and set you to sewing up your new dress. All right?"

"Oh, yes, my strong, brave husband," she responded, batting her eyes for effect. "I will stitch and bake—and weep for joy when I hear your footsteps on the *portal*."

"You do that."

Chuckling, Noah tucked Isobel under his arm and hurried her down the muddy road toward the adobe home. But it occurred to him as he studied her golden head and her cotton skirt fluttering around his legs that he wouldn't mind it if he had a woman to sew and bake and wait for him to come home at night. He wouldn't mind it one bit.

Chapter
7

Isobel had never stitched a dress in her life. For that matter, she had never allowed cheap cotton fabric to touch her skin—not until the day she became Noah Buchanan's wife and was forced to wear one of Susan Gates's simple ginghams. But she had to remember she was no longer Maria Isobel Matas, daughter and heiress to a wealthy Catalonian family. She was Belle Buchanan, wife of a poor cowboy.

After a quick breakfast Susan patiently taught Isobel to thread the black Wheeler and Wilson treadle sewing machine. Using a borrowed pattern that had been the model for nearly every woman's dresses in Lincoln Town, Isobel learned to lay out the blue fabric and cut it to size. The bodice took some adjusting, for she insisted her bosom be tightly encased in hooks all the way up to her throat. She may have succumbed to Noah's charms the previous night, but she could not allow such intimacies to become commonplace.

As she snipped and pinned and tried her hand at finishing seams, Isobel turned their physical encounter over and over in her mind. What could she have been thinking of? She had made an arrangement with Noah—a mercenary one only. Each would use the other to get what was needed. How then had she tumbled so willingly into his bed and surrendered to his caresses?

Oh, his caresses . . . and his kisses . . . and the warm fire of his fingers . . . She shut her eyes as the memory of his hands fondling her breasts seeped through her. Her thighs began to tingle. Her breath shortened.

"Are you planning to gather that skirt or not?"

Susan's voice shattered the image of sun-browned fingers on pale flesh. Isobel looked up, flushed, and resumed sewing. Her feet tilted up and down to work the treadle, while her fingers guided the fabric. The soft *cush-cush-cush* of needle biting through fabric lulled her. As the full skirt ruffled beneath her fingers and the long hours stretched on, she formed pictures of Noah in her mind—his chest as solid as stone and his dark face moving with the rhythm of his body as he thrust deeply within her.

"So, how are you and Mr. Buchanan getting along?" Susan asked. Night was setting in, and the lamps cast a golden glow over the swaths of fabric that had taken shape during the day. "He sure seems like a nice man."

"Nice, yes . . ." Isobel wet the tip of a thread with her tongue, knotted it, and began to hem. Her voice carried the soft melody of her daydreams. "Nice . . . but . . . common. He reminds me of the laborers who worked the cattle on our ranch in Spain. Strong and powerful but also rough."

"So, you still have your sights set on Don Guillermo Pascal?"

Isobel smoothed the hem and leaned back in her chair. "Noah sent Guillermo a telegram last night. There has been no reply."

"Well, maybe he just hasn't had time—"

"A man doesn't wait to consider consequences if he truly plans to make a woman his wife. He goes to her. He rescues her. He cares for her in the midst of trouble."

"You think Guillermo—"

"He doesn't want me, Susan. And how can I blame him? I have nothing to offer."

"You sure are pretty."

Isobel laughed. "For a common man, a wife need only be

pretty. But for such a family as the Pascal, wealth and land are necessary to forge a marriage."

"So . . . what are you planning to do? You've come all this way to marry the fellow."

"I always knew that first I must find my father's killer. I must regain my lands and jewels. Then I shall decide."

"Well, you *are* married to Noah, and he's a good man. You might consider—"

"Oh, Susan, what a silly head you have! To think that I would ever consider Noah Buchanan in any serious way. It's only an arrangement we have." She lowered her head and tried to remember all the original reasons she had rejected Noah. "He's just a *vaquero*, and so plain. He has no land . . . and . . . and he's like a bull . . . clumsy . . ."

"Clumsy?"

Isobel thought of the expert way his fingers had moved over her body, touching and teasing her to arousal. Noah was anything but clumsy. "Well . . . his hands are large and rough. A working man's hands. He's just . . . he's beneath me, Susan. How can I explain it?"

"You just did." Noah's voice echoed off the adobe walls of the little sewing room. Isobel and Susan started, lifting their heads at the unexpected intrusion.

"Noah," Isobel gasped.

"I came for you. It's almost dark out."

She fiddled with the hem of her dress. Had he heard the horrible things she had said about him? Things she knew were lies and lame excuses to hide the surge of need she felt every time she thought of him?

"We were just finishing the sewing." She studied his face, trying to read it.

"Yeah."

"Isobel's learned a lot today, Mr. Buchanan," Susan said, filling the silence. "She threaded the Wheeler and Wilson. She's fine with a straight seam. And her hemming just—"

"Well, I sure do hate for the *marquesa* to have to wear such common, low-class duds."

Isobel stood, her face hot and her heart thudding in a dull rhythm. "This dress will suit my purposes until I've found my father's killer and my trunks arrive. Shall we go, Noah?"

He shrugged, then glanced at Susan. "Good night, Miss Gates. I hope you have a pleasant evening."

"Oh, Mr. Buchanan, do you suppose I might have a word with you? That is, if Isobel wouldn't mind waiting a moment."

"Happy to oblige you in any way I can, Miss Gates. Isobel—will you excuse us?"

Isobel saw the flush creep up the schoolteacher's cheeks as she eyed Noah. Grabbing the blue dress, Isobel bundled it into her arms and waltzed out of the sewing room. Well, why should she care if her friend had cast a roving eye on Noah? First Susan was "in love" with Dick Brewer, and now the red-head blushed and tittered over another man. Perhaps Susan was just man-hungry.

But what difference could it make to Isobel if Susan or any other young lady fancied Noah? Their marriage was no more than a bargain, and he had plainly stated he would want an anullment. So? Let Susan Gates have the *vaquero*.

A moment later Isobel felt him take her elbow. "Nice night," he commented, leading her out of the McSween house and onto the freezing road.

She chose not to respond. Now that she was able to see things more clearly, she realized what had happened the night before. She had simply been carried away by the insanity of her situation. But that was all in the past. She knew what she had to do. She knew Noah's place in her life. And she had mapped out her plans.

"Chilly," he said as he opened the front door of the Patrón home. "Too damn chilly."

When they had crossed through the empty front room to their bedroom door, Isobel turned, but Noah was already speaking.

"I heard what you told Miss Gates about me," he said. "That I'm just a plain, clumsy *vaquero*. I'm low-class and beneath you. I reckon it's all true, too."

"Noah—"

"Hear me out. I thought maybe we were on to something kind of good last night. But now that I know how you felt about it, I aim to give you plenty of elbow room. You stay here tonight, and I'll head back to Mac's place. He's got room for me to bunk down."

"It's really all right——" She gestured emptily toward the bedroom, realizing that the magic they had created the night before had been swept away by her careless words.

"I may be a common cowboy, Isobel," he said, "but I've got my pride. Now, if you'll excuse me."

Settling his hat on his head, he strode through the silent living room and left Isobel alone to wonder whether her husband would seek other, warmer arms that night.

In the morning Isobel slipped her new blue cotton gown over her head. She stood on tiptoe, tilting and swaying as she tried to see herself in the tiny mirror. It was not a bad dress, she realized—though hopelessly out of fashion. The full skirt begged for a bustle, and Isobel knew bustles had not been in style for years. Nor, for that matter, had full skirts. The latest illustrations she had seen showed tight, straight ankle-length gowns—sometimes with fish-tail trains that swished when a woman walked.

Oh, well, she mused, Lincoln Town had never heard of style or fashion. She patted her bottom flat and smoothed the gathers that tended to emphasize her hips. Tightly corseted, her waist felt taut and hard as iron. Above it, of course, her bosom stood out almost unchecked. Beneath the thin pink chemise she had brought from Spain, her nipples distended in the crisp morning air. They reminded her of the way they had looked after Noah's lips had covered them. Flush. Taut. Eager. Attempting to dismiss the image, she worked at the hooks until her breasts were primly secured all the way to the high neck ruffles that rustled beneath her chin.

As she brushed her hair, stiff bristles sliding through golden waves, she wondered how she could make the best use of her day. She could try to speak with Squire Wilson or Constable Martínez. Or she might try to find Sheriff Brady—though she could hardly trust what a man like that might tell her.

Sweeping her hair into a knot, she had just begun to pin it when someone knocked on the door. Dropping the mass of hair, she swung around, fingertips at her throat.

"Yes?"

"Buchanan here."

Annoyed at the flutter that began in her chest at the sound

of his deep voice, she marched to the door and opened it. Though images of Noah had drifted through her mind all night, she was unprepared for the sight of him. A clean chambray shirt collar showed beneath the ankle-length canvas duster coat he wore. His denim trousers clung to his thighs and then skimmed down to the black boots on his feet. A red bandanna was tied at his throat.

"I've come to take you for a buggy ride," he announced, as if she had no choice—and she supposed she hadn't. "Bring your shawl. It's cold out."

Moving without protest, Isobel swept the white shawl from the foot of the unmade bed and wrapped it around her head and shoulders.

"Better straighten the bed," Noah said. "It's polite, you know."

Isobel had never made a bed in her life, but at Noah's words she set to work smoothing sheets, blankets, and pillows. All the while her thoughts reeled. Why this sudden change in him—this desire to take her for a buggy ride like a man might take a woman he intended to woo? And where had he been all night? With Susan?

She glanced at Noah. He certainly looked fit and chipper. His square jaw gleamed from the morning's shave. His blue eyes glowed with the brilliant hue of the morning sky outside her window. He smelled of scent—a manly cologne that hinted of herbs and spice. A tingle started in the base of her stomach.

"You have a buggy?" she asked, moving toward him again. She felt timid suddenly, as though courting for the first time. But Noah showed no outer signs of tenderness.

"I borrowed a rig from Alexander McSween." He took her arm and hurried her through the living room. "Had breakfast?"

"No."

"A *marquesa* might choose to sleep late, but around these parts a woman gets up early." He stopped in the kitchen long enough to bundle a stack of freshly baked tortillas in a white napkin and hand them to Isobel. "Thanks, Beatriz," he said to Juan's petite wife. "If we aren't back by sunset, send out a posse."

Busy with her housework, the woman waved them on. Noah hustled Isobel across the portal and into the waiting buggy.

Saying nothing, he drove. He absorbed the familiar feel of the clear morning beginning to warm up. A pale yellow sun rose to light the Capitan Mountains, which guarded the Rio Bonito's narrow valley. Purple shadows faded. Greens began to stand out. Noah figured he'd take Isobel away from town and turn the buggy into the woods, where he could talk to her about the things that needed to be said. And being so far out, he'd have time to calm her down before she did something fool-headed. At least he'd try.

My, but Isobel looked fine this morning. Her new blue dress with all its ruffles and gathers showed off her sumptuous curves in a way that made it hard for him to concentrate on what he had to tell her. She sat up straight and tall on the buggy seat, her chin held high, her bosom rising and falling, her dark gold hair all atumble around her shoulders. As a matter of fact, she looked as sweet and mild as barnyard milk.

But he knew better. Beneath that demure facade lay a woman with a tongue as sharp as barbed wire. He'd felt its sting the night before when she hadn't known he was listening to her chatter with Susan Gates. It didn't take much to set Noah Buchanan on the straight track. And Isobel had done just that. So much for all the daydreams that had been rolling around in his head since the night he'd made a woman of her. Daydreams weren't worth a barrel of shucks.

"Where are you taking me?" Isobel asked as the buggy passed the Dolan store with its group of Fort Stanton soldiers lounging around on the porch.

"Thought we'd go for a ride."

"Where?"

"Out of town."

She didn't seem to cotton to his evasiveness, but Noah decided he didn't care. He wasn't about to start talking to her this close to population. As the buggy left the road and began to near the river, the sparse New Mexico vegetation thickened. Yellow-green cedar shrubs mingled with olive-colored piñon trees and blue-green, rough-barked junipers.

Grama grass and bunch grass, ungrazed by cattle this far

away from town, had grown thick and tangled during the past summer. Now dry and gray-brown, it crackled beneath the buggy wheels. The rig bumped and jolted along a rutted trail. Bare-leafed oak brush stretched gray stems toward the sky. Chinese elms and aspens clustered near the riverbank. As Noah turned the horse off the trail, he saw that the ground was littered with long, brown pine needles, still damp from melting snow.

"There are people in Lincoln I need to talk with today," Isobel said finally. "I hope you aren't planning for us to be away long."

"Why don't you eat one of those tortillas? Do you good."

"Noah—"

"Go on. Eat up. Nothing better than a warm tortilla on a cold morning."

She studied his face for a moment, wondering how she had come to accept orders from this sort of man with such acquiescence. Perhaps she felt bad about having insulted him last night. Perhaps she should apologize. At least she wouldn't have to live with this knot in the pit of her stomach. "Noah—" she began.

"If you aren't going to eat, hand me over one. That Susan Gates is a bum cook. Good thing she's set her mind on teaching."

"You ate Susan's breakfast?"

"Tried to." A smile crossed his face at the memory of the men who were staying at McSween's as they hunkered down for their morning meal. "Eggs looked more like cowchips. And the bacon . . . well, a man could break a tooth on the stuff."

Isobel frowned. "Poor Susan."

"Aw, well, she's a sweet gal."

Susan. Isobel wondered what words had passed between the two of them when she was sent away. What might have happened during the night at the McSween house? The thought of him touching another woman's body . . . of his fingers slipping across other skin, other breasts . . .

She watched Noah's hands work the leather reins. It was a wonder, she realized suddenly, how much like this land Noah was. He seemed a part of it. His work-worn hands were rough and sunbaked. A pair of lines creased outward from the corner of each blue eye. When his face was still and solemn, she could see the paler skin in each crevice. But a smile erased every sign of tender flesh and left only the tanned skin of his face showing. He must smile often, she reasoned.

"Whoa, now." He pulled the horse to a stop in an open glade at the edge of the rushing, olive-green water. "How's this?"

"For what?"

"For talking." He jumped down from the buggy and walked around to Isobel's side. When he extended a hand, she stood, lifted her skirt, and descended. She felt shaky. Had he brought her here in the woods far from human eyes to play with her and woo her? Or to punish her for her villainous words? Or perhaps to tell her some news about himself and Susan?

"What will we talk about, Noah?" she asked.

He looked into her golden eyes, swallowed, and hitched up his shoulders. "Well . . . how about we spread a blanket and sit a spell? Kind of warm our toes in the sunshine?"

"Noah, what do you have to tell me?" She felt a river of unease course through her at his evasiveness. "Has something happened? Is it about Mr. Tunstall's murder?"

He rubbed a palm across the back of his neck. "I'll spread that blanket."

She stiffened as he set about unloading a coarsely woven wool blanket from the buggy and spreading it on a patch of grass. She felt sick inside. Sick with the knowledge that what he had to tell her was going to be painful. She walked toward him, picking her way over smooth, gray river stones embedded in the dry grass.

"Noah." She looked at him, her mouth dry.

"Come here, Isobel." He patted the blanket. Taking her by the hand, he eased her down beside him. She seemed to melt into a puddle of poufy blue cotton. "What I have to tell you isn't about Tunstall, Isobel."

"Then who?"

He took a deep breath. "I'm pretty sure I found out who killed your father."

"My father?" It was the last thing she expected him to say. "Who? Tell me!"

"Before you get bees in your britches, I want you to hear me out, Isobel. And I want you to do your best to think straight."

He noticed that she'd clumped her skirt in knotted fists, but she nodded, trying to obey his request. "Last night after I left you at Patrón's house, I went looking for my buddy, Dick Brewer. He's been staying over at McSween's place until things cool down around here—him being Tunstall's foreman and all. Dick and I sat out on the porch and got to talking about this and that. Finally I led him around to telling me about the day he came across that massacre on the trail."

"My father?"

"Yep. Well, Dick let loose with a secret he'd never told before. He said that when he found the coach, the guard who was still alive gave him a fair description of the man who shot your father. Dick figured out right away who the killer was. But he reckoned as how that fellow would be long gone by the time the story could come out, so it wouldn't do much good to tell. Anyway, Dick knew the law would try to drag the man back to Lincoln, where no one wanted him to be. 'Course . . . now he's back in town whether we like it or not."

"Who, Noah?"

"It *was* the Horrell Gang that attacked your father's party. The same bunch that killed Juan Patrón's dad. But the guard told Dick that the man who pulled the trigger on your father had a low-slung jaw, a flat nose, spiked-out red hair, and slanted yellow eyes."

"Snake Jackson," she whispered.

"You'd be hard put to find a man to match that description better than Rattlesnake Jim Jackson. I know for a fact he was riding with the Horrells back in seventy-three. This morning I got Juan to confirm it."

Isobel shut her eyes. *"Madre de Dios,"* she mouthed.

Noah watched her inner struggle and tried to imagine how it would feel to learn the name of a man who had murdered someone you loved. He'd never known his own parents—not that he could remember anyway—and it was hard to figure how Isobel might be feeling. He felt an urge to put his arms around her and hold her close, to kiss away the pain and try to ease the agony of her loss.

But then he kept remembering what she really thought of him. To Isobel he wasn't someone worthy of giving comfort. He was just a no-account cowboy, and he'd better learn to keep his hands off.

"Now, Isobel," he said finally, shoving his hands into the pockets of his coat to keep from touching her. "I think you'd better look at this situation straight on. Snake Jackson may have murdered your father, but he just murdered John Tunstall, too. He's in a heap more hot water about that second killing right now. And he already has his eye out for the mysterious Spanish woman who saw him put a hole in Tunstall's chest. If he ever pins you as that woman, you don't stand much of a chance of survival. And if he links you up to the Horrell business, too, then, honey, your days are numbered."

Isobel couldn't speak. Staring at dry grass that blurred into a brown fog, she alternately pictured Snake Jackson shooting the Englishman . . . and then imagined him killing her own father. His face, ugly and misshapen, faded in and out. She could hear his voice shouting threats over the wall of the *torreón*. His yellow eyes seemed to stare at her in the dim light of the Dolan store as his mouth formed words that dripped with evil . . . *"You always wear that white shawl?"* . . . *"Strange accent you got there"* . . .

"Take me back to town, Noah," she said with finality. "I must kill Jim Jackson."

He lifted his head. "*Kill* him? I just told you your life isn't worth a plug nickel, woman, and you want to ride into Lincoln and try to hunt the man down? A man who's in league with Dolan and Evans and the rest of those sidewinders?"

"What choice do I have, Noah? Snake killed my father!"

"Here's a choice for you. Take your pick. You can either ride on up to Santa Fe and marry your fancy don—or head back to Spain and settle down with your nice, safe little family."

Isobel sniffed and looked away. "I don't suppose you've had a telegram from Guillermo Pascal?"

"Not yet. But that doesn't mean a thing. Those Pascals are a bunch of . . . what I mean to say is, the Pascals have a lot going on. Irons in the fire, you know. They stay pretty busy, what with this and that they've got their sticky fingers into. Maybe he just hasn't had time."

Isobel shrugged. *A man of honor would make time.*

"Anyway, why don't you head back to Spain?" Noah was asking. "I bet your mama'd be tickled pink to see you again. And your brother . . . and that horse of yours that can jump over all those fences."

"I'm not wanted in Spain. No more than I'm wanted by Guillermo Pascal."

Noah let out his breath and lay back on the blanket. Well, here was a fine to-do. She wouldn't go to Santa Fe because her don didn't want her. She wouldn't go to Spain because her family didn't want her. So what did she plan to do—stay in Lincoln? Who wanted her around here?

He settled his hat on his stomach and shut his eyes. Not him, that's for sure. Well . . . he wouldn't deny he'd enjoyed that tumble the other night. But if she thought she could treat him like a piece of dirt under her fingernail and still expect him to stick by her and protect her and keep her around . . . just because nobody else wanted her . . .

"What do you see?" she asked.

He lifted his head and squinted at her. "I had my eyes shut."

"No—I mean here, in this place. In Lincoln. What do you see here that makes you stay?"

"Aw, hell, Isobel, haven't you been here long enough to figure out this is God's country? What I see in New Mexico is elbow room. Clean air and plenty of sunshine. Blue sky. Rich, chocolate-colored earth. Trees that have stood up to wind and rain and drought. It's a tough land. Tough people, too. I like that."

"Tell me about these people."

"Most of them are hard as old boot leather. They've worked hard and lived hard. Even played hard. Not too many of them you can't figure. They're either good—honest, thrifty, hardworking folk. Or they're bad—shifty, cheating, lying scoundrels. It's not hard to tell them apart. Kind of seems to show on their faces, you know. I've often thought . . . well . . ."

"What have you thought, Noah?"

"Crazy notion, maybe. I have an idea that the way a man's heart is . . . the state of his soul . . . eventually starts creeping out onto his face. The older he gets, the more he begins to look like the person he really is inside."

Isobel pondered this, sifting through the people she knew. The more she thought of it, the more Noah's idea seemed to hold some validity. There were the evil—Snake Jackson, with his lantern jaw and yellow eyes; Jimmie Dolan, with his dark hair and bulbous face.

There were the good—her father, with his golden hair and soft smile; Dr. Ealy, with gentle gray eyes and peaceful expression; Dick Brewer, with the classic face of a Greek god. And Susan Gates.

"Susan is lovely," Isobel said.

"She's easy on the eyes."

"Perhaps you'll marry her."

Noah sat up and plopped his hat on his head. "Marry Miss Gates?"

"She seems to like you." Isobel gazed into the blue eyes that stared at her with such frank shock. "I think Susan would make you a good wife."

"Well, Isobel, near as I can figure, you've got two problems with your little notion. Number one is that Miss Gates has set her sights on Dick Brewer, and he's returning the compliment. Fact is, she wanted some information about him from me last night after you left the room in such a huff. And I had only good things to tell her. Dick is twenty-seven years old, he's got a fine ranch, and he's respected by nearly everybody in town. I don't imagine it'll be too long before we hear wedding bells."

"A wedding?" Isobel didn't know how it was possible she had miscalculated everything so badly.

"The second hitch in your scheme," Noah went on, "is that I'm already married—in case you forgot."

"I didn't forget," she said.

"Neither did I."

They looked into each other's eyes, each trying to read the message hidden there. Isobel swallowed and folded her hands in her lap. She felt hot suddenly, as if the morning sun had focused its rays on her shoulders.

"Noah, how do I look to you?" she asked. "Am I one of those whose face shows the hardness of her heart?"

He took one of her hands from her lap, opened the fingers, and studied them for a moment. "When I first saw you hiding behind that juniper, I thought you were a might chilly-looking. All those shiny green ruffles, you know? And those red boots. I guess I have you pegged as hardheaded, stubborn, afraid of tying yourself to anybody, and scared to trust folk. That stuff shows on your face, Isobel. It does."

She lowered her head.

"On the other hand," he continued, "being strong-minded and independent will serve you well out here in the West. A woman's got to be a little tough or she won't make it."

She watched him toying with her fingers, rubbing the knuckles, absently squeezing each white nail. In her mind Isobel pictured herself growing harder and more craggy through the years, until finally she turned gray and became dead and solid as one of these river stones. And she realized she didn't want to be that kind of woman.

But what sort of person could she choose to become? She knew no other way to approach life. Taking a breath, she plunged into the speech she had rehearsed all night—the one she knew must be said.

"Noah, last night you heard me say . . . harsh words . . . cruel things about you."

"Like I told you, I reckon most of them were true, Isobel."

"They were lies." She looked into his face, trying to make him see that what she was telling him came from her heart. "You're the best man I have known since the death of my father. You're kind and gentle. But also brave and strong. You have intelligence."

"Well, go on. Sounds good to me."

She grinned. "You *are* a good person. You agreed to watch over me even when you didn't want to. You can cook and wash dishes and sweep—"

"Hold it there, now. You're edging out of tough-man territory."

"Noah, I'm sorry. About what I said last night. I'm sorry."

He studied her hazel eyes and wondered if the shine in them came just from the sun or if she really meant her apology. "Isobel, if you didn't mean what you told Miss Gates, why'd you say it?"

Nervous, she lifted the hair from the back of her neck and ran her hand over her damp skin. Her long eyelashes fluttered down as she struggled to voice feelings she didn't understand herself.

"I . . . I can't allow myself to think too well of you, Noah," she said finally.

"Why? Because I'm low-class?"

"No!" She whirled on him. "That has nothing to do with it. What is there for me here, Noah? Nothing! I have no future. My paths to Santa Fe or Spain are blocked. My only hope is to find Snake Jackson and get my land titles from him. I have nothing. I am nobody. How can I allow myself to look at anything but my *revancha*?"

"Revenge? Listen, Isobel. I'm not letting you get anywhere near Jim Jackson. How many times do I have to say it before you hear me? That bastard will kill you!"

"So what will you do with me, Noah?"

"Right after the funeral tomorrow, I'm taking you to Chisum's ranch. That's final. No arguing."

"And then? What then, Noah? What will become of me? You can't keep me there forever. You don't want me any more than my family or my betrothed do. I heard you say you didn't want—"

"I want you, Isobel. I'll be damned if I understand it myself, but ever since I first laid eyes on you, I've wanted you. I don't know about the future. Right now everything's about to blow sky high in Lincoln. I've got to get Chisum out of jail and settle things with him. I can't think about the future. All I can think about is right now. And right now I know I want you, woman."

Isobel let out her breath slowly. "If you want me . . . take me, Noah. Take me now."

Chapter

❧ 8 ❧

The blanket beneath her naked back felt cool and soft as Isobel lay upon it. Noah had eased apart the hooks on her new dress, and she was forced to smile as she remembered the protection she had imagined that flimsy barrier. No, mere clothing could not douse the fire that sprang up each time she was touched by Noah Buchanan . . . touched by his words or by his hands.

He was a temptation. A man who looked as he looked, who spoke as he spoke could not easily be resisted. At each memory of his mouth on her full flesh, she had melted a little inside. And now, with his fingertips stroking the soft rise above her chemise, she felt a flood of warm need between her thighs. The tingle that had begun in the pit of her stomach that morning now shivered up her back and down her legs and out to the tips of her breasts.

"Noah," she whispered. "Touch me, please."

Noah had thought he had himself pretty well under control. But looking down at this vision on the blanket, he realized he was getting mighty tangled. Her pouty lips called for his kisses. Her warm hazel eyes were soft with desire. A rosy flush had spread up her bosom and onto her neck. When she murmured her words of hunger, he knew he didn't stand a chance. What man would?

Thoughts of the uncertain future went clean out of his head as he bent to kiss the swollen rise of first one breast and then the other. If he was going to take Isobel again, by golly, he'd do it right this time. Slow and easy, the way he knew a woman wanted to be loved.

Starting with the pink bow at the top of her corset, he worked his way down the row of tiny hooks that held it together. As the whalebone undergarment spread and she could breathe more easily, her chest began to rise and fall in quick gasps. She was ready . . . ready for him now. And he'd barely begun.

He lifted her pink chemise and began to fondle her breasts. But she was mewing with need for him. "Noah, Noah, please, I can't bear this!" she begged. Her hands groped at his trousers, fingers fiddling blindly with the metal buttons.

Giving up the slow and tender preparation, he shrugged out of his coat and ripped off his shirt. In a split second she was covering his chest with hot, sweet kisses, her tongue working circles on his nipples and dipping in and out of his navel. He thought he was flat going to die right then and there.

"Isobel, darlin'." But she had worked apart his fly and was reaching for his flesh. He let out a groan as her hands covered him. Soft and pliant, they kneaded and stroked his hunger until he felt like a burning brand. "I have to at least get us out of these clothes, honey."

Her eyebrows lifted in the slightest sign of surprise at the notion, but she quickly accepted the idea and began to lower his trousers. Her dress, corset and chemise melted beneath his hands. Her boots and stockings, his underwear, wool socks, and leather boots soon lay in a haphazard pile on the grass. The slight late-winter breeze playing off the river mingled with the warm early-spring sunlight to create a bower fragrant with the bloom of sweet clover. In their silent haven Isobel and Noah touched and stroked, kissed and caressed . . . a world away from the fear, bloodshed, and anger pursuing them.

Noah found sweet release in the chapel of Isobel's body. She arched and cried aloud with pleasure as he worshiped her with his hands. And as they slipped together through a boundless ecstasy, each was certain of heaven.

It seemed with the shedding of their clothes that all boundaries and reservations had fallen away. After their loving, Isobel lay in Noah's arms, her cheek on his chest, her dark gold hair soft against his shoulders. Their legs twined, toes nestled, hips pressed flush. She gazed at the tangle of dark chest hair growing around his brown nipples. Sunlight sifted through the coarse curls and blended them into mist. Despite their springy texture, they felt soft against her ear.

"Noah." Her breath stirred his skin. "The first day we met, you went searching Dick Brewer's cabin for paper."

She sensed the slightest tension ripple through the muscles in his chest. "Yeah . . . I did."

"What do you write, Noah?"

His fingers laced through her hair, weaving among the golden waves as he pondered her question. Finally he let out a breath. "Not much yet," he said.

She lifted her head and studied the uneven, sun-hardened planes of his face. "The moment I first saw your hands—when you saved me from the bullet's path that day on the trail—I knew," she said.

"What did you know?"

"I knew you were more than a cowboy. I knew you were an artist. Your hands are those of a poet."

He smiled a lazy grin, his eyes never leaving her face. "I'm no poet, Isobel."

"Then tell me what it is you write. Please, Noah."

After a moment's hesitation he shrugged. "Aw, stories mainly. They're all up here. In my head. Not a one of them's written down on paper yet. So I can't call myself a writer. Not really. I just have patches of ideas floating around. Stories about life on the trail. About things that can happen to a man when he's living off the land, when he and God and the lowing of the cattle are his whole world. Yarns the men spin while they're sitting around the fire after a long day." He paused and laughed. "It's probably a crazy notion."

She regarded the cowboy with his blue eyes focused somewhere far above on things she couldn't see. And she began to understand that what to her was a rough, untamed land was to this man a place of dreams. As his poet's hands slipped up and down her back, her heart grew and opened toward him.

"It would be crazier *not* to write down your stories, Noah," she said softly.

"Maybe so, Isobel. Maybe so."

A white butterfly drifted over their heads. Noah watched, wondering how it had emerged from its cocoon so soon. Too soon. A frost would no doubt end the fragile creature's life before summer. The white wings trembled, and the butterfly alighted on the creamy round swell of Isobel's bottom. She didn't notice. Noah smiled.

He liked Isobel this way, he mused. Of course, not many men wouldn't. She was soft, feminine, delicate. She was fleshly and giving in a delicious way that made him want to do things he'd tried to put clean out of his mind. Things like protect, honor, and provide for her. He wanted to keep her at hand so he could touch her hair and run his lips across her open mouth. He'd like to know her sweet thighs were waiting for him at the end of the day.

If he could keep her just like this . . .

"You must take me to town now, Noah," she was saying, hazel eyes heavy-lidded and so seductive he figured he'd do near anything she asked. "I must find Jim Jackson before dark. I cannot be denied *la venganza*."

It took him a moment to sift through the sunlit imaginings that had spangled his reality. *"La vengan—"*

"My father's murder, Noah—I must avenge it. I have to find the land grant titles that Snake stole from the *familia* Matas. Now that you've told me the name of the assassin, I have no choice."

Noah groaned and sat up, easing Isobel's shoulders forward until she was at a safe distance. He forced himself to look into her eyes, never mind that her peaked breasts were tempting him beneath the tangle of her hair.

"I want you to hear me once and for all, Isobel. You're not a Matas any longer. You're a Buchanan. You're under my protection. I swore an oath to keep you safe, and I aim to abide by my word. For decency's sake, I'm going to Tunstall's funeral tomorrow. But the minute it's over, I'm taking you to South

Spring River Ranch. No arguing. And none of this business about revenge against Snake Jackson, understand?"

"I understand, Noah," she said. *But*, she thought to herself, you *do not*. Not at all.

That evening in Lincoln Noah refused to let Isobel out of his sight. She insisted on a visit to Susan, but he barred her way. Their dinner with the Patróns was strained. Juan was worried that the Dolan group would attend the funeral the following morning. With Alexander McSween's party there—along with John Tunstall's closest friends and employees—violence could be expected.

While Noah and Isobel had been away that morning, Juan explained, Sheriff Brady had allowed the Fort Stanton soldiers to feed their horses hay from the Tunstall store. In an outrage over the action, Alexander McSween had immediately gone to Squire Wilson and charged Brady—along with others in his bunch—with the unlawful appropriation of Tunstall's property.

Once again an arrest had been made. Brady was bound over to the grand jury at the coming term of court. The feeling in town, Juan told Isobel and Noah, was that Sheriff Brady now sided squarely with Jimmie Dolan. And that meant trouble.

After dinner that evening Noah and Isobel retired for the night. But Noah couldn't bring himself to enjoy the company of the woman who awaited him in their narrow bed. Armed, he paced the front of Patrón's home and store. He circled the house through the night, checking windows and doors. Dawn found him sprawled on the wooden couch in the living room, his black hat on his stomach, his eyes shut, and his hand resting on the handle of his gun.

Isobel read the concern on his sleeping face. Brows drawn together, he snored softly, his huge shoulders wedged against the wood surface of the couch. She woke him with a gentle touch.

After a breakfast of *atole* and warm tortillas, they and the Patróns joined the stream of people moving down the muddy road. Alexander McSween had selected a burial plot to the east of Tunstall's store, just behind the land for the church Dr. Ealy planned to build.

"John Henry Tunstall," Dr. Ealy said to begin the solemn service, "was a young man barely twenty-four years of age at the moment of his untimely death. The son of John Partridge Tunstall of London, England, our dearly departed friend was the brother to three sisters whom he loved with an extreme devotion. Minnie, the oldest of his sisters, was closest to John in age—and he often spoke of her with the most tender affection. Many are not aware that John was blind in his right eye, but he overcame this handicap with the air of the gentleman he was."

Isobel studied the row of heavily armed men who made up the Dolan faction, though she didn't see Snake Jackson among them. They stood clumped at the other side of the open grave beyond the pile of newly turned earth. The casket, a simple pine box, rested on the ground. Eyes wary, the Dolan men glanced back and forth at the friends of John Tunstall who had gathered to mourn him. Noah had put his arm around Isobel, yet—like the other men in the McSween group—he rested his fingertips lightly on the holster that hung at his thigh.

A detachment of Company H, the 15th Infantry, had been sent by Captain Purington from Fort Stanton, and the soldiers kept a watchful distance from the proceedings. Lieutenant Delany had evidently instructed his men well, for Isobel sensed that their respectful but obvious presence was the only thing keeping the two angry groups in a truce.

"My text today is from the Gospel of John, Chapter Eleven, verse twenty-five." Dr. Ealy cleared his throat as he opened the heavy black Bible and began to read. "Jesus said unto Martha, 'I am the resurrection and the life; he who believeth in me, though he die, yet shall he live.' Clearly we are to understand by these words that those who believe in the Lord Jesus Christ will live with Him in heaven after their earthly death."

Noah glanced at Dick Brewer, who was standing protectively beside Susan Gates. Both men knew full well that John Henry Tunstall had been more than a mite contemptuous of organized religion. Still, it seemed to Noah that there was hardly a man who had ridden through the beauty and grandeur of New Mexico Territory who could discount the power of the Creator. So maybe young Tunstall was resting in heaven now. Noah sure hoped so.

"I'd like to ask now," Dr. Ealy said, "that we close this service with a hymn. As we have joined together here beside the peaceful flow of the Rio Bonito, let's lift our hearts together in song. Noah Buchanan, I understand you're blessed with the best voice among us. Would you please lead us in singing 'Shall We Gather at the River'?"

Isobel felt not a moment's hesitation from Noah as he raised his head and began to sing. His deep voice drifted over the gurgling stream and seemed to roll across the grassland to the flowing mountains.

"Shall we gather at the river, where bright angel feet have trod," he sang, "with its crystal tide forever, flowing by the throne of God?"

The entire company—even the Dolan men—joined him in the chorus. "Yes, we'll gather at the river, the beautiful, the beautiful river; gather with the saints at the river that flows by the throne of God."

Not knowing the words as the others did, Isobel shut her eyes and absorbed the vibrations in Noah's chest. Though it was a funeral, she felt at this moment more peace than she had known the entire sum of her life. She was gathered in the arms of a man who had sworn to protect her. Sweet golden sunlight streamed over her face, warming her eyelids and the crest of her nose. The anger that had driven her to this land had faded and left in its place the gentle lull of tranquility.

"Soon we'll reach the shining river, soon our pilgrimage will cease," Noah sang. "Soon our happy hearts will quiver with the melody of peace. Yes, we'll gather at the river, the beautiful, the beautiful river; gather with the saints at the river that flows by the throne of God."

Dick Brewer was weeping, his head bowed low and his curly hair resting against Susan's. Alexander McSween mopped his eyes with a large white handkerchief. When the song ended, the lawyer cleared his throat and announced that he had something to pass along—a message from Billy Bonney.

The Kid, Isobel knew, was still in jail, as was Fred Waite. The crowd perked up uneasily when Alexander began to read. " 'Though I cannot be present for the burial of John Henry Tunstall, I want it known that he was as good a friend as I ever had. When Mr. Tunstall hired me, he made me a present of a fine horse, a good saddle, and a new gun. He always treated me like a gentleman, though I was younger than him and not near as educated. I loved Mr. Tunstall better than any man I ever knew.' Signed, William Bonney."

Alexander folded the letter and placed it on the casket. As the pine box was lowered into the ground, Noah turned Isobel away from the scene. Dick Brewer, eyes red and face drawn, caught his friend's elbow.

"There's to be a meeting at McSween's house," he whispered. "The men want to discuss the situation in town."

Noah nodded. "Wait here a minute, Isobel." He left her beside a juniper tree and walked a few paces away to confer with Dick. "What's this about now?"

"It's Sheriff Brady," Dick explained. "Folks are mad as hell that he won't arrest anybody for John's murder. And he won't allow any arrests to be made by anybody else. I think we ought to ask Brady outright just what he means by it."

"I'm with you, Dick, but I can't stay for the meeting. I've got to get Isobel out of town. I told her about Snake Jackson murdering her father, and she's hot for blood. The woman's a spitfire, Dick. I've got to get her away from—"

"Noah!" Dick grabbed his friend's shoulder. "It's Snake. He's talking to Isobel by that tree."

Noah swung around, fingers sliding over the handle of his six-shooter. "Snake!" he shouted, feeling half sick with fear. "What the hell do you think you're doing with my wife?"

The heavy-jawed man straightened. His yellow eyes shifted to the tall man approaching. "Buchanan, this Mexican ain't your wife."

"She damn sure is." Noah reached the tree just as Isobel opened her mouth to speak. He grabbed her arm, stopping her words, and jerked her behind him. Dick took her shoulders and squared her against his chest. Then he turned and marched her quickly out of earshot—and pistol range.

"You stay away from my woman, you ugly snake in the grass," Noah growled. "If I see you near her again, I'll bore a hole in you big enough to drive a wagon through."

"Forget it, hombre. The jig's up with your little Mexican *chiquita* now. This morning a pile of fancy trunks got dropped off at the hotel. Jimmie Dolan read the name on the trunks for me—Miss Maria Isobel Matas. Later on along come that uppity Mexican so-and-so Juan Patrón a-wanderin' into the hotel. He took one look at the trunks and then, all sneaky-like, he made new name markin's on every one of 'em. Mrs. Belle Buchanan."

He gave Noah a triumphant smirk. "All through this sorry funeral," he continued, "I been studyin' her from behind them trees over there. And I got it down for a fact. She's the señorita who was in the woods the day we laid Tunstall out, ain't she? She was wearin' this Mexican veil." He shook the fragile white *mantilla* in Noah's face. "And you know what your woman just told me, lover-boy? She thinks I'm the man who done in her Mexican papa a few years back. Well, guess what?"

Noah glanced behind at Isobel. She was staring whitefaced, her hazel eyes luminous with terror. Dick and Susan were attempting to lead her out of the clearing, but she resisted.

"What have you got to tell me that I don't already know, Snake?" Noah asked.

"Just this. I *am* the man who made her papa a free lunch for the coyotes. And I'm the man who's got what she's come to Lincoln lookin' for—her package of fancy little papers. And I'm the man who's gonna pull her picket pin the minute your back is turned. So watch out, Buchanan. The next funeral you sing your pretty songs at is gonna be hers."

"Why, you lowdown—"

"Now, just a minute here, gentlemen." The burly lieutenant stepped between the two men. "Jim Jackson. Noah Buchanan. Haven't the two of you got better things to do with yourself this morning? Especially here in the presence of the dearly departed."

Noah glanced at Tunstall's grave. It was nearly filled with dirt now, and the reality of it struck him like a bolt out of the blue. "Lieutenant Delany," he snapped. "This man here is the one who shot John Tunstall down in cold blood."

"Now, you don't know that, Buchanan," Delany insisted. "You weren't even there."

"I was there, all right. And I've got a witness who'll swear to the name of the man who pulled the trigger on Tunstall."

"Aw, hell, Buchanan, quit your jawin'." Snake gave a menacing laugh. "Why, Tunstall's own men swore out a statement about who was at the site of the killing, and your name weren't on it. Neither was the name of the mysterious witness you think you got tucked away fer good measure. And if Tunstall's men didn't say neither of you was there, how you gonna convince a judge of it? Huh?"

Noah glared at Snake. "Don't sell me short, Jackson."

"Go on your way, Mr. Buchanan," the lieutenant said. "And you, too, Snake. Captain Purington charged me with the protection of life and property around here, and I mean to carry out my orders. Now, get along, the both of you."

Snickering, Rattlesnake Jackson lumbered across the clearing. He gave Isobel a sideways glance and formed his fingers into the shape of a gun. As he walked past her, he aimed at her heart and pulled the imaginary trigger. Tossing his head back in laughter, he sauntered along the side of Tunstall's store toward the Dolan mercantile.

"If you know something about him, Buchanan," the lieutenant said, "'you'd better watch your back. That man's so mean I reckon he's got a reserved seat in hell."

The faint trace of a smile crossed Noah's face. "You're right about that, Delany."

"You know he used to run with the Horrells, don't you? And now he's in deep with Jesse Evans and the Dolan bunch. Steer clear of him, that's my advice."

"Thanks, Lieutenant." Noah tipped his hat and headed for the Tunstall porch, where Dick stood guarding the women.

Isobel jerked free of Dick's grip and raced across the bare ground toward Noah. He caught her waist. "Why'd you tell him, Isobel? Why'd you tell Snake you knew he shot your father?"

"I was so frightened when he came suddenly from behind the tree. He grabbed my arm and began to accuse me of terrible things!" Tears filled her eyes. "He called me unspeakable names and threatened to . . . to use my body in a horrible way. He told me that a Mexican gang had murdered his parents in Laredo and now he would kill everyone of Mexican blood he could lay hands on. If I ever say a word about what I saw in the forest, he promises he will strangle me and then bury a knife in my stomach. And then he'll shoot me between my eyes. And . . . oh, Noah, I was so afraid. My fear became anger, and I told him that I knew he had murdered my father. He began to threaten my life. But then you came and stopped him."

She bent and buried her face in her open hands. Sobbing, she allowed Noah to draw her into the fold of his arms. "Noah," she cried, "I have no choice now. I must kill that man before he kills me."

"Come on, now," he murmured. "You're not going after Snake Jackson, Isobel. You're a woman. And a woman's place is somewhere safe and secure and quiet."

"The pair of you better get out of Lincoln fast," Dick said, joining them. "If Snake's got you marked, you don't need to make it easy for him. Why don't you two go on up to Santa Fe? Or head over to my place and hide out a while."

"Thanks, Dick, but I'm taking Isobel to Chisum's ranch. It's a good distance from the trouble, and I know I can keep my eye on her there."

Susan touched Isobel's arm. "After the funeral Mr. Patrón told me your trunks came into town this morning. They're at the hotel, Isobel."

"My trunks . . ." She looked at Noah.

"I'll borrow a buckboard from McSween. Dick, will you help me load up?"

"Count on it."

The two men began walking down the long covered wooden porch in front of Tunstall's store. Susan lifted her skirts and hurried to catch up to them, but Isobel stood in silence for a moment.

She turned and watched the men stomping soil on the mound that covered John Tunstall's grave. She remembered the peace she had felt at the sound of Noah's voice lifted in song. She remembered Dr. Ealy's words of hope for a future life.

But Isobel knew she wasn't ready for a celestial paradise. She had tasted such bliss here on earth. For the first time in her life she had touched the fringes of serenity, of ecstasy, of union. She had found her heaven in the arms of Noah Buchanan. And she wasn't ready to let her promised land slip away. Not yet.

It took four full days to drive the loaded buckboard to John Chisum's South Spring River Ranch. Opting for the main road rather than a trail, they bumped and jolted southeast along the edge of the Rio Bonito before making the slow climb over the foothills that bounded the Rio Ruidoso. They passed first Barlett's Mill and then the Fritz ranch. Isobel asked whether they might spend the night at the second home, but Noah shook his head.

"Charles Fritz's brother died nearly four years ago, and the wrangle over his estate was the start of the mess in Lincoln," he explained. "Alexander McSween, being a lawyer, was trying to settle Emil Fritz's will when Jimmie Dolan stepped in and claimed that all the money was owed to his store. See, Fritz had once been part owner of the store. When McSween refused to give over the inheritance, Dolan accused him of stealing it. Funny thing . . . Charles Fritz seems to believe Dolan instead of McSween. Most folks think Charles has sided with the Dolan bunch now."

Isobel eyed the rambling adobe home nestled against the foothills of the Capitans. The setting sun splashed an orange glow over its mellow brown mud walls. Wooden vigas projecting from the roof cast long black shadows down the sides.

"I can hardly keep it all straight in my head." She sighed. "It seems everyone has accused everyone else. One man arrests another . . . and then is arrested in turn. Sometimes I wonder which side is right and which is wrong."

Noah took her hand and squeezed it lightly. "The main thing to remember is that you and I have no part of either side. Once I settle you at Chisum's ranch, we'll just bide our time until the trouble blows over. After we see how it comes out, you can make a decision as to what you want to do with yourself."

"And what about Rattlesnake Jackson? Shall I be content to let him get away with my father's murder and the thievery of my family's lands?"

"You have no choice, Isobel. If Dolan's bunch wins this

feud, Snake will have everything, including the law, on his side. If McSween's group comes out on top, they'll lock Snake up without needing your testimony. Snake said something to me when we were talking back at the funeral—and he had a good point. All the affidavits sworn right after Tunstall's murder don't mention you or me."

"But we wanted our names left out for our protection."'

"Looks like our good idea might have backfired. See, we can't come along now and say we were there in the woods all along. We can't just up and claim you saw the whole murder. No judge'll believe that. It's too convenient."

Isobel fell silent. She felt trapped. Cornered. Held hostage by a man who deserved the worst fate she could wish upon him. But she knew that a trapped animal—one with spirit and fire to live—didn't lie down and die. No, it fought. It snarled and slashed and bit. And perhaps . . . perhaps turned the tables on the trapper.

A silver pistol nestled in the folds of her emerald-green silk gown. The gown lay in the trunks that rode the back of the buckboard. Isobel knew how to use that pistol. She had the skill and the desire. Now all she needed was the opportunity.

Glancing down, she mused over the large brown hand that covered hers. Fingers thick and hardened. White nails shortened by work rather than by the fine scissors of a manicurist. A palm almost crusty with calluses. This was a good hand. It held the promise of protection, nurture, sensuality.

And what of Noah, the man who possessed such a sturdy hand? Isobel sensed he wanted her to be at peace. He hoped to mold her into the sort of woman to whom a simple blue calico dress and white wool shawl might belong. He believed he could take her away and erase every need in her life but the need for him.

As darkness settled over the road, she studied his profile beneath the black felt Stetson. His nose, a shade too long, was outlined in the last ribbons of golden light. A blue ray lit the iris of his eye. A gray shadow dusted the plane beneath it, then veered sharply over the ridge of bone and fell to form the deep black wall of his cheek. His chin jutted forward, capturing just a trace of gold, but his neck and the red bandanna were painted in ebony.

As the hours and days had passed, Isobel realized, Noah had shed his common, dusty *vaquero* image. She had almost forgotten the dark-bearded stranger who had swept her onto his horse. In his place she saw a real man. A human being who held hopes, dreams, feelings, and needs in the palms of those rough hands.

It frightened her to think how much of herself she had given to him—and how little she really knew him. For the hundredth time, she mused over the interplay between the two factions in Lincoln Town . . . McSween, the lawyer . . . Dolan, the merchant banker. How could it be that the law in this territory supported Dolan? The men who seemed most honest and trustworthy belonged with McSween. Who was good; who was bad? Who was right, and who wrong?

Perhaps Noah knew best. Maybe she should step out of the fray and hope that Snake received the fate he deserved at the hand of another. But this was not the way she had been brought up.

"Noah," she said as they rode on through the darkness. "You told me I have no choice but to abandon the revenge that calls me."

"That's right. No choice at all. You just give up the notion like any woman with a thread of common sense would."

"Noah, what do you know about my people? About Catalonia?"

He pondered this a while, thinking that what he knew about it could fit in a thimble. "Well, I reckon it's part of Spain. That means everybody speaks Spanish—"

"We speak Catalan."

When Noah frowned at this revelation, she went on. "Catalan is a Romance tongue that traces its roots to Provençal . . . the language of the French troubadours. The Catalan tongue has been forbidden to us, but we speak it anyway. We are a creative, artistic, political people, Noah. The Catalan nation is a leader in the production of textiles. Barcelona has grown and spread far beyond its fifteenth-century walls. Most of us wish for autonomy from the Spanish government."

"Autonomy? You mean you folks are thinking of civil war—like the one we went through a few years back?"

"Exactly. The rest of Spain is poor and ignorant. But we are a high-minded, cultured people. Have you heard of our *Jocs Florals*—the Floral Games?"

" 'Fraid not."

"They're public poetry contests in Catalonia. Huge prizes are awarded. We have great numbers of choral societies. We are a people in search of fraternity and liberty."

"Sounds like revolution words to me."

"We have nationalist movements and anarchist movements. Noah, I'm trying to explain that we, in Catalonia, do not sit calmly by and wait for our future. We have a heritage of progress. Change. We're willing to fight for our freedom."

"So, what are you telling me here, Isobel?" Noah tried to read her face, but it was shadowed by the utter darkness of the roadway.

"What I'm telling you is this," she said in a voice so low the sound of the buckboard wheels almost drowned it. "I am a Catalan. I have a noble spirit and a blood of fire. My father has been murdered and our family heritage stolen. These are crimes I cannot allow to go unavenged."

"Isobel—"

"I must prepare myself, Noah. I must find Jim Jackson. And then I must kill him."

Chapter
❦ *9* ❦

Noah wasn't much in the mood to chat or do anything else by the time the buckboard pulled into San Patricio. It was almost midnight according to the moon-silvered hands on his pocket watch. The little town nestled in the valley where the Bonito and Ruidoso rivers joined to create the Rio Hondo was shut down tight. The buckboard passed the Dow Brothers store, but Noah elected not to stop. Instead he pulled into a wooded copse and set the brake.

Isobel sat shivering while he built a fire of dry wood by the river's edge. They spoke little, Noah musing over the firebrand he'd gotten himself yoked to, and Isobel pondering the mulehead she'd married. By the time they'd eaten the supper of tortillas and roasted meat Beatriz Patrón had packed for them, both were feeling positively hostile.

"Shall I sleep in the buckboard?" Isobel asked after washing the supper dishes in the chilly stream while Noah banked the fire.

"Unless you'd rather pack a rifle and stand guard over your fancy dresses all night," Noah shot back.

Isobel tossed her head. "Better to appear foolhardy and defend one's possessions than to be so concerned for safety that one loses everything. To run is cowardly."

"Who're you calling a coward, woman?"

"Certainly *I'm* not the one who chose to flee the face of danger."

"As I recall, you're the one who was so scared she blabbered everything we'd worked so hard to keep under wraps. And then we were left with no choice but to get out of town."

Isobel could hardly argue there. She *had* collapsed in front of Snake Jackson. But with the clarity of reflection, she realized she should have stood her ground with him. She should have insisted to Noah that they stay on in Lincoln.

"Sometimes even a brave person may have a moment of weakness," she asserted, "but it is your continuing stubbornness that may prevent me from my goal. Good night, Noah." She climbed onto the back end of the buckboard and settled in a pile of blankets in the midst of the trunks. She could hear Noah muttering as he checked the horses.

"*Me* stubborn?" she heard him snort. "She's so ornery she wouldn't move camp in a prairie fire. Cussed Spanish hothead."

She pulled the blanket over her head, but his words drifted through the thick wool. "Thinks she's going to kill Jim Jackson. . . . It'll be a cold day in hell before I let her near that snake. . . ."

And then he was singing in a low, almost inaudible voice. "On the margin of the river, washing up its silver spray, we will walk and worship ever, all the happy golden day. Yes, we'll gather at the river, the beautiful, the beautiful river; gather with the saints at the river that flows by the throne of God. . . ."

On the second day Isobel and Noah drove along the Rio Hondo past the Sanders–Frank Coe farm. At Casey's Mill they stopped to spend the night. There Isobel learned that once again the hostility in Lincoln had left its mark.

Three years earlier, Noah told her, the owner of the mill, Robert Casey, had been murdered. His death had been tied directly to the political aspirations of Lawrence Murphy, a man for whom Jimmie Dolan had worked. The murderer had been tried and hanged. John Chisum—Noah's boss—had recently helped the widow Casey sell off her cattle.

Indirectly John Chisum tied Noah to the Casey family, which in turn pitted him against Dolan.

The more Noah thought about it, the less he liked the fact that he was being drawn into the bloody tangle in Lincoln. First it was Chisum's connections with McSween. Then it was Noah's own agreement to protect Isobel.

All he really wanted to do was buy some land. Settle down. Write a book.

Humming under his breath, Noah settled Isobel in one of the bedrooms at the Casey house and set up watch outside the door. Mrs. Casey and her five children had taken a herd of cattle to Texas, so the house was empty. The place felt eerie and sinister to Noah without the usual patter of young ones running about, without the smells of cooking that wafted from the kitchen, without the echoes of laughter from the dining room.

Like most settler families in the area, the Caseys had borne more than a fair share of hardships. As Noah settled back on the pine chair beside Isobel's bedroom door, he reflected on the calamities that could befall a single family in this rough country.

On their way to New Mexico, the Casey family had met up with raiding Indians who had robbed them of most of their cattle and provisions. Later, Robert Casey had been murdered. The Horrell Gang—the band of ruffians who went on a murderous rampage killing Mexicans, including Juan Patrón's father and Isobel's father—had descended on the Casey mill one night. Though they left in peace, their presence had caused the family much concern.

Noah knew that in the past two years the Caseys had undergone the same plagues as the rest of southeastern New Mexico—locusts first, then cabbage lice and fleas. Finally black smallpox had hit the area. Four-year-old Mollie Kathleen, youngest of the Casey daughters, had died. Her little grave was in the family cemetery beside that of three other Casey children who had died five years earlier of diphtheria.

Lord, it was a rough country. Why couldn't he make Isobel understand that Lincoln County was no place for a tenderfoot woman who'd lived all her life in high society? Why couldn't she just leave the fighting and the avenging to the men? If only she'd look the facts square in the face, she'd understand why a man like Noah wanted no part of trying to raise a family under such conditions. And she ought to see that out here a woman's life was no round of *bailes* and *fiestas*.

As he shook his head, Noah fingered the rifle that lay across his thighs. Nope, there was only one way to look at this situation. Until the trouble in Lincoln was over, he'd lay low at Chisum's place. He'd make sure Chisum sold him the land he'd been after. Then he'd pack Isobel off either to Santa Fe or to Spain.

Most important, he'd have to keep himself away from her. Sure, it was easy to excuse his behavior the two times he'd lost his head and made love to her. Isobel was one pretty lady. She was exciting and she was willing. More to the point, he'd been without a woman for more than a decent period of time before he'd met Isobel. How much temptation could one man be expected to handle?

But if he intended to send her away, he'd better learn to keep his hands off. Not to mention the practical problem a baby would introduce, there was the simple fact that Noah had never been the type of man who could spend much time around a woman and not start to feel a mite attached.

He'd never allowed that sort of thing to hobble him in the past. But with a woman like Isobel around day after day, looking as beautiful as a spring morning, hair golden as the sunrise, smile as sweet as honey, body just begging to be touched . . . well, he could see Isobel becoming a real problem.

Noah settled his black Stetson on his lap and scratched the back of his neck. No, sir, he'd better just back off. Way off.

The third day's travel took Noah and Isobel along the north bank of the Rio Hondo. No homes or ranches had been established in this deserted stretch of the road that led east toward the town of Roswell.

It might have been a good day for talking. The sun was bright, and the smells of an early spring hung in the air. A light breeze played across the Hondo Valley, dancing through bare-limbed poplars and scattering dry leaves along the trail.

That morning before they set out, Isobel had bathed at the

Casey home, so she felt fresh and clean. She had dug out a tan cotton riding skirt from one of her trunks. Smelling of the lavender she had pressed between its folds, the skirt allowed her to relax and ride more comfortably on the rough buckboard seat. With the skirt she wore a white blouse and a pair of riding boots that fit her feet like a pair of gloves.

But talking was not the order of the day for Isobel and Noah. The farther they traveled from Lincoln, the worse Isobel felt. She realized she was being taken from her only hope in life. If she lost track of Snake Jackson, she would never regain her lands in northern New Mexico. And now that Snake knew she was in the territory, he might work harder to speed up the transfer of the property from her name to his. If she lost her land titles, what future did she have?

Noah was absorbed in his own thoughts. To Isobel he seemed distant, as though he had drawn inside himself and shut doors of iron between them. She didn't mind. The more she could emotionally separate herself from the man whose very presence she had come to crave, the greater her chances of staying focused on her goals.

That evening they camped along the Hondo River. Noah dozed but remained sitting upright all night—his rifle and six-shooter at the ready. The following day the buckboard rattled through the dusty settlement of Roswell. Situated six miles north of Chisum's ranch, the town was a motley collection of three adobe houses, their corrals, the shingle-roofed Smith Mercantile, and a rough hotel.

It was just after lunch when Noah drove over the river and down the trail to the home of John Simpson Chisum. At once Isobel descended from the buckboard, her face glowing with pleasure at the sight of the rambling adobe house that had been built around a central patio.

"But this is lovely!" she exclaimed.

"She's a tough old place, all right." Noah slapped the side of the house with a gloved hand. "She's set on low ground, so she's kind of damp and leaky. But buried inside these walls are long planks so that Indians and thieves can't saw a gap with a rawhide or horsehair rope. See the roof? It's flat and made of dirt brought down from the north. And there's a parapet, too."

"A *pretil*," Isobel whispered, aware that the three-foot wall dotted with portholes could protect a great number of armed men from attackers. "This is a fortress."

Noah nodded. "And it's where I aim to keep you safe from Snake Jackson."

Isobel turned and looked at him fully for the first time in many hours. "Is this where you stay, Noah?"

"I've got a house up north a ways. I've nearly got it built, but it's not near as fancy as John's place."

"Take me there. I want to see your home."

Noah's brow lifted a touch. "You're going to stay right here where you'll be safe, hear? And while we're on this subject, I've got a few things to tell you."

"These are the things you've been thinking about as we traveled? The things that have made you frown and scowl at the world?"

"I reckon so." He took off his hat and wiped his forehead with the back of his hand before settling the hat on his head again. "Isobel, I've had to try to straighten things out about you. So here's what I've decided. First, until John gets out of jail, we don't have to pretend we're married. Which is good because I think we let things get a little out of hand in that respect."

"You're unhappy because we played together in Juan Patrón's house and then again beside the Rio Bonito?"

He forced himself to meet her eyes. "Played together . . . well, yeah. It's just not a real good idea, Isobel. We set up this arrangement for convenience's sake, and we plan to end it one of these days, right?"

"Yes," she whispered. But it came into her mind as she spoke the word that she could not imagine the day when Noah Buchanan would ride out of her life as swiftly as he had ridden into it. She gazed into his blue eyes and wondered how he had come to fill such a large part of her heart.

"So," he was saying, his large hand patting the side of the buckboard, "I reckon I'll head over to my place and check on things while you stay here. You'll be safe. Nobody's getting into John Chisum's house."

"Or out?"

"Or out."

"Then you intend to imprison me."

"I look on it as protection—not as a jail sentence. When John comes home, we'll act married again for a while. After he's sold me the land and we've found out what's become of Snake Jackson, we'll go our separate ways. I don't imagine it'll take too long to work it all out."

"And then you'll be rid of me."

"You'll be rid of me, too, darlin'." He touched her chin with the tip of one finger. But fearful that he would see things in her hazel eyes he couldn't bear, he drew away. "So, I'll settle you in and then head upriver."

From the house and the nearby corral some of Chisum's men drifted toward the newly arrived buckboard. Isobel stood aside as Noah directed them in the removal of her trunks. Respected for his position of authority in the ranch hierarchy, Noah moved and spoke with a quiet nobility that Isobel had never noticed before. His long canvas coat, black hat, and leather gloves and boots gave him some resemblance to a military officer. Tall and powerfully built, his physique put him above the other men. But it was the confident air with which he gave orders that showed his true rank.

Isobel watched, trying to memorize him, yet trying to force herself to look away. Trying to accept that what he had told her was the truth. Their arrangement had been nothing . . . their marriage was nothing . . . their lovemaking had been nothing at all to Noah.

She moved her feet toward the house, failing to notice things that would have cheered her on another day. She didn't see the hundreds of rosebushes waiting for warm mornings to stir their blood to life. Nor did she see the willows and cottonwoods. She missed the huge orchards that John Chisum had laid out year by year—apple, nectarine, cherry, peach, pear, and plum trees by the score.

Instead she tramped across the tile floor and stepped into the front room. "Mrs. Buchanan?" The voice that halted her was friendly and hearty.

Isobel looked up. The small, plump woman who extended a hand wore a grin that would have warmed even the heaviest heart.

"I'm Mrs. Frances Towry, John Chisum's housekeeper. My

husband, Tom, and our son, Tom Junior, moved here from Paris, Texas, a while back." She was rattling with information Isobel hardly cared to hear, but her chatter was so full of life that the young woman felt compelled to listen. "Tom runs the harness and saddle shop, and Junior works on the range. He's a good friend of your husband. 'Course, I don't know a soul who ain't fond of Noah. You got yourself a fine man, Mrs. Buchanan. Mighty fine."

"Thank you," Isobel said, mustering a smile as she shook the woman's pudgy hand.

"Welcome to South Spring River Ranch. And this here's our cook." She gestured to the chocolate-skinned man who had wandered in to see what all the commotion was about. "Dick, say howdy to Mrs. Buchanan."

As they greeted one another, Isobel began to see that John Chisum had developed the same sort of lifestyle in which she had been reared. The house was large, cool, and well appointed with modern furniture and lovely carpets. Mrs. Towry prattled on as she led Isobel to a fine bedroom.

"I'm gonna put you and Noah right here in Mr. Chisum's room. Now, don't look so shocked. You see this wonderful bed I got for him?" She pointed out the elaborately carved wooden bedstead covered by a mattress, feather tick, bolster, pillows, and shams. "He won't touch this. None of it. Every single night he spends in this house, he sets his camp bed on the floor and uses it as a pallet."

"But why?"

Mrs. Towry smoothed a hand over the delicately embroidered shams. "He says it's too much trouble to fold up the beddin' and arrange everything. He tells me that when he wants to go to bed, he wants to go to sleep right then and there. No fussin'." A twinkle lit her gray eyes as she glanced at Isobel. "Now, Mr. Chisum is known for the jokes he likes to pull on folks. So . . . if he don't like his own bed, I reckon we'll just settle you and your husband into it. See how that suits him."

Isobel couldn't see how this sort of a joke was going to win her over with John Chisum. But before she could protest, Noah had come into the room, and Mrs. Towry had scuttled out.

"Everything okay?" he asked, jamming his hands into the pockets of his denims to keep from touching Isobel. She was standing alone in the middle of the huge room. She looked lost and vulnerable.

"It's good," she said.

"Okay, well . . . I'll tell Mrs. Towry I'm leaving you here at Chisum's until I can get my place into the kind of shape a man would want to bring his wife home to. After I talk to her, I'll head out."

She was staring at him, her eyes large and luminous. He took a step closer. Her fingers were knotted together in front of the brown skirt she wore. Her mouth parted, and she tried to smile.

"I'll be back to check on you in a couple of days," he said. "Don't go anywhere."

"Where would I go?"

"Well, you've given me fits about heading back to Lincoln and trying to chase down Snake Jackson."

"If I leave, then everyone here will know I'm not Belle Buchanan. I'll ruin your chance to buy land from John Chisum, won't I?"

"Isobel." He moved closer. "I'll get my land one way or another. That's not the reason I don't want you to go back to Lincoln. Snake will kill you. How many times do I have to say it before it sinks in?"

She shrugged. "If I'm dead, then you won't have to bother with me anymore."

"Damn it, woman." He took her shoulders in his hands. "I swore I'd protect you, and I'm not backing down on that."

"You also swore to be my husband."

"Well, I'm *not* your husband."

"You're my lover."

"I *was* your lover. Don't tempt me, Isobel."

"How do I tempt you? Tell me, Noah."

"Your eyes . . . your hair . . . your lips . . ." He drew her against him, wanting one last time to feel the press of her breasts against his chest. He imagined them, soft and full in his palms. He thought of the long days he'd spent beside her on the buckboard, smelling the scent of lavender in her clothes and wanting to touch her so bad it was all he could do to keep his hands on the reins.

"Noah," she murmured. "I, too, decided some days ago that we must never be lovers again. I must keep my eyes on my future."

"That's right." But her eyes were on his face, searching each plane and hollow. Her dark lashes fluttered gently, their tips stroking the underside of her eyebrows as she looked up into his eyes. "Isobel," he said.

"We are so very different, Noah. And we want such different things from life."

"Isobel . . ."

"Kiss me once, Noah. Before you go."

"Isobel . . ." But his mouth covered hers in a kiss that broke the flimsy barriers of restraint they had tried to build.

His tongue stroked over her teeth. He nipped at her bottom lip. She ran her hands up his bare neck and into his hair. Her breasts crushed his duster coat against his chest. Their hips came together, pelvis against pelvis, and he slid his hand over her bottom to wedge her against the need that had welled instantly inside him.

"Aw, Isobel . . ." he protested again, but he felt her tongue slide inside his mouth, test his teeth, dip into the soft, damp hollows. She gently drew his tongue into her mouth and suckled, encouraging his hunger with every caress.

Finally breaking free of him, she lifted her head. "Go now, Noah Buchanan, to your safe little home. Run away from me. Run from every danger in your life."

His breath ragged, he looked into her face. "You think I run from danger, Isobel? Well, you're damn right. Steering clear of calamity is how I aim to keep myself alive, keep myself free, and make my dreams come true."

"And going *mano a mano* with calamity is how I will make my dreams come true, Noah."

He shook his head. "Isobel . . . Isobel . . ."

"Good-bye, Noah Buchanan."

She turned from him lest he see the tears that welled in her eyes. For she knew that this was the last time he would ever hold her, the last time their lips would touch. Their destinies called them in opposite directions, and each must obey the beckoning whisper.

By moonrise that night Noah had settled into the four-room adobe *jacal* he had built at the edge of the Pecos River. He checked on the old milk cow and the dozen hens he kept penned in a roughshod barn. It looked like his neighbor down the river, Eugenio Baca, had been taking care of things in fine style. The house was clean enough, the cow milked, the grass cut away from the edge of the portal, and the chickens mostly untouched by varmints.

By lantern light Noah meandered down to the old bare-limbed cottonwood tree and dug up his pail of money. It was all there—ten years' worth of scrimping and saving. More than enough to buy the acreage adjoining his home. As he reburied the pail and shifted the heavy slab of limestone back into place, he couldn't help but smile. He had the money. He had the wife. And pretty soon he'd have the land.

The following morning, a Tuesday, Noah set to straightening up his place. He swept and mopped and dusted, gathered eggs and milked his cow. Woman's work, but he was used to it. He sure couldn't imagine Isobel doing the common chores that made a house into a home. No, sir, she probably expected to have servants obeying her every command. Good thing she was settled in at Chisum's place. Far away.

On Wednesday Noah sharpened his pencils and set up his inkwell. He spent the morning writing out the main ideas for the story that had been tickling his thoughts ever since Tuscon. It was about a brave cowboy who would stand up to a desperate bunch of men who had ridden down on him to rustle his cattle. The cowboy would shoot them, all but one—the leader of the gang—who would get away. The cowboy would marry some sweet gal. But all of a sudden the old enemy would return.

Noah stayed up half the night, his blood boiling and the precious oil in his lamp burning, as wrote out the story. Damn, it was good. He could hear the men talking inside his head; he could smell the acrid tang of gunpowder and taste the dry dust in his mouth with each new sentence, each paragraph, each page.

He wrote all day Thursday. Forgot to milk the cow. Forgot to eat breakfast. Forgot to chop wood for the wood box. A late snowfall began outside his window, but Noah didn't see it. He was out on the prairie, sun beating down on his shoulders, sweat trickling from his brow, wind chapping his lips into thick slabs of leather. He was shooting wild turkeys and riding a fiery black stallion and bunking down at night with an Indian blanket 'twixt him and the ground. Stars by the million twinkled overhead. The smell of blooming cactus filled his nostrils by day. The low of the cattle and the roll of hoofbeats made music in his ears. Hellfire, this was a great story!

Around three o'clock the following morning, Noah fell asleep at the kitchen table. His lamp flickered out an hour later. Snowflakes slipped in under the front door. Once inside they didn't melt. It was far too cold. Fingers of frost crept up the new glass windowpanes Noah had installed the summer before. With every breath a vapor puffed from his nostrils. The steam settled on the thick growth of black whiskers that shaded his upper lip and jaw. As the frigid air hit the moisture, it froze, creating a beard of crystalline ice that rimmed Noah's mouth.

The smells of hot coffee and bacon on the campfire wafted through his sleep. The sweet kisses of a beautiful, golden-haired woman dripped across his tongue. And then the thunder of gunfire shattered the dream.

"Noah? Are you in there?"

Not gunfire. Someone was hammering on his front door. He lifted his head. Running a hand across his chin, he knocked some of the ice crystals from his beard. Scowling through puffed lids, he stared at the door. It shuddered on its hinges from the severe pounding outside.

"Noah Buchanan! Open this door at once!"

No mistaking that voice. "Isobel," he croaked. "Get your fanny back to Chisum's, where I left it."

"I've come with my furniture, Noah."

What the hell was that supposed to mean? he wondered as he pushed away from the table and tried to stand. Damn, he must have forgotten to light a fire. He wandered across the room to the door, his knees aching and his joints stiff from the cold. He felt hungry enough to eat a saddle blanket. The iron doorknob, when he grabbed it, near froze his hand solid.

"Isobel, what the hell are you . . ." He was growling as he dragged the door open, but the sight of her stopped his words.

Oh, the woman was a beauty. Dressed in an emerald-green wool cloak with the hood pulled up, she stood on his portal looking like a queen. Her red gloves and red boots were the only spots of contrasting color, save her bright pink cheeks and lips. Her hazel eyes flashed at him as one dark gold eyebrow lifted.

"You have been drinking, Noah Buchanan," she announced.

Pushing past him with a sweep of her red-gloved hand, she stepped into the icy room. What a disgrace! What a horror! The pathetic little house looked as if it had lived through a tornado. Blankets piled here, dishes there, a bed in the living room, two broken chairs by the door, the stove unlit, and the dining table piled high with papers.

"Shame, Noah," she scolded, stripping away her gloves and heading for the wood stove. "I let you out of my sight for five days, and you become a *borrachón*. What have you been drinking? Whisky? Rum?"

"Rum? Now, see here, Isobel." Noah watched in amazement as she clanked open his stove door and began to build a fire. A damn poor fire. No doubt it would smoke up the house before it caught flame.

"I had hoped we might never see each other again," she was saying. "You made it clear you no longer needed me. And I knew you planned to keep me from my appointed task."

"Killing Snake Jackson is not your appoint—"

"Unfortunately my furniture arrived at Mr. Chisum's house before I could set out for Lincoln. Of course, the dear imprisoned man cannot be expected to store it for me. And so I decided I must bring it here."

As a prickly feeling wandered up his back, Noah took a look out the front window. Sure enough, two oxcarts loaded high with large crates waited by the portal. "You drove those over here in the snow?"

"It wasn't difficult. We'll spend the day unloading and arranging. It's the least you can do for me after all, Noah. If you don't intend to help me capture Snake Jackson—"

"I never said I'd help you capture Jackson. I said I'd keep you safe."

"*And* help me find the man who murdered my father. I remember that was part of the bargain."

They stared at each other.

"Well, you look damned good anyhow, Isobel," Noah said.

She averted her eyes. He looked terrible, but she didn't want to say it. His hair tumbled over his head as if he hadn't combed it for days. His shirttail hung almost to his knees. With the dark hair and beard framing his face, his blue eyes glittered like the ice on the window.

Isobel's glance fell on the littered pine table. She took in the reams of scribbled paper, the inkblots, the pencil shavings, and the open penknife. Lifting her eyes, she stared at Noah in surprise.

"You have been writing."

"Finished my first story last night." Suddenly enthusiastic, he strode to the table and grabbed the sheaf of paper. " 'Sunset at Coyote Canyon.' That's the title. I've been writing it for a few days now. You just wouldn't believe the ending. See, there's this no-good skunk of a fellow who sneaks up, and then . . . well . . ."

"And what happens?" Isobel had settled on a chilly wooden chair, water from her cloak puddling around her feet as the room began to warm.

"Well . . ." Noah stammered and set the pages back on the table. "Aw, hell . . ."

"Are you ready to mail your story to the publishers in New York? I'll take it to the post office when I return to Lincoln."

Noah tapped the stack of paper, staring at his scrawled handwriting, at the blotches of ink and the side scribbles of pencil where he'd added ideas that had come to him along the way. "No, it's not anywhere near ready."

"I will cook breakfast," Isobel announced. "You read the story to me."

Without giving him opportunity to protest, she shed her cloak, rolled up her sleeves, and set to work.

"Read, Noah!" she commanded.

He cleared his throat, settled into a chair, and began to speak aloud words that once had been only in his mind. " 'A round blue moon hung over the canyon. Travis Kent struck a match and lit the brown cheroot he had pulled from his pocket'."

Isobel smiled as she tapped a spoonful of grease into the black iron frying pan. Noah's deep voice settled into her bones. She peeked at his long body sprawled across the rickety wooden chair, boots caked with dried mud heavy on the floor. He needed a bath. And food. His home needed her touch. So did he.

" 'Up on the ridge a coyote began to howl,' " Noah read, " 'a sound that blended with the whine of the wind and the soft call of the owls. Travis lifted his head and blew a puff of smoke into the black night.' "

Isobel cracked six eggs, one by one, into the sizzling grease.

Chapter
❧ *10* ❧

" 'Opal stood between Travis and Buck. In her arms she carried the newborn babe.' " Noah's voice lowered as he read the words. " 'She looked into the eyes of the stranger who had come to kill her husband. "You'll have to shoot me first, Buck Shafer," she said. "I won't be parted from the man I love." Her voice never wavered.' "

Noah lifted his eyes from the stack of papers he held. Isobel was absently stirring the third batch of scrambled eggs she had made that day. Her eyes were closed and her face raised as she listened to the final passage of his story.

Noah decided it didn't matter that they'd eaten eggs for breakfast, lunch, and now supper—nor that she'd burned them the first two times. What mattered was that Isobel was listening. She was transported into his tale. She felt it, just the way he had felt it when he'd written it.

" 'Travis gazed into the face of his wife,' " he read on, " 'and at the tiny, cherubic smile of his newborn son. He knew he couldn't allow Buck Shafer to tear apart their family. "Hold on, Opal!" he shouted suddenly. At the same moment he pushed his wife aside and fired his six-shooter. The baby's howl was the only sound in the house as the pungent gunsmoke filled the air. "Opal," Travis called. "Opal, sweet-heart." He knelt and swept his fallen wife and child into his arms. "We're all right, Travis," Opal whispered. "We're all right." They cuddled against his chest as he stared at the man who lay dead on the floor. Then Travis strode out the door and into the flaming orange sunset of Coyote Canyon.' "

Noah placed the last page upside down on the rest of his manuscript. He felt bleary-eyed and hoarse from reading most of the day. Worse, he'd seen a lot of mistakes in the story, more mistakes than he could count. Reading it out loud that way, it hadn't sounded half as good as he'd imagined it would.

"In my mind," he said slowly, "it came out better. The words flowed more smoothly, and things kind of went to-gether like water down a stream. But on paper it got jumpy and disconnected. Like when Travis shot Buck there at the end . . . well, when I thought it up, it was stronger. It had a lot more impact, you know? And Opal and the baby . . . now that part . . ."

His words drifted off, and he sat staring at the table. He felt kind of sick inside. It was like everything had been wrung out of him while he wrote down the story. But then when it was on his tongue, it was just a bunch of scrambled words, like Isobel's half-burned eggs.

"Hell," he muttered.

A pair of arms came from behind him, slipped around his neck, and down his chest. A cheek pressed against his. A wet cheek.

"It was a good story, Noah," Isobel said.

He turned and shut his eyes, resting his forehead against her neck. Isobel was crying. Crying real tears over his writing. "Well, I'll be damned," he whispered.

"If I read this story in Catalonia," she said, "I would know New Mexico. I would understand this country. I would see these people."

"What about Opal? I bet you think I should have let her blast Buck Shafer to kingdom come, like you would have done."

Isobel came around Noah and knelt beside his chair. "Opal did what was right for her. She had to protect the child—but she showed her love by standing between Travis and his enemy."

Noah nodded. Isobel understood. She saw the point of the story—and it had moved her. Maybe his writing wasn't so shabby after all. He flipped the corners of the stack of paper, pondering his first effort.

"Isobel, why'd you come here to my place?" he asked suddenly, wanting to understand everything, wanting to understand her.

"My . . . my furniture." The hesitation in her eyes told him what he needed to know.

"It wasn't your furniture that brought you to my house. You came because of me, didn't you?"

"No." She shook her head, trying to make herself believe that what she said was true.

"You've gotten yourself in quite a tangle. You want to be bold, brave, shoot-'em-up Isobel Matas. But somewhere inside yourself there's a Belle Buchanan who likes fixing up a house and learning to cook and wash dishes. There's a woman who cries when a story comes out right. And there's a woman who can't stay away from the man she wants. The man she needs."

"I don't need anyone, Noah Buchanan," Isobel insisted.

"You need me." He cupped her jaw in his palm when she started to shake her head. "Yes, you do. And that's why you came all the way out here in the snow with your two oxcarts full of furniture. Because I've got something nobody else has ever given you. And you need it."

"No," she said, but her body betrayed her. Her lips parted, and her eyes melted when he looked into them. "Oh, Noah."

"There'll be other men for you, Isobel. Men who'll fit into your schemes better than I do."

"Yes." But she knew he was wrong. There were no other men. Not only because she was already considered a spinster, but because in the days apart from him she had realized she wanted no one else. She wanted Noah Buchanan . . . his kiss, his caress, his strong hands, his poetry . . .

"Isobel, you're going to have to get on back to Chisum's," he was saying, trying to put her off. "See, I've got things to do around here. I've let the chores go. And the cow—"

"The cow, the chores!" She pushed away from him and stalked toward the stove. "These are *your* excuses. You think you're so strong and independent. You think you need no one. The truth for you is the same as for me. You need me, Noah. You need me and you want me."

"Well, what if I do?"

"Don't you act on your needs?"

"Not always. I don't have to let my hot blood control me, Isobel. If I'm mad or vengeful, I give myself time to cool down. If I find myself wanting a woman who's no good for me, I back away."

"I'm no good for you?"

"You're so damn good I can't stand to be this close and not touch. But, Isobel, what could come of it?"

She knew the answer. It didn't matter how she felt inside. It didn't matter that when she looked at Noah Buchanan, she saw her match in spirit. He might need her, but he didn't want her.

"Then we shall bring in my furniture," she said, whirling away from the stove and stalking past him to the door. "Stop gawking like a schoolboy, Noah. It's growing late, and I have many things outside in the snow. Come along."

As Noah scooted the last velvet-upholstered chair across the oxblood-and-dirt floor of his house, he decided he had never seen so much furniture in his life. A huge wooden bed, broken down into pieces that could be reassembled, rested against one wall in his kitchen. A couch and three chairs filled half the living room. Rolled carpets were piled in the bedroom. Cupboards lay on the floor next to crates of dishes and fine linens. Straw stuffing had gathered in every corner. An enormous, gold-framed mirror almost filled one wall.

Noah was muttering as he headed out the door to milk his cow just before midnight. He could hear Isobel singing Spanish ditties in the house and happily sliding things here and there. She had already filled one of his cupboards with her brightly painted plates and cups. All his tinware lay in a heap at the bottom of a drawer. One of her wool rugs—in some fancy Oriental-type of design—now covered the floor in the living room. When he'd walked out to tend the milking, she was setting knickknacks on the shelves where he'd always kept his gun-cleaning supplies.

He'd thought she was storing her stuff at his place, not moving in and setting up housekeeping. But she just *had* to arrange things a little, she'd insisted. She just *couldn't* let her precious furniture lie around in heaps.

As Noah kneaded his cow's udder, he stared blankly at the stream of hissing milk. How had his perfectly comfortable life gotten into such a mess? There was a time when he'd gone out on the trail for months, then come home and settled in for a few weeks before heading out again. Everything had been straightforward and simple.

Now? Now he was hooked up with a hot-blooded señorita who was bound and determined to shoot Snake Jackson full of holes; he had a head full of stories that wouldn't hush until he wrote them down; he had a boss in jail and a best friend sitting on a keg of dynamite in Lincoln; and he had rooms full of frilly, velvet furniture.

As he walked back to the house, warm creamy milk slopped onto his boots and then dripped into the fresh snow. He paused outside the door to put out the lantern. From inside the house he heard a strange sound—*aclickety-click-click, aclickety-click-click, ding, clickety, clickety, click.*

What now? He shouldered into the front room. Isobel was seated on a puffy chair with rollers on the legs. She was bending over a strange machine that sat on his pine table. Her fingers bounced around, clickety-clacking on the machine as her eyes scanned his manuscript.

"What in tarnation—"

"It's my Remington!" She beamed the prettiest smile he'd ever seen. She spun around in the twirling chair seat and lifted her feet in the air. "This is a machine for making letters and numbers in type. Like printing. I've owned it for three years."

"What *for*?" Frowning at the small contraption, Noah set the milk pail on the floor and ran a forefinger along the cold steel case.

"For transactions on my father's farm in Spain. I keep all records on this—but it came from America. See, E. Remington and Sons of Ilion, New York."

With a healthy amount of suspicion Noah studied the rubber platen and the smaller rubber cylinder set parallel to it. Strange springs, ratchets, pawls, and levers jumbled in among a pair of spools and an inked ribbon. "So, what do you aim to do with it here in my front room?" he asked.

"I aim to put your story into type before we post it to New York. Look, the first page is finished."

She held up a neat, clean sheet of white paper with capital letters sprawled in a straight line across it. SUNSET AT COYOTE CANYON BY NOAH BUCHANAN.

"Well, I'll be damned." He whistled softly and sat down beside her as she began to touch the keys again. He couldn't see what was happening, for the printed words hid way down inside the machine as they were made. But when his own story began to appear at the top of the unrolling paper, he got downright excited.

"How about that?" he murmured, his chin resting on her shoulder as she worked. "Did I write that? Reads pretty good, as a matter of fact. Well, well . . . how do you like that?"

"I like it," she said. Her slender wrists moved back and forth in a graceful dance. Her long fingers waltzed across the keyboard. "It makes the story look good. *Sí*? And when we send it to New York, they will think so, too."

A smile playing about her lips, she *clickety-clacked* until a second page rolled out of the Remington. Forgetting the milk pail, Noah leaned one elbow on the table and watched her work. He felt strange inside . . . as though his already skewed sense of order had just taken one more tilt off-balance.

Hadn't he planned to stow Isobel safely away at Chisum's house? Hadn't he decided there was no future in wooing her? She'd made it plain she didn't want to be hooked up with some dusty cowboy for the rest of her life. And he knew he'd never wanted to be hobbled by a wife and family.

So why did her fancy Spanish furniture feel suddenly just right in his adobe house? Why did her dishes look so good on his shelves? Why had it warmed his heart to walk in the front door and find Isobel seated at his table? And why in hell was she typing out his story for him?

He studied the gold ringlets that fell artfully from the bun at the back of her head. He looked at the way the lamplight turned her earlobe a soft pearly white. She was wearing the blue dress again. The one she and Susan Gates had made that day in Lincoln. Little ruffles clustered around her neck. Little hooks marched down her bosom. Little cuffs clasped her slender wrists.

"This part I like," she said softly. "This part you wrote about the coyote. It makes me shiver."

Noah stifled the groan that welled up inside him at the thought of what a shiver would do to her full breasts. Lowering his head, he ran his nose over the soft blue calico that puffed at her shoulders. Eyes closed, he leaned closer and drew the scent of her neck into his nostrils. The *clickety-click* began to slow as he trailed damp lips up to her ear. When he took her lobe gently between his teeth, the typing stopped altogether.

She stayed still and quiet as his tongue dipped into the cup of her ear. Shivers, he thought. *Oh, Isobel, I want to make you shiver.*

His hands came around her waist, testing its narrowness and the firm corset beneath. Her breath coming in shallow gasps, she shook her head.

"Noah . . . you said you didn't . . ."

"But . . . I do."

His hand cupped over the ripe mound of her breast and felt its hardened tip press into his palm. She shivered.

"Noah," she whispered, trying to make herself think despite the whirlwind growing inside her. "Noah, I'll type your story tonight and leave for Chisum's in the morning like you asked me to. You go to bed and sleep. Your brain is tired."

"My brain may be tired, honey, but the rest of me is just waking up." He took her shoulders and turned her to face him. "I know what we said, Isobel. And I know we meant every word. But there's no way in heaven or hell I can be this close to you and not start thinking about what it's like to touch you . . . to feel your lips on me . . . to hold your sweet body against mine. I want you, darlin', and if that means I have to break my own rules, then so be it."

Isobel gazed at the rough-knuckled, sun-bronzed hand stroking her thigh. Perhaps she was too daring, too reckless. Perhaps her heart would always disobey. But one thing she knew now . . . and she must confess it.

"Noah, I came to you for this. For the loving." She lifted her head and made herself meet his eyes. "When you left me, I sat alone in the big house of John Chisum and I thought about my life. I thought about the future. Noah, death runs close behind me. I feel its breath on my skin. I feel its tongue licking my heels."

"Now, Isobel, I told you I'm going to take care of you. Stop thinking that way about dying and all."

"Listen to me, Noah. I have nothing to claim as my own. Nothing. Death or murder are my only two paths. My heart is desperate. And I know that if such a fate awaits me, I want to live my life now with some happiness."

"Aw, Isobel—"

"Noah, will you take me to your bed? Will you love me? For a few short days can you let me pretend to be Belle Buchanan? I want to know what it means to cook and clean and mend a husband's shirts. I want to feel a man's arms around me in the night, and I want to see a man's face on my pillow when I wake. Will you give me that gift before I go?"

"Now, listen here. You're making this out to be a lot worse than it really is."

"Please!" She took his hands, gripping them with all the anxiety that had led her to him. "Please, Noah. Put yourself in my place. What would you do?"

He stared into her brown-green eyes. He heard the tremble in her voice. And he knew the answer.

"I'd go after the man who stole my land," he vowed, his voice low. "I'd track down Snake Jackson. And while I waited to snare him, I'd live for the moment. 'Cause I'd know each day could be my last. And if I had on hand a woman who looked like you and smelled like you . . . and tasted like you . . ."

He bent and brushed her lips with a kiss. She slid across the seat of her chair into his lap. His hands covered her thighs, cupped her bottom, nestled her into him. Draping her arms around his neck, she covered his neck with her mouth. Oh, he smelled the way she remembered, of spice mingled with fresh air. His flesh was warm against her lips. She dipped her nose in his hair.

The gray plaid flannel shirt he wore came easily apart, for

its mismatched buttons hung on loose thread. Two buttons at the neck were missing. Isobel slid her hands against his chest and kneaded the rock-solid muscle. She heard his breath grow raspy with need as she pushed her breasts into his skin.

Noah was male in every hard, masculine, rough sense of the word. And yet his calloused hands moved with a dancer's grace as he unclasped the hooks down the front of Isobel's bodice. She saw the artist's softness in his eyes when he let them rove across her face.

As he held and kissed her all the way into his small warm bedroom, she lowered her eyelids and tried to block anything but the feelings he was giving her. Things that once had seemed foremost in her life had given way before the powerful surge of need she felt for this man who had rescued her from a bullet's path just ten days before.

Once she had been a noblewoman, the betrothed of a don, a lady of high breeding and exquisite taste. Now, with her life turned upside-down, she felt little desire for her privileged past. It was this rugged land that moved her, the sloping mountains and flowing streams she had once thought so paltry. It was this man she ached for, a man she had once considered common and vulgar. The beast who had been transformed into a prince.

His magic fingers stripped away her garments; his damp lips made fiery pathways down her body; his poet's soul spoke words that turned her heart to liquid butter. She ran her tongue over his corded chest and tested his flat nipples with its tip. Her hands molded to the steel sinews that rippled in his arms. Setting her naked hips against his leather belt, she slowly worked away his clothing as his fingers gripped her pale buttocks. She danced her breasts against his flesh, setting them afire. She drank in the scent of bay rum that lingered on his skin. And when he sagged onto the bed, his body rigid with need, she moved to mount him.

"Mercy, Isobel," he groaned as she sheathed him deeply inside herself. The soles of her feet stroked his thighs. Her heavy breasts glowed before his eyes, milky white tipped with roses. He lifted slightly and began to lick.

"Noah," she pleaded. Splaying her hands across his chest, she rose and fell upon him, allowing his body to stroke her deepest desires. Oh, this was what she had craved. This communion of the physical and spiritual. The sound of his deep, animal moans slipped through her veins and set them singing.

From above she watched the expression on Noah's face as he absorbed her ministrations. His mouth was parted, his eyes closed. His head tilted backward on the white feather pillow, and she could see the tendons in his neck strain as he struggled against his need for release.

Wild, his hands worked her body, kneading her bottom, molding her breasts, stroking the length of her arms. Their fingers interwove and his eyes came open. He gazed at her, rapt.

"Isobel, darlin' . . ."

"Noah, *mi amor, mi cariño, contra viento y marea mi esposo . . . ayudamé . . .* help me . . ."

Her body, pierced by his, rose on a wave of passion. She cried aloud. Her back arched and her head rolled against one shoulder. Sheets of fire tore through her, splintered her with tingles of ecstasy, branded her with curls of flame. And then he broke free inside her, his own fire raging out of control. They writhed with the ultimate pleasure of surrender, their arms, legs, tongues twining, and their bodies damp.

Then Isobel sagged, gasping for air, her cheek pressed to Noah's chest. His hands covered her back and began to slowly stroke her shoulders as breath returned to his lungs.

"Isobel . . . I'm not ever going to let you go," he murmured. "I hope you know that."

She shut her eyes and nestled into the fur on his chest. "Perhaps, Noah. Perhaps."

In the next three days no word of past or future was spoken between Noah and Isobel. These were the first days of March, and in true New Mexico style, a gale of wind ushered them in. The snow quickly melted, the remaining leaves on every tree whisked away, the dry grass along the Pecos River bent low.

Noah kept his wood stove hot with freshly chopped logs. The stove in turn warmed the entire four-room house. While Isobel continued the unpacking and arranging that lifted her spirits higher than he'd ever seen them, Noah went hunting. There was no scarcity of wild game along the river, and in no time flat he had bagged a brace of rabbits. He managed to snag

Isobel away from the cupboard she was analyzing long enough to teach her how to skin and clean a rabbit.

"Oh, Noah," she said, her eyes suddenly bright with unshed tears. "It's just a bunny."

"It's food, darlin'. After one day not eating and a second with only three slim helpings of eggs, I'm in need of a meal."

He handed her the knife and supervised while she skinned and carved the rabbits. Then, with a kettle of simmering water, a handful of withered turnips and carrots out of the root cellar, and a sprinkling of pepper and salt, he taught her to make stew.

By the time the meal had begun to waft its aroma through the *jacal*, Isobel had stripped and cleaned Noah's almost barren kitchen shelves. She lined the edges with strips of delicate white lace she had brought from Spain to wear in her hair. Then she reorganized all his utensils and set them neatly on the bright shelves.

"Curtains," she said aloud, musing on the new glass windowpanes. "We must have curtains."

Noah straightened from the bowl of cornbread batter he was stirring. "What for? Nobody's around here to look inside the house except us."

"Oh, a home must have curtains. They soften . . . and frame . . . and let in the light just so . . . ."

Noah scratched the side of his face where he'd shaved that morning. "Let's see now. When Mrs. Allison passed away a few years back—"

"She's dead? Your Mrs. Allison?"

He nodded. "Some kind of a fever got her. Just like the one that got my mother." His eyes lowered for a moment, then he lifted his head. "Anyhow, Mr. Allison sent me a trunk from Texas. Stuff that Mrs. Allison wanted me to have. I took one look inside the trunk and shut it quick."

"But why?"

"Aw, hell, it was just the kind of stuff Mrs. Allison loved. You know, the tea and biscuits sort of thing. I think there were some fancy curtains in there—along with framed prints of pink roses and sets of silver spoons. I knew I'd never get a minute's use out of those things here in New Mexico. . . . And it made me feel kind of . . . sad to look at them. Being as they were Mrs. Allison's prized possessions and all, you know?"

Isobel watched the flicker of pain that crossed his face, and she knew that the delicate, childless Englishwoman had been the only mother Noah had known. "Please show me the trunk, Noah," she said softly.

Abandoning the cornbread makings, he led her into the extra back room where he kept all his stores. After shifting aside an old wooden water bucket, a tub, and a dough-raiser, he uncovered the trunk. He flipped the two snap-over catches and unfastened the iron lock before raising the trunk's domed lid.

Isobel caught her breath the moment she saw inside. "*Lace* curtains! But these are the finest. They're from Nottingham in England! Oh, Noah."

She lifted the stack of soft white fabric and hugged it to her breast. A small grin tugged at Noah's mouth. "Exquisite, huh?"

The remainder of the trunk revealed a most delicate collection of treasures. A silver tea set, now darkened for lack of polish. Sugar tongs. A silver toast rack. Porcelain cups and saucers. Framed prints. Fine bone china candlesticks. A pink-flowered hair receiver. Crystal salt dishes and knife rests. Heavy white linen napkins and tablecloths. A brass bedwarmer. An inkwell. And at the bottom, a heart-shaped pewter box.

Isobel lifted the box, her heart thudding with pleasure at the array of fine things. She lifted the latch.

"Noah—here's a letter. It's for you."

During her exploration of the trunk, he had wandered away to dust mice droppings from the top of his grain bin. Now he swung around and took the folded sheet on which his name had been written in a fine hand.

" 'Dear little boy,' " he read aloud. He cleared his throat. "Mrs. Allison always used to call me that—dear little boy."

For a moment he couldn't read. Then he slowly began to speak. " 'I lie near death in a foreign land, far from my England and far from those I love the most. I think of you and pray each day as you ride the cattle trails for Mr. John Simpson Chisum. Do be careful, dear Noah. I am sending you these things, though I know they will not fit well into your trail life. But they are all I have. Dear little boy, please remember our sunny afternoons reading books in the library. I know you remember me, for I have saved every letter you wrote, one from each . . . from each week you have been away. Dear little . . .' "

Noah swallowed. He gazed at the letter, the muscles in his jaw working as he fought for control. " 'Dear little boy,' " he whispered, " 'I love you so much. Mrs. Allison. Jane.' "

He refolded the letter and stuffed it into his shirt pocket. Clearing his throat, he lifted his head and looked at Isobel. "I'd be pleased to hang those curtains for you now," he said.

The days filled themselves with cooking, cleaning, typing, and moving furniture. The nights filled themselves with sweet passion. As Noah milked his cow that Sunday evening, he decided he couldn't remember a time he'd felt so downright happy.

Not to say that Isobel wasn't more than a mite stubborn and bossy. She was mule-headed and hot-tempered. But the fact was, Noah didn't care a lick. In fact, he sort of liked the way she took charge of things around the house. She knew what she wanted, how she wanted it, and when she wanted it. She unearthed the copy of *Beeton's Book of Household Management* that Mrs. Allison had given him the day he set out for New Mexico. Before he knew it, the determined young *marquesa* was elbow deep in pots and pans.

"Have you curry powder and mushrooms?" she had asked that morning while he sat reading his Bible at the pine table, as he always did on a Sunday.

"Not hardly."

"Bacon? Wine?"

"Bacon, yes. Wine, no. But I've got whisky."

"Then we shall have ragout of rabbit. With whisky sauce."

Listening to the ping of the milk hit the bottom of his pail, Noah had to smile. She was bent on making cheese and butter. She'd scrubbed all the bottles, pails, and tumblers in the house and had set them on fence posts to dry. And she'd hinted about wanting him to turn over a patch of ground outside the kitchen.

Did the highfalutin señorita really mean to plant a garden?

The idea of her staying on at his place—and forgetting about the things that had driven her to New Mexico—had begun to sit nicely with Noah.

They had spent only three days together, but the words that ran ragtag around inside his head were sounding better and better all the time. Mr. and Mrs. Buchanan. Noah and Isobel. The Buchanan family. Well, well. Could you beat that?

Monday morning, March 4, 1878, started out to be the prettiest day so far. The sun appeared. The wind died down. The buds that hadn't frozen in the last snow began to swell.

Isobel had finished typing Noah's manuscript, had bound it in cloth, and sewn the packet shut for mailing. She decided to teach herself laundering with the ribbed wooden washboard and tub on Noah's front portal. Noah was saddling up the horses in preparation for the ride he had planned. He wanted to take Isobel out on the range and show her the cattle he owned—and the land he intended to buy.

Her hair slicked back in a tight bun, Isobel had just bent over the washtub when an uluating holler rippled down the river valley. Chilled, she straightened. Noah came charging out of the barn, his six-shooter drawn.

"What the hell was that?" he shouted. "Isobel—get in the house!"

"Where's the rifle? I'll stand by your side."

Noah was just about to give her what-for when he saw Billy the Kid's horse thunder up the bank, followed close behind by a band of mounted men—Dick Brewer, Waite, Middleton, Macnab, Scurlock, Bowdre, and a slew of others from the McSween camp.

"Buchanan!" Billy reined his horse and swung down. "How're you and the señorita gettin' on? Looks like it's gettin' mighty homey 'round here!"

He let out a hoot as the others joined him on the portal. Noah had holstered his gun, but he felt a sense of dread growing inside. Dick's face wore a worried look, and all the men were armed to the teeth.

"Last I heard, you were in the lockup, Kid," Noah said.

"Aw, me and Waite got out the day after Tunstall's funeral. Hell, they didn't have nothin' to keep us in for."

"So, what's going on, Dick?" Noah asked, turning from Billy.

"Things are looking bad, Noah. Alexander McSween wrote out his will last Monday. He's made John Chisum executor without bond."

Noah's face fell. Chisum was still in jail, yet McSween's action made the rancher deeply involved. It was clear whose side Chisum would take.

"McSween and Deputy Sheriff Barrier left Lincoln on Tuesday," Dick went on. "They went into hiding somewhere outside of town. We thought they might hunker down at Chisum's, but we went by the ranch this morning, and they're not there. Mrs. McSween's heading for Kansas."

"What about Dolan?"

"Nobody's made a move to arrest any of John Tunstall's murderers. Snake Jackson's on the loose. He's going to get away scot-free if somebody don't bring that murderer to justice. William Morton, Frank Baker, Jesse Evans—they're at liberty, too. We got word they're all down the Pecos hiding out at Dolan's cow camp. So we've formed a band, and we aim to round up every one of them and see that they get what's coming to them."

"A band? Hellfire, Dick. That sounds like trouble."

"It's not like you think. We call ourselves Regulators. We've taken an oath to stick together no matter what happens. We'll make arrests, but we've sworn we won't shoot on sight. We plan to take Snake, Evans, and the rest of them into custody and deliver them to Lincoln. They'll be tried at court in April. I'm the leader of the Regulators. Squire Wilson made me a constable."

"And the rest of us are official deputies!" Billy hooted.

Dick eyed his friend. "We've ridden out to ask if you'll join up, Noah. We want you on our side."

Images of the lace-curtained windows, the packet of pages bound for New York, the spring garden began to wither. "Aw, damn it, Dick." Noah kicked his heel against the edge of the step.

"You're the best shot in these parts, Noah. We could use you."

"You know I made a promise to Isobel, Dick. I've got to

stay here and protect her like I swore I would. If Snake got his hands on her—"

"We will go with them, Noah." Isobel's voice rang out from the shadows of the portal. Noah saw Dick's eyes widen as he turned.

There stood Isobel—the old Isobel Matas—dressed in a pair of his denim trousers, her riding boots, a chambray work shirt, and his worn-out leather coat. She had slung his rifle over one shoulder.

"Isobel—what in the name of thunder do you think you're doing?"

"Snake Jackson not only murdered John Henry Tunstall," she addressed the group of men, "he murdered my father. It happened four years ago when he rode with the Horrell Gang. Just ask Dick Brewer." The Regulators gaped at Dick, who shrugged and rolled his eyes at Noah.

"Snake Jackson killed my father and stole my lands," Isobel stated. "My desire to find him and bring him to justice is as great as yours. I shall ride with you."

"Hold on, now, Isobel—" Noah began.

"We can't have a woman in the Regulators," someone protested.

"Señorita, please—"

Isobel marched to the edge of the portal. Inside her heart, she felt the flickering flame of retreat, the urge to run to Noah's arms, to forget the past that haunted her. But she smothered the impulse, knowing that the days with Noah had been only a wonderful, magical game. With the arrival of the Regulators she understood at last that she would never be truly free . . . not until she freed herself.

Shouldering the rifle, she took aim at one of the tiny glass bottles she had set on a fence post to dry. In rapid succession she blasted away at the row of bottles. Each shattered in a spray of glass. Out of ammunition, she held up her hand.

There was a moment's hesitation, then Billy the Kid set his own six-shooter in her palm.

"One, two, three, four, five, six," she said, calmly exploding the rest of the bottles.

No one moved. A faint breeze lifted the white smoke from

the end of the revolver and sent it drifting over the heads of the men. Billy let out a low whistle.

"The señorita can ride at my side any day," he said finally.

"That goes for me, too, Noah," Waite added.

Dick studied his friend. Noah was staring at Isobel.

"Why?" he whispered. "Why, Isobel?"

She let out her breath. "How can I have a future when my past is unfinished? I must go with them, Noah. I have no choice."

He shook his head and settled his hat lower on his brow. "I guess knowing you ought to have taught me one thing. Once you set your mind on something, there's not a thing I can do to change it, is there?"

"I'm sorry, Noah."

"Well, looks like you've got yourselves a couple more Regulators, men," he said, his voice tinged with resignation. "Now, Dick, if you'll excuse me for a minute, I reckon I'd better go take the cornbread out of the oven."

Chapter
~ 11 ~

The Lincoln County Regulators—now eleven men and one woman strong—set out from Noah Buchanan's adobe house on Monday, the fourth day of March, 1878. Each person's horse packed a heavy supply of arms and ammunition. Food was plentiful along the Pecos River, and the weather was warming as spring crept into New Mexico Territory. The Regulators planned to make camp each night after dark in the hills where they would be well hidden.

If Noah and the others expected trouble from the female in their midst, they didn't know Isobel. An expert rider, she had no trouble keeping up with the rest of the Regulators.

They took the main road south past Chisum's South Spring River Ranch toward the little community of Seven Rivers. The first day brought the group almost as far as the Rio Feliz crossing. They might have gone faster, but at the slightest sound they turned off the road and into the wilderness, for they suspected that by now Jimmie Dolan must have heard of their organization—and they knew he wouldn't just sit back and rest.

That first night Isobel bedded down alone on her own pallet among the men who lay beside the fire. She had sensed

Noah's wariness, his constant vigilance as he rode beside her, his tendency to hover after they had made camp. It burdened her to know that this man, who preferred to spend his life tending cattle and writing tales, had been forced back into the bloody war. And it was all because of her.

Where the other men had only to scout for enemies and protect their own lives, Noah held himself responsible for Isobel. Though he said nothing, his blue eyes constantly scanned the woods. He noted every track that crossed the muddy road. Now and then his hand whipped toward his pistol, fingers positioned to draw and shoot.

The second day passed without incident. On the road that followed the Pecos River, the Regulators crossed the Rio Feliz and headed toward the Beckwith Ranch, which lay just north of Seven Rivers. They spent that night a few miles up from the Rio Peñasco crossing.

"Noah," Isobel whispered from the folds of her blanket as she lay beside the banked fire.

He lifted his head, every muscle instantly tensed. "What is it? You hear something?"

"No. She reached out and touched his arm with her fingertips. "Noah, I'm . . . I'm thinking of dying."

He scowled. "What in thunder are you thinking about that for?"

"If I am killed, Noah, and if my lands are ever recovered from Snake Jackson, I want you to have them." She rested her chin on her folded hands for a moment. "You have been very good to me, Noah Buchanan. I thank you for that."

"Great ghosts, Isobel, don't go spooking yourself into getting shot. You're not going to die. I make that a promise, okay?"

Ignoring his avowal, she gazed into the intense blue eyes. He looked haggard, his hair mussed from a day under a hat and the lines in his face etched more deeply than usual.

"Noah," she whispered again. "You are a good man."

He reached out one long arm and touched her hair with the tips of his fingers. "Go to sleep, Isobel. It'll be all right."

The next day's travel was uneventful until about four in the afternoon. Dick Brewer and his group had just crossed the

Peñasco when around a crook in the road they came upon five of Jimmie Dolan's men, riding hellbent for leather.

"It's Buck Morton!" Billy the Kid shouted from his position at the point of the Regulators. Hearing the familiar voice, the Dolan five wheeled their horses, broke into two groups, and took off overland at a gallop.

"Let the others go. After Morton, men!" Dick hollered. "He's one of Tunstall's killers."

Weapons drawn, the Regulators gave chase. Isobel caught no sign of Snake in the group, so she spurred her horse after the three who included Buck Morton, Frank Baker, and Sam Lloyd. Noah's horse matched hers neck and neck. They rode up and over a ridge, then skirted a patch of yuccas and thundered toward the river. Mud flying from their hooves, the horses pounded along the soft bank. When Morton swung west, the Regulators followed in hot pursuit.

They'd ridden about five miles when Sam Lloyd's horse suddenly gave out. Stumbling, it fell to the ground in a tangle of thrashing legs. The rider gave a cry for help, but Morton and Baker rode on without him.

"Leave Lloyd!" Dick shouted. "He wasn't in the posse that shot Tunstall. Stick with Morton, men!"

Oddly pleased at being referred to as one of the men, Isobel lowered her head and guided her horse in a flying leap over the prone figure of Sam Lloyd. Grinning, she turned to Noah.

"Yeah, yeah, just watch where you're going, hothead!" he called over the rumble of hoofbeats. Then he softened his words with a quick wink.

Their own horses flagged with the effort of the long chase, and it was all the Regulators could do to keep up the pursuit. As they ascended the brow of a low hill, they realized Morton and Baker were no longer in view.

"They've give out!" the Kid hooted. "I bet they're hiding in that patch of *tule*. Who's going in with me?"

Not one of Dick's riders hesitated to follow Billy down the slope into the shallow depression. As Regulators closed in, an arm waving a dirty white handkerchief rose out of the *tule*.

"Hold your fire, men!" Dick shouted. "Morton—is that you? You aiming to surrender in peace?"

"Brewer, we give up! Don't shoot us, man."

"We won't shoot. Every one of us took an oath to round you snakes up and take you back to Lincoln to stand trial."

The very pale faces of Morton and Baker appeared in the midst of the *tule*. At that moment Billy released the safety on his rifle. In the depression the click sounded as loud as thunder.

"Put it down, Kid!" Noah grabbed the barrel and jerked it upward, taking the aim away from the prisoners' heads.

"Hell, Buchanan, we've got two of Tunstall's murderers," Billy argued. "Worst of the lot, as far as I'm concerned. Let's kill 'em right now and be done with 'em."

Dick assessed the skinny, buck-toothed boy. "To tell the truth, I'm sorry they gave up, too. If we'd have shot it out, we could have finished them. But we took an oath before Squire Wilson, Kid. I promised to protect any prisoners I captured and transport them to Lincoln. Alive."

Billy spat into the ground. "Shoot 'em between the eyes right now and save the court's time. That would avenge Tunstall's death."

"No, Kid. I'm not gonna let you do it." Dick nodded to Noah and the others. "Take their weapons, men. Let's head for Lincoln."

They spent that night at one of Chisum's cow camps near the Pecos. It bothered Noah that they had failed to capture three of the five men. He knew the position of the Regulators was tenuous. All it would take was a word from Lloyd or one of the others, and Dolan's men would ride after them.

As he watched Isobel sleeping, he wondered how big a mistake he had made. If Dolan's bunch came to rescue Morton and Baker, it would be tough for the Regulators to hold up. He honestly didn't know how well he'd fare at protecting his own hide, let alone Isobel's. Sure, she was good with a gun, but being hunted down by a bunch of heartless desperados was a hell of a lot different than shooting glass bottle targets.

He was still awake when the sun slid over the Pecos and warmed the others out of their sleep. With the two prisoners riding toward the front of the line, the Regulators made their way back up the Pecos toward South Spring River Ranch.

They reached Chisum's place by nightfall that Thursday.

There they learned that Dolan had organized a posse of at least twenty men in Lincoln—and the sole aim of the posse was to chase down Regulators.

Though Noah's boss still had not been released from jail in Las Vegas, another man joined the group at the Chisum ranch. His name was William McCloskey, and Isobel saw at once that he was neither well liked nor trusted by Noah, Dick, and the others.

"Fact is," Noah explained to her in a low voice as they rode toward Lincoln the following day, "McCloskey *says* he's joined up with the Regulators, and I know for a fact he once worked a short time for Tunstall—but last month he rode with Mathews's posse."

"But those are the men who shot Mr. Tunstall!" Isobel glanced warily at the broad shoulders of the man who had become a part of their group. He rode to the front of the bunch, along with the two prisoners, the Kid, and several of the other Regulators.

"McCloskey wasn't in the gang that killed Tunstall," Noah said. "He was in the group that rode over the ridge right behind Snake, Evans, and them. But all the same, I don't feel good about him."

"What if he's a spy for Jimmie Dolan?" She felt edgy and uncertain suddenly. If Dolan's posse was preparing to track down Regulators, it wouldn't matter that Squire Wilson had made Dick a constable. "Noah, even if we turn Morton and Baker over to Sheriff Brady as we promised, he'll release them. He's on Dolan's side!"

Well, Noah thought, at least Isobel was getting the picture. "Hey, Dick!" he called. "What do you say we take the north trail up ahead?"

Dick slowed his horse until he was moving alongside Noah and Isobel. "You think Dolan's posse may try to ambush us and rescue Morton and Baker?"

"I'd say that's a real good possibility. If we take the main road into Lincoln, we'll play right into their hands. This way we'll be coming in by a different route. And, since it takes longer, we won't get to town until after dark."

"Sounds like a good plan to me, Noah." Clapping his friend

on the shoulder, Dick gave one of his mesmerizing smiles, then spurred his horse forward to join the others.

As the riders left the main road onto the trail that led through Blackwater Canyon, Isobel felt once again the overwhelming sense that in New Mexico she had at last come home. No, this was not her beloved Catalonia, but here the sky was large and blue, a giant porcelain bowl covering the earth. Here trees grew tall, needles long and fragrant, bark as rugged as the land itself. Here rivers rushed gurgling across the desert. Here deer leapt over fallen logs, wild turkeys gobbled, jackrabbits nibbled grass wet with morning dew, rattlesnakes lay sunning on huge gray limestone slabs, and coyotes lifted their heads to cry out to the moon.

This was a place as raw and untamed as the spirit that flamed inside her breast. Oh, yes, she loved her fine furnishings and her fancy silk dresses, but she knew without the slightest doubt that somewhere deep within the cultured, educated Isobel Matas and the homespun, nestling Isobel Buchanan beat an outlaw heart.

Gripping the horse with her denim-clad knees, she relaxed the reins and studied herself for a moment. Noah's shirt and trousers—far too large—felt soft and warm on her skin. His thick leather belt and heavy holster tugged at her waist with a satisfying weight. With her hair braided and tucked under one of Noah's black Stetsons, her riding boots hooked in the stirrups, and her hands encased in a pair of warm gloves, she felt as if she had discovered herself at last.

This was the real Isobel. Spirited. Game for adventure. As tough and skilled as any man. Yes, this was who she was.

"I thought I'd let the others get ahead a ways," Noah said, leaning toward her a little. "Never did get to say thanks for all the typing you did. I put the story in my saddle bag so I can mail it when we reach Lincoln."

Isobel lifted her head from the scrutiny of herself and faced the warm blue eyes of Noah Buchanan. In that instant the feisty vixen full of *machisma* evaporated.

Oh, how much she had enjoyed the days with him in his little brown adobe *jacal*. Images of herself stirring eggs, arranging china plates, and sipping hot tea by the stove scampered through her mind. Images of him flitted by. Noah carrying a shiny pail of white milk, setting fresh logs in the stove, stirring cornbread batter, reading his story.

"I enjoyed the typing," she said, half-amused and half-dismayed that one look at Noah had wiped away the headstrong, trigger-happy adventurer she had been so sure of. "I . . . I liked your home very much, Noah."

He smiled, strong white teeth a contrast with his bronzed skin. "We had a good time."

As he reached to take her hand, the sound of gunfire rang through the canyon. Noah whipped his six-shooter from his holster. His left hand reached to shelter Isobel as he spurred his horse ahead of hers. A few paces ahead, Dick Brewer reined, glanced back at them, and then spurred his horse toward the sounds of shouting and more gunfire.

"Kid!" Dick shouted. "What's up?"

Noah and Isobel rounded the bend in the trail moments after Dick. On the ground lay three bodies splattered with fresh crimson blood. Buck Morton, Frank Baker, and William McCloskey. Dead.

"Damn it—who did this?" Dick barked. "Billy, you responsible here?"

The Kid shrugged and glanced at the other men who had been with him at the front of the band. He scratched his chin with the shooting end of his pistol.

"I'm lookin' for answers here, Billy," Dick demanded. "We promised to bring back prisoners—and now we got three dead men."

Isobel slid from her horse. Once again, death. Holding her breath, she walked among the horses to where the three men lay sprawled on the ground. As she took off her hat, her golden braid tumbled down her back. "Three," she whispered.

"Isobel . . ." Noah took her arm, but she drew it free to kneel beside the latest victims of Lincoln County's violence.

"See, Dick, here's how it happened," Billy was saying behind her. "Morton, there, was ridin' with McCloskey up front ahead of all of us. Now, you know as well as we do that McCloskey weren't one of the original Regulators. We didn't invite him to join up, he just took it on hisself. And he was part of them that murdered Tunstall, even though he didn't pull the trigger."

"So you just shot him down for bein' in the wrong posse, huh, Billy? Is that what you did?" Dick asked.

"As a matter of fact, no. It was Morton that done it. He grabbed McCloskey's gun and shot him with it." Billy glanced at the others for confirmation. "That's what happened, ain't it, boys?"

"Yeah," the others assented slowly.

Warmed up now, Billy began to talk fast. "See, Morton was aimin' to make a gitaway. He grabbed McCloskey's gun and shot him. Then Morton and Baker took off, tryin' to escape. So we shot 'em."

Isobel stood and rubbed her bloodstained fingers together. "Nine bullet holes," she said. "Buck Morton was shot in the back nine times."

"Like I told you," Billy insisted. "He was tryin' to git away. *'Course* we shot him in the back."

No one said a word as they stared at the three dead men. Isobel felt sick inside. There was a period in her life when she had been sheltered and naive. Now she had seen the face of death four times. Death was not as she'd imagined while reading books or contemplating the noble revenge of her father's murder. These deaths were ugly.

Once-vital men lay on the ground, their faces shattered, their sun-tanned skin stained red, their eyes open but sightless, their lips parted and sagging. Oh, she knew at least two of them had helped kill John Tunstall, but she didn't feel the expected sense of relief at seeing his murderers slain.

"Fine way to regulate the law in Lincoln County," Noah said finally, his voice tight. "Makes me damn proud to be called a Regulator."

"What's the matter, Buchanan—you been lookin' at the world through lace curtains a little too long?" Billy jeered.

Noah gave him a deadly stare, then moved toward the corpses. "Let's get these men buried."

Morton, Baker, and McCloskey had been shot in Blackwater Canyon, just five miles below Agua Negro Spring. At a cow camp not far from the site Dick Brewer arranged with a group of Mexicans to bury the bodies. His mood obviously growing blacker by the minute, Dick spoke not a word as the Regulators rode the canyon trail.

With night setting, Billy Bonney announced he'd had enough of his leader's ire. He and the others responsible for the three deaths would ride cross-country to the town of San Patricio. Leaving Dick alone, they'd hide in the hills until he had settled his business with the law in Lincoln. Then, when all was clear, the Regulators could regroup and make new plans.

"At least we got rid of three of the scum that killed Tunstall," Billy said as he waved a hand and led the rest of the men off the trail.

Noah and Isobel elected to remain with Dick for the ride to Lincoln. When Dick protested, Isobel insisted she needed to find out what had become of Snake Jackson. Yet she knew the real reason for not leaving Dick Brewer had nothing to do with her personal motives.

By now she had come to know Noah Buchanan well enough to see that he had no intention of leaving his closest friend to face a possible ambush by Jimmie Dolan. Noah was a man who stood by those he loved—encouraging, defending, protecting. Even at the cost of his own peace . . . or his own life.

Riding the long, winding canyon trail, it took the three another full day to arrive in Lincoln Town. As they tied their horses to the post outside Alexander McSween's house, Isobel found herself recalling the Sunday exactly one week before when she had watched Noah reading the Bible at the pine table in his house near the Pecos.

How much had happened since that peaceful morning. She had ridden miles over the rugged territory of southeastern New Mexico. She had helped chase down two murderers. And she had been only paces away when those men had in their own turn been killed. The silence of Noah's adobe house, the faint rustle of worn pages turning, the smell of bacon frying seemed far away indeed.

Isobel sighed and stepped onto the portal of Alexander McSween's home.

"Isobel!" Susan Gates flew through the door and into her friend's arms. "Is it really you? Why, you look exactly like a *man* in that getup. Oh, Isobel, I was so afraid I'd never see you again! What's happened? What's become of . . . of . . ." She looked around, scanning the faces. "Oh, Mr. Brewer . . . how nice to see you."

Isobel wiped the smile from her mouth as Susan struggled to contain her joy at finding Dick alive and well. The handsome cattleman made no such pretense. He took two strides toward Susan, lifted her in his arms, and kissed her soundly on the lips.

"Miss Gates, I'm back," he announced, setting her on the porch. "I'm here to tell you that I've done some thinking in the past hours. In front of all this company, I want to say that I love you and I aim to marry you. That is, if you'll have me."

"Mercy!" Susan's eyes lit up as she stared open-mouthed at Isobel. Then, with a tiny whoop, she clasped her hands at her breast. "Why, yes, Mr. Brewer. I'll have you. Indeed, I will."

There was a moment of silence before Dick cleared his throat. "Thank you kindly, Miss Gates. And now, if you'll excuse me, I need to talk to a good lawyer."

"Reckon I'll do?" Alexander McSween asked from the shadows of the doorway. "I decided to come out of hiding for the time being. Figured no one would be bold enough to shoot me in the back—what with Governor Axtell in town these past few days." A great smile lit the lawyer's gentle face as he clasped Dick's shoulder and led him into the house.

Susan was still standing stiff and wide-eyed, staring after her newly affianced, when Isobel kissed her cheek. "*Felicitaciónes*," she whispered with as much tenderness as she could muster under the circumstances. "I wish you much happiness, my friend."

"Congratulations, Miss Gates," Noah said, brushing past her to follow Dick and Alexander into the firelit front room.

"My stars, what a shock!" Susan giggled as she gestured toward the tattered wicker chairs on the portal. "Come sit down, Isobel, and tell me—if you can—what brought that on. I've never seen Dick so bold."

"Dick Brewer is a bold man, Susan. Bold and brave. You'll do well with him for a husband."

As Isobel settled on a weathered cushion, she realized how tender her posterior had become after days of endless riding.

Her body felt as if it were still in motion, her legs bent at the knees, her back stiff and her neck swaying to the rhythm of the horse's gait.

As briefly as she could, she explained the events of the past days. Susan listened, the light in her eyes growing dimmer and the smile on her face fading as Isobel recounted what had befallen the Regulators.

"So what *did* happen to Morton, Baker, and McCloskey out there in Blackwater Canyon?" Susan asked at the end of the tale. "Were they really trying to escape? Or . . . did Billy just take it into his head to shoot them and get it over with?"

Isobel shook her head. "I don't know. Perhaps it was just as Billy told Dick. But perhaps it was not. I think we may never have the full truth."

Susan tapped her feet on the wooden floor. Her face crestfallen, she began to rub the bare ring finger of her left hand. "I guess you ought to know what's happened here in Lincoln while you've been away," she said softly. "With all the hulla-baloo, Governor Axtell decided to come down from Santa Fe for a visit. Of course, he's good friends with Jimmie Dolan, so you can imagine how it all came out. The governor flat-out refused to interview anybody on our side. Mr. McSween even risked his life to come back to town, but the governor wouldn't see him."

Isobel noted the way her friend had spoken of "our side"—and she realized that Susan had become as deeply involved as she. "Did the governor actually do anything about the situation?"

"I'm afraid so. He took away Squire Wilson's position as justice of the peace. Said the squire's appointment was illegal and void."

Isobel lowered her head, thinking of the man whose careful record-keeping had helped her trace the events of her father's murder. "What else?"

"He revoked the appointment of Robert Widenmann as U.S. marshal. He gave all the legal power in the area to Judge Bristol. And . . . he said that nobody's to enforce *any* legal process except Sheriff Brady and his deputies."

Realizing the chilling significance of that final statement, Isobel lifted her head just as Noah stepped onto the portal. His face was dark. He had hooked his thumbs in his pockets, his well-worn boots heavy on the wood floor. Leaning one muscled shoulder against the doorjamb, he set his eyes on Isobel.

"Governor Axtell outlawed the Regulators," he said. Silence followed as the import of his words sank in.

"Then . . . Dick had no authority to round up Morton and Baker?"

"Not as of March ninth, the day Morton and Baker were shot in Blackwater Canyon."

"Dios mio." Isobel breathed the prayer.

"We're outlaws. Every last one of us."

Susan grabbed Isobel's arm as she stood. Noah straightened his shoulders and surveyed the woman he had married. His voice was even, toneless. "I'm offering you a choice Isobel. You can ride for Santa Fe tonight or you can stay here under Alexander McSween's protection."

"And you?"

"Dick and I are heading for his farm on the Ruidoso River. We'll hide out there until court convenes April second."

"But that's three weeks away! I'll go with you."

"No, you won't, Isobel." His words left no room to protest. "I can't promise I'll be able to protect you in that kind of situation. You'll stay here and be accorded the same treatment as the other women or you'll ride to Santa Fe. Which'll it be?"

Isobel gazed into the blue eyes and knew she was not ready to leave them. Not yet.

"I'll stay here," she answered. "Here in Lincoln Town. And I'll wait for you to return."

Isobel settled in comfortably with the Ealy family and Susan Gates. They had been her companions on the trail to Lincoln, and she trusted them without reservation. In the absence of his wife, Alexander McSween had opened his home to the missionary doctor, Mrs. Ealy, their two young daughters, and the schoolteacher. This arrangement gave the Ealys access to goods from the Tunstall store and room to move about freely. Of course, it also set them squarely in the Tunstall-McSween camp.

Susan tried her best to interest Isobel in discussions of the wedding she was planning. She and Dick Brewer had spent not five minutes alone together before he and Noah had set off for Dick's farm. But that time was enough to convince Susan that Dick meant business. He wanted her for his wife—and the sooner the better.

Isobel followed Susan into the empty Tunstall store to study the array of fabrics that might be fashioned into a suitable wedding gown. She tried to pay attention while her friend held bolt after bolt of cloth under her chin. "The blue, do you think?" Susan would ask. "Or the pink?"

But Isobel's thoughts were not with Susan Gates. Her mind's eye saw not rolls of bright fabric and gay wedding gowns, but a man whose face was imprinted on her soul.

Dressing each morning, she recalled the way his large fingers had so deftly worked the hooks on her bodice. Brushing her hair, she remembered how his head had lifted a dark gold tress from her shoulder, turning it this way and that. Helping Mary Ealy put on the breakfast, she seemed to hear the clatter Noah made as he searched for bowls, a frying pan, spoons.

Isobel had only to gaze out the window, and the scene brought Noah to her thoughts. Riding into town that first evening. Sliding off her horse into his arms. Striding down the frozen streets with Juan Patrón. Lincoln, New Mexico, had become a part of her life. Her life and Noah's, together.

"You've come to care for Mr. Buchanan," Susan said almost a week after the men had ridden away. "Haven't you, Isobel?"

Isobel gave a weak smile. "The last time I told you how little Noah meant to me, he was standing just outside the door. Now . . . I wish he were here again."

Susan gathered and folded the voluminous swaths of yellow silk fabric against the sewing machine. Reaching out, she covered Isobel's hands with her own.

"You *are* married to him," she said. "It's all right to care."

"No." Isobel sucked in a breath, then let it out as she began to speak again. "Noah doesn't want me, Susan. He wants his freedom, his writing, and his cattle. He wants land. He wants peace. He doesn't want a wife."

"But you want a husband? You want Noah?"

"I try to tell myself that I want only my future. I try to put my vision on the capture of Snake Jackson and regaining my land titles. That's where my hope lies, Susan. I must accept it." She gazed at their intertwined hands. "But . . . Noah is the only man I've ever wanted. I cannot imagine my life without him now."

"Isobel . . ." Susan leaned forward and whispered so that no one in the busy house could hear. "Isobel, could you be carrying Noah's baby? Have you had your monthly at the right time?"

Isobel lifted her head. How Susan knew that she and Noah had been intimate she couldn't imagine. Did her face betray her so easily?

"The day the men left for Dick's farm, my time began. I have no child."

"Thank goodness! Isobel, you must be careful what you allow with Noah. If you're certain he won't have you as his wife, you mustn't let him get you with child." Susan squeezed her friend's hands. "You can't stay in this state of indecision much longer. If Noah Buchanan is too much of a loner to make a good husband, then you must stop thinking about him. You must decide what to do. Can you go to Santa Fe and ask the Pascals for help in getting your land back?"

"There has been no telegram from Don Guillermo."

"Maybe you could tell Alexander McSween the whole story. Since he's a lawyer, I'm certain he'd—"

"I've got news." Dr. Ealy strode into the room through the back door, his coattails flying in the March breeze. Mary Ealy and the others left their work to gather around him. He adjusted his spectacles and smoothed the pouf of thick dark hair on his head before beginning. "It's about Jesse Evans—one of the men who shot John Tunstall."

"Have they caught him?" Mary Ealy asked, her voice filled with hope.

"Evans, Tom Hill, and some of the others in their band have been hiding out in the Sacramento Mountains. A few days ago they sneaked down to old John Wagner's place near Tularosa. He's a German sheepman, they tell me. Evans and the others decided to raid and loot Wagner's camp. Since nobody was around, they were having a merry time of it, when all of a sudden old man Wagner returned to his camp on the sly. He

grabbed Tom Hill's rifle—which was leaning against a tree—
and fired away."

"Who was shot?" Isobel asked. She had realized at once
that Snake Jackson normally rode with the Evans gang.

"Wagner killed Tom Hill and wounded Jesse Evans. Shot
him in the wrist and the lungs."

"Lungs!" Mary Ealy exclaimed. "Oh, he can't last long."

Dr. Ealy snorted. "Guess again. Evans escaped and rode all
night until he got to friendly turf in the Organ Mountains. He
hid out there a few days, and just this morning he decided to
give himself up to the commanding officer at Fort Stanton. So
there he lies—safe from the Regulators and receiving the finest medical attention in these parts. Save for my own skilled
hands, of course."

"Is Evans a free man at the Fort?" Isobel asked.

"He's under arrest until court convenes in April. They'll try
him under one of the old warrants he's racked up. Or maybe
one of the new." Dr. Ealy mused for a moment, then shook his
head. "Want to hear the best part of it all? Jesse Evans has declared that Tom Hill was the man who pulled the trigger on
John Tunstall that day in the woods."

"Tom Hill!" Isobel exploded. "But it's Snake Jackson and
Jesse Evans who are the murderers."

"Yes, ma'am. But Tom Hill—who was once a loyal member of the Evans gang—is now dead as a doornail. So who better for Evans to pin the murder on?"

Clenching her jaw, Isobel swung away from the group and
strode outside into the bright sunshine. Tom Hill. Jesse Evans.
The real object of her mission was a man named Rattlesnake
Jackson.

If she could have no part in Noah's life . . . no station as a
doña in the Pascal family . . . no rights to her father's land in
Catalonia . . . then she had no choice but to take the only open
path. She must find Snake Jackson.

And only one man would know where he was hiding. Setting her eyes on the rolling green hills that rose above the
river, Isobel made her decision. She must ride for Fort
Stanton. At once.

Chapter
❧ *12* ❧

Isobel knew that if she told Dr. Ealy and his wife about her plan, they would forbid it. Instead she took Susan aside and carefully explained the situation. If she could confront Jesse Evans while he was under arrest at Fort Stanton, she could force him to tell her where Snake Jackson was hiding out.

"And what then?" Susan asked, panic raising her voice to a much higher pitch than usual.

"Then I shall find my father's killer."

"*Then* what, Isobel?"

Isobel lowered her head and studied her riding boots. "Only God knows," she whispered.

Susan's protests did no good. Isobel knew she had come to New Mexico to find her father's murderer and to avenge his death. She knew her revenge would be complete with the recovery of the land-grant titles that had belonged to her family since the earliest days of Spanish exploration in the New World.

True, other events had come into her life to attempt to dissuade her from the solitary goal of vengeance. She had witnessed a murder. She had lost hope of marrying into the Pascal family. She had become the wife of an American *vaquero*. She had formed friendships and bonds. But when she peered through these vines of entanglement, she saw again that she had no choice.

Clad once more in Noah's denim trousers, chambray shirt, and leather coat, Isobel settled the black Stetson over her gold braid and mounted her horse.

Reaching down, she took Susan's hand in hers. "I shall return in a week," she said. "If not, you must write to my uncle at Fort Belknap and to my mother in Spain. Tell them I tried."

"Oh, Isobel—"

"And tell Noah . . . tell him that I loved him. Truly, I did." Unable to face the pain and fear of her own future, she spurred her horse onto the main road and rode west toward Fort Stanton.

The newly rebuilt fort—constructed mainly of stone—lay nine miles from Lincoln. Once under the authority of Kit Carson, it was now commanded by Captain Purington. As Isobel rode toward the gate of the bastion, she saw on one side the towering snow-covered peak of Sierra Blanca. On the other lay the mountains of El Capitán.

Entering the fort with little notice from the guards, she took stock of the adobe barracks, irrigation ditches, and spaded garden plots. Homes and other buildings dotted the enclosure, and Isobel noted more women and children than she had expected to find. Bony dogs scampered and played with dusty, giggling toddlers. Aproned mothers took laundry down from lines that stretched between trees.

A large number of black soldiers were stationed at the fort, and Isobel noted the stunningly uniformed men standing guard throughout the area. These men were members of the 9th Cavalry Regiment—one of four black regiments that had been organized following the Civil War. From Noah Isobel had learned that companies F, H and M of the 9th Cavalry were stationed at Fort Stanton. These soldiers were highly respected by the local settlers and were often called to defend them against attacks by Apache Indians.

Noah had also explained to Isobel that the fort provided more than protection in southeastern New Mexico. A great deal of the military's supply business went to farmers and ranchers in the area. Not only did the garrison of soldiers need meat, vegetables, ground wheat, and wood, but Fort Stanton was also charged with providing food to the nearby Apache reservation.

In fact, five years earlier, Jimmie Dolan and his partner, L. G. Murphy, had been the primary suppliers to the fort. Accused of duplicity in their dealings and defrauding the government, however, they had been ordered to leave. Finally, under a great deal of duress, they had been ejected by a party of soldiers.

Isobel assumed that this meant the fort commanders would be unsympathetic to Dolan's side in the troubles of Lincoln Town.

She was wrong.

Though the military tried to remain objective, the past weeks had shown that its orders—if not its sympathies—lay with the law in New Mexico. And the law upheld every movement Jimmie Dolan made.

Aware of the eyes that followed her across the open courtyard, Isobel tied her horse and strode onto the portal of a building that housed the fort's store, hotel, and post office.

"Help ya?" The voice came from a row of mailboxes where a man was sorting through a stack of envelopes. "Name's Will Dowlin. I'm the trader and postmaster here at the fort."

As he spoke, he swung around to peer at his customer. The sight of the young woman clad all in baggy denims caused him to pause. He raised, then lowered his spectacles, all the while examining her.

"I've come to speak with a medical prisoner," Isobel said. "Where may I find such a man?"

"You're speakin' of Jesse Evans, I take it? He's under guard at the hospital. Go on over to headquarters and ask to speak with the officer in charge." The postmaster moved toward the counter. "Will you be needin' a room for the night . . . ma'am? Or is it *sir*?"

"My name is Isobel Matas Buchanan. I'm searching for Jim Jackson, the man who murdered my father. And no, thank you, I won't need a room."

Isobel made for the door, but as she prepared to step outside, Dowlin called to her. "Miz Buchanan—I wouldn't go spreadin' that around about bein' on the lookout for Snake Jackson. He's liable to start lookin' for *you*."

She tipped her head. "I certainly hope so, Mr. Dowlin."

It took more than a little negotiating for Isobel to convince Captain Purington to let her interview Jesse Evans. In fact, she might not have been allowed at all had not the colonel been so frustrated with the War Department. He was tired of being fettered in his efforts to control the situation brewing in Lincoln County. Purington told Isobel that if she was fool-headed enough to hunt down a man wanted by the law for stealing horses and committing murder, so be it.

Late that night Isobel was ushered into the Fort Stanton hospital. Dr. Appel, the physician who had been paid a hundred dollars to examine John Tunstall's body for the Dolan faction, pointed out Jesse Evans. The chunky outlaw sprawled between clean sheets, his wounded wrist and chest bandaged in white. Isobel might have felt a measure of sympathy for the injured man, but she had heard from too many reliable sources that he was a horse thief, cattle rustler, murderer, and robber.

Approaching the bed, she touched the place on her thigh where Noah's six-shooter had hung. Now the holster was empty.

"Mr. Evans," she said.

The man turned toward her. Heavyset and dark-skinned, he stared, saying nothing. She perched on the edge of a nearby chair, glanced at the guards who stood at the door, and cleared her throat.

"Mr. Evans, I'm looking for Rattlesnake Jim Jackson." She watched for a reaction in the dark eyes, but there was none.

"What fer?" he asked finally.

She noted that he spoke with difficulty, his chest laboring to take in air. "He murdered my father."

Jesse Evans's eyes rolled toward the ceiling. "Oh, Lord. Not *you*."

"I'm the daughter of Albert Matas. My father was shot and killed at the hand of Jim Jackson five years ago—when he rode with the Horrell gang."

Evans took to coughing. He spat a globule of bright blood onto the white sheet. A groan emerged from somewhere deep inside his chest. Glancing at the guards, Isobel saw that none of them intended to move.

"Here," she whispered. She grabbed a clean towel and blotted the outlaw's chin. Then she tucked the linen around his throat. When she sat back in her chair, he was staring at her.

"Snake aims to kill ya, miss," he said. "Hates Mexicans."

"I'm from Spain."

"Don't matter. Some of you folks done in his family when he was a kid. And . . . o'course, there's the matter of you bein' out in the woods that evenin'.''

"When you murdered John Tunstall? Yes. I saw it all."

Evans scratched the side of his face and coughed again. "I reckon if I tell you where Snake is and you go after him," he wheezed, "you gonna git yerself killed."

"It could be."

"I reckon you couldn't be no government witness if you was dead, now, could ya?"

"Certainly not."

"Well, now . . . that sits all right with me, I guess." He coughed again. "I'm not the kind to go squealin' on my pals' hideouts. Nor do I like the thought of sendin' a purty young gal to her grave. But in this case—"

"Where is Snake, Mr. Evans?"

"He's up at the old L. G. Murphy ranch about ten miles northwest of the fort. Take the road to White Oaks."

Standing, Isobel regarded the outlaw. "Thank you, Mr. Evans," she said.

"Good luck, señorita. Yer gonna need it."

Dawn was casting pink and purple lights over the mountains when Isobel dismounted at the edge of the main road. She could see the Murphy ranch house some distance away atop a small grassy knoll. At this early hour no one was stirring.

Perspiration broke out on her temples as she drew her gun and crept through the scrub piñon and oak brush toward the dwelling. A rooster crowed. The sudden sound sent ice down her spine. Pausing, she wiped her brow with the back of her hand.

She knew she couldn't kill Snake Jackson without first

learning what he had done with her land grant titles. Not that she really wanted to kill the man. If she could round him up and take him to the fort, she felt sure Captain Purington would put him under guard until court convened in Lincoln. Then the law could hang him.

Her breath sounded loud in the crisp morning air as she knelt beside a rail fence near the house. Swallowing, she leaned her head against a post. Whispering a quick prayer, she brought to mind the faces of her father, her mother, her brother . . . and the gentle smile of Noah Buchanan. *Oh, Lord, keep him safe. Always.*

Cradling her gun, she flipped open the chamber and counted the six bullets. As she clicked it back into place, a gloved hand clamped over her mouth. Hot, hard, smelling of leather.

"Don't scream. Don't move." The voice was muffled and husky.

Fear knotted Isobel's throat. She wrestled, struggled, but the hand gripped tighter. Her lips twisted. Her nose bent beneath the pressure. She craned her head, wanting to see the man who had trapped her. A dark hat, a bandanna, shadowed eyes.

She held her breath, waiting for the shot that would tear open her back.

"Isobel." Still gripping her, the man jerked the red scarf from his nose and mouth. A strong nose. Sensual lips. Unshaven chin. And now she saw the blue, blue eyes.

"Noah!"

"Hush." He clapped his palm over her mouth again. "Muleheaded woman," he breathed. "What do you think you're doing out here?"

"How did you find me?"

"Susan Gates sent for me, of course. You didn't think she'd let you ride off to your death, did you?"

"But . . . but I told her—"

"Enough's enough, Isobel. You're coming back to Lincoln with me."

"Noah—look!" She caught his arm.

The front door of the Murphy house had swung open. Scratching his rumpled auburn hair, Snake Jackson wandered onto the porch. He wore only a red union suit, its buttons half undone. In one hand he carried a rifle. As he stretched and yawned, a thunderous belch erupted from his chest.

"Ah-h-h," they heard him sigh.

Noah gathered Isobel in his arms as Snake leaned the rifle against a sagging porch post. Gazing out across the landscape, his body facing his hidden enemies, he began to undo the fly of his union suit.

"Turn your head, Isobel," Noah whispered.

But she watched as Snake ejected a long yellow arc over the porch rail and onto a bed of pansy blossoms. At that moment Isobel wrestled free of Noah's arms and rose from behind the fence.

"Jim Jackson!" she shouted, leveling her six-shooter at his flaccid organ. "Where are the titles to my lands?"

"Get down, Isobel!" Noah hissed from his crouching position at her ankles. "There may be others in the house." He drew his own gun and aimed it at Snake's head.

"I am the daughter of the Spanish nobleman, Albert Matas, whom you murdered five years ago," Isobel continued, ignoring Noah. "Tell me where you have put my family's land titles and jewels. The ones you stole from my father's coach."

"Ga-a-a . . ." Snake made a move toward his rifle, but Isobel cocked her pistol. "All right, all right, señorita. Hold yer horses now."

"Shall I shoot off your pitiful *pene*? Or will you talk?"

"I'll talk, all right. I recognize you. Yer the Mexican that seen our posse the day Tunstall got shot. Yer the one with the fancy lace veil."

"Yes, I saw you murder John Tunstall. I saw it all. Now tell me where you put the titles, or I'll blast off your *cojones*!"

"And I'll blast off yore sassy head!" Grabbing his rifle, Snake made a flying lunge onto the porch floorboards.

Isobel pulled the trigger. The bullet smashed into the open front door. She aimed at Snake's bobbing red rear end as he wriggled toward cover. The instant she squeezed the trigger a second time, Noah grabbed her by the waist and hurled her onto the ground. A bullet zinged past her head and *thwapped* into a tree trunk behind them.

"Someone's firing from upstairs in the house!" Noah shouted.

"You made me miss my shot!"

"Head for that arroyo." Jerking Isobel's arm, Noah began to haul her toward the protection of the nearby ditch.

Isobel aimed at the face in an upper window and fired her third bullet. A return shot whizzed into the fence post. A spray of sawdust and splinters exploded around her head. Sliding backward across the rough ground, one arm clamped in Noah's fist and her feet dragging, Isobel shot at Snake as he scampered around the side of the house.

"Asesino!" she hollered. "Murderer! Thief!"

A bullet plowed into the dirt beside her. Another hit a rock and ricocheted off.

"I want my land!" she screamed.

As Noah was tugging her down into the ditch, a bullet tore through the flesh of his left forearm. Like a burning knife, it severed muscle, vein, and sinew. Blood spurted from the powder-singed hole.

"Bastardo!" Isobel shouted, firing her remaining bullets at random. "Oh, Noah—if I could only get my hands on that man—"

Her words hung in her throat as she caught sight of the spreading crimson stain on Noah's arm. Paying little attention to himself, he was attempting to keep them covered while he scouted the landscape for the quickest escape route. His blue eyes darted back and forth, his mouth a grim line of determination.

"This way!" he shouted, jerking her roughly.

"You're . . . you're wounded! You've been shot, Noah!"

"Yeah, that's what sometimes happens when folks take aim and fire at you darlin'. It's a hell of a thing. . . . This way— now!"

Running in a crouch, they raced through the low shrubbery toward the road. Her mouth dry, Isobel followed at Noah's heels. The fire in her blood still pumped like lava through her veins. But the chilling ice of realization that the man she loved had been shot because of her settled in a cold lump in her heart.

"Get, now! Get on!" Noah shoved her rump onto the waiting horse. In almost the same motion he slid a foot into his own horse's stirrup and swung his leg over the saddle. "Go, Isobel! Ride like the wind, damn it!"

Obeying for once, she leaned into her horse and spurred it down the road. Noah kept his own stallion just paces behind hers. Pistol drawn, he rode with his face turned toward the house behind them. If Snake and whoever was with him decided to give chase, he knew it was going to be a close shave. Isobel's horse, though a good one, was no match for the rugged, sinewy steeds the outlaws rode.

Turning, he glimpsed her just ahead, her blond braid bouncing against her back, her shirttail flying and her boots kicking out an even rhythm on the horse's flanks. Despite the oversized denim trousers, her round bottom looked fine as it settled into the saddle. She guided the horse in a leap over a fallen log, then she swung around, pulling on the reins.

"Are you badly hurt, Noah?" she called.

"I reckon I'll live."

"Then let's return now!" Her face was alight and her hazel eyes sparkling. "We'll ride around behind the house. They'll never expect it!"

Busy thanking the Creator for a relatively safe exit—as well as admiring Isobel's firm little behind—Noah didn't quite catch her drift at first. His arm felt like it was on fire as he attempted to rein his galloping stallion.

"This way!" Isobel was crying, one long finger pointed in the direction of the Murphy ranch house. *"Por la venganza!"*

She spurred her horse and set off through the forest. For a moment Noah sat stock still, watching her golden braid fade away into the brush.

Maybe it was the loss of blood, but his head didn't feel quite right. Hadn't he just *rescued* Isobel? Hadn't he just dragged her across the ground to safety as bullets flew around their heads? Hadn't he just gotten himself shot trying to get her away from Snake Jackson?

Then where in hell was she going?

"Isobel!" he hollered, goading his horse into action. "Isobel, damn it, get back here!"

A branch raked his hat from his head as he followed her horse's flying hooves through a thicket. Muttering curses, he lowered his bare head against his stallion's black flank. *All right, this is it. This is going too damn far, Isobel.* "We'll take cover there!" she cried, wheeling her horse around. "Behind the privy. You on the left side. I on the right."

"Isobel—"

But she was off again. Her horse thundered across a stretch of denuded ground. Instantly shots rang out from the Murphy house. Isobel's horse shied, reared, danced sideways. Whinnying, it fought for freedom with as much determination as Isobel fought for control.

"Caballo loco!" she shouted, wrestling with the reins. "It's a crazy horse!"

Gritting his teeth, Noah plunged across the cleared ground after Isobel. Bullets seemed to be coming from every direction—fortunately from just a little too far away to be terribly accurate. Feeling vulnerable without his hat, he hunkered down against his horse. He held his breath as he approached the bucking mount.

"Isobel!" he shouted over the hiss of bullets.

"Noah—to the outhouse! My horse will follow yours!"

"Are you nuts? We're getting out of this deathtrap!" He grabbed for her horse's reins.

"I can't leave now. I'm too close."

"Close to getting yourself killed."

"No, Noah!"

Faced with the reality that his wife was certifiably *loco*, Noah grimaced and turned his six-shooter on her. "I said move it, darlin'."

"Noah! But—"

"Now!" He released the safety and gave her bottom a nudge with the end of the pistol. "Get your fanny out of here, Isobel! I ain't joshing."

A veil lowered over her eyes and face as she swung her horse away from the line of fire. He followed a pace behind, his gun leveled at her—just to keep the situation clear in her mind. They backtracked through the forest, steering clear of the main road in case Snake and the others might try an ambush.

When they had ridden two miles without hearing gunfire and were approaching Fort Stanton, Isobel finally turned toward Noah. Her face was set in anger, and she glared at him for a full minute before speaking.

"Where are you taking me?" she snapped.

"Home."

"I have no home! And you just made certain of it."

"Snake Jackson isn't going to give up those land titles, Isobel, even with you shooting at him from behind a privy."

She gave a little *humpf* and looked away. "How little you understand me, Noah Buchanan."

"You can say that again."

They rode for a few more minutes, neither speaking. Finally Isobel muttered something under her breath.

"What?" Noah asked.

"I said—at Fort Stanton, I will gather soldiers. *They* will be brave enough to fight by my side against Snake Jackson."

Noah snorted. "We're not stopping at Fort Stanton, Isobel. Or at Lincoln. Or anywhere else along the line. I'm taking you to Chisum's ranch if I have to do it at gunpoint."

"You will have to keep your gun on me *vaquero*, because I intend to return to the Murphy house. I know my place."

"So do I, señora."

Cradling his wounded arm, Noah reached to lower his hat against the morning sunshine. He ran his hand across his damp hair and let out a sigh. No hat. No breakfast. A hole through his arm. And one *loco* spitfire. This arrangement was turning out to be some kind of fun.

Isobel had meant every word she said. If she thought she could escape from Noah Buchanan, however, she was mistaken. He watched her like a hawk, his blue eyes never wavering from her back. He kept his pistol holstered most of the time, but if she showed the slightest inclination toward bolting, he whipped it out and aimed it at her heart.

As angry as she was at being captured and treated in such a foul manner, Isobel couldn't allow Noah's wound to go untreated. Within an hour of their leaving the Murphy ranch, she had insisted on bathing his arm in the clear icy water of the Rio Bonito. God had been with him—it was a clean wound. The bullet had passed through, tearing flesh but breaking no bones.

In his saddlebag Noah carried some ointments which Isobel applied to the broken skin. She tore into strips a clean linen towel from her own bag. Then she bound them tightly around his forearm to staunch the flow of blood.

Though she couldn't understand why he had taken her away from Snake Jackson when she was so close to the battle, it bothered her to face the reality of Noah's wound. She didn't like to think that such a man could ever be hurt in any way. He had always seemed so strong, so invincible. Like her father.

But there were other matters that she forced into precedence over her concern for Noah. When she lined up these items in her mind, they seemed such a barrier between herself and him that she could not imagine ever overcoming them.

As they rode the last few miles toward Chisum's South Spring River Ranch, she decided to speak her thoughts freely. It would define their arrangement.

"First," she began without preamble, "you have no understanding of me or my goal, Noah. Second, you have treated me in a boorish manner. Third, I perceive of you as a coward."

He turned his head, blue eyes piercing. "A coward?"

He was silent for more than a minute, and she began to wonder if she had pushed him too far. Then he gave a little grunt. "I reckon I must be sliding down the social ladder. First I was a dusty, no-count *vaquero*. Now I'm a coward."

"If you had stood by my side—"

"I expect you're right. We should have fought it out with Snake and his cronies from behind the privy. Then, when someone came to claim our rotting bodies in a week or so, they could say, 'Yup, these two are dead as doornails, but they shore was brave.'"

"I have no intention of dying at Snake Jackson's hand," Isobel shot back.

"What do you think you have—some kind of holy halo around you that's going to keep the bullets away?"

When she considered his retort, it occurred to Isobel that Noah had come very close to the truth. She knew her father had been killed, and she had seen four murdered men. But the thought that *she* might actually be felled by a bullet . . .

Perhaps it was her youth or the knowledge that she was a fine rider and could shoot with such accuracy—but she fully expected to die in her sleep at the age of ninety-seven or so. When the bullets had hummed past her head, she had felt no fear. Only anger. Only determination. So close to the possibility of death, she had never felt more alive.

"I will never back away from my destiny, Noah," she said finally. "I have tasted the presence of death. I am not afraid."

"Well, that's a good thing," he answered in that calm, slightly cocky voice she had come to know so well. "You and destiny and death can all get together and have a little tea party one of these days. But until our arrangement is over, I plan to keep you right here, safe and sound, locked in your room with a guard at the door if I have to."

Lifting her head, Isobel saw that they had come almost to the gate that led to John Chisum's house. With March nearing an end, spring had set in, and the sight before her nearly took her breath away. The one hundred rosebushes had leafed out and were beginning to bud. The grass had brightened from a wintery yellow-gray to a fresh soft green. The stream rushed high and swift, gurgling through the peaceful valley.

Isobel had the sudden sense that the recent past had been no more than a dream. A nightmare. This was the land that softly cradled her. This was the place where she and Noah had been happy. She remembered their sweet, clean days and their nights filled with ecstasy.

Now he had brought her here again. If she went to his home, she would fall into that world again. It would absorb her and rob her of her dream. Or was that world her dream? Did a life with Noah beckon her more strongly than the call to reclaim her own legacy?

She studied him as he leaned over the gate and worked the latch. It seemed forever since her hands had stroked his broad shoulders, an eternity since her fingers had slipped through his hair. A palpable ache began to throb in the pit of her stomach when she watched him straighten from the gate.

"Noah," she said, looking into his face, "when will our arrangement be over?"

His hands relaxed on the saddle as he regarded her. "When things calm down in Lincoln and I'm sure you're safe from Snake Jackson. And when I convince Chisum to sell me the land I want."

She nodded, wondering how long it would be until those things were accomplished. Half of her hoped she would be free of Noah soon. Half of her hoped a day would never come when he looked into her eyes and bade her farewell.

"Howdy!" The laugh from the portal of the house drew their attention. It was easy and hearty, as if its owner had not a care in the world. "Buchanan? Is that you? Where's your hat, partner?"

A slender, mustached man with deep brown eyes and thinning hair was waving to them from the steps. At least fifty years old, he was making his way toward them with the stride of a much younger man. He wore no holster. No gun. And yet he moved with the pride of a king.

Noah's spirits lifted as his focus settled on the gentleman. "Looks like we may wind up our arrangement sooner than we thought," he said to Isobel. "That man there is John Simpson Chisum."

Chapter
❧ 13 ❧

"I've been away from the ranch, thinking how much everybody's missing me," John Chisum greeted Noah and Isobel. "But then I come back to find myself nearly shut out of house and home. Why, I daresay I thought I was one of the three bears for a minute. And this must be Miss Goldilocks!"

He took Isobel's hand and kissed it grandly. His thick brown mustache—each end waxed into a curly point—brushed over her bare skin.

"What are you talking about, you old coot?" Noah asked as he and Chisum embraced in a massive bear hug.

"I'm talking about your wife usurping my fine bed. What did you mean bringing your bride all this way and then dumping her at my place and heading off on your own? Mrs. Towry told me all about it, Buchanan—and I was mighty ashamed of you. Especially when I realized that your bride had taken to sleeping in *my* brand-new bed, wrinkling my pretty embroidered pillow shams, and leaving my wardrobe full of her shiny silk dresses."

Noah gaped at Isobel, who had blushed a deep red. "But Mrs. Towry said—" she began.

"Now, a man like me just doesn't cotton to such behavior in

his employees, Buchanan. Don't you know I've been cooped up in a Las Vegas jail for three long months? Eating grub that ain't fit for man nor beast. Sleeping on a hard prison bed. Why, I've been just *living* for the day I could get back here and stretch out on one of those fancy embroidered pillow shams of mine."

"Oh, Mr. Chisum, please—" Isobel interjected.

"Yessir," he went on, ignoring her, "now that your bride has gone and messed things all up, I reckon I'll just have to get back to sleeping on my poor old camp cot on the floor."

"Mr. Chisum, I'm terribly sorry. I had no idea. And certainly Noah—"

At this the cattle baron slapped his knee and burst into a gale of hearty chuckles. "Oh, I got you good there, didn't I, Miss Goldilocks? I had you thinking you'd got your husband into a heap of trouble, huh? Haw, haw, haw! Fancy embroidered pillow shams! Haw, haw! Camp bed on the floor—why, that's where I *always* sleep! Haw, haw, haw!"

Noah instinctively tucked Isobel under his arm and gave Chisum a good slap on the back. "You had us plumb tongue-tied, you old joker. I should have guessed what you were up to the minute you started in on her."

It took a moment for Chisum to control his laughter over the grand joke he had pulled. Isobel had yet to see anything humorous in the situation. She felt used by Mrs. Towry and then doubly abused by Mr. Chisum with their silly antics.

"John, I'd like you to meet Belle Buchanan," Noah was saying as his boss collected himself. "We got to know each other while I was on that Arizona run. Came all the way back here right after we got married. She's brought her furniture over, and we're settling in at my place."

"Pleased to meet you, Mrs. Buchanan. Don't you mind me, now. Everyone around here knows how I love a joke. Welcome to the family."

She mustered a smile she didn't particularly feel.

"Noah Buchanan," Chisum said as his sharp brown eyes studied Isobel. "I never would have figured you to settle down. Not for a minute. But now that I've seen this enchanting young bride of yours, I can understand how it all happened. . . . Well, you folks come on into the house, now."

As Isobel and Noah followed Chisum up the steps, he turned and fixed them with a frown. "Where've you been, anyway?" he asked. He glanced at Noah's arm. "You know how I feel about gunfighting, Buchanan. A six-shooter will always get you into more trouble than it'll get you out of."

Without waiting for a response, he turned and strode through the double doors into the cool shadows of his front room.

Isobel was starting to think that John Simpson Chisum must be the most eccentric man she had ever met. He swaggered when he walked. His speech was peppered with sarcasm and loud hoots of jeering laughter. He loved practical jokes that were funny only to him.

But as Isobel entered the cattleman's rambling, opulent home for a second time, she was reminded that as odd as he might be, John Chisum was also a shrewd, insightful businessman.

His ranch—stretching two hundred miles along the Pecos River—was the largest in the territory. Mrs. Towry had told Isobel that Chisum ran over 40,000 head of cattle. Though much of the stock remained on the Pecos, three years earlier Chisum had sold the lot to the firm of Hunter & Evans for almost $300,000. Gradually Noah and the other trail bosses were transferring the cattle to Kansas or Arizona. This arrangement made John Chisum not only wealthy but powerful.

Yet, there was another side to the strange man. Isobel had inferred from studying his home and fields that those Chisum loved were privileged indeed. His employees fairly worshiped the ground he walked on. He treated them with fairness and honor. His friends were deeply loyal. And he had taken great pains with his livestock and grounds.

As she entered the great room, Isobel gazed out the window in admiration. Long irrigation ditches between the rosebushes and the orchards flowed with clear water.

"We'll have watermelons, come summer," a voice said close to her ear. Isobel started and glanced up to find Chisum leaning near her. "You and Noah can come over for a visit."

"Thank you," she said uncertainly.

Chisum fiddled with the waxed end of his mustache for a moment. "To tell you the truth, I'm glad you made use of that damn-fool bed of mine, Miss Goldilocks. In fact, if you and Noah need—"

"No, thank you, sir. I've brought my furniture with me, as Noah mentioned."

"So, tell me about yourself. Where you came from. Your family. What possessed you to up and marry my best trail boss."

Isobel found Noah across the room. He was talking to Alexander McSween, who evidently had sought refuge at Chisum's ranch from the furor in Lincoln Town. Though the lawyer was whispering intently to Noah, the cowboy's eyes hadn't left Isobel for a moment. He looked as if he wanted to break away and come to her rescue. But he didn't.

"I married for love, of course," Isobel replied, turning her head and meeting Chisum's frank appraisal. "As to my family—my father owned land, but he was killed five years ago. Now my mother and my brother see to the family property."

"In Tucson."

Isobel hesitated only a moment. "Near Tucson," she replied, remembering how much Noah wanted to buy a section of land to start a ranch. She knew it was up to her to make John Chisum believe that Noah was now a happily married husband.

"You reckon you're going to like it out here in the territory?"

"I have no doubt."

"Reckon you'll be starting a family any time soon?"

"As soon as possible."

"Reckon you'll manage to settle down ol' Noah Buchanan?"

"I already have."

"Then how'd he wind up with that bullet hole in his arm?" Chisum asked, leaning closer.

Isobel was ready. "Noah was protecting me—as a good husband should."

Chisum grinned beneath his mustache. "I like you, Miss Goldilocks. You have spunk. We're going to get along fine."

After patting her on the back, he clapped his hands. At the signal everyone fell quiet. For the first time Isobel noted the other people seated in the room. Other than Alexander McSween, however, she recognized none of them.

"Noah Buchanan, Belle," Chisum said, holding out his arms in a warm manner that belied the tart way in which he had originally greeted them. "I'd like to introduce you around. You know Alexander McSween, of course. And this is his wife, Sue. She's just returned from St. Louis."

A perky woman with mounds of tightly curled chestnut hair and a pair of sloping, almond brown eyes stood to greet them. Her small lips and rather large nose gave her a definite plainness, but her elegant blue brocade dress trimmed in white ruffles at the neck and sleeves revealed the McSween wealth and stature in the county.

"These gentlemen," Chisum continued, sweeping a hand to indicate the three, "are Mr. Simpson, Mr. Howes, and Dr. Leverson. Dr. Leverson has just come down from Colorado, hoping to establish a colony of settlers in our area."

Everyone stared at the man whose ill-fated timing had led him to Lincoln County in a most unpropitious month. When the other guests resumed their chatter, Noah started for the front door.

"Buchanan, where are you off to in such a hurry?" Chisum asked, casually blocking his path.

"Thought I'd head over to my place and check things out." Noah nodded in Isobel's direction without actually looking at her. "Reckon I'll leave Belle with you, John. With all the restlessness in the county, I figure she'll be safer here. You wouldn't mind keeping an eye on her for me, would you?"

"I certainly would." Chisum glanced at Isobel and then gave a little sniff. "Not that I wouldn't appreciate the company of such a lovely creature around the house, Buchanan, but she's your wife. You've already gone off and left her here once. I don't want you making that a regular habit. . . , No, sir, I reckon you'd better pack her up and take her with you. Besides, you'll need someone to help tend that bullet hole of yours. *Adiós*, partner."

Laughing that hearty laugh, Chisum hailed McSween across the room and swaggered away, leaving Noah standing in the lurch.

* * *

"You make one move to get away, and I swear I'll hogtie you to this post," Noah avowed as he and Isobel wrapped their horses' reins around the hitching post outside Noah's adobe *jacal*.

Marching across the cool portal, Isobel decided she would not lower herself to respond to such a vulgar comment. The very idea that Noah believed he could tie her up . . . Of course, not so long ago he *had* held a gun at her back and threatened to shoot her. And that was in the midst of his mission to prevent her from attaining her revenge against Snake Jackson. Or had Noah actually been trying to save her life, as he had insisted?

When she pushed open the front door and stepped into the familiar room, her anger wavered. She hadn't expected the house to smell so evocative—the dust on the floor, the crisp starch in the lace curtains, the old leather coats on the rack, the cedar wood shavings from Noah's abandoned pencils on the pine table. From the kitchen had filtered the aromas of ground coffee, cinnamon, and lye soap. From the bedroom drifted the scents of the eucalyptus and lavender Isobel had packed among her clothes, and the bay rum cologne Noah sometimes wore.

She shut her eyes and stood for a moment, swept away from the recent past to memories bathed in soft, golden light. Laughter, as she and Noah hung curtains too long or too short for the windows. Giggles over too much garlic and not enough onions in the rabbit stew. The soft *swish-swish* of the straw broom. The *clickety-clack* of the Remington.

"I mailed your story to New York," she said when she felt Noah moving behind her.

"I forgot all about the thing in the rush to head for Brewer's place, and then my chase up the river to Murphy's ranch," he said. He was silent for a moment, before speaking again. "Thank you, Isobel."

She turned to him and looked into his blue eyes. "It seems we go in opposite directions, Noah. You are for the quiet life. The life of peace. I am for *la venganza*."

He nodded, staring at the oriental carpet that stretched beneath the velvet sofas. "On the other hand, I remember a few days when you seemed happy with my way, Isobel. Days right here in this house."

"I remember, too." Once again, their eyes met. "So perhaps there is a Belle Buchanan who sometimes moves in the direction of the quiet life, the life of peace. But will there ever be a Noah who might turn—even for a time—toward the pursuit of justice and right?"

Noah studied Isobel's golden hair and shining eyes. He could feel the pain inside her as much as he could feel the need for quiet inside himself. He knew how she hurt. He knew how lost she felt.

"I've lived a rough life, Isobel," he said finally. "It's been a man's life. Rounding up cattle. Warding off rustlers. Doing without decent food at times. Living off stagnant water when it was all that could be found. I've used my gun plenty of times on the side of justice. Though it's not something I like to talk about much, I'll admit that bullets from my six-shooter have sent three men on to their rewards. Two were cattle rustlers. And the other was trying to steal my horse." He paused a moment, trying to figure a way to make himself clear to her. "I'm no coward, Isobel. And I'll always stand by law and order. It's just that I've got to follow my own dreams. It's time."

He watched her face mirror every emotion she felt. He read the sadness, the anxiety, the need. Mixed into it, he read something new. Something maybe he hadn't allowed himself to see in her before. He saw in Isobel's eyes a softness toward him, despite everything he'd just told her. She cared for him. She wanted him. Maybe . . . maybe she loved him.

"So we'll just keep apart," he said quickly, apprehension a tight cinch around his chest. "While you're at my house, you just do what you want, and I'll do what I have to. In a few days we'll head back to Chisum's place and talk to him about the land I want to buy. We'll check out the news from Lincoln, and as soon as we hear Snake is in jail, you can get on with your own business."

"Yes," she said softly. "I understand."

But as she began removing her shawl, coat, and bonnet, Noah realized that every word he'd spoken had been just so much rubbish. He didn't want to stay away from her. He didn't want to send her off. No . . . what he wanted was Isobel.

* * *

Isobel knew for certain now that Noah had no use for her. He couldn't have made himself more plain. Though he understood her, he would never help her. When the time came, he expected—and wanted—to be rid of her.

And yet there were eggs to be collected, milk to be churned into butter, clothes to be washed and mended, meals to be prepared, and cleaning to be done. Without really intending it, Isobel slipped into each chore as though it were something she had done all her life. She discovered that she enjoyed cooking, and with *Beeton's Book of Household Management* at her fingertips, she found she could create surprisingly tasty dishes out of the simplest foodstuffs.

Noah slept out in the barn while Isobel took up residence in the comfortable bedroom. But each day they found themselves side by side at their chores. The house soon wore a new coat of caliche whitewash on the inside walls. The windowpanes sparkled. The floorboards squeaked of fresh wax. Noah repaired his fences, shored up the sagging portal roof and gave the small barn a fresh coat of red paint.

Knowing Noah would bar any attempt she might make at escape, Isobel channeled her urge for revenge into labor. She spaded the deep rich river soil beside the kitchen. In Noah's storage bins she found the seeds for corn, beans, peas, and chiles. She cut the eyes from the old cellar potatoes and planted them in rows beside the onion bulbs. Then Noah taught her how to dig irrigation ditches from the river to her garden.

In the second week Noah woke one morning with the idea of taking Isobel out to see the land he hoped to buy. He couldn't deny that she'd settled back into his home more comfortably than he'd imagined. She seemed to belong. Every morning when he walked into the house, his milk pail heavy by his side, and smelled the eggs frying and the coffee bubbling, his heart lifted.

And there she always was—Isobel. Freshly scrubbed from her morning bath. Dressed in her blue cotton dress or one of the fancy Spanish outfits she'd refashioned. Her hair gleaming like sunshine. Her lips ready with a smile. Her head filled with plans for the day—ideas that spilled out in a sort of gurgling stream as she and Noah ate their breakfast at the white-clothed table.

Yes, Noah decided, he'd like to show Isobel the land. Of course, he knew she wouldn't want to stay on. No, he had no illusions about that. Many a sunset he had seen her standing on the back portal, staring in the direction of Lincoln Town. He'd seen the way she kept her little pistol handy beside the bed. And he knew—though he'd never had to hogtie her— that, given the slightest provocation, she would ride out again in search of Snake Jackson and *la revancha.*

"Can you leave your laundering for a day?" he asked that morning as they cleared the breakfast dishes.

She lifted her hands from the hot, soapy water. "Why?"

"I thought we might go riding."

"To Chisum's?"

"No. Just out on the range." He hung the iron frying pan on its hook. "Thought you might like to see the land I want to buy."

She scrubbed the entire kettle before answering.

"All right," she said at last.

The final days of March had brought both rain and sun, and as the horses cantered through belly-high green grass, Isobel was sure she had never been so content. Dressed in her riding skirt, shirtwaist, and boots, she had placed one of Noah's old hats on her head for protection from the sun. She felt comfortable, free, relaxed.

She watched Noah riding just paces ahead, his broad shoulders perpendicular to the straight line of his back and neck. In the time they had stayed at the *jacal*, the wound in his arm had almost healed. Now he made use of the muscle as if it had never been torn by a bullet.

His hair had grown too long. In the back it hung over the chambray collar of his shirt. She had considered asking him if he would like her to cut it, but they had not touched each other the entire time they'd spent at Noah's house. The thought of lifting his hair in her fingers, of sifting it as she snipped with her scissors, of smoothing it with a comb . . . No, she could never cut his hair.

"I own a few head of cattle," Noah said, turning and beckoning her forward. "I bought them from Chisum, and for the most part they range with his herds. Now and again I round them up, see how many calves have dropped, and then send a few beeves to the railhead. I've managed to save a little bit of money. Enough to buy a spread, anyway."

"A small one, like Dick Brewer's ranch?"

"Smaller. Chisum's not going to let go of much of this land, you know. He staked his claim on it and has fought off rustlers for too long to let it go just like that. Besides, he's got brothers who'll want their share."

"But you want to buy here—along the Pecos?"

"Sure I do. Can't you see why?" He surveyed the rolling green grasslands dotted with pink and yellow wildflowers. Yucca spears in a deep olive shade shot heavenward, their creamy flowers clustering at each shaft. Delicate pink cactus blossoms had erupted amid spiny thorns, and almost every tree was in bud. The turquoise sky spread overhead like a clear lake. Wispy white clouds drifted in lazy bands against the blue.

"There are times out here I almost think I can see straight up to heaven," Noah said. "Sometimes, you know . . . I believe I can see God. This is the place I want to make my home."

"I have never seen my lands," Isobel responded, her voice as soft as his. "They lie in the north. Near Santa Fe."

"Good country. Rich soil. Snowcapped mountains. You'll like it."

But she knew she might never own that land. Not unless she returned to actively pursuing it. But Noah had ridden beneath a huge, green-leafed tree and was waving her forward.

"This is a cottonwood," he called as she approached. "Remember what I told you last month?"

"You said the leaves would sound like a rushing river."

"Listen."

Together they slid from their saddles to the ground and stood in silence, heads bowed and eyes shut. For a moment Isobel thought Noah had been mistaken. The only sounds she heard were the thudding of her own heart and the brush of breeze through the grass. Then she heard it. Whispering, rushing, fluttering. The gurgle of cool, clear water.

"Yes," she whispered. "Yes, Noah."

She lifted her head and let the winds play across her sealed eyelids. Dappled sunlight warmed her cheeks. Grass swished against her riding skirt. The scent of soil and sunshine and ripeness filled her nostrils. A warm mouth covered her lips.

"Noah!" Her eyes flew open, and she stepped backward.

"Isobel, don't keep moving away from me," he said, taking her waist and drawing her near. "This has been hell—you and me together day after day. Working and laughing but never touching. Isobel . . . give it all up. Forget about your lands. Stay here with me. I'll protect you, I swear it. I'll give you a home. Maybe it won't be grand and rich like your Santa Fe don's. Maybe you won't have your big *fiestas* and your fancy *bailes*, but I'll give you what I can. I'll give you shelter and food. Put all of this other stuff behind you."

"Shelter and food? Is that what you think I want from you, Noah?"

"Well, it's better than what you've got now, isn't it? It's better than nothing."

"Oh!" Pushing away from him, she walked around the cottonwood tree and leaned against the trunk. How could he be so blind? Didn't he see the love in her eyes as she cooked for him? Didn't he know of her love by the way she mended every tiny tear in his thick denim trousers? Didn't he feel her love in his freshly polished boots, in the ruffles of white lace lining his kitchen shelves, in the neat rows of the new garden she had worked so hard to plant? Didn't he know what she wanted from him? Didn't he sense that what she needed was not his shelter and his food? She wanted his love.

The hope of possessing Noah's love gave her the only hope she had of healing the burning wound inside her, the wound that drove her ever toward a violent fate.

"Isobel, now I reckon I just offered to make good on this marriage of ours," Noah said suddenly, coming around the cottonwood trunk, his head lowered like an angry bull's. "I reckon I've stepped over my own bounds to a good extent. I've offered you a home and all that goes with it. Now I want to know what gives you the all-fired uppityness to huff in my face and then go marching off like I've said something wrong?"

"Oh, Noah . . ."

"Well?"

They stared at each other. Her heart throbbed in her throat as she watched his blue eyes roam over her face and down her body. She moistened her lips, and his gaze darted to them.

She could sense the animal power in him, the male need emanating. His stance, shoulders set, legs spread, feet planted firmly, jaw locked, said nothing would get past him now. He wanted honesty. He wanted answers. And he wanted her.

"I suppose you think a woman in my destitute circumstances cannot be selective, but—"

"You're saying I'm not good enough? We're back to that dusty *vaquero* business?"

"I'm saying I want more in my life than food and shelter, Noah Buchanan."

"Well, what in hell do you want?" he practically bellowed.

She stamped her foot and tossed her head. "I want passion!"

"Passion? Why didn't you say so?" He took her and brushed his open mouth across her lips. "I've been pussy-footing around you so long I'm about to go stark raving *loco*. Food, shelter, and passion are three things I can manage, darlin'. Now come here and kiss me."

Though her heart cried out that he misunderstood—that she needed something more, something deeper from him—her body would not be restrained. As his hands roved down her bosom, cupping and kneading her breasts, she moaned aloud with the utter pleasure of his touch. Their mouths met again and again, wet and seeking. Her fingers wound through the thick dark hair at his nape. Holding his neck, she kept his lips pressed against hers as she sought to slake her need.

He nudged apart the buttons of her white shirtwaist while she worked the buttons of his chambray. Laughing at their fumbling haste, they came together yet again, tongues meeting, suckling, roaming over lips and teeth and into the soft hollows of ears and necks. His fingertips slid beneath her chemise and closed on the tight buds of her nipples.

It happened so quickly that an instant melting weakened her stomach and sent ripples down her buttocks. Then he loosened the tiny bow on her undergarment and lifted her breasts up and over the corset she wore.

"Yes," he murmured. "This is what I've been dreaming of every single night out there in the cold barn. I've wanted you so much I had to get up and take long walks. I even jumped in the river a couple of times. Darlin', you're enough to make a man forget whatever burdens he bears."

He bent and kissed the dark tips of her breasts, wetting them until they puckered and hardened. "Stay with me, Isobel," he murmured against her flesh. "We can make it work, darlin'."

"Yes," she echoed as his tongue lapped in circles around each dark pink areola. "How can I say no when you do these things to me, Noah?"

"Feel me." He took her hand and placed it over the rock-hard mound beneath his denims. "This is what you do to me, Isobel. This is why we're good together. This and everything else that's happened between us in that little house."

Knowing what swelled between his thighs, knowing the pleasures awaiting her, Isobel moved into him and pushed her pelvis against his. "Now you feel me, Noah," she whispered.

His blue eyes grazed over her bare bosom as his hands worked apart the fastenings on her skirt and corset. As they fell to her feet, he slid his hand beneath the soft folds of her bloomers. She wriggled in anticipation. He watched her breasts shimmy and tilt toward him. Her nipples just touched the skin of his chest as his fingers slid into her.

She gasped aloud at the unbearable liquid sensation as he stroked and fondled and taunted her. Her knees went weak, and she was sure she could no longer remain standing. But as she sagged, he caught her buttocks with his free hand and began to massage.

For a moment she had been so carried away that she wandered in a golden fog. Now, with her own urgency mounting, she reached for him. Loosening him from his trousers, she stroked him up and down. Her eyes delighted in his taut length and the masculine thrust of his rigid flesh. Toying with him, she smiled as he too forgot where he was and lost himself in her ministrations.

Head thrown back, he could only groan in hunger. His chest

rose and fell as he sucked in air. The muscles in his arms stood out in relief. His fists clenched the soft mounds of her buttocks.

"Oh, Isobel," he breathed, "oh, darlin' . . ."

She knelt to free him of his trousers. As she did, she could not resist allowing her lips and tongue to stroke over his tumescence. He stood taut with pleasure as her mouth worked magic on his body. Then she rose, stroking her naked neck and breasts and belly up him.

Their mouths came together again, and this time he caught her beneath her thighs, spread her legs and lifted her high against his waist. She held her breath as she felt his body searching for hers. Then slowly, with infinite ecstasy for both of them, he lowered her.

Writhing with need, she slipped up and down. Though he was holding her entire weight with his big hands wrapped around her thighs, he remained standing, his face shot with rapture as her softness stroked him. She pushed her breasts against his chest, then lifted them with her own hands and touched her nipples to his in small, sweet kisses.

"I need release," she pleaded as he licked lines of fire up her neck. "Please, Noah."

Smiling, he let her legs slide to the ground. Now his flesh fully stroked the essence of hers. As he thrust into her, she felt each caress as a flame of torment. Rising higher on a plateau of ecstasy, she could hear her breath coming in tiny gasps. She could feel herself mounting a peak from which she thought she would never descend.

But then he chose to lift her breasts and tug their tightly beaded tips with his fingers. At that moment she slipped over the plateau in a roaring, crashing wave of ultimate passion. Her body danced and shivered against his. He caught her lips as her release brought on his own. Together they surged and slid and finally tumbled in a heap into the grass.

"Oh, Noah." Isobel sighed, her eyelids heavy and her mouth swollen. "Noah, how can I ever leave you?"

"Don't leave, Isobel." He lay silent for a moment. "Listen to me. . . . We'll head for Chisum's right now. I'll get him to sell me the land."

She gazed across the plain of his chest and studied the nodding heads of the silver grasses. Why not? She lifted her head, kissed his lips, and nodded her own head.

"Why not, Noah Buchanan?"

He ran a hand over her fanny. "Not a reason in the world."

Arriving late that afternoon at the South Spring River Ranch, Noah and Isobel walked hand in hand up the steps of the front portal. From inside John Chisum must have seen them, for he was the one to open the door before they had a chance to knock.

"Why, it's Goldilocks and Papa Bear!" he said, laughing. "Come on in, you two!"

But Noah was not in the mood for any of Chisum's fun and nonsense. He took his boss's shoulder and spoke in a voice so low that the other guests in the front room couldn't hear him.

"John, I want to talk to you."

"Sounds serious."

"It is."

Isobel decided that for all his hearty ways, John Chisum knew when a man meant business. He immediately held out a hand in the direction of the private library off the front room. "Kindly excuse us, Mrs. Buchanan," he said.

Isobel nodded, watching them go and wondering whether Noah's dream would come true at last. Dusting her bottom from the long ride, she sat on the edge of a blue sofa.

"I don't suppose you've heard the news?" Sue McSween asked.

Isobel looked around her at the earnest faces of the lawyer, his wife, and the other three guests. A chill slid into her stomach where recently only Noah's warmth had been.

"News?" she responded softly.

"Rumor has it that Sheriff Brady has threatened to place my husband in confinement."

"Jail," Alexander McSween clarified.

"As you may know, the jail in Lincoln is no more than a hole underground." Sue glanced at her husband. "It's being spread about that the sheriff intends to run water into the jail and drown Mac."

Isobel's mouth dropped open as she turned to the lawyer. "Then you cannot allow yourself to be taken."

"I'm duty bound to be in Lincoln for the opening of court on April the first. That's only three days hence. We plan to leave tomorrow morning."

"But I was told the opening date for district court was April eighth," Isobel insisted.

"The whole thing's been garbled." Sue McSween's face clearly revealed her anger and distrust. "We think District Attorney Rynerson—that great hairy ape—may have switched it deliberately so that in the confusion Mac could be arrested. Or ambushed and shot."

"No!" Isobel said, standing. "Not another good man. We won't allow it."

"We're all riding with Mac, Mrs. Buchanan," Dr. Leverson announced. "Mrs. McSween, Mr. Chisum, these two gentlemen. All of us."

Isobel looked at the men who hoped to provide protection—every one of them soft-handed and pale. Not one wore a gun. She knew not even Chisum would strap a holster to his thigh. The whole situation was tantamount to suicide for Alexander McSween.

"Well, Miss Goldilocks," Chisum said loudly, coming out of the library. "Looks like you and your husband are landowners—soon as Buchanan digs up his pot of gold and brings it to me, that is. Congratulations!"

Isobel glanced at Noah and saw his broad smile. There was utter peace, utter hope in every plane of his face. "I'm so happy," she said, going to him and wrapping her arms around his waist.

He drew her against his chest and, ignoring the gathered company, he planted a kiss on her mouth. "I reckon I'm the luckiest man alive," he said. "A beautiful wife. Land. And good friends."

"Hear, hear!" Alexander McSween cried. "Our best to you, Noah."

"Let's head for home, honey. I've got some digging to do."

Isobel stared at her feet for a moment, then lifted her head. "Noah," she said with the barest of sighs. "We must first escort Alexander McSween to Lincoln Town. Sheriff Brady plans to kill him."

Chapter
❧ 14 ❧

Isobel quickly recounted her conversation with the McSweens. While she spoke, Noah studied the determination in her face, the hope in the eyes of Sue McSween, the fear in the posture of Alexander McSween, and the lily-white visages of the other three. Then he turned to Chisum.

"You go on home, boy," the cattleman said. "Plow your land. Buy some cattle. Start that family you mentioned wanting. We'll take care of Mac."

But Noah knew he could never allow an innocent man to ride into an ambush. "No," he murmured. "I'll go with you. You'll need protection."

Chisum cleared his throat. "Well, as a matter of fact . . . some friends of yours will be taking care of things for us in Lincoln Town. They were here yesterday."

"The Regulators?"

"If that's what you call them, yes. They rode over to check on Mac. Billy Bonney, Frank Macnab, John Middleton, Big Jim French, Fred Waite, and Henry Brown."

Noah glanced at Isobel, knowing these were the names of the men who had vowed revenge for John Tunstall's murder. "What about Dick Brewer? Was he riding with them?"

"Nope. I reckon Dick's still at his farm mending fences and keeping a sharp eye on his own back."

"Then the Regulators have gone ahead to Lincoln?" Noah asked.

"Just to keep an eye on the situation for us."

"You'll still need protection on the trail, John."

Chisum quirked up his mouth and eyed the ceiling for a minute. "Buchanan, you just spent a good quarter of an hour in my library explaining how you planned to lay down your six-shooter and start a family. How you're a loyal husband now. How you want to be a peaceful rancher. You don't mean to tell me you're changing your mind, do you? I'd hate to have to change mine."

Noah bristled. "I will lay down my gun, John. And I do mean to ranch. But I'll be damned if I'm going to let you and Mac and Sue ride straight into Sheriff Brady's trap without my protection."

"All right, all right. Calm yourself." Chisum clapped Noah on the back. "You can ride with us—you and your wife. We'll make it a jolly jaunt, how's that sound?" Turning suddenly, he roared in the direction of his kitchen. "Mrs. Towry, we've got more company! And tell the cook to add two extra places to the dinner table!"

The three-day journey passed uneventfully. Isobel found herself in the company of Sue McSween, while the men insisted on riding protectively in front of and behind the two women. The high-bosomed wife of Lincoln's lawyer soon revealed a personality that tended to match Isobel's in spirit and hotheadedness. She had an opinion about every participant in the growing turmoil.

Mention Jimmie Dolan, and Sue McSween labeled him a "beady-eyed, Irish-Catholic dog who doesn't have a clue how to run a business." Sheriff Brady was "another Irish Catholic, foot-licking servant of Dolan and his thugs. He's got a Mexican wife and a bunch of half-breed spawn." In fact, by the time the party was approaching Lincoln Town, Isobel had heard more gossip, more slander, and more out-and-out vituperation than she had imagined could come from the mouth of such a small woman.

Noah had decided that he and Isobel should journey into town together ahead of the others. They would scout out the situation, make certain that nothing new had happened to change the outlook, and see that the Regulators were in place to guard the arrival of the McSween party.

"Noah, what do you think of Sue?" Isobel asked early that first morning of April as she and Noah walked their horses toward the sleepy town.

He shrugged. "Never gave her much thought, to tell the truth."

"Do you like her?"

"She's nice enough, I reckon. Most folks think she's smart . . . canny in the business end of things."

Isobel rode for a while without speaking. Then she blurted what she had been wondering for three days. "Am *I* very much like Sue?"

Noah glanced at her, startled at the intensity behind the question. "Sure you are. You're smart. You're determined."

"And I'm also angry. Opinionated. Spiteful. Always wanting vengeance."

"Well . . . that's sometimes true, too."

"Noah," Isobel whispered, "I don't like Sue McSween."

"Aw, you've got to understand about this bunch here. Mac and Sue and most of their friends are all fierce Scottish Presbyterians. They have aims to get a Protestant church and school started up in Lincoln. In fact, that's why they asked their mission to send out Dr. Ealy and Susan Gates. On the other hand, Dolan and his bunch are Irish Catholics. So that puts them on opposite sides of the fence, so to speak."

"But, Noah—"

"Hear me out, Isobel. Sue McSween just has this little idea in her mind that religion is behind some of the troubles. She's got a few problems with the Catholic way of doing things. And her holier-than-thou attitude has led to the troubles she's had with some of the Mexicans in town."

"I know she doesn't like Catholics or Mexicans, Noah. But you don't understand. . . ." She faded off, feeling miserable. "In Sue McSween I saw a mirror of *myself*. I saw a woman driven by the need for land and power and wealth. I saw a woman filled with anger, bitterness, revenge. Noah, I don't like what I saw."

He reached across the space between their horses and covered her hand with his. There were a lot of things he could have said—quick assurances and shallow denials—but he was beginning to appreciate what he saw in Isobel's face. A softness was growing, a melting of the anger, a gentleness blossoming.

"Perhaps," she said softly as they rode into town past the jail and Juan Patrón's house, "I shall wipe away the reflection that I saw, Noah. Perhaps it is time for me to change."

She had just spoken the last word when Noah's hand squeezed on hers. "Look—there's Brady."

The sheriff, his goatee and heavy mustache neatly combed and his pouf of dark hair gleaming in the morning sunlight, strolled on foot down the winding street. Four of his deputies walked with him, two at either side. Heavily armed, they wore an air of purpose and importance. Sheriff Brady carried a large rolled sheet of white paper in one hand.

"Let's see," Noah said under his breath, "that's Billy Mathews, George Hindman, George Peppin, and John Long. What a bunch. They must have just come from Dolan's place. I wonder where they're headed."

"The courthouse maybe?"

"It could have something to do with the mix-up of the court dates."

Isobel studied the little town as she and Noah rode past the *torreón*. "What time is it? Hardly anyone seems to be about."

He pulled out his pocket watch and flipped open the case. "I have nine o'clock."

An uneasiness hung over the street. The usual morning scents of piñon smoke and baking bread were absent. No children laughed or played in the streets. No women with baskets on their arms bustled toward the shops. "Do you see any of our people? Dick or Billy?" Isobel asked.

"Yonder's Squire Wilson hoeing onions. And there's his kid, Gorgonio, out in front of the Wilson house. But as to the Reg—" Noah stopped short when he noticed a Winchester rise over the high adobe wall of John Tunstall's corral. Just behind it emerged the face of Billy the Kid.

"Isobel!" Noah shouted.

At that moment a row of rifles appeared from behind the wall. Then a row of men—Macnab, Middleton, French, Waite, Brown. A fusillade of gunfire splattered the street. A dozen bullets slammed into Sheriff Brady. For a moment he hung in midair, mouth frozen open in a death grimace. Then he toppled to the street, his body riddled. George Hindman, one of the deputies, staggered toward the courthouse, moaning for water. The other lawmen fled.

Noah drew his own Colt revolver as he grappled for Isobel's reins. Trying to control her horse, she watched in horror.

"Take cover!" he was hollering, though the shooting had already stopped. "Move, Isobel!"

She gazed in shock as Ike Stockton ran from his saloon with a mug of water for the bleeding Hindman. A child was screaming. Billy the Kid jumped the adobe wall and ran into the road where Brady's body lay. He bent to grab a fallen rifle.

"This is *my* gun, you bastard," the Kid snarled into the blank face with its neat goatee covered in blood. "It's mine and I want it back." Then he tore open the dead sheriff's coat and began searching through his pockets.

"Billy!" Noah warned. At that moment a shot cracked from the window of a nearby house, and a bullet ripped through the Kid's left thigh. He yelped. Skipping for cover, he left a trail of blood in a spotted line across the dirt road.

"Noah—it's Squire Wilson!" Isobel cried, observing the hunched man lying in the garden patch. "He's been hit."

Abandoning her horse, she scampered across the road. The squire lay in a fetal curl, his hands wrapped around the backs of his thighs. "I was just hoeing onions," he moaned. "In this godforsaken town, can't a man even hoe his onions in peace?"

Though fear quivered in the pit of her stomach, Isobel rolled the squire over. She passed a hand across the raw flesh where the bullet had torn through both his legs. "You must come inside, Squire," she whispered. His face white with shock, the little boy lifted his father's left arm while Isobel supported the man's right side.

She glanced around in search of Noah as she led the bleeding squire toward his house and the hysterical wife who waited in the doorway. On the street a half-dozen men had gathered around Sheriff Brady's body. Another four huddled at the feet of the dead George Hindman, who had not lived long enough to drink his water.

"It's a massacre! A massacre! An ambush!" the squire's wife was shrieking. She grabbed for her husband and jerked him into the house along with her son. "Oh, Green—are you gonna die? Gorgonio, did you see all that? Oh, my stars, it was a massacre."

Isobel had just stepped off their front portal when a steel arm swept her from her feet and hurled her across a saddle and a pair of rock-solid thighs. "I thought I told you to take cover!" Noah shouted overhead. "I turn my head for one second, and you're gone. Just your horse milling around the street, damn it!"

Isobel nearly lost her breakfast as Noah's black stallion galloped across the road, scattering people left and right. He tore through the gate of the McSween's house and thundered to the back, where the Ealys were living.

Without dismounting, Noah hammered with the butt of his rifle until Susan Gates flung open the door. "Isobel! Lord, are you shot this time?"

Still half-angry at the scare Isobel had given him, Noah grabbed her bottom and thrust her off the horse. "She's not hurt. Now, get her inside and keep her safe. Tie her up if you have to."

Susan took Isobel's shoulders as Noah wheeled his horse about. He had started back toward the front gate when he saw Billy Bonney stagger through the back entrance. The young man's face was ashen. His upper lip had glued onto his buck teeth, and sweat streamed from his sideburns.

"Buchanan! 'S the doc in?" he hissed. "I'm hit."

Noah had half a mind to let the Kid take what he deserved for pulling a dirty game like that on Brady and the deputies. But when he saw the wounded-animal look in the youth's faded gray eyes, he dismounted. "Come on. He's in here."

Noah pounded on the door again, and this time Mary Ealy opened it just a hair. She took one look at the face of Billy the Kid and tried to shut it again. "Mrs. Ealy," Noah said, supporting the boy with one arm. "Please. He's got to have a doctor."

The two men made their way into the back room. Isobel rose from the bed where she was huddled with Susan and the other members of the Ealy family.

"I've brought Billy," he explained. "He took a bullet in the leg. Where's Doc Ealy?"

"When the shooting stopped, he went into the street to see if anyone needed medical help," Isobel said. "I told him about the squire."

A thin, bearded, pasty-faced young man emerged from the shadows. "Dr. Ealy asked me to keep watch over the women," he said, looking as if he'd rather be doing almost anything else. He awkwardly held a rifle in one hand as he studied the bleeding Billy.

Noah recognized him as Sam Corbet, the clerk who had manned Tunstall's store before the murder of its owner. "Well, Sam, I expect you and I will have our work cut out for us in a few minutes. The law is sure to come looking for Billy."

Noah lowered the wounded Regulator onto the narrow bed. Staring, mouths clamped shut, everyone in the room gathered around. The Kid grinned weakly at the two little Ealy girls. "Don't never get shot, ladies," he breathed. "Hurts like hell."

"So what happened out there, Kid?" Noah asked, anger evident in his words. "You did a damn fool thing gunning down Brady like that."

"It's not like it looked, Buchanan. Me and the other Regulators snuck into town last night to keep an eye on things for Mac." Billy grimaced as Mrs. Ealy began cutting away the lower half of his trousers. "And then this morning we see Brady headin' our way . . . and we thought about how he was planning to arrest Mac and then flood the jail . . . and how he had organized the posse that murdered Tunstall . . . and how he'd never arrested nobody for the killin' . . . and how since Brady *was* the law, he wasn't never gonna get his just deserts . . . so we just took it into our heads to settle the matter with him."

"But that was just a *rumor* about flooding the jail—" Isobel began.

"Then why the hell were you going through Brady's pockets?" Noah interrupted.

"I was lookin' for the warrant for McSween's arrest. I knew Brady had it with him, but I didn't have time to find it before one of them Dolan bastards shot me."

"Did McSween have anything to do with this?" Noah demanded. "When the Regulators were over at South Spring the other day, did McSween and Chisum order you to ambush Brady?"

"Aw, Noah . . ." the Kid stopped speaking when Dr. Ealy hurried into the room.

"George Peppin has declared himself sheriff," the doctor puffed, jerking off his spectacles and rubbing them on the tail of his frock coat. "He's one of Dolan's men, of course. They're all fighting mad about the ambush. They think McSween is behind it, even though he's not in town. Peppin has said he's going to send to Fort Stanton for Captain Purington and some troops." The doctor slid his spectacles onto his nose. "They've sworn to arrest McSween and all the Regulators—especially Billy the K—"

"Why me?" Billy hunched up onto his elbows as the doctor, seeing him clearly for the first time, gaped. "There was a whole passel of us shooting at Brady. Why am I takin' all the blame?"

"Oh, my." Dr. Ealy glanced at his wife, then at each of the faces surrounding the bed.

"Can you patch Billy, Doc?" Noah asked.

"I'd . . . I'd be harboring a criminal . . . but Christian duty binds me. . . . Mary—fetch my bag."

While Noah looked on, Dr. Ealy drew a silk handkerchief through the raw hole in Billy Bonney's leg. Isobel and Susan took brush and mop and scrubbed the trail of blood that had trickled across the wood floorboards from the back door to the bed. Mary Ealy kept an eye on the windows while Sam Corbet sawed a hole in the McSweens' floor.

"Here comes George Peppin!" Mary cried out in the midst of the scramble to ready the house. "He's coming through the back gate with some deputies and a bunch of others. It looks like they're following the trail of blood. Oh, Taylor! What shall we do?"

When Peppin began pounding on the back door, Dr. Ealy hastily tied the bandage around Billy's leg. The doctor and Noah helped the wounded man into the adjoining room. Isobel followed, watching as they lowered Billy into the hole Sam had cut, handed him a pair of pistols, and then slammed the boards into place.

While the men ran into the back room to delay Peppin, Isobel smoothed the carpet over the floorboards, scooted an ornate rocking chair directly over the space where Billy lay, and sat down in the chair.

"Susan!" she called. "Come here and bring the Ealy girls with you." When the pale teacher hurried into the room, Isobel directed her onto a nearby stool. The two little girls crawled onto the women's laps. "Give me the Bible on that table, Susan."

Taking the heavy book, Isobel flipped it open in the middle and began to read in a soft, comforting voice. " 'The Lord is my shepherd, I shall not want. He maketh me to lie down in green pastures. He leadeth me beside the still waters. He restoreth my soul.' "

Peppin stalked into the room, his boots heavy on the wood floor. "We seen the trail of blood leading to the back door, Mrs. Buchanan—and we aim to find out where Billy Bonney has got to."

"I assure you you're wasting your time here, sir," she answered. "You can see that we're reading the Good Book and trying to calm the children."

Peppin snorted, and his deputies began overturning furniture, tossing pillows onto the floor, and ripping aside silk curtains in their search for the Kid. Isobel took Susan's icy hand, planted a kiss on one of the little Ealy girls' rosy cheeks, and continued reading. " 'Yea, though I walk through the valley of the shadow of death, I will fear no evil, for Thou art with me.' "

She rocked and rocked on the loose floorboards while the men tore up the house. It occurred to Isobel that if the vitriolic Sue McSween was unhappy with Dolan's men before, she was going to be furious when she saw what they had done to her home.

The ornate furnishings were in total disarray. China plates had been smashed, velvet upholstery torn, ferns uprooted, bamboo screens tattered. The piano and the organ had been shoved from their places and had, no doubt, lost their fine tuning. The place was a shambles.

But Isobel just rocked on, unspoken but genuine prayer mingled with her Scripture reading. Susan sat in silent fear, her arms locked around the Ealys' toddler. Isobel rested her cheek on the soft golden hair of the other little child. When all the deputies had stormed from the house, Isobel's voice still moved across the room.

" 'Surely goodness and mercy shall follow me all the days of my life,' " she said softly. " 'And I shall dwell in the house of the Lord forever.' "

The McSweens' home was raided two more times that day in search of Billy the Kid. The final scrutiny was undertaken by Captain Purington and his troop of black cavalrymen who had ridden down from Fort Stanton. But Billy remained safely hidden with his pair of six-shooters in the hole in the floor beneath Sue McSween's carpet, her rocker, and the Bible-reading Mrs. Belle Buchanan.

Leaving Isobel at the house, Noah intercepted Mac and Sue McSween, John Chisum, Dr. Leverson, and the other two of Chisum's guests as they drove into Lincoln. Hearing the news, the party immediately elected to stay at the home of their sympathizer, Isaac Ellis, who lived on the outskirts of town. But Peppin, Captain Purington, and the twenty-five soldiers wasted no time in marching to the Ellis house to arrest McSween on the warrant retrieved from Sheriff Brady's body.

Though Mac refused to surrender to Peppin on the grounds that Brady's death canceled his status as deputy, he gave himself up to the Fort Stanton regiment on the condition that he be taken to the garrison and held in protective custody until court opened a week later.

As Noah and Isobel lay in bed that night in the spare bedroom at Juan Patrón's house, Noah related the shouting match that had taken place between Captain Purington and Dr.

Leverson—who, as it turned out, was a fiery Englishman with friends in high places. *Very* high places, for Leverson claimed as acquaintances the United States secretary of the interior, Carl Schurz, and the President of the United States, Rutherford B. Hayes.

"Leverson accused Captain Purington of going against the U.S. Constitution by illegally searching the Ellis house without a warrant," Noah explained, chuckling. "Here was this little Englishman shouting at the captain about how he was breaking the law. Leverson kept hollering about unlawful search and seizure, and due warrant—that sort of stuff. Finally the captain hollered back, 'Damn the Constitution and you for a fool!' When Leverson heard that, he started in on the soldiers, urging them not to obey a captain who would show such contempt for the Constitution. By that time, Captain Purington was mad as a rattler on a hot skillet."

Isobel smiled at the image of the two men shouting each other down. Noah stroked a finger along her bare shoulder as he continued. "The captain shouted at Leverson, 'Shut up! You're making a damn ass of yourself.' And then Leverson shot back in a real huff, 'God knows, I would not live in a country where such outrages as these I have witnessed this afternoon are countenanced.' And Purington snapped, 'Sir, you have my permission to suit yourself.' " Noah laughed again. "It was quite a scene."

But Isobel saw little humor in the situation. "Oh, Noah, everyone in Lincoln is so angry. The tension is stretched to the breaking point. I'm . . . I'm afraid Noah."

He drew her closer and kissed her forehead. "I'm here with you, darlin'. Nothing's going to happen to either of us. I promise."

"Do you think Mr. Chisum or Mr. McSween told Billy and the others to assassinate the sheriff?"

Noah studied on the question for a long time. "I don't know. I hope not. I'd like to think the men we're in this with are better than that. But Isobel . . . I'm just not sure."

"Noah, will things settle down now that the soldiers are involved?"

"I expect so. Up at Fort Stanton Captain Purington's got a twelve-pound mountain howitzer and a Gatling gun. Maybe knowing that will keep folks in line. Leverson has vowed he's going to write letters to the U.S. Government and get it involved. And with district court starting in a week, there'll be a lot more people in town who don't want to get shot at."

Isobel stroked her hand over Noah's bare chest and wondered how she fit into this horrible muddle. She had no idea where Snake Jackson was now, nor what had become of her land-grant titles. She had witnessed two more murders that morning, bringing to six the number of men who had been killed almost before her eyes in the two months she had been in Lincoln County.

An image of Noah's little adobe house filtered across her mind as she lay in his arms. She wondered how the cow and the hens were faring. The lace curtains would need a thorough washing after all the wind and dust March had brought in. Would the corn and beans have sprouted in her garden? How high was the river flowing? And had it rained?

Her sigh drew Noah's attention, and he cuddled her closer. "Isobel, I've got my land and I've got you beside me. I'm not going to let those slip away. Not for anything."

"What will we do, Noah? Can we go home?"

"When Jim French sneaked into the McSween's house this evening to fetch Billy out from under the floor, he told me Dick Brewer has called a meeting of all the Regulators. I think Dick has in mind to settle the boys down. The ambush of Brady this morning isn't going to sit well with folks around here. The sheriff may have been a Dolan man, but he wasn't a bad fellow. I suspect the Regulators are going to be more than a little unpopular in Lincoln Town."

"Do you think Dick wants to disband the group?"

"I bet he does. Dick's never been a man for violence." Noah brushed a strand of dark gold hair from Isobel's shoulder. "I'd like for us to ride to the meeting place and hear what Dick has to say. You know how I feel about him. He's my best friend and I trust his judgment. I'd lay down my life for the man."

"All right," she whispered.

"The meeting is at a site a good safe distance from Lincoln. Things will be peaceful there, Isobel. I'm sure of it. It's a place called Blazer's Mill."

* * *

To reach Blazer's Mill, the Regulators rode through friendly territory. They took the shortcut trail south to Dick Brewer's farm, where he was waiting for them. As they began the journey west past the farms of other Regulators—Charley Bowdre and Doc Scurlock—they picked up five new sympathizers, among them Frank Coe and his cousin, George Coe.

Isobel rode her bay beside the mounts of Noah and Dick and listened on as the two friends discussed the situation in Lincoln. Dick was furious over Brady's murder. He felt that by killing the sheriff, Billy and the others had betrayed the true purpose of the Regulators.

Dick wanted to call a halt to the group and disband. But the situation led him to believe the Regulators were still needed. Members of the posse who had shot John Tunstall continued to roam loose. A couple of the murderers were said to be hiding around the little town of Tularosa, which was not far from Blazer's Mill. Dick had also heard that a huge number of Tunstall's cattle had been stolen and driven to San Nicolas Spring near the Organ Mountains. The spring, too, could be reached from Blazer's Mill. To complicate matters further, Dolan had put a bounty of $200 on any Regulator. If the group dispersed, bounty hunters could pick them off one by one.

Isobel studied the two men, one slender and finely carved, the other massive, as if hewn from stone. Noah and Dick seemed many notches above the rest of the riders. Both spoke with control and earnestness. Both kept themselves clean, their guns polished, their horses groomed. Both were men of high intelligence and skill, yet both advocated avoiding violence.

As she rode along the grassy train that followed the bubbling Rio Ruidoso, Isobel formed in her mind a picture of the future. At first her thoughts seemed childish and silly; but as she adjusted them and accustomed herself to the notions, she began to long for her dreams to become reality.

She and Noah would live in the adobe house beside the Pecos River. They would own land and run cattle. She could imagine their children scampering through the front yard, playing on the shady portal or wading in the irrigation ditches . . . little girls in pigtails and soft white dresses . . . little boys with dirty knees, with tiny fingers clamped around a treasured stone or stick. A lush garden grew beside the house, rich with peas, beans, corn, chiles. Laundry flapped on a line, the New Mexico sun bleaching the linens a pure, brilliant white. Chickens scratched in the dust. The aroma of *bizcochitos* drifted from the kitchen window. Lace curtains billowed in the breeze.

Perhaps now and again Dick and Susan Brewer would drive out in their buckboard full of children to the Buchanan home. Laughter and happy chatter would fill the house as the two families joined for dinner and singing. She and Susan would sew and embroider while discussing their children and their latest recipes. Noah and Dick would linger on the portal after all the children had gone to bed. They would speak in low voices, sharing ranching and farming ideas, and talking over new methods.

"To tell you the truth," Noah was saying, "I'm afraid Billy's the troublemaker in the bunch. He was a good enough kid before. But ever since Tunstall got shot, he's been wild. He's angry, reckless, hotheaded. He's not thinking about the future. All he wants is revenge."

Dick nodded his curly head. He glanced behind at the youth, who seemed little the worse for the shot that had torn up his leg a few days earlier. "Billy loved Tunstall, you know. They were pals. Tunstall was the first fellow who accepted the Kid for who he·was and tried to help him."

"I know."

"Well, I'll have a talk with him after lunch. Maybe I can settle him down a little. Talk some sense into him."

Noah checked his pocket watch and saw that it was about eleven o'clock as the horsemen rode past Blazer's sawmill and up the slight hill toward Dr. Blazer's home. They rounded a pile of logs beside the mill, then rode into the corral near the foursquare building with its small tower on the roof.

Noah dismounted and helped Isobel down from her bay. He had noticed that she wore a strange look on her face this morning, a sort of peaceful and faraway gaze. It worried him. Isobel's usual fire-and-ice demeanor seemed to have evaporated, and Noah wasn't sure just why.

She had even chosen to leave off wearing his old denim trousers and shirt. Instead she'd put on a black riding skirt and a white shirtwaist. She wore a little black vest that showed off her curves in a becoming, feminine way. At her neck she had pinned a silver brooch that seemed to set her hazel eyes to sparkling.

She had refused his hat. Instead she had fixed her hair high on her head, all swooped up in curls and waves. Ruffles of gold tumbled down her neck, and little tendrils wisped around her forehead.

Of course, all this had caused Isobel to take on a new light with the Regulators. She already had their respect for her shootings and riding skills—today she won their devoted admiration of her beauty. Noah knew most of these poor, woman-starved cowboys wouldn't know what to do with Isobel if they had her. She certainly wasn't the typical frontier wifely type. Nor was she the sort of woman who frequented saloons. But the men flirted and made eyes at her all the same.

Noah had to acknowledge, too, that some of the men in the bunch were said to be downright handsome. Fred Waite with his thick black hair, blue eyes, and handlebar mustache had been known to make women nearly swoon. Noah had heard that ladies thought the Kid was a real charmer. He could dance better than any man Noah knew; when he felt like it, he could flirt the pants off anything that moved; and as long as you didn't pay too much attention to those buck teeth and droopy eyes, Billy had a nice enough face.

Isobel had shown no interest in the flirtations of the other men. In fact, she made it plain she belonged with Noah. Even though most of the Regulators had been in the woods the night of the arranged marriage and knew it was a sham, Isobel slept under Noah's blankets each night on the trail. She rode at his side. She followed him with her eyes.

Now, at Blazer's Mill, she was introducing herself to Mrs. Frederick Godfroy, the wife of the Indian agent who rented the house from Dr. Blazer.

"I'm Mrs. Buchanan," Isobel said. Then she added, "Noah's wife."

The woman smiled, her small eyes darting back and forth between the pair. "Mr. and Mrs. Buchanan, would you and the rest of these gentlemen like some dinner?"

The dentist, Dr. Blazer, had leased his house to the U.S.

Government as headquarters for the Mescalero Indian Agency. Mrs. Godfroy was known for serving up a fine lunch to travelers, and all the men had been looking forward to eating there before they hunkered down to talk things over.

They were settling around the table for a big meal of stew and cornbread when Noah happened to glance out the window. A trail of dust drifted up from the road along which the Regulators had just ridden. Noah squinted to make out the lone mule and rider. He was a small man, loaded down with pistols, cartridge belts, and rifles. He carried his right arm at an odd angle.

A wash of ice slid down Noah's spine. "Boys, looks like we've got a visitor," he said. "Here comes Buckshot Roberts."

Chapter
❧ *15* ❧

"Buckshot Roberts!" The name went up around the room like a war cry. Abandoning their steaming bowls of stew, the men pushed away from the table and went for their weapons.

"Roberts was in the posse that shot Tunstall!" Billy Bonney shouted, grabbing his rifle and angling toward the window. "Let me at him. I'll pick him off!"

"He's a bounty hunter," someone else said. "He'll be after that two hundred dollars Dolan put on our hides."

"Hold it, boys!" Dick cried. "I've got a warrant for Buckshot's arrest. Let's try to talk him into surrendering."

"Aw, hell," Billy muttered. "I could put a bullet through him right now!"

"Coe, you know Buckshot Roberts pretty well." Noah addressed Frank Coe and ignored the Kid. "Why don't you go outside and talk things over with him? Let him know Dick wants him to turn himself in."

"All right." Frank glanced around the room before buckling on his six-shooter and heading out of the building before Buckshot had a chance to come inside.

Inside, Noah handed Isobel her Winchester. "Buckshot Roberts may be short and so crippled he can't lift a rifle to his shoulder," he said, "but he'll stand up to all fifteen of us if he's pushed to it. He's fought Indians, Texas Rangers, and anyone else who stood in his way. Isobel, I want you to stay right with me through all of this, understand?"

She nodded. It was hard to imagine such a great number of armed men in a dither over a single bounty hunter riding a mangy mule. But she saw the serious set to Noah's jaw, and she knew she would obey him. Still—what could one man do against fifteen?

"All right," Dick said suddenly from the window where he had been watching Frank Coe attempt to talk with Buckshot outside on the porch. "Frank has just moved out of my line of vision, and I sure as hell don't trust Buckshot to keep calm as a toad in the sun. George, Middleton, Bowdre—you three head out to see what's going on. And arrest that little spitfire, would you, boys?"

By this time Mrs. Godfroy was in a tizzy. "Oh, Mr. Brewer, you can't shoot your guns around this place, hear? Those men outside on the porch are standing right next to a door that leads into one of Dr. Blazer's storage rooms. He's got a Springfield and a thousand rounds of ammunition in that room. If Frank Coe or Buckshot Roberts were to get into that room—"

"Roberts, throw up your hands!" The voice of Charley Bowdre outside the window cut off Mrs. Godfroy's frantic speech.

"No!" Buckshot Roberts shouted.

A blast of gunfire shattered the valley. Mrs. Godfroy screamed. She, Noah, Isobel, Billy, Dick, and the rest of the Regulators hightailed it out the back door of the house. Noah grabbed Isobel's hand and ran behind a water trough near the corral. They hunkered down, breathing heavily. Without stopping to talk, they loaded their Winchesters.

"Buckshot has been wounded!" Isobel whispered as she peered around the corner of the trough. Noah jerked her back to cover, his blue eyes flashing with sudden anger.

"You stay put, Isobel! I'm telling you, Buckshot is a dead-eye shot with a rifle."

"But he's been hit. I saw him on the porch dragging some kind of a mattress into the doorway of that room Mrs. Godfroy told Dick about—that storage room with all the ammunition. It looked like his stomach was covered with blood."

"His stomach? Oh, Lord. A gut shot." Noah took off his hat and wiped his brow with the back of his hand. "He can't last too long."

As he spoke the last word, Charley Bowdre and George Coe dashed around the edge of the water trough. "Damn little spitfire!" Bowdre spat. "He drew on me, so I shot him in the innards. But he won't quit! Look—he blew off my cartridge belt. And he mangled George's finger."

George Coe was already binding off his hand with his bandanna, all the while muttering exactly what he thought of Buckshot Roberts. "Blasted off my trigger finger right at the first joint, mean little son of a—"

"Middleton took a bullet in the chest," Charley Bowdre breathed. "I don't know where he's got to. I think Buckshot hit Billy, too."

Isobel peered around the corner of the trough a second time and stared in amazement at the small man who had managed to shoot four men in a matter of seconds. He lay stomach down on the bloodstained mattress, his rifle aimed in the direction of the trough.

Perspiration trickled down the inside of Isobel's corset between her breasts, and she knew more than the heat of the day had brought it on. She scanned the landscape behind her in search of the other men. Most of them had hidden a safe distance from Buckshot's rifle range.

Dick Brewer, head down, was running toward the trough. As he slid in next to Noah, he took off his own hat to wipe his brow.

"How many shot here?" he asked.

"Two. Coe and Bowdre," Noah answered. "But they'll live."

"Middleton's been hit in the lung. He's hurting bad. A shot shaved Billy's arm. He says it matches the one that went through his leg the other day. He's all right. Mad as a hornet, though."

"Where's Mrs. Godfroy?"

"She's safe. But she keeps insisting Buckshot's in a room full of ammo. Listen, Noah. I'm going to head over to that pile of logs by the sawmill. I'll be able to see Buckshot better from there. I'll try to get him to surrender."

Noah reached out and grabbed Dick's arm. "Let me do it. You round up the others and head out. You've got to get Middleton to a doctor."

"If I don't talk Buckshot into surrendering, he's going to die up there on that mattress. I'm the leader of the Regulators, Noah. I'll do it."

Without waiting, Dick crouched and ran across the road, through the corral, and down the creek toward the logs. Isobel watched with bated breath as he huddled behind the pile of wood barely a hundred yards from the doorway where Buckshot Roberts lay.

Noah had been handing Bowdre fresh ammunition since the man's gunbelt had been shot off. He lifted his head and peered across the clearing.

"Isobel, where's Dick now?" he whispered.

"He's behind the logs," she answered. "See, he's raising his head to get a bet—"

"No!" Noah roared.

It was too late. Dick lifted his head just above the line of logs. Buckshot took aim and fired. The bullet struck the middle of Dick's forehead, right between the eyes. He fell.

"No! No!" Noah's anguish filled the valley. "Dick!"

He started across the open ground toward his friend, but Bowdre and Coe dragged him back to cover.

"He's gone, Buchanan. Dick's a dead man," Coe barked. "We better get the hell out of this place before Buckshot kills us all."

As if to confirm the prediction, bullets suddenly splattered across the trough, splintering the sides and splashing into the water. "Move!" Bowdre shouted.

George Coe grabbed Isobel's arm with his bloody hand. Bowdre shoved Noah toward the corral. Most of the Regulators had already mounted their horses. Noah's black stallion, Isobel's mare, and the other horses stood at a safe distance from the line of fire. And fire it was. Bullets rained across the open space from the doorway where Buckshot Roberts lay.

George boosted Isobel onto her horse. Three men hauled Noah onto his and then one grabbed the reins to keep him from heading back toward the Blazer house. As the Regulators galloped down the road away from the mill, Buckshot continued firing.

"Dick," Noah groaned, his voice coming from the depths of his chest. "We've left Dick."

"Brewer's dead, Buchanan," Billy Bonney answered. "The Godfroys will bury him. We've got to get the hell out of here, man."

Noah pulled his bandanna over his nose and lapsed into silence then. But when Isobel gazed at the man she loved, she saw that the red cloth was soaked with tears.

When the Regulators arrived at Dick Brewer's ranch, they agreed to stop and hold a short meeting. The men gathered on the porch, and Isobel settled beside Noah. For almost two days he had said nothing. His mouth clamped shut, his eyes red-rimmed, Noah had ridden blindly with the others. Now, his hat in his hand and his eyes on the porch floor, he sat a short distance from where the others had huddled.

"We need a new leader," Billy started off. "Now that Dick is dead, we got even more reason to round up them Dolan snakes and blast 'em all to kingdom come."

"You sayin' you want to be leader, Kid?"

"Sure!"

A good amount of disgruntled muttering followed Billy's announcement. Then Frank Macnab stood and surveyed the group.

"I'm puttin' my name in the ring, boys," he said. "I'd like to head up the Regulators. Everybody here knows I'm a cattle detective. Makin' war on cattle rustlers is my job—and I see the Dolan bunch as no better than a pack of thieves. I work for Hunter and Evans; I have dealin's with John Chisum; and I reckon I can get myself deputized easier than any one of you."

"He's right," Charley Bowdre stated. "Most of us ain't canny enough to know the Dolan game. But Macnab is used to handlin' that sort. I'd stick by Macnab as leader."

"Me, too," someone added.

"Aw, shoot," Billy said, flinging down his hat.

Noah stood and walked among the gathered men. "I'm going to round up Dick's cattle and take them to Chisum's ranch for safekeeping," he said. "I'll throw in my lot with Macnab."

"You gonna stick with the Regulators, Buchanan?" Bowdre asked. "Nobody'd think you were yeller if you wanted to leave now. With Dick gone—"

"With Dick gone, I've got a job to do," Noah spat. "It's called *revenge*."

He glanced at Isobel before stalking off the porch and heading for his horse.

Late that evening Isobel heard Noah's boots on the front porch of Dick Brewer's cabin. She had heated the oven and baked a batch of fluffy white biscuits. A pan of thick cream gravy simmered on the stove. It wasn't much of a meal, but she knew Noah liked it.

He came into the front room, head lowered and eyes to the floor. Winding up his lariat, he hung it on a nail by the door. Never once looking at Isobel, he sat on a stool and pulled off his muddy boots. He took off his duster and slung it over a chair.

"Noah," Isobel said from the stove. She felt cowed by his utter silence, by the unfamiliar change in him. "Noah . . . I cooked supper."

He said nothing, but he came to the table and sat in one of Dick's rickety chairs. Isobel found herself trembling as she filled a chipped crockery plate with biscuits, split them with a fork, and ladled gravy over the top.

All evening in the cabin she had been remembering the first hours she and Noah had spent together. Here, in Dick's cabin. She remembered the way Noah had drawn her bath. The look in his eyes when she had risen naked from the water. The way they had snapped and fenced with each other. The gathered evergreen boughs in the cup on their table at breakfast. The way he had taught her to wash dishes, their hands touching now and then in the soft, soapy warm water.

But somehow, with the death of Dick Brewer, the gentle Noah had slipped away. She wasn't sure who had come to take his place. All she knew was that this silent, angry bull of a man frightened her.

"Will you have more biscuits, Noah?" she asked.

He shoved his plate in her direction. Glancing up, she saw that he wasn't even looking at her. Quickly she filled his plate a second time and ladled on the gravy.

"How many days will it take to round up the cattle?" she asked.

He chewed a bite so long she thought he wasn't going to answer. Then he lifted his head. "You know, you were right all along," he said. "When someone you care about gets killed, you don't just stand back and wait for things to take their course. You don't wait for the law—not in Lincoln County. One time you told me that a person ought to take action on things. I said I took pride in holding myself back. I was wrong. You were right."

"Noah, what are you saying?"

"I'm saying that Dick Brewer got killed this morning. And Dick Brewer was as fine a man as any to walk God's green earth. I'm saying that Buckshot Roberts deserves to die for killing Dick. I'm saying that Jimmie Dolan, Snake Jackson, Jesse Evans—the whole passel of them—deserve to die. And I'm saying, Isobel, that I aim to bring them to justice."

"You mean you'll try to kill all those men yourself?"

"I mean I *will* kill them all. I'll see that justice is done." He pushed his plate back and stood. "I understand you, Isobel Matas," he said. "Finally I understand."

He went into the bedroom. Though he left the door open, Isobel sat at the empty table for a long time. She stared at the chipped plates. She blinked away tears.

Never had she imagined a day when she and Noah would have changed places so completely. Visions of their little adobe home on the Pecos began to wither. She knew her kitchen garden would never bear fruit. There would be no laughing children, no laundry flapping, no sweet *bizcochitos* baking. Susan and Dick would never drive up to visit.

Ashes. The dream had burned to ashes.

Dick Brewer had not owned many cattle. Even so, the drive from his place to Chisum's South Spring River Ranch left Noah and Isobel exhausted. They took turns during the night, one sleeping while the other kept watch over the herd. It was almost more than two of them could manage to keep the cattle out of the river and see that they continued moving constantly toward the east.

Noah figured that caring for Dick's few dozen cattle was the least he could do for his friend. Farming was all Dick had ever wanted to do. And after meeting Susan Gates, he had told Noah about his dream to raise a ranching family on the lush New Mexico range. Dick had longed for sons to rear in the honest, hardworking pattern of his own life. He'd confided to Noah that he hoped every one of his children would have Susan's red hair and dark gray eyes.

Choking down the knot in his throat that rose every time he thought of Dick, Noah rode to the head of the herd. Isobel had kept to the river's edge, urging the cattle to keep moving. She had been skillful and determined to pull her weight on the drive.

From a distance now, Noah studied her. The fine black vest and riding skirt were dusty and worn from days in the saddle. Her white shirtwaist hung loose, its lace frayed and tattered. The long golden tresses that had once turned the men's heads were shoved beneath one of Dick's old hats that Isobel had found at his cabin. She wore a blue bandanna over her nose and heavy leather gloves on her hands.

By all accounts Isobel had returned to her rough and ready ways. She had borrowed one of Dick's holsters, and like a man's, her pistol now hung at her thigh. A thick leather cartridge belt studded with bullets girdled her hips. The Winchester Noah had given her was secured at the saddlebags. If not for the softness in her hazel eyes each time she looked at him, Noah could have figured her for as tough and trustworthy a trail partner as a man could want. But where was the fire?

None of the avenging amazon lurked in the gentle smiles Isobel cast Noah's way as they settled for a silent supper. Her hands softly cradled the bowl of stew she had cooked for him. Her fingertips spread his blanket on the thick green grass each night. She never once tried to make him speak of things she knew he couldn't bear. Instead she dusted his Stetson, laid a bouquet of sweet pansies by his blanket, and read aloud from his Bible as they sat beside the campfire.

Her tenderness toward him was almost enough to weaken him to the point of shedding the tears that pushed against the dam of anger he had built inside himself. But when he lay on his blanket, the fragrant pansies faded as an image flashed before his face. Dick. Dick rising from behind the stack of logs. A bullet slamming into Dick's forehead. His body jerking backward. Crumpling.

No!

Justice had to be done, and Noah knew he was the man to deliver it.

Noah and Isobel drove Dick Brewer's cattle out onto one of John Chisum's ranges. They left the herd under the watchful eyes of some of the men Chisum employed, then rode their horses back to Chisum's square ranch house.

Neither Chisum, Alexander and Sue McSween, Dr. Leverson, nor the others who had ridden to Lincoln were at the house. But plenty of news awaited the travelers. Mrs. Towry, the housekeeper, had already heard all about the shootout at Blazer's Mill. In New Mexico it seemed that news traveled faster than the horse's hooves that brought it.

"Buckshot Roberts died the day after you left the sawmill," she said as they sat on the sofa in Chisum's front room.

"Gut shot," Noah grunted.

"Major Godfroy and Dr. Blazer sent to Fort Stanton for a doctor. I don't know why they wanted to save the rotten bounty hunter. Him shooting Dick Brewer like that . . . Anyway, Dr. Appel drove down to the mill from the fort, but it was too late to do any good. The Godfroys buried Buckshot Roberts right beside Dick Brewer's grave."

Noah suppressed a curse. He clenched his jaw and stared out the window.

Mrs. Towry continued. "Mr. McSween is still at Fort Stanton, under protection of the soldiers. Today's the eighth of April, so district court was to start in Lincoln this morning. Last I heard, the judge—Warren Bristol—hadn't made it to Lincoln. But he might be there by now. Everyone thinks Judge Bristol will be staying at Fort Stanton for protection. There'll be soldiers in Lincoln every day to stand guard over the court. The town should be safe enough, I'd imagine."

Isobel glanced at Noah. What was he thinking? She could read nothing on his hard, blank face.

The days of endless silence had worn on her nerves. She had begun to think that the best thing for Noah would be to explode. Anger and pain were boiling inside him, barely leashed. Perhaps she should unleash them.

"I'm going to Lincoln," she said on an impulse. "I want to be there for the trials."

Noah's eyes darted to her face. If she expected the usual resistance, she was not rewarded. Noah made no move to dissuade her. The anger she hoped to provoke stayed buried.

"All right," he said. "We'll go."

Mrs. Towry took in a breath. "But Mrs. Buchanan has been on the trail for days, Noah, riding with those reckless Regulators and then herding cattle like a common cowboy. It's just plain indecent the way you've treated your bride. Why don't you take her out to your house for a while? District court is bound to carry on for weeks. Besides, you need to tend to things. The fellow who looks after your place while you're gone told me some kind of varmint got into your chicken coop. Your milk cow got scared and broke loose. He hadn't found her the last I heard. If I was you, I'd head out and check on things."

"Well, you're not me, Mrs. Towry," Noah said, standing and slinging his saddlebag over one shoulder. "I have business in Lincoln."

The housekeeper gave a little sniff. "I suppose you'll be wanting dinner before you ride off?"

"Thank you, Mrs. Towry," Isobel answered for Noah, who had ambled out of the room. "Dinner would be wonderful."

She waited a moment while Mrs. Towry plumped the sofa cushions and recovered from her snit. Then she started down the hall after Noah.

"It is one thing," she said, throwing open the door through which he had vanished, "to grieve and mourn your loss. It is quite another to be rude to an innocent, well-meaning person."

She looked around the empty room. At first she thought her imagination was playing tricks on her. Then Noah emerged from behind an ornate bamboo screen, his chambray shirt in his hands and his face dripping wet.

"What?" he snapped.

"You were very rude to Mrs. Towry." Isobel tried to keep

her eyes on his face, not on the hard chest that stirred untoward emotions inside her. "She was only trying to help."

"And I was only trying to get my point across." He flung his shirt on the bed, then turned and went back behind the screen. Amid splashing water, she could hear him talking. "That little house is part of the past. Gone. Crazy idea anyhow. Writing stories and all that damned nonsense . . . garbage . . . Lincoln County is outlaw territory . . . kill or be killed . . ."

Isobel marched around the screen. Noah was bent over the washstand, his face and hair dripping. While he muttered, he ran a bar of soap through his hair. The washbowl filled with bubbles as he scrubbed.

"Buckshot Roberts . . ." he mumbled into the water. "Jimmie Dolan is the man behind this . . . and Dick would want me to take care of it . . . loyalty . . . honesty . . . can't let dreams stand in the way . . ."

Spluttering, he came up for air. As he blindly reached for the towel, his hand inadvertently touched Isobel's shoulder. He pulled back. She took the piece of white linen from its brass hook and thrust it into his open palm. For a good minute he rubbed his hair and face.

Then he lifted his head and stared at Isobel. Bright blue eyes shone in a face as worn and tortured as any she could have imagined. His whiskers formed a dark shadow around his jaw. His damp hair stuck out in spikes around his head.

"Noah," she whispered. "Noah, what has happened to you?"

"I'm mad as a hornet, that's what."

"Your anger is only a mask, Noah." She followed him around the screen, trying to make him listen. "Always anger is a mask. It's the curtain that hides the true feeling."

"The only true feeling is that I'm mad as hell. Last week the best man I ever knew got the top of his head blasted off. And now he's buried next to his murderer. If you don't think that turns my stomach—"

"You're in pain. For you the anger hides the sorrow. You loved Dick. Now that he's dead, you don't know what to do about the emptiness inside you. So you've covered it with anger."

Noah flipped open the flap on his saddlebag and pulled out a fresh shirt. "Masks and curtains," he muttered, fumbling with the buttons.

"Sit down, Noah Buchanan," Isobel commanded suddenly. She would take no more of his nonsense. Setting a chair in the middle of the room, she pointed one finger at it. "Sit. Now."

"I'm getting dressed."

"Sit!"

Casting her a black look, he dropped the shirt on the bed and sat in the chair. She snapped open a new linen towel and drew it over his shoulders and around his neck, tying it in back.

"What the hell—"

"It's time for a haircut," she said. "You may choose to behave as a barbarian, but you won't look like one. Not in my presence."

She rummaged through the drawers in the dresser until she found a pair of scissors. They were small and fragile—sewing scissors, she imagined—but they would have to do. She took up her brush and swiftly pulled it through the thick tangle of Noah's dark hair. Then she raised the comb.

"When I was a little girl," she began, snipping his sideburns and trimming over his ears, "I was afraid."

He said nothing for a time. Then he spoke. "Afraid of what? You lived on your fancy hacienda with your rich clothes and your rich parents. What was there to be scared of?"

"Oh, many things." She smiled as she drew the comb through his hair and cut the ends. "I was afraid of my horse."

"Your horse? The one that—"

"The great jumper. Yes, I was terrified of him. He was so big and I so small. One day my father took me aside and brushed away my tears. He told me, 'Isobel, *mija*, you must change your fears into anger. Anger will make you strong. And with strength, you will control your horse.'"

She worked at the back of Noah's hair for a while, but when he said nothing, she continued her story. "So I did what my father had taught me. From that time on I took my fears and hid them behind the curtain of anger. I became strong and powerful. No one, nothing, could frighten me. I turned the murder of my father into anger. I have pursued Snake Jackson with that anger—never letting anyone see the fear beneath it."

Noah had shut his eyes, relaxing beneath the sensitive touch of her fingers sliding through his hair. But when she finished speaking, he looked up at her. She was working on the front now, running the comb down his part and trying to tame the thick mane. He could see her bosom rising and falling beneath the dusty black vest she had worn so many miles. He could see her throat, long and pale and slender.

"Are you afraid of Snake Jackson, Isobel?" he asked. "Is that the fear you had to change into anger?"

"No," she whispered. "I'm afraid of losing the ones I love."

He reached up and took the hand that held his comb. Drawing it down, he touched her bare neck.

"You lost your father. I lost Dick." He spoke the words as she knelt on the carpet in front of him. "You hide your fear. I hide my pain. What's so bad about that kind of anger, Isobel?"

She searched his bright blue eyes, hoping for answers she wasn't sure of herself. "Once a man taught me that there is more to life than fear and pain and anger," she said. "Once a man showed me how to laugh at bubbles in the dishwater. How to smell the evergreen boughs in a chipped cup. How to weep over the beautiful tale of a man's love for his wife. How to feel *other* things inside me than fear, pain, anger. Better things."

Noah stood suddenly, knocking back the chair as he strode away from her to the window. From her crouched position Isobel watched as he leaned his head on his arm, the fist clenched.

Rising, she moved across the room to him. She touched his back, running her open palm down the taut muscles along his spine. He let out a breath and turned to her, his eyes red.

"That man died, Isobel," he whispered in a hoarse voice. "The second that bullet smashed into Dick Brewer's forehead, the old Noah Buchanan died. Buckshot Roberts's bullet blew away that part of me. I don't feel it anymore. I feel only the anger."

She saw in his eyes that he meant every word. "Come, Noah," she said, taking his hand and running it down the front of her bosom. "Let me remind you of other things."

Isobel said nothing while Noah dumped the dirty water from the washbowl and refilled it. She remained motionless while he unbuttoned her shirtwaist and slid it from her shoulders along with the black vest. Yes, she was exhausted and emotionally worn, but she wanted to give Noah the only gift she could think of that might lift away some of the blackness.

Still clad in his denims and boots, he stripped off all her clothes until she stood naked before him. Then, taking up a cloth, he dipped it in the warm water and began to rub it over her body. Rivulets ran over the crests of her breasts, down her stomach, and into the triangle of curls at the apex of her thighs. The cloth slid around each nipple, bringing it to heightened stimulation. Then he took soap and began to stroke.

Isobel shut her eyes, unable to believe that at a time like this she could instantly feel such need for him. The throbbing became intense. Her breath shortened. Her head rolled back as she sighed with pleasure.

He kissed her neck, running his tongue up the length of her throat. His mouth covered her ear, and his tongue flickered in and out of the pearly cup. She reached for him, drawing his naked chest against her bare breasts. He felt stiff and tense, but she rose on tiptoe and pressed her taut nipples against his.

The slippery soapsuds stuck their skin together in a sensual way that left Isobel's head reeling. If only he would hold her breasts, cup them in his palms. If only she could feel the surge of his need against her pelvis. She ran her hands around his back and pulled him toward her.

"Noah," she murmured. "Noah, it's so good . . ."

She laid one palm against his flat stomach and began to work her fingers beneath the waistband of his trousers. But when her fingers touched his flesh, he suddenly jerked her hand away.

"No, Isobel," he growled, his eyes icy, distracted. "I can't, don't you understand?"

"Noah—"

"I'm sorry, darlin'. Right now I've got other things to attend to." Pushing away from her, he strode across the room. She heard the door slam as she stood alone, naked, needing her husband.

Chapter
❧ 16 ☙

On the long ride to Lincoln, Isobel considered her future—with or without the silent man who rode at her side. Though she believed Noah spoke the truth when he told her that Dick Brewer's murder had changed him forever, she also felt certain that deep inside his heart Noah would always remain the same. The intensity of the pain he felt over the loss of his friend proved that his gentle nature had not been erased.

But he was a man, taught from birth to hide his feelings, told to hold his tears and sneer at hardship. He had always been urged to focus on the practical and not the emotional. Thus, his matter-of-fact remark on the third day as they neared Lincoln did not surprise Isobel.

"I've been considering," he said. "I think it's time we broke off our arrangement."

Isobel tried to squelch the dismay that rose inside her. "And why is that?"

"The way I see it, we've more or less wound things up. I've helped you find out the name of your father's killer. I've protected you from Snake Jackson and the others. You'll be safe now because these district court trials in Lincoln are bound to put an end to the trouble in the county. Dolan may go free because of his connections in Santa Fe, but I suspect most of his scalawags—including Snake Jackson—will wind up behind bars."

"And I helped you to get the land you wanted from John Chisum. So we are even."

"Looks that way to me."

Isobel nodded, but inside she felt frantic to sort out the real meaning behind Noah's words. Did he want to be rid of her? Did everything that had passed between them suddenly have no meaning? Or did he really care about her and fear for her safety if he followed his plan of revenge for the death of Dick Brewer?

"So what will you do, Noah?" she asked. "Will you go back to riding the Arizona cattle trail for Señor Chisum?"

He scowled at the sun-dappled road. "You know what I'll be doing."

"You told me the court would bring justice to Dolan's men. And Buckshot Roberts is dead. What more do you want, Noah?"

"I want to bring Jimmie Dolan down."

"How?"

"Any way I can."

"Will you ambush him and murder him on the streets like Billy the Kid did to Sheriff Brady? Will you become no better than that bounty hunter, Buckshot Roberts, who killed Dick?"

"I'll do what it takes, Isobel. All I know is, Dick wasn't going to let John Tunstall's death rest. I'm not going to let Dick's death rest. And the man behind those murders is Jimmie Dolan."

"And what is to become of me while you are off making yourself into a cold-blooded avenger?" she snapped.

"Look, I didn't take on your entire future the night I married you in the woods, Isobel. We struck a temporary bargain, that's all. You're free to do whatever you want."

"Then I shall ride with you in pursuit of Jimmie Dolan."

"No, you won't!" He whirled on her, his blue eyes flashing. "I've already lost Dick, and I'm not going to lose . . . I just . . . I don't want any more killing going on, you hear? You stay at the McSweens' house through the trials if you want. Susan

Gates is probably in a fix over losing Dick. She'll need comforting."

"And what about you, Noah?"

"I don't need your comforts, Isobel. You saw that three days ago."

"Three days ago, I saw a man whose best friend had been murdered. I saw a man in deep mourning, a man whose pain was still too raw to heal. One day you'll want my comforting, Noah."

"No. No, I won't. If there comes a time I need a woman, I'll get one the way I always have. With no strings attached. I don't want to be tangled, Isobel."

"And I tangle you."

"Yes, you do."

"So. You will throw away your stories, the lace curtains, the kitchen garden, the milk cow, the chickens, the warmth of your wood stove on a winter night—all for the satisfaction of bringing Jimmie Dolan to justice. Those days with me in your adobe home meant nothing to you. Our times of laughter and cooking and riding—"

"Don't. Just don't talk about that, Isobel. I don't want to hear it."

"You told me not many days ago that you wanted to make our marriage real. You took me to John Chisum's house to buy land for our home and our future."

"That was before Dick got killed. That was before I saw how things really stood." He reined in his horse and looked at her evenly. She could see the evidence of strain in the lines at the corners of his eyes. She could see the intense strength it took for him to hold back the flood of feelings inside himself.

"I'm sorry, Isobel," he said. "Sorry I steered you wrong. Sorry I got you to thinking about me like there was going to be a future for us. Like I was something good for you."

"You are good for me."

"No. You don't know what kind of people I come from. All this time I've been telling you about Mrs. Allison and her fancy tea parties in the library. But you ought to know who I really am. My daddy was a gambler. He ran off and left the family not too many years after I was born. My mother turned herself into a common whore just to keep food in our bellies.

Then she died of a fever and left all us kids orphans. I don't come from good breeding stock, Isobel. To tell the truth, I'm no better than Snake Jackson. His folks left him an orphan, too. It was only the luck of the draw that got me a job as a stable hand with the Allisons in Texas and taught me some of the things you think you like about me."

"Are you saying you're not the man who wrote 'Sunset at Coyote Canyon?' Who was that, if not you?"

"I'm saying I've got my daddy's roving blood, Isobel. I'm a wanderer. That's why Chisum didn't want to sell me any land. He thought I couldn't sit still long enough to keep it up. He thought I was too wild. And he was right. I may have fooled you into thinking I was sort of a gentleman, but the truth is, I've got an outlaw's heart."

Isobel blinked at the tears that blurred her vision of the narrow dusk-shrouded street of Lincoln. So this was how Noah would choose to end their union.

"It is your choice, Noah," she said, meeting his level gaze. "Just as both Isobel Matas and Belle Buchanan are parts of me, the outlaw and the gentleman are parts of you. You have the power to become either. Choose well, Noah."

Lest he see the tears that spilled down her cheeks, Isobel dug her heels into her horse's sides and galloped down the darkening street toward the home of Alexander McSween.

Susan Gates had fallen into a swoon upon hearing the news of Dick Brewer's murder. Though she had regained consciousness, she was very ill. Nothing Dr. Ealy tried had been able to restore her health.

Isobel spent hours by the bed of her friend, comforting her as she mourned. It came to Isobel as she held Susan's trembling shoulders that it would have been much better had Noah allowed himself to cry out the anguish of Dick's death. Instead, he kept it buried inside him.

As the two women clung together, Isobel knew her own tears were not so much for the loss of Dick Brewer but for the emptiness inside her heart. How could Noah have let her go so easily? How could he have given up what they had begun to build? *La venganza* was not worth such sacrifice.

Days passed, and Isobel saw nothing of Snake Jackson or

the wounded Jesse Evans and their bunch. Though the town was swarming with citizens and soldiers, she escaped to the small cemetery to sit beside her father's grave and—for the first time—to accept that Don Albert Matas really had died and she would never see him again. His golden hair, laughing smile, and hazel eyes were no more.

Several times she wandered to the courthouse. Though she went on the pretense of learning about the proceedings, she really hoped to catch a glimpse of Noah. But the room was crowded to overflowing, and Noah was nowhere to be seen.

By the time the district court concluded on April 18, Isobel learned that the trials had turned out mostly for the good of the McSween faction. John Copeland, a man sympathetic to the McSween side, had been appointed sheriff by Judge Bristol.

For the killing of John Tunstall, indictments were brought against Jesse Evans, Jim Jackson, and several others as principals, along with Jimmie Dolan and J. B. Mathews as accessories. Unfortunately, of the principals only Jesse Evans could be found. He was arrested and put under a $5,000 bond. Dolan and Mathews were also arrested and placed under bonds of $2,000 each. All the cases were continued.

For the killing of Sheriff Brady and his deputy, four indictments were brought in. The men named were Billy Bonney, John Middleton, Fred Waite, and Henry Brown.

For the killing of Buckshot Roberts, only Charley Bowdre was indicted. Since neither Bowdre nor any of the other Regulators were to be found in Lincoln, no arrests could be made. Sheriff Copeland held the warrants.

Alexander McSween was entirely exonerated from any criminal charges. The press expressed general public feelings in the New Mexico Territory toward the lawyer. Most newspapers that carried the trials stressed that Alexander McSween had been a victim of his enemies. Fort Stanton quickly released him and everyone else for whom the grand jury had not returned indictments.

Finally the grand jury brought an indictment against Jimmie Dolan and his mercantile for encouraging cattle stealing.

Isobel breathed a sigh of relief when Dr. Ealy came in with a summary of all the court news one evening. Surely Noah's

predictions had come to pass; Dolan had been exposed and arrested. Sheriff Copeland held warrants for the arrest of
Dolan's rowdies. And, though Isobel sensed that Billy and the
other Regulators felt their ambush of Sheriff Brady had been
justified, she believed they had been wrong to murder him. It
was only fair that they, too, be punished.

She had settled in a rocker beside Susan's bed to discuss the
outcome of district court with her friend when someone began
hammering on the back door. Reminded of the day of Brady's
killing when she had hidden Billy the Kid from Peppin and his
men, Isobel tensed as Taylor Ealy hurried to the door to see
who was outside.

"Why, Mr. Buchanan!" the missionary declared with some
surprise.

Noah stepped into the room. "Evenin', Dr. Ealy."

Isobel had not seen Noah for almost two weeks, and somehow she had forgotten how tall and imposing a figure he cut.
He swept off his black Stetson but not the canvas duster that
concealed his six-shooter from the Ealy children playing near
the piano. His blue eyes cast about the room until his gaze fell
on Isobel.

"I need to talk to you," he said by way of introduction.

Susan squeezed her hand as Isobel stood.

"What is it, Noah?" Her heart had begun to thunder the moment she had set eyes on his face, the chiseled planes and
granite jaw. She swallowed, trying to suppress the surge of
emotion that flooded through her as she ran her eyes over his
lips and down his neck.

"Would you step outside with me for a minute?" He gestured toward the door with his hat.

Isobel glanced at Susan, as if for reassurance. But the ache
she saw in her friend's eyes only mirrored what she saw in
Noah's. Lifting the skirt of the new pink dress she had sewn,
Isobel walked across the room, aware that everyone's attention had focused on her and Noah. She took her white shawl
from the peg by the door and stepped outside.

Noah shut the door behind him. For a moment he eyed the
sliver of moon that hung over the roof of the McSweens'
house. Then he took a breath.

"I'm riding for Santa Fe tomorrow morning," he announced. "I'll take you to the Pascals' hacienda if you want to go."

"Santa Fe, Noah? But why?"

"Jimmie Dolan posted bond and left Lincoln this afternoon. I'm told he's headed for Santa Fe. Speculation has it he's on his way to talk to Governor Axtell and Tom Catron. Catron's the United States District Attorney for the territory. He's practically a dictator around these parts, thanks to all the property mortgages and loans he holds. They say Axtell and Catron are both in the Santa Fe Ring. If Dolan gets their help, he can turn things around to his favor pretty quickly down here in Lincoln County."

"And you mean to stop him?"

"Legally, if I can. If not . . . Yeah, I mean to stop him."

Isobel studied the grim moonlit face. She ached to touch Noah, to feel his arms slip around her and his lips brush her neck. She shivered. "Why must you be the one to pursue Dolan? Why can't Billy? He's always so hot for blood."

"The other Regulators are hiding out. Sheriff Copeland's a friend, but he does hold warrants for their arrest. None of them wants to make a move until they're sure where they stand . . . Besides, nobody's after me, and I know how to talk to bigwigs like Catron."

Isobel tried to review the consequences of riding with Noah to Santa Fe. She knew it was a thoughtful gesture on his part to take her to safety, and she wasn't sure exactly why he had elected to reverse his decision to end their separation.

But what would happen if she and Noah were together day and night during the long northbound journey? Would they talk? Could she break down some of the barriers between them?

Then she considered Guillermo Pascal, whose portrait lay abandoned at the bottom of her saddlebag. Her betrothed had never responded to the telegram Noah sent so long ago. Guillermo would not be expecting Isobel to appear on his doorstep like some windblown beggar. He would not want her.

When she lifted her eyes, she met Noah's blue gaze. "Yes," she whispered. "I will go with you to Santa Fe."

* * *

The sun had not yet risen when Isobel mounted her bay and rode through Lincoln Town at the side of Noah Buchanan. She had thought herself warm and full from the hearty breakfast Mary Ealy had prepared. But the moment she had peered out the McSweens' window to see Noah riding up on his black stallion, her stomach had begun to flutter.

Susan had risen from her bed and embraced Isobel. "Don't let him get away from you," she had whispered as Noah walked through the doorway. "Make him love you, Isobel. He's a good man."

Isobel said nothing in response, only hugged her friend. But as she rode onto the trail, she wondered about Susan's encouragement. What good had it done the petite redhead to fall in love? Dick Brewer had been killed as easily as Noah might one day be killed, and now Susan was worse than before—for she had to live with her loss for the rest of her life.

But studying the broad expanse of Noah's back, the noble set to his spine, the fine control of his mount, she knew that she had no choice but to acknowledge her longing. Against all better judgment, she loved Noah Buchanan. Could she ever make him love her?

She knew that she had only days in which to rekindle the passion that had sprung up between them. Otherwise, he would turn her over to Guillermo Pascal.

There she would face the Pascal family's rejection, the final realization that she had lost her land grants, and the certainty of being sent back to Catalonia with nothing but heartache to show for all her months in New Mexico.

More important than the things that had brought her here was the fact that she loved Noah. Though she knew she could live without him, she also knew that she didn't want to.

God had given her one week in which to win back the heart of her husband.

Noah had chosen the more difficult northern passage over the mountains to Santa Fe. He was hoping Jimmie Dolan might have opted for a longer but safer route up the Pecos River. If Noah had his way, he intended to beat the Irishman to the capital and speak with Catron before Dolan could.

Climbing the mountainous trail with Isobel only a few feet

behind him gave Noah plenty of time to reconsider what he'd
done. The more he thought about it, the less sure he was of
what had driven him to the McSween house the night before
to propose such a venture.

The moment he'd stepped through the front door and had
seen Isobel sitting on that low stool by Susan's bed, he had a
sure feeling he ought to back right out the door and run.

Great stars, she was a beauty! Her long waves of golden
hair hung shimmering over her shoulders like a waterfall out
of fairyland. She must have sewn herself a new dress, for there
she sat swathed in a pink confection with ruffles at the wrists
and ruffles around the neck and a deep-cut bodice that showed
off a little more than might be thought respectable in some circles.

Oh, but she looked good enough to eat. Seeing him, she'd
risen from the stool with her damp lips parted and her hazel
eyes shining. And when he'd taken her out under the moonlight, it had been all he could do to keep from gathering her up
in his arms and kissing her long and deep the way he wanted
to.

He turned around now, on his stallion, and glanced at her
riding behind. She'd put on dark Spanish riding clothes that
morning—a black outfit that covered her neck and swung
down to her boots. She had swept her hair up into a tight knot
high on the back of her head.

But Isobel was no *marquesa* on this ride. Around her waist
hung a belt studded with a row of silver bullets. Dick Brewer's
old hat dipped low on her brow. A pair of Noah's leather
gloves covered her hands. She looked ready for battle.

Letting out a breath, Noah shifted and tried to make himself
focus on the winding trail and the obstacles that lay ahead of
him. He knew he had to block out the persistent images of
Isobel lying beneath him, soft and warm, her breasts thrusting
against his chest. He had to force away memories of their days
in the little adobe house by the river. He had to forget the letter
that had come to him in Lincoln telling him that his story had
been received by the publisher and passed along to a magazine
editor in New York.

There was no room for fantastic imaginings in the real
world—and he had damn sure better not forget it. Too many

years now he'd allowed his dreams to encroach on reality. He'd believed people were better than they were. He'd hoped for a peaceful future. He'd expected to become a writer.

But that was all nonsense. He finally understood. It had taken the death of his best friend to bring the truth to him. People could be liars, cheaters, murderers. And if you were a man who chose to live in the West, you could almost bet your bottom dollar that a bullet would put you into the grave.

Therefore, Noah reasoned, there was no point in getting attached to people—especially not to a pretty blond Spaniard who made a fellow lose sight of the way things really were. He clenched his jaw and made up his mind that he could last one week on the trail alone with Isobel and not get tangled. He had to.

With the help of the Good Lord, he knew he could keep his mind on the job at hand—Dolan. He knew he had to resist taking Isobel into his bed . . . and into his heart . . . again.

It seemed that heaven chose to favor Noah Buchanan, or perhaps the cowboy's determination not to become entangled was stronger than the *mujer's* efforts at temptation. Oh, she had bathed naked in a stream, brushed her hair in full view, attempted to start at least a hundred conversations, even complained of the cold and made as if to snuggle into his pallet with him.

But Noah kept Isobel at a distance. He knew he had to avenge Dick's death, and he couldn't be besotted with a woman. He had to be clear-thinking, footloose, and fancy-free.

So it was that Noah and Isobel had traveled from Lincoln to the small town of White Oaks. From there they journeyed north to a tiny settlement named Gallinas and then to Anton Chico on the Pecos River. From Anton Chico they continued north to Las Vegas, then swung west toward Santa Fe. Finally their journey took them—on the first day of May 1878—down the dusty trail to the hacienda of the *familia* Pascal.

As they approached the house in the rolling foothills of the Sangre de Cristo Mountains, Isobel had the oddest sense that her imagination had taken root and sprouted to life. The Pascal home was a long, rambling, whitewashed affair with a flat roof and, along the facade, a row of vine-entwined arches. Red tiles covered the *portal* floor on which sat carved wooden chairs of the finest order. From its perch on a pole in the shade of a flowering purple lilac bush, a green parrot eyed the two approaching riders.

Isobel caught her breath at the sight of the nearby corral. Arabian horses and steeds of lesser heritage pranced and turned for their trainers.

Fat, sleek cattle, belly-deep in thick green grass, dotted the foothills. Among the herds rode mounted *caballeros* with dark leather chaps and fine wide-brimmed hats.

When Isobel and Noah dismounted, an elegant, slow-moving gentleman met them on the *portal*. He nodded in greeting, then held out a silver salver, as if expecting to receive a calling card.

"I've brought Isobel Matas," Noah explained. "The Pascals are expecting her, I reckon. I sent a wire from Lincoln almost two months back."

The gentleman peered at Isobel, his dark eyes sweeping up and down her dusty black riding clothes, leather holster, pistol, and battered felt hat. Then he held out a hand. "Won't you come inside señor, señorita?"

Isobel waited nervously on the sofa of a grand salon while Noah paced in front of huge glass-paned windows. She watched him stalking back and forth, his hat swinging in one hand, the other hand jammed into the pocket of his denim trousers. Through the glass he studied the rising hills and the herds of cattle; then he surveyed the interior of the richly furnished house.

"Looks like your dream's about to come true," he said finally. His deep voice echoed off the thick wooden *vigas* on the ceiling.

Isobel swallowed. "The Pascals have a very nice home."

"Well . . . I reckon you'll be happy, then."

For a moment she fiddled with the string that bound her holster to her thigh. "How long will you be in Santa Fe, Noah?"

"Aw, don't give me another thought. You just do your best to get this fellow to take you on, hear?"

"Are you that eager to be rid of me?"

His eyes darted to her face. There was a moment of silence between them, each gazing at the other.

"Well, sure," Noah said finally, beginning to pace again. "This was the plan all along, wasn't it? I was supposed to get you up here to the Pascals so you could marry your fancy don. That was the agreement."

Isobel stood. "But, Noah, that was before—"

"Buenas tardes." The chocolate-rich voice drew their attention to the doorway. Isobel knew the man at once.

Tall, with shiny-slick black hair, a thin mustache, and crackling brown eyes, Don Guillermo Pascal studied the pair of strangers in his salon. For a moment he said nothing. Then he removed his pressed-straw hat with its carved leather band around the crown and gave the slightest of bows.

"Señorita Matas," he said. "What a lovely surprise."

Noah stood watching in the background while Isobel took her first long look at the man who was supposed to be her husband. And a dandy he was. He wore a brown suede suit with black leather trim and rows of bright buttons. Every line of the outfit skimmed over his sleekly muscled body like a second skin. At his hip hung a pistol with a carved ivory handle. Every inch of his holster and gunbelt had been tooled. At his neck he wore a thin black bow tie with five-inch strings hanging down the breast of his white shirt. And on his feet gleamed the shiniest pair of pointed-toe boots Noah had ever laid eyes on.

Noah glanced down at his own leather boots, crusted with dried mud and worn down at the heels. His denims might be tight-fitting, but only because they'd been washed a thousand times and were halfway threadbare to prove it. His own chambray shirt wore a sweat stain around the collar—a darker strip that would never come off. The sleeve cuffs had frayed so badly there was no hope for mending them. To top it off, a layer of fine dust had settled on his hat, and his duster smelled of saddle leather and old horseflesh.

Don Guillermo moved without haste toward Isobel and took her hand. Lifting it to his lips, he planted a delicate kiss on her fingertips.

She smiled.

When the Spaniard lifted his head and saw that flash of white teeth and those full lips, Noah knew right off Isobel had won her man. His brown eyes sparkling, Don Guillermo bent for a second kiss.

"*Cariña*, you must be exhausted from your journey," he said smoothly. "Come, let me call *mamá*. She will want to meet you, of course. And then you must be given a *sala* and opportunity for bathing and refreshment before dinner."

Isobel smiled again. Don Guillermo swung around, smugness written on his face, and proceeded toward the door. As he was stepping into the hall, he paused and addressed Noah.

"You may go, señor," he ordered. When Noah made no move, he frowned. "Do you wish payment?"

"No."

"Then you are dismissed. Señorita Matas will have no further need of your services." With that he went, bootheels ringing sharp *rat-a-tats* on the tile floor.

Noah studied Isobel. Her high cheekbones held a flush that told him she'd been pleased by the attentions of the fancy señor. He tried to flatten the rising revulsion he felt at the thought of the Spaniard ever touching Isobel again. His prickly little mustache poking into her lip as he kissed her. His long, thin fingers toying with the buttons at her bosom. His slim-hipped body pressed against hers . . .

"Isobel—"

"Noah—"

Their words overlapped. Each stopped and looked at the other. She cleared her throat. He stuffed his Stetson on his head and crossed his arms over his chest.

"Well . . ." he said.

"You will leave me here?" It was more a plea than a question. She heard her own voice waver over the words. Would Noah actually walk away and leave her in the hands of this . . . this perfumed, pompous bombast?

"Reckon I'll head out," he said.

"Noah . . ."

He started for the door. "Take care now, Isobel."

She watched him step into the hall just as Don Guillermo Pascal and his mother swept through the door.

"Ah! Señorita Matas—*que bonita*!" The hefty doña waddled across the room, her black lace *mantilla* billowing behind her as she made for Isobel. *"Bienvenido, cariña!"*

Isobel was smothered in the folds of a red flower-embroidered *mantón*, the rich scent of rosewater, and the fleshy bosom of the señora as she heard the front door slam shut, leaving her alone with the *familia* Pascal.

Noah rode toward the huge gate thinking how glad he was to have Isobel off his hands. Yes, sir. No more need to look out for somebody else's skin. No more wild-goose chases after Snake Jackson. No more . . .

Well, he had to admit she hadn't turned out to be that much trouble after all. Not like he'd expected at first. Noah grinned, remembering how Isobel had jumped out of that tub of water and pulled her pistol on him. And then when she'd refused to wash the breakfast dishes . . . but that had turned out all right, too.

As a matter of fact, they'd had a good time together all in all. The cowboy and the señorita . . . yes, sir. Pictures filtered through his mind—the first time he'd seen her in her new blue dress, the time she'd slipped off her horse into his arms and he'd kissed her, the way she'd typed page after page of his story, the hours she'd spent digging up that kitchen garden, the nights they'd rolled on the bed . . .

Of course, now she was where she'd always wanted to be. Right here in Santa Fe with Don Guillermo Pascal. She belonged with a dandy Spaniard a hell of a lot more than she belonged with some old dusty . . . what had she called him? . . . *vaquero.*

Yes, sir. Isobel didn't need to be out riding the trail, hiding from bad hombres like Snake Jackson and sleeping under the stars. She deserved a fine hacienda, fat cattle, the *fiestas* she'd always wanted. She deserved a man like Guillermo Pascal . . .

Noah reined his horse and looked over his shoulder at the hacienda.

Chapter

❧ 17 ❧

Doña Maria Pascal elected to give her eldest son the privilege of showing their visitor around the house and grounds. Isobel removed her leather gloves as she walked down the flagstone path amid gardens of blossoming red roses, purple lilacs, and golden forsythia.

When Don Guillermo extended a hand to assist her over a bridge beneath which ran a mountain stream, she had no choice but to take it. Then he tucked her fingers around the inside of his elbow, drew her against his side, and chatted, his voice filled with great élan.

"So you have come all the way from Catalonia?" he asked finally, after a great deal of discourse on the wonders of the Pascal estates.

Isobel nodded. "I . . . I sent a telegram from Lincoln."

"A telegram?"

She couldn't tell whether or not he was feigning ignorance. "I've been in New Mexico for more than two months."

"But *cariña*, you should have come directly to Santa Fe. If I had known—"

"Known what!" she snapped, losing patience suddenly. "You knew my father had been murdered and the land-grant titles stolen. My family sent you a letter saying that I was traveling to New Mexico—so you knew that, also. What did you not know, señor?"

"We speak honestly, I see." He paused and took a breath. "Very well, Señorita Matas. I did not know you were so beautiful."

The honest avowal took her off-guard. "How can my appearance possibly matter in this situation?"

"It matters very much. To me." Stroking his narrow black mustache, he eyed her. "I am Don Guillermo Pascal, you see. With my father's death last year I became the head of our family. I lack for nothing. Your land grants appealed to me when your father first offered them as a part of the betrothal agreement. But I've acquired a great deal of property since that time. If I'm able to regain the titles—which I have no doubt I can accomplish—I will simply absorb those lands into my own. The jewels, of course, would also be of benefit. Lands, jewels . . . these I have in plenty. But women are scarce in this rough land."

"Especially beautiful women?"

He smiled, only the slightest upcurve of his lips beneath his mustache. "And you are a beautiful woman with a quick mind. I think, perhaps, our fathers knew best when they arranged our marriage."

"Then you intend to follow through with the agreement, Don Guillermo?"

"We shall see, Señorita Matas. Only time will tell."

Time had given Noah a head start in his crusade against Jimmie Dolan. Representing himself as an independent land and cattle owner in Lincoln County, Noah made appointments with both Governor Axtell and District Attorney Catron.

He settled in at a local hotel. With some of his cattle drive earnings, he bought himself a fine new suit, a pair of shiny boots, a spanking clean hat, and a stack of local newspapers to fill him in on the latest events. Then he turned on his lamp and began to write.

But this was no fictional tale of the West Noah intended to tell. This was his persuasive argument in favor of the downfall of James J. Dolan. And with each stroke of his pen, Noah forced his longing for Isobel Buchanan deep inside his heart. There he buried away that burning desire, with the hope that it would stay hidden forever.

Isobel, too, spent much of her time nosing through local newspapers. They seemed the only link with the world she had lost—the world that had claimed her heart.

Doña Maria would grunt in dismay when she waddled past Isobel's room, only to find the young woman scanning and marking the latest events in Lincoln County. Don Guillermo had little patience for Isobel's lack of interest in him, and he quickly threatened to discontinue the family's subscriptions if she didn't participate more fully in the activities of the estate.

Isobel made an effort to play her part as a proposed future doña in the *familia* Pascal. After all, she reasoned, she had once made a marriage of convenience—why not again? But the answer was obvious. She had grown to love Noah Buchanan with a passion that she knew could never be matched.

Guillermo Pascal had no overtly unpleasant side. His appearance did not turn her stomach. His manners were impeccable. But what attraction could she possibly feel for such a self-absorbed, petty man?

And so she read her newspapers. From the *Cimarron News and Press*, she cried over the letter Alexander McSween had written in memorial to Dick Brewer. The glowing praise of the young rancher served to remind her how deep a loss both Noah and Susan must feel without him.

Letters in the *Santa Fe New Mexican*, the *Trinidad Enterprise and Chronicle*, and the *Mesilla Independent* volleyed the situation in Lincoln County back and forth—some writers lauding Dolan, others glorifying the bravery of McSween and the Regulators.

Jimmie Dolan himself began to express his defense in the newspapers; but in Isobel's opinion his letters did nothing more than reveal his own weaknesses. In fact, the man sounded more like a whining child than a business magnate.

It was the small notice she found buried in an issue of the *New Mexican* that gave her hope for Noah's cause against Dolan. The letter stated that James J. Dolan & Co. was temporarily shutting the doors of its mercantile in Lincoln due to the unsafe condition of affairs there. Perhaps, Isobel mused, the outcome of the district court had actually driven the tyrant from the county.

In addition to the good news of the closing of the Dolan Mercantile, Alexander McSween published the information that he had been authorized by John Tunstall's father in England to offer a reward of $5,000 for the apprehension and conviction of his son's murderers. This, of course, could do nothing but enhance the job of the Regulators—even though they themselves had been outlawed. Isobel knew now that bounty hunters—she shuddered to recall Buckshot Roberts—would set their sights on Snake Jackson, Jesse Evans, and the rest of Dolan's bunch.

In fact, Isobel's lightheartedness took the entire Pascal family by surprise. Though she had confided none of her past experiences to them, they had surmised that she held a keen interest in the affairs of Lincoln County.

While Guillermo was spending a great deal of time in Santa Fe looking after his properties, Doña Maria took to joining Isobel on the patio. At first the two women did little more than enjoy the sun and fresh air wafting down from the Sangre de Cristo Mountains. But eventually the canny old doña could not resist leafing through Isobel's newspapers and engaging her young guest in discussion.

"Now, this cannot be good for the side of the Regulators," she commented one evening as she was flipping through the *Cimarron News and Press*. "Men have begun the murdering again in Lincoln County."

"Who?" Isobel wadded the Santa Fe paper in her lap in an effort to read the news over the doña's shoulder.

"Look here. There was a shooting at the Fritz ranch on the Rio Bonito. This man Frank Macnab got himself killed."

"Macnab! But he was the new leader of the Regulators." Isobel scanned the story in dismay. "Who shot him, Doña Maria?"

"A band of men from the Rio Pecos. They are called the Seven Rivers Gang. Along with these hombres were a Peppin and a Mathews. Ah, yes . . . I remember. They were the ones who killed the Englishman, Tunstall."

Isobel didn't know whether to be more taken aback by the

doña's knowledge of events or by the events themselves. It was appalling to think that more men had joined the Dolan forces. And now Frank Macnab had been murdered, leaving the Regulators leaderless a second time.

"Oh, my," Doña Maria said, bending lower to read the tiny print. "More trouble here. Look, this hombre George Coe, has shot somebody from the Dolan side. And here . . . here it says that the soldiers of Fort Stanton have returned to Lincoln to keep order. Hmm . . . those Seven Rivers men surrendered to the soldiers."

"Does Captain Purington hold them at the fort, then?"

"It says here a Colonel Dudley is now running the garrison." The doña sniffed and glanced up at Isobel. "You favor this man Dolan or this one McSween?"

Isobel debated only a moment before releasing her true feelings. "Both sides have greedy, ambitious men, Doña Maria. But Alexander McSween seems to be both good and honest. He wants to do right. He carries no gun and he tries to make peace. Jimmie Dolan has already cheated the United States Government through his mercantile. So much cheating, in fact, that his business was driven away from Fort Stanton. Now he tries to play his games of deceit on the landowners. His men are murderers and thieves. I don't trust him."

The old woman adjusted her *mantilla* and settled her heavy bosom against the table as she leaned forward, bright brown eyes sparkling. "It's like a bullfight, yes? One—strong and brave—struggling against another, also strong and brave. Who will win?"

"I don't know, Doña Maria."

"Together we shall watch this bullfight, Señorita Matas, you and I?"

"Yes," Isobel said, feeling the first spark of companionship since her arrival. "We shall watch together."

The doña laughed and clapped her hands. *"Ole!"*

Time passed quickly for Isobel as she sat with the matriarch on the portal, reading the newspapers. But she quickly realized that any dreams she might have held for becoming an active participant in the running of the Pascal hacienda held no substance.

No one in the family would hear of her riding out on the ranges. She was kept in the house, pampered, fed, clothed by the finest tailors in Santa Fe, and encouraged to stitch, plan meals, and play at cards with the doña.

In all, Isobel felt bored nearly to the point of tears. Or was it merely boredom that brought on the tears, the long periods in which she felt no urge to laugh or even to smile? Day and night she thought of Noah Buchanan. No matter how hard she tried to force herself into the role of the dutiful betrothed, she could not erase the cowboy from her heart and her thoughts. Was he still in Santa Fe? Surely not after all this time. But what had become of his quest for justice against Jimmie Dolan?

Almost a month had passed since Noah had ridden away from the Pascal hacienda. The newspapers had contained no mention of his name. Though Susan Gates had written to Isobel twice, she had said nothing about Noah. Isobel assumed it could only mean that the Regulators were still being hunted, and Susan did not want to give away Noah's whereabouts. Mail was never secret, especially in the territories.

Standing on the portal feeding sunflower seeds to the green parrot one morning at the end of May, Isobel heard someone open the front door and step out of the house. She assumed it must be Doña Maria, for they regularly sat together at this time of day to read and embroider.

Isobel had decided, finally, to approach the older woman about her decision to return to Spain and rejoin her family as a confirmed *soltera*. So it was with some surprise that she saw Don Guillermo's slender brown hand slip around her elbow.

"Señorita," he said.

She glanced at him and at once decided she did not like the look of intensity in his eyes. "Señor?"

"I wish to speak with you regarding the arrangement of our future."

Isobel tried to quell the feeling of dismay that rose inside her.

Don Guillermo folded his hands behind his back and began to pace along the garden path. "I have spoken with territorial officials in Santa Fe regarding your family's stolen land titles. It seems I shall have little trouble restoring them."

"But we were told the thief had already started transferral proceedings. That was more than three months ago. How can you have settled it all so easily?"

"I have connections, *cariña*." He winked at her, then cleared his throat and reassumed his businesslike tone. "As to other matters . . . I find it agreeable that we should wed. I have arranged for the ceremony to take place at the end of three weeks."

"Three weeks!"

"Have no concern, Isobel. I have arranged everything. The food, the entertainment, your gown, the priest. The first banns have already been published in this morning's *Santa Fe New Mexican.* You and my mother will, I am certain, peruse the announcement at your leisure." His thin upper lip lifted in a hint of a grin at his own small humor.

"I have written to your mother confirming all the details," he continued. "Of course the marriage ceremony will have been concluded before she receives my message, but that cannot be helped. Doña Maria is amenable to the union, as are my brothers."

"And what about me?" Isobel demanded. "Did you think to ask for my consent, Don Guillermo?"

"You gave your consent five years ago when you agreed to the betrothal."

Isobel crossed her arms. "Five years was a long time ago. I cannot deny that I have come to care for your mother and for the Pascal family. Once, Don Guillermo, becoming your wife would have been the summit of my aspirations. But in the past three weeks I've had time to consider my future. . . . I intend to return to Spain."

"Spain? That's preposterous! I won't allow it. Our families have signed a legal, binding betrothal contract. I've already begun proceedings of land transfer from your name to mine. The wedding is arranged, señorita, and you *will* marry me."

"Hell, that's not much of a proposal, Pascal." The deep voice from behind a boxwood hedge visibly startled Isobel. She clutched the parrot's stand and swung around to look.

"Noah!" She caught her breath as the cowboy rode his black stallion around the hedge and straight into the formal garden.

"No, don't draw your gun, señor." Noah's six-shooter already weighed in his own hand. Its barrel was pointed at the Spaniard.

"What is the meaning of this outrage?" Don Guillermo blustered, stepping protectively in front of the young woman.

"I've come for Isobel."

"I beg your pardon! The Señorita Matas is my betrothed. She will go nowhere with such a *vaquero* as yourself."

"Fact is, Isobel here is my wife—and you might as well forget the *señorita* business and get used to calling her Mrs. Buchanan. She's a *señora* and has been for more than three months. I married the lady on February 18, 1878—the day we met."

Guillermo's dark eyes flashed to Isobel's pale face. "Can you explain this man's utter nonsense—"

"I've come for you, darlin'," Noah interrupted. "You and I have urgent business in Lincoln County."

"Noah—what's happened?" Isobel could hardly breathe for the shock of seeing the man she had believed she would never lay eyes on again.

Noah holstered his gun. "It seems like you just attract snakes wherever you go, darlin'." Though he was speaking to Isobel, his blue eyes never left Guillermo's face. "Tom Catron—who's one of the territory's major snakes himself—let slip a tiny fact the other day while we were chatting. Seems his district attorney's office has been working on behalf of the Pascal family to secure a packet of stolen land-grant titles from a fellow named Jim Jackson."

"Snake!" Isobel's eyes darted to Don Guillermo.

"A couple of years back," Noah explained, "Snake Jackson went to Jimmie Dolan and told him he had the Matas family's Spanish land-grant titles. Dolan took the matter to his pal Catron in Santa Fe. Catron then approached the Pascals to see if things could be turned under the table in a way that everyone could benefit. Don Guillermo could lay his hands on the land without having to get hitched to a spinster—seeing as he's always been known to enjoy the plentiful company of loose women. And then Catron, Dolan, and Snake could each take their share of the profits."

"But I appeared in New Mexico to upset your plans," Isobel

spoke up, confronting Guillermo. "And then you decided you liked me well enough after all."

Noah grunted in agreement. "He realized he could up and marry you to get the titles. That would cut Catron, Dolan, and Snake out of the picture. And with Pascal's connections with other members of the ring, he soon figured out he wouldn't have much trouble doing just that. Didn't you, Señor Pascal?"

"The ring?" Doña Maria's voice sounded shrill across the garden. "Of what do you speak here?"

"Never mind, *mamá*." Don Guillermo held out a hand to stop his mother from approaching. "It is merely business between Señor Buchanan and myself."

But the old woman bustled forward, her embroidery bag in one hand and a stack of newspapers under her other arm. She elbowed past her son until she was staring up at Noah. "Speak frankly, señor. Tell me what you know about this ring of which I have been hearing rumors."

Noah peered at the little woman for a moment, but knew her short stature did not diminish her role as matriarch and ultimate power in the Pascal family.

"Your son is a member of the Santa Fe Ring, Doña Maria," Noah said. "He's in league with Governor Axtell, Tom Catron, and the rest of the scalawags who are trying to own New Mexico. You know Guillermo has nearly doubled the Pascal family land holdings since your husband's death. That ought to give you a clue that he's in with the ring. Nobody gets land in the territory that easily anymore. A person has to have connections."

Isobel stared at Guillermo as she recalled his words to her only minutes before. He had connections, he had avowed, winking slyly.

The doña's plump face had suffused a bright red, and her eyes narrowed. "You accuse my son of such evil, *vaquero*?"

"This man is a liar, *mamá*," Guillermo interjected. "Not one word from his mouth is the truth. Why, the fool even claims to have married Señorita Matas!"

Doña Maria turned to Isobel. "Who is this man?"

Glancing at Guillermo, Isobel realized the deep significance of the next move she made. She could deny everything Noah said. If she did, she could marry Don Guillermo. She

could have her hacienda, horses, gardens, *fiestas*. Her children
would be of pure Spanish blood.

Then she turned and looked into the cowboy's blue eyes.

"Noah Buchanan speaks the truth," she whispered. "The
vaquero is my husband. For my protection from the villains in
Lincoln County, we were wed in haste by a traveling priest.
Later I came to your hacienda in good faith, planning to marry
Don Guillermo and put my confused past behind me. But now
I see your son for the man he really is, Doña Maria. I told him
this morning I wanted to return to Spain. I must go now."

"But the wedding? And grandchildren! And what about our
newspapers, Isobel?"

The young woman held the matriarch's rounded shoulders
and kissed her gently on each pudgy cheek. "You have been
good to me, Doña Maria. I thank you."

Her face alight, Isobel placed her hand in Noah's. He
swung her onto his black stallion, and they left at a gallop
from the gardens of the *familia* Pascal.

"But, Isobel—all your new dresses!" the doña cried behind
them. "And who will feed the parrot?"

Isobel turned to wave and saw the old woman clobber her
son with her embroidery bag. "*Imbécil!* The Santa Fe Ring?
What is this now? Do you ruin your father's good name . . ."

Isobel relaxed into Noah's arms and shut her eyes. It
seemed that God had chosen to smile upon her after all.

"So I just kept after Catron every day until he started to
look more closely into Dolan's finances," Noah was saying as
he and Isobel sat on a blanket beside their flickering campfire
on the silent trail to Lincoln. "The more Catron checked into
things, the more he began to put together the extent of Dolan's
financial troubles. Of course, I helped matters along by telling
Catron a lot of the stuff that McSween had confided to me
about the Dolan Mercantile from the early days when he used
to represent it."

Isobel studied Noah and tried to concentrate on what he was
telling her as she secretly reveled in their companionship.
How easily they spoke together. How natural it had seemed to
cook, wash the dinner dishes, and settle their camp. Inside her

heart the flower of determination to return to Spain and rejoin her family began to fade.

"Turns out," Noah continued, "that Tom Catron has been involved in endorsing Dolan's business notes to the tune of over twenty thousand dollars. Their connection has been in effect since last year. Our young Irish devil is deeply in debt to the district attorney. A few months back, Dolan mortgaged all his property—even his personal possessions—to Catron as security for the notes. And he got a new note for twenty-five thousand dollars. This month in Santa Fe he took out a second mortgage from the bank. Fact of the matter is, Dolan's mercantile is insolvent."

"Then the man is ruined."

"Business-wise. Catron's been trying to keep Dolan afloat. He doesn't want to be saddled with all the Irishman's debts, but the fact is Dolan has shut down the store. And I reckon the things I told Catron will do him in for good."

"What did you tell him?"

"A lot of things. Among them that Dolan's been defaulting on his deliveries of flour and beef to the Mescalero Agency."

"So what's happening in Lincoln, Noah? I can't keep it all straight." Of course, part of the reason things looked muddled to Isobel was because she hadn't been concentrating very well. As Noah talked, she had, in fact, been studying the deeply tanned skin of his throat and wondering how it would feel to slide her lips along it.

"Basically, Dolan's ruined. If he leaves Lincoln County broke and defeated, I guess I'll feel like Dick's death has been avenged. Also, Doc Scurlock took over the Regulators after Macnab was killed. That's good news. Scurlock's a decent man. The bad news is that Governor Axtell removed Copeland from the sheriff's job. He's put George Peppin in."

"But he's a Dolan man. He's the one who came looking for Billy Bonney that day at the McSweens' house."

"I know. The man's a varmint. I'm just hoping that with Dolan ruined his faction will fall apart and things will settle down in Lincoln. It's what I've been trying to accomplish all the time I was in Santa Fe."

"It seems as though you were successful."

"I nearly went and let you marry that Pascal skunk." Noah

flipped a twig into the fire. "When I saw the wedding announcement in the paper this morning, I knew I couldn't sit still. I'd already found out enough about Pascal to hook him into the ring. And I surmised he was the silent partner Catron mentioned as the one planning to take over your land grants. 'Course, I didn't know for sure till I bluffed him this morning. He sure sounded guilty to me."

"All that was a bluff?"

Noah shrugged. "A good guess."

"But why didn't you leave me there with the Pascals? What good has it done you to take me with you again, Noah?"

He dusted off his thigh and stared at the fire a full minute before answering. "I couldn't let you marry Pascal, Isobel, not knowing what kind of fellow he is. You deserve better."

"And what sort of man do I deserve, Noah Buchanan?"

"I heard you mention heading back to Spain. Maybe that's what you ought to do. You could find a decent fellow there."

"In Spain I would live my life as a spinster. With the Pascal betrothal broken, my name will be besmirched. I have no doubt Don Guillermo will see to it that the story of my hasty marriage to a *vaquero* is spread about in Catalonia. Even with the annulment you and I planned from the beginning, in Spain I'm considered too old to marry."

Noah lifted his head and studied the young woman. He couldn't imagine any man in his right mind turning her down. Not one thing about Isobel failed to move him. Her freshly brushed hair lying dark gold on her shoulders. Her smooth neck. The hint of her full bosom swelling over the edge of the dark green satin dress she wore. Long arms. Long legs.

But there was more to Isobel than a woman's succulent body.

He'd almost forgotten how easily they could talk. She made him laugh and think and create and dream and want. He desired everything about the woman. But he wasn't sure now how she felt about him. After all, he'd backed out on the settling-down plans he'd made with Chisum. He'd abandoned Isobel to the Pascals in Santa Fe. He'd given her no promises, no tender words of love, no hope for a future with him.

He didn't know that she'd want to spend her life with him. He didn't know that he would have a life to give her. If Jimmie

Dolan somehow rode out his troubles, Noah knew he couldn't let the matter go. He still felt Dick's death like a knife in his gut. No home, no wife, nothing would change that.

"Now that your *venganza* against Jimmie Dolan is complete, how will it be between you and me, Noah?" Isobel was asking, her voice soft against the rush of the river past their campsite. "Will it be as before—at home by the Rio Pecos and cooking in the kitchen? Or will you drive me away again?"

"Isobel . . ." It was more a sigh than a word. "Great stars, woman, you make things hard on a man."

"And you make things hard on a woman."

Their eyes met and held. "Darlin', what do you want?" Noah asked, his voice low. "Do you want to try to get your land titles from Snake before Pascal takes them over? Do you want to own your own spread and be the ranching queen of New Mexico? Do you want to go back to Spain and live a quiet safe life away from all the guns and killing? Or do you want to be hooked up with a dusty cowboy who can't promise you one damn thing about tomorrow?"

"I'm old enough to realize I may never live happily ever after, Noah," she whispered, "but I want to live happily today. I want to feel alive again."

"Come here, Isobel." He took her hand, drew her into his arms, and settled her on his lap. "You know I made a fine show of myself in Santa Fe. Bought some fancy duds, ate good food, slept on clean sheets every night. Every day I carved Jimmie Dolan's empire into pieces. I buried away everything that reminded me of painful stuff. You. Dick. My stories."

"Were you happy?" Isobel turned her head and studied his face as she spoke.

"Miserable. Walked around looking like a throw-out from a footsore remuda." He shook his head and chuckled. "I thought revenge was supposed to feel good. Hell, *you* sure made it look like fun."

"By now you know what kind of woman I am, Noah . . . when I want something, I cannot stop striving until I have it. It's my nature."

He slid one hand along her thigh, thinking about the way she'd told him with her eyes that she wanted him to make love to her. He hadn't touched a woman since the last time with Isobel. All his urges had seemed dead—killed along with Dick Brewer.

Sure, women had made eyes at him in Santa Fe. But every time he considered the situation, he found out that who he really wanted was Isobel. And nobody else.

Now, just holding her, he felt a rush of need stronger than he'd ever known. It centered in his body in a physical way that told him he could satisfy Isobel. But the need ran deeper than that. Something inside his soul longed to connect with hers. A spiritual ache had resurfaced the moment he saw her that morning standing in the garden in Santa Fe.

He ran his hands up her bare arms and over her shoulders. She nestled into him, her head rolled back on his arm and her body limp against his. Splaying his fingers over her ripe flesh, he stroked her bosom above the green dress bodice.

"Noah," she murmured, her lips damp with desire, "I couldn't let Guillermo Pascal come near me. It was impossible for me to think of any man but you."

He ran one finger down inside the front of her dress and caressed the warm skin between her breasts. "The minute I saw your name on that wedding announcement, I starting throwing things into my saddlebags. Didn't even give it a second thought. Just hopped on my horse and headed out to fetch you. I had to have you with me again."

"Oh, Noah . . . I don't know how it can be that I once thought of you as just a common man. Now . . . and each day that I was without you . . . Noah, I ached for you . . ."

"Darling Isobel," he whispered, kissing her lips, sliding his hand up her throat, slipping his fingers into her hair. "I missed you like crazy."

He drew the straps from her dress and ran featherlight fingertips over her skin while his lips sought hers. Their tongues danced as their passion grew, until Isobel heard herself moan with the intensity of the hunger inside her. Noah had caught her breasts in his palms and was stroking their tips, rolling each nipple between thumb and forefinger. At his touch she throbbed with instant, burning desire for him.

"Will you let me touch you this time, Noah?" she begged.

In answer he stretched across their blanket and allowed her

to fondle the hardness she had provoked beneath his denims. As she worked apart the brass buttons, she felt him shudder with pleasure and need.

He gathered her skirt around her hips and began to ply the tender skin of her inner thighs. Then his fingers slipped beneath the strings that held her undergarments at her waist. Drawing away the filmy cotton lingerie, he sought the moist depths of her aching body.

"Noah," she pleaded, "oh, Noah."

He covered her flushed nipples with his mouth as he urged apart her thighs. Slowly, slowly he licked her flesh in tingling circles. His body positioned over her, he eased into her sweet tenderness. She arched with pleasure, her eyes heavy-lidded and her hands hot along his bare back.

Rising and falling against him, Isobel opened her eyes and gazed into the face of the man she loved. This was the union, the bonding, the oneness she needed. Shivering, she lifted onto her elbows and rubbed the tips of her breasts into his chest. She spread her legs, curled her feet around his thighs and lifted into him, needing the utter pleasure of the stroking of his shaft against her velvet.

"Isobel . . . oh, sweetness." He'd never known such pure ecstasy. Her whole body had come alive against his. Her golden hair tangled in his fingers as he sought to translate his own passion to her.

Mouths meeting, kissing, sucking, nipping, they rolled across the ground. Now she rose above him, her breasts outlined in the blue moonlight. He caught her waist, then slid his hands around her until his knuckles had pushed her breasts high and tilted upward. He took their tips in his fingers again, stroking and teasing until she was crying his name aloud.

Then he turned her again, this time sliding his chest over her back and entering her from behind. She sighed as his hands reached around her to cup her pendulous breasts. The intensity of his body from this position was almost too much. She laid her forehead on the blanket. His palms circled her thighs, then his fingertips reached to stimulate her ecstasy.

"Noah," she moaned as his hands made swirls over her tiny moist pinnacle.

She could feel him swell inside her as she neared her own

moment. Clutching the blanket in her fists, she wriggled her hips against his thighs. He let out a groan of release just at the moment she slid over her own apex. Together they danced, writhing with the mutual joys of sweet surrender.

Then Isobel collapsed onto the blanket, and Noah tumbled beside her. He gathered her in his arms, unable to believe the sheer fullness inside him. "I'll stay with you, darlin'," he murmured in her ear. "Come hell or high water, sweetheart, you're mine."

Chapter
❧ 18 ❧

Isobel and Noah took a languid two weeks to make the journey from Santa Fe to Lincoln. It was neither the threat of Indians nor fear of outlaws that slowed them, but simply the pure pleasure of the New Mexico summer.

While picnicking by a stream, Noah would start combing Isobel's hair through his fingers. Then she would lie back on the blanket and begin to unbutton his shirt. Before long the trip was forgotten, and evening shadows had crept over the trail.

Noah's desire to write came back in a flood, and it was all he could do to keep it under control. Once they camped on the green, grassy slopes of a mountain where he spent two solid days roughing out an idea on a pad of paper he had tucked into his saddlebag. This idea had nothing at all to do with revenge against Jimmie Dolan. It was, rather, the tale of a cattleman on the western trail.

Noah felt he'd done well with his story, which included a young orphan boy, a wily rattlesnake, marauding Apache, and all sorts of twists and turns. When Noah read it to Isobel, she declared it was even better than his Coyote Canyon story.

They spent their final night on the trail in the little town of

White Oaks. The following morning Noah saddled up for the ride to Lincoln while Isobel purchased supplies at the local mercantile. She had hoped to learn news of Lincoln from the shopkeeper, but her words froze when she saw Noah run into the store, his pistol drawn.

"Isobel!" he called. His face wore a look of anger and dismay. "He's here, damn it! Come on."

Grabbing her arm, he followed the storekeeper's pointed finger toward the back door—evidently a common escape route. Isobel ran, too out of breath to ask questions. Noah practically hurled her onto the saddle of the horse they had bought in Las Vegas. He leapt on his own stallion and put his spurs into its flanks.

"It's Dolan," he called over his shoulder, his blue eyes bright. "He's come back to Lincoln County from Santa Fe. And he's brought the Kinney Gang with him."

Isobel strained to see around the corner of the hotel as they galloped past, but Noah kept the horses headed for the woods. When they had splashed across a stream and were safely into the thick woods, Noah pulled his horse to a halt.

"It's Kinney," he said, breathing hard. "Damn it all—Dolan's got Kinney."

"Who's Kinney?"

"John Kinney. He's a ruffian, a cattle thief, a murdering outlaw, and a robber. Hangs out around Doña Ana County and El Paso. Likes to haunt the Rio Grande valley. Kinney's ten times worse than Jesse Evans or Snake Jackson ever thought about being. It looks like Dolan's hired him and his gang to do his dirty work now."

Isobel felt the color drain from her face. Did this mean that Noah's revenge for Dick Brewer's death had failed? Did it mean that once again the cowboy would put her aside and return to his single-minded pursuit of vengeance?

"Let's go back to Santa Fe, Noah," she begged, her love for him stronger than her fear. "Let's stay away from the trouble."

He took off his hat and wiped his sleeve across his brow. "I have to warn McSween and Chisum about Kinney. With Peppin as the sheriff of Lincoln, Dolan back in town, and the Kinney bunch roaming the place, things look bad for the Regulators." He sat for a minute, then slapped his hat against his thigh. "Damn this mess!"

Isobel's shoulders drooped as she felt her dreams begin to sift away once again. Noah was staring up through the trees at a patch of sky, as if God were going to give him an answer to the dilemma.

Finally he stuffed his hat on his head and turned to her. "I'll take you to Chisum's ranch. It's the safest place I know."

"You won't have time to warn McSween if you ride with me all the way to South Spring. Noah, I'll go with you—"

"No! I'm not going to lose you, Isobel. Not again."

"You may lose me if you don't take me with you. Don't force us apart again. Please, Noah."

He could tell by the spark in her hazel eyes that she meant what she'd said. Besides, the truth was, he didn't want to leave her alone at Chisum's. He knew his boss had been planning to head for St. Louis during June to treat an old leg injury that had bothered him for years. With Chisum away, the guard at the house would be down.

Maybe Isobel would be safest at Noah's side—even if that meant riding into the thick of the Kinney Gang.

"All right," he said. "We'll head for Lincoln together. But, darlin', I'm afraid things are shot to hell again."

"Everything is going to be all right. We're together, aren't we, Noah?" she said, breaking into that smile that warmed his racing heart.

Riding at breakneck speed, Noah and Isobel barely beat Jimmie Dolan and John Kinney from White Oaks to Lincoln. They just had time to warn Alexander McSween and the Regulators of the outlaws' imminent arrival. Most of the Regulators had gathered at the McSweens' house, where they had been living for almost a month. Noah realized they had been enjoying a relative amount of peace. But any serenity in Lincoln shattered with the thunder of horses' hooves.

The Regulators rode out of town as if the Devil himself was after them. The Kinney Gang rode in, hellbent on murder. Noah watched the comings and goings from behind the curtains that covered the windows at the front of John Tunstall's store. Isobel had insisted on a quick check on Susan Gates, who was living with the Ealy family in a couple of rooms at the back of the store.

Though Noah had the definite instinct that he and Isobel ought to hightail it out of town with the rest of the Regulators, Dr. Ealy wouldn't hear of it. The missionary wanted to keep Isobel under his wing—said Susan had been morose without her—and then he launched into a list of the things that he and God had accomplished in Lincoln during the peace since Dolan had been away.

Noah grunted with anger as he watched John Kinney riding up and down the single street in town, as if to say, "Look folks, I'm here and I'm in charge."

For all Taylor Ealy's good intentions, Noah knew Sunday school, church, and prayer meetings didn't mean a damn thing to an outlaw like Kinney. Even though the good people of Lincoln may have set their sights on holy ground, once John Kinney took to shooting them up, they'd have to respond in kind.

A hand on Noah's arm drew his attention away from the window and his dark musings. Isobel leaned against his shoulder to kiss his cheek. "Susan tells me she's better these days," she whispered. "She has started teaching school to the children of Lincoln. That seems to have taken her mind from Dick Brewer."

"I'm glad, darlin'." Noah gave her a little squeeze. Maybe Susan had recovered from the death of her fiancé, but Noah knew it would take him a lifetime to get over the loss of the man who had been his closest companion for so many years.

"Dr. Ealy wants me to stay here, Noah," Isobel was saying, "but I don't think it's wise. I want to be with you."

"Let's ride for Chisum's. Some of the Regulators told me they'd be heading there to hide out. The rest of them went to San Patricio. If we ride fast, we may be able to catch up with the Chisum bunch."

Once they had agreed on a plan, it took only moments for Isobel to bid farewell to her red-haired friend and the missionary family. Then she and Noah slipped out the back door to the hitching post in the corral where their horses had been tethered.

"Listen," Noah warned, "Kinney and his men are roaming

all over this town, Isobel. I want you to ride close to me. We'll make for the woods and stay under cover until we're clear."

She nodded, her heart already thundering with the thought of impending danger. Urging her horse, she followed Noah through the gate on the eastern end of the corral. The gate led straight onto the street, but Noah cut his stallion at once to the side and rode down the slope toward the Rio Bonito. Isobel was trailing not five paces behind when she heard a cry ring out behind her.

"It's Buchanan!" someone shouted from the street. "After him! He's a Chisum man!"

Noah whipped his pistol from his holster. "They've spotted us, Isobel. Ride around me!"

She spurred her horse forward while Noah covered them with his gun. Behind her she could already hear horses crashing through the underbrush. Her gelding charged into the river. Water sprayed around her head in bright silver spangles. Holding the reins with one hand, she pulled her pistol from the holster tied to her leg. Branches raked her arms. A bullet smashed into a tree trunk just ahead of her. Splinters flew into her hair.

"Ride, Isobel, ride!" Noah was shouting behind her as he fired at their pursuers.

She lowered her head to the horse's neck. On the hill above the stream the Huff house and the *torreón* flew past. Then the Baca house and corral. "I'm making for the hills, Noah!" she cried. "Follow me."

Her horse galloped out of the streambed and began the climb toward the foothills. She glanced behind to see Noah riding just a few yards ahead of the outlaws. At their head rode a hulk of a man . . . a man with a huge lantern jaw and slitted yellow eyes.

Snake Jackson.

Muffling the scream that rose in her throat, Isobel watched the outlaw gang break into two parties. "Rattlesnake, you and your men stay with these two!" the black-haired John Kinney shouted. "We'll ride south for San Patricio and round up the rest of the bastards!"

"Keep going, keep going!" Noah flew past Isobel and gave her horse's flank a slap. "Snake's after you."

At that moment all the fear, anger, and outrage inside Isobel's heart broke loose. She buried her head against the horse's neck and rode for her life. With each yard of ground they covered, she saw her father's face, his golden hair, his beautiful hazel eyes. She saw John Tunstall in his dapper tweeds. She saw blue-eyed Dick Brewer, curly hair tossing in the breeze. And she saw Snake Jackson's evil face. She heard his mocking cries. His hoots of derision. His jeering laughter.

A bullet splatted into the dirt alongside her. She swung around. Noah was returning Snake's fire, his arm stretched out behind him and his six-shooter blazing.

Chisum's ranch was three days away, Isobel realized, reason making inroads into her panic. How could she and Noah possibly hold off Snake Jackson and his men for three days? Darkness was hours away. Their horses couldn't keep up this pace much longer. In a moment Noah would be forced to reload.

She scanned the hills for some kind of cover. Nothing but piñons, cedars, and junipers. The horses crashed through evergreen branches, scenting the air with the sweet smell of their sap. But Isobel's nostrils were filled with fear. She was about to die like a dog at Snake Jackson's hand—just as her father had died—all because she had grown weak and relaxed. In her besotted love for Noah Buchanan, she had forgotten her true goal. Now she would pay for her failure with her life!

Gritting her teeth, she whirled around and fired three shots at Snake. The bullets whanged into tree trunks and rocks. Snake lifted his head and whooped. "Missed me, señorita!" he shouted. "But I'm gonna git you!"

"Damn it, Isobel," Noah hollered, flying past her once again. "Stay in front. Let me do the shooting!"

She lowered her head and surged past the cowboy. This time her mind had regained its focus. She berated herself for having grown lazy. Sentimental. She and Noah had dallied on the road from Santa Fe. Then she had waylaid them to comfort Susan Gates. Now they would both suffer for her weaknesses—unless she could will herself into action.

Her horse pounded around a bend, hooves kicking up dirt and old pine needles. The mount, used to long rides on the trail and not racing from outlaws, had begun to slow. Noah rode against her again and slapped the horse's flank. Blue fire shone in his eyes.

"Find cover!" he called. "Your horse is going down."

She rode around the base of a second hill. This time she spotted a stone outcrop halfway up. Pointing so that Noah could see without giving them away, she led the two horses through the trees toward her objective.

Head low, she maneuvered toward the crag. Wheezing, foam dripping from its mouth, her horse had slowed to a trot. Fear acrid on her tongue, Isobel slid from the mount and began to run the few paces toward safety. She clambered over a boulder and slid across a shelf of pebbles.

At that moment a burning pain tore through her shoulder, shattering flesh and bone. She tumbled behind the rock.

"Isobel!" Noah's whispered voice drew her out of the momentary blackness.

She opened her eyes, only to feel the searing pain in her right shoulder once again. Reaching, she clutched at the wound. A warm damp liquid seeped onto her fingers.

"Snake winged you." Noah was peering between two boulders as he spoke. "They're coming this way. I need your help, darlin'. Please try."

She attempted to sit up, but her stomach turned and bile rose in her throat. "Noah," she groaned.

"Can you load this, Isobel?" he asked, tossing a six-shooter into her lap. "Just try to stay with me on this. If I can turn Snake and his men back, I'll have time to fix your shoulder. But if we can't keep them off—"

A bullet sprayed them with rock fragments. Isobel clenched her jaw and flipped open the six-shooter's chamber. Breathing heavily, she pried the cartridges from their loops on Noah's cast-off gunbelt. Then she slid the bullets into their slots and clicked the gun shut.

Noah grabbed it and tossed a second, empty six-shooter into her lap. The hot metal burned through the thin fabric of her clothes, but she lifted the gun and began to reload.

Things blurred after that. Bullets slammed into the stone around their heads. Cries rang out through the hills. Horses galloped past. Noah's two six-shooters, his rifle, and her own small pistol alternately blasted, then fell into her lap for reloading. Pain fogged her mind. Blood soaked through her sleeve and trickled onto her fingers. Dark clouds lowered, then rose briefly, then lowered again.

Now and then Noah's eyes peered into her face, his eyes turning dark blue with fear and worry. "Isobel, darlin', hold on for me," she heard him whisper. "Don't give up on me now, sweetheart."

Then the sound of firing stopped. Smoke cleared. The acrid smell of gunpowder lifted. Warm arms came around her. She was stretched onto the ground, her head resting in a pile of soft pine needles. Above, she saw the sky—streaks of orange, blue, purple. Noah's face appeared amid the colors.

"Rest now, darlin'," he murmured. "Snake's gone, and I'm going to patch you up."

She heard her sleeve tear, but her arm had gone numb. She shut her eyes.

"Okay, now." The voice drifted in and out. "Dear Lord, the bullet's still in here. Damn." The words filtered through the fog. "There's barely enough light to see . . . but Isobel . . . Isobel, darlin' . . . I've got to take this bullet out . . . Hold on, precious woman."

The searing pain of a knife sliding into her shoulder cut through the fog and brought her sharply awake. A scream rose in her throat. Then it faded away as swiftly as did the pain, the knife, the bullet, and the murmured words. Blackness swam up and blocked the agony.

Isobel opened her eyes to find Noah seated on top of the rock outcrop. Legs bent, he rested one arm on each cocked knee. He had lifted his head to the heavens, but his eyes were shut. His lips moved silently. Brilliant blue sky framed his profile, the straight nose and square jawline, the sweep of dark hair, the felt Stetson.

Shifting a little, Isobel tried to ease the throbbing pain in her shoulder. Noah heard the movement and glanced down into the sheltering cove among the rocks.

"Isobel?" He scrambled from his perch and crouched beside her. "Isobel, darlin', are you awake?"

She tried to speak, but no words came out. Her mouth and

throat felt as parched and scratchy as desert sands. Noah bent over her and smoothed the hair from her forehead.

"I got the bullet out," he whispered. For a moment he dug around in his shirt pocket. Then he held up a flattened piece of lead. "Take a look at that, would you?"

She tried to grin, but her lips had stuck to her teeth. The pain in her shoulder pounded unbearably. She tried to shift again. Noah leaned across her and adjusted the wool blanket he had folded to form a pillow beneath her head.

"You've lost a hell of a lot of blood, darlin'. Now that you've come to, I need to get you back to Lincoln."

"No!" she croaked. Snake and Kinney would find her and Noah there in an instant. She wanted to go someplace safe—someplace where she could be with Noah and forget all about the past.

"Doc Ealy is the only one around these parts who can patch you up right. Looks to me like you need sewing. And you've got to have some medicine to keep infection away. I've seen gangrene, Isobel, and I'm not going to let that happen to—"

"No!" She grabbed his arm with her good hand. "Not Lincoln."

"Well, we can't stay here. My guess is Snake'll be back. And soon. I've got to get you out of here."

"Chisum's," she whispered. "Please, Noah."

"That's a three-day ride for a fit horse and a healthy rider. I don't imagine you can even sit up straight, and you've been in and out of consciousness all night. There's no way—"

But the thought of being that close to the little adobe house drove Isobel to struggle up from the pallet. Blood siphoned from her face, but she forced herself to throw the blanket back from her knees.

"All right," Noah said, grabbing her shoulders before she swooned. "I always knew you were mule-headed, Isobel, and I can see you mean business. Come on, you'll ride with me."

He tethered her gelding behind his horse and then settled Isobel in his arms. For all its strength the black stallion moved slowly under the burden of its double load. Noah kept to the brushland, away from the river's edge for fear of ambush. They stopped often to drink water, rest, or mop the blood from Isobel's shoulder. More often than not, she rode in a semiconscious fog, her head lolling on Noah's chest and her legs dangling against the stallion's side.

Noah regularly checked her forehead for fever. In the midst of her daze she could hear him muttering curses against Jimmie Dolan and Snake Jackson. In between the curses she heard the whispered refrains of hymns.

Once she heard Noah praying out loud, a fervent plea. He spoke in that conversational tone she had heard him use before—not as though God were some unreachable omniscient deity, but as if God were a father with whom a man could talk about his deepest needs.

Somewhere in the feverish mists, she remembered the wedding ceremony the itinerant priest had performed in the Lincoln County forest. She recalled her later fears that God would punish her for such a hasty, selfish union. Perhaps this was God's chastisement—her wounded shoulder, her terrible fears, her deep yet hopeless love for Noah Buchanan.

Yet as she pondered the nature of a God who would wreak vengeance on his wayward flock, she heard Noah's voice lifted in song—"God is love; his mercy brightens all the path in which we rove; Bliss he wakes and woe he lightens: God is wisdom, God is love."

Several times each day Noah bathed Isobel's shoulder and changed the dressing. She found that she could not move her arm at all. The slightest jolt sent a searing pain through her that nearly made her scream out loud. Noah had fashioned a sling to hold her arm close against her body. When she tried to eat, she could keep little of the food down. Only water from the Rio Hondo kept her feverish body functioning.

Each night Noah bedded Isobel beside him, holding her close beneath the blankets. Their journey had taken many more than three days already, but they could move no faster. Accepting that, she nestled against him, her mind wandering from memories of her father to memories of the estate in Catalonia to memories of sweet lovemaking. Her thoughts drifted over hanging lace curtains, typing pages of a story, galloping along mountain trails, baking *bizcochitos*, washing dishes.

Through these memories wove a deep baritone voice, "E'en the hour that darkest seemeth, will his changeless goodness prove; Thro' the gloom his brightness streameth: God is wisdom, God is love."

They had been on the trail almost a week, and June was nearly gone when Noah's horse trotted the last few yards down the road to Chisum's house. The scent of blooming roses suffused the air with a heady perfume. Apple trees glowed a light green among the orchards. In the corrals, horses pranced and fed on sweet alfalfa.

Noah's spirits lifted in spite of his fears for Isobel. He'd done a lot of thinking on the trail, but his thoughts always came around to notions he was afraid she would object to. About the only words she'd said during the entire trip had to do with how much she wanted Noah to stay with her, never leave her, always be near.

As hard as it was for him to acknowledge to himself, Noah now knew without a doubt that he loved Isobel Matas Buchanan. In the frozen instant he'd watched her tumble behind that pile of rocks, his heart had nearly stopped. When he'd made it to her side and had seen her life's blood pumping out of that shoulder wound, a red rage had filled him. The thought that he was going to lose her had been all it took to convince Noah that he loved her.

If Dick Brewer meant a lot to him as a pal and confidant, Isobel meant one hell of a lot more. She was his friend, supporter, companion, lover. They could laugh together, talk about anything, even cry together. He'd shared his dreams with her, his writing, his ambitions and hopes. And she'd shared hers with him. The thought of losing her was more than he could handle.

Trouble was, Noah knew this business with Snake Jackson could go on and on unless somebody stopped the evil reptile. With Jimmie Dolan and now John Kinney fueling his fires, Snake wasn't about to tone down. All three needed a dose of strong medicine. Lead poisoning would do the trick, and Noah knew just the man to deliver it.

"I want you to know I'm thinking about going to Lincoln after I settle you here," he whispered into Isobel's ear as they rode the final paces to the hitching post along the front of the Chisum house. "No—don't get your feathers ruffled about it,

Isobel. When I see that you're in good hands, I'm going to take off after Snake and Dolan."

"Noah!" Her hazel eyes were filled with terror. "Noah, they almost killed me. Please don't go."

"I'm going *because* they almost killed you." He cupped her chin and turned her face to his. "Listen here, Isobel, the only way to stop killin' is to kill. You were right about that. All my big words about being strong enough to stay out of the trouble were like spittin' in the wind."

"Noah—I can't lose you. Not again." But her words fell on deaf ears. Noah was already handing her down to the waiting arms of Mrs. Towry and the others who had rushed to meet the riders. She saw the faces of several of the Regulators slide before her eyes. Then she was bundled into a cool room, tucked into bed with a damp cloth on her forehead, and abandoned.

"Noah!" she croaked. "Noah, please!"

But her voice only echoed off the bare walls.

Chapter
❧ 19 ❧

Noah sat at Isobel's bedside for another three days. She was still groggy and exhausted from the ride. But her pain had lessened, and the shoulder wound seemed to be healing with no infection.

Mrs. Towry proved herself a marvel, tending Isobel like a mother hen. Tongue clucking, she bustled back and forth fetching ointments from John Chisum's medicine box, chicken soup, fresh bandages, and cool, sweet lemonade. Finally Isobel was able to sit up on her own. Shortly afterward, she began to walk about the room while leaning on Mrs. Towry's arm.

One morning after breakfast Noah settled on a wooden chair by Isobel's bed. In his large hands his Stetson hung between his knees. His blue eyes twinkled.

"Today's the Fourth of July," he said. "Know what that means?"

"The Independence Day of the United States." She smiled, aware of the patriotism Noah must feel, despite the fact that New Mexico was a territory rather than a state.

"When I lived in Texas, Mrs. Allison used to fix up a big picnic for everybody. Feel up to a picnic today, Isobel? Me and some of the other Regulators thought we'd ride over to the Pecos and relax a little."

"How many men?"

"There're twelve Regulators here, not counting you and me. Some would have to stay here to keep an eye on the place. Sheriff Peppin has mustered a posse of fifteen men—mostly the Seven Rivers Gang—under the command of a couple of deputies named Marion Turner and Buck Powell. A real pair of rascals. The posse's stationed at Roswell."

"That's close by!"

"Aw, the Regulators have been riding back and forth between the Pecos and the ranch house without any trouble from the posse. And since this is a holiday, I just thought it might be fun to get you out of the house. 'Course, the cook's fixing a feast for dinner here at the house, so there's that to look forward to. But if you wanted to take in some fresh air, you could ride in the buckboard. Think you're up to going?"

The thought of a day in the crisp mountain breeze and sweet yellow sunshine brought a light to Isobel's eyes. If she were to ride in the buckboard, she could wear a dress. Just the idea of putting on her corset and petticoats, brushing her hair into artful waves, setting her feet in a pair of slippers instead of heavy leather boots—"I'd love it!" she exclaimed.

He bent over the bed and kissed her cheek. "I'll give you half an hour. Mrs. Towry's putting a basket of grub together. She thinks she might want to come along with—"

"Noah!" Billy Bonney knocked open the bedroom door and charged into the room. "Noah—hit the rooftop! It's Buck Powell and the Seven Rivers Gang."

"Buck Powell?" Billy's words took a moment to sink into Noah's brain. He'd so expected to spend the day relaxing with Isobel that he couldn't fit his image with the reality of gunfire.

"Me and the Coe boys was ridin' back from Ash Upson's store this mornin'." Billy brandished his six-shooter as he spoke. "Twelve of the gang jumped us! It was a runnin' gun battle all the way back to the house. And now they're takin' potshots at the boys on the roof. You gotta get up there and get to shootin' afore somebody gets killed!"

Noah glanced at Isobel, but he didn't like the look of wariness in her eyes. Before she could say anything to try to hold him back, he stuffed his hat on his head and drew his gun.

"Stay away from the windows, Isobel!" he shouted as he and Billy bolted out of the bedroom. "And don't go looking for trouble!"

Isobel watched the door slam shut and heard the boots pounding down the hall. "I found trouble when I married you," she murmured, settling back against her pillows. "And you found it when you married me."

The shooting went on all day and most of the night. The picnic was abandoned, of course, though somehow the big holiday feast got on the table as planned. The Regulators took turns coming down from the parapet roof to grab a bite of dinner before heading back upstairs.

It was clear to Isobel that the men felt supremely confident in their position. With Chisum's fortifications and their large supply of ammunition, they were having no trouble holding off Buck Powell and his men. Isobel and Mrs. Towry spent the night in the central courtyard of the house. If not for the occasional burst of gunfire, it would have seemed idyllic.

The roses in full bloom scented the air. The beds dragged out onto the patio remained outfitted with down comforters, pillows, bolsters, shams, embroidered sheets, and every necessity. But the two women sat up most of the night, wondering aloud how the battle was proceeding and worrying about the men.

At dawn the following day Noah found Isobel sleeping fitfully, her blankets tossed from her bare legs. He smoothed the covers into place and woke her with a gentle hand on the shoulder.

"Buck Powell and the others have gone," he said when she had rolled over and opened her eyes to find the two of them alone in the courtyard. "We think they've gone to Lincoln for reinforcements."

She took his hand. "Has anyone been hurt, Noah?"

"Not a soul. We've had the upper hand the whole time." He gave her the hint of a smile, then his face grew solemn. "Listen, I've been talking with the others, Isobel. The Regulators. Everyone agrees there's no chance to end this without all-out war on the man who's behind all this mess in Lincoln County. Jimmie Dolan."

"War?" Isobel moistened her lips.

"Revenge, darlin'. It's the only way to settle things. Dolan is responsible for too many deaths. He ordered John Tunstall murdered. He was behind Buckshot Roberts' bounty hunting, and that makes him a party to Dick's killing. He got Copeland thrown out as sheriff and Peppin put in. We're sure he sent the Seven Rivers Gang here to Chisum's to hunt Regulators. In a roundabout way Dolan's even responsible for the deaths of Sheriff Brady, Deputy Hindman, Morton, Baker, and McCloskey."

"Billy the Kid and the Regulators shot Brady and those others, Noah. You know that."

"But they wouldn't have felt the need to shoot if Dolan hadn't threatened to get Sheriff Brady to throw McSween in jail and then drown him. As for Morton, Baker, and McCloskey—they were part of the renegade posse that shot down Tunstall in the first place. Any way you look at it, Isobel, Dolan's got to be put away."

In silence she gazed at the embroidered coverlet, pink-lit with the sunrise. She ran one finger over a red rose entwined with green leaves.

"And then there's *you*," Noah added before she had a chance to speak. "Snake Jackson is not going to rest until he kills you, Isobel. That's the upshot of it. What's he got to lose by pulling your picket pin? Nothing. What's he got to gain— the land titles, the money from Pascal and Catron, peace of mind, and one less 'Mexican'—"

"I'm Spanish."

"Isobel!" Noah clenched her hand tightly. "Hear what I'm saying. Your life is in danger, woman. Now, the Regulators are riding to Lincoln this morning. A couple of the boys will head down to San Patricio and round up the rest of the group. Everyone's going to meet at McSween's house and decide how to finish this business. Isobel . . . I'm going with them."

"What's happened to you, Noah? What has become of the man with the gentle hands and the soft eyes who lifted me away from the path of a bullet? Where is the man who would rather leave a fight to others than shoot down an enemy?"

"That man is long gone."

"Oh, Noah . . ."

"Look—I've been around a few years, but I didn't learn what was what until I met you. Crazy as it may seem, the fact of the matter is, Isobel Buchanan . . . I love you." His eyes locked with hers as he laced their fingers together, squeezing so hard he nearly stopped the blood. "I'm not going to let Jimmie Dolan or Snake Jackson or anybody else hurt you. Not ever again. What I realize now is that the only way to fight fire is with fire. Gunfire."

"Noah, please—"

"What's happened to my spitfire? When I met you, Isobel, you believed in revenge. Fighting. Bloodshed. I keep thinking if I'd supported you, instead of trying to stop you, Snake Jackson might be dead right now—instead of you with your arm half shot off. You were right. It's time for revenge."

He stood suddenly, knocking back the wooden chair. She tried to read his face, but he brushed a hand over his eyes and then settled his hat on his head.

"So, I'm going." He shoved his hands in his pockets. "Heal up, now, Isobel, you hear?"

He started across the patio, but she called his name. When he turned, she saw that his face was grim.

"I love you, too, Noah," she whispered.

From her bed Isobel heard the drumroll of horses' hooves as the Regulators set off for Lincoln Town. She slid aside the embroidered coverlet and eased herself to the floor. In the week since the shooting, her arm had grown stronger, and she was able to move it a little more comfortably now. She seemed to have recovered from the loss of so much blood, and she was able to make her way into her bedroom and walk to the window with no assistance.

As she gazed outside, she saw only the light cloud of brown dust along the road as it spread in a line under the blue sky. She opened the window and leaned out, breathing in the sweet fragrance of roses in full bloom. But the poignant scent brought her no happiness. Instead she felt an overwhelming loss, a certainty that what she had known and loved of life was about to end.

Mrs. Towry shuffled past the window, a basketful of roses on her arm and a pair of garden shears in one hand. Seeing Isobel, she waved and approached. "Shootin's over. It's safe to move around. Feelin' better today, Mrs. Buchanan?"

Isobel tried to smile. "I'd like to walk with you in the garden."

"You sure you're up to it? You still look mighty pale."

For a moment Isobel studied the whitewashed adobe bricks surrounding the window. Then she lifted her head. "Noah went with the others, didn't he?"

Mrs. Towry's face grew solemn as she nodded. "Such high talkin' those boys was doin' in the front room this morning. Great stars, I wish Mr. Chisum was here to preach some sense into the fellers. They think they're gonna be heros or somethin'. Shootin' up Lincoln and killin' all their enemies. What next?"

She paused for a moment before continuing. "Yes, Noah went with 'em, Mrs. Buchanan. Good thing, too, to my way of thinkin'. Noah's the most levelheaded of the bunch. They ought to have made him leader of the Regulators. Not that Doc Scurlock is a bad feller, but Noah Buchanan's got horse sense. The minute I met that man, I knew he had his head on straight. In fact, he reminds me a lot of Mr. Chisum himself—smart, peaceable, strong, and brave. I sure do wish Mr. Chisum would get back from St. Louis right about now. . . . Well, honey, come on out to the garden, and let's walk."

Isobel left the window and went behind the bamboo screen to change out of her nightgown. But as she slipped the white garment over her head, she felt none of its warmth. Inside her heart she knew only a chill, only the icy heaviness of dread.

"Mrs. Buchanan! Mrs. Buchanan! Look here what come in the mail from Lincoln! I bet it's from your husband."

Mrs. Towry had made it only halfway across the portal when Isobel ran to grab the letter from her hand. A week had passed since the Regulators' departure—an eternity of silence. After tearing open the envelope, Isobel spread the crisp white sheet of paper.

" 'Dear Mr. Buchanan,' " she read aloud. " 'It is my great pleasure to inform you that your novelette, "Sunset at Coyote

Canyon," has been accepted for publication in our monthly magazine, *Wild West*. The novelette will run in ten installments, one each month beginning this December. Congratulations. Enclosed please find a check for the sum of fifty dollars. *Wild West* would like to see more of your fine writing, Mr. Buchanan. Sincerely, Josiah Woodstone, Editor.' "

Isobel lifted her head and stared at Mrs. Towry. The older woman frowned as she took the envelope. "This ain't from Mr. Buchanan," she said. "It's *to* him from somebody in New York. The post office at Lincoln must have got the letter and sent it out here to the ranch."

"Noah's story," Isobel whispered. "It's going to be published."

"Mr. Buchanan writ a story?" Mrs. Towry started to laugh, but seeing the look on Isobel's face, she caught herself. "Ain't what I expected of a rough and rugged cowboy like him, but there's fifty dollars to prove it's true. That ought to go a good way toward payin' off the land he bought from Mr. Chisum."

Isobel turned without hearing. Noah's story would be published. His dream would come true. But where was Noah now—this man with a gift so few possessed? He was probably riding into Lincoln Town this very moment, and chances were good that someone would put a bullet through his gentle heart.

It was all her fault, she thought, tucking the letter into her pocket. If she hadn't been so fiery and headstrong—if she hadn't been so determined to seek out Snake Jackson—Noah would never have gotten involved in Lincoln's troubles.

When she had met him, he was on his way home to buy land and write stories. Novelettes. He was the man Mrs. Towry had described—peaceable, gentle, strong, and brave. But thanks to his untimely marriage to a Spanish spitfire, he had tossed away that mantle and assumed the one she had brought—revenge. All because of her, he was chasing down Jimmie Dolan with the bloodlust of an outlaw.

She had ruined Noah. While he had taught her the beauty of life, the sheer pleasures of simplicity, she had taught him to seek vengeance. From Noah she had learned to love lace curtains, to cook meals that would satisfy, to build a home, to plant a garden. She had learned that what she wanted most in life was not land titles and jewels. Not revenge for her father's death. Not riding and shooting and hiding from enemies.

What she wanted was love. Noah's love. She wanted their marriage and their home. She ached for his arms, his voice, his eyes, his smile. Nothing else in the world mattered.

"Mrs. Towry," she said, turning to where the housekeeper was arranging a vase of cut roses. "Mrs. Towry, I—"

"Why, Mrs. Buchanan, what's wrong? You look plumb white as a sheet. Are you gonna faint?"

"No." Isobel held the housekeeper away with one hand as she walked toward her room. "Excuse me, please."

Isobel hurried into the cool shadows of the chamber where she had spent so many endless days. She heaved her saddle-bag from the floor to the bed. Unbuckling the brass clasp, she groped around inside. Yes—her pistol. She drew the weapon into her hands and contemplated it. Then she tossed it onto the bed.

Quickly she changed from her dress into a riding outfit complete with leather boots. She transferred Noah's letter from the New York publisher into a pocket. After stuffing jackets, socks, and clean shirtwaists in the saddlebag, she re-fastened it and slung it over her good shoulder. Unarmed, she slipped out the door.

Arranging roses, Mrs. Towry hummed on the portal as Isobel hurried toward the back door that led out from the kitchen. She ran down to the corral and selected a horse that had not yet been unsaddled from a morning's ride. Tossing her bag behind the saddle, she swung her foot into the stirrup. Pain again shot through her shoulder as she hauled herself onto her mount.

"Now," she breathed as she goaded the horse's flanks, "take me to Lincoln. Please. I have to save Noah."

Though Isobel knew the trail well enough, travel was much more difficult than she had anticipated. She was alone, for one thing. That meant she had to be especially alert for signs of the Apache, Comanche, and outlaws who often roamed Lincoln County's roadways.

In addition, she had brought no food. Nor had she brought her gun. She did discover a long knife in a sheath tied to the saddle. Perhaps she could use the knife to cut fruits or dig for tubers along the river. She had eaten well at John Chisum's ranch house. But now, to preserve her strength, she spent part of each day searching out edible food. For most of the journey she survived on river water and a small supply of beef jerky she found in the pocket of Noah's jacket that she was wearing.

Perhaps it had been foolish not to bring her pistol, but Isobel felt certain that she never again wanted to see or touch such a weapon of destruction. In fact, as she rode she could only think of the words she ached to say to Noah.

I was wrong! Wrong! Revenge is not the way. Leave the hatred and the bloodshed, my love. Come home with me to the little adobe house by the river. We'll live there in peace.

Would she ever get the chance to say those words to Noah?

For the first time in her life Isobel prayed not the repetitious, stilted prayers of her childhood, but the deep and soul-wrenching prayers of her heart. She prayed as she had heard Noah pray. "Please, dear God—let Noah live. Give me the chance to atone for the error of my ways. Allow me to lead Noah away from the violence and into a life of love."

Each night she lay bundled in blankets and listened to the rush of the river. As she gazed at the stars through the piñon branches, Isobel recounted her life and its many blessings. Noah Buchanan was the greatest blessing of them all. Before it was too late, she had to convince him to leave Lincoln.

Each day while she rode along the trail, she exercised her arm. The shoulder had regained much of its strength and flexibility, but she knew all too well how easily the pain could resurface. Jerked the wrong way or lifted too high, the shoulder throbbed in agony. The scar she would bear for the rest of her life—a round patch of smooth, tender skin, a reminder of the man who had killed her father and had tried to kill her.

Isobel spent her fourth night on the trail at the spot where the Rio Hondo met the Rio Bonito. She knew Lincoln lay only a few miles to the north, but she felt too exhausted to make the final leg in the dark.

Her sleep was restless as she turned over in her mind the following day's plan. She would ride into town and find Noah. Then—no matter what it took—she must convince him to leave with her.

Early the next morning she struggled up from the blankets just as dawn was breaking over the mountains. In the pale purple light she dressed in a clean shirtwaist and brushed the dust from her boots. She dipped her comb in the river and slid it through her hair again and again. With nimble fingers she wove the damp tresses into a tight chignon. Then she set Dick Brewer's old hat on her head.

Isobel saddled and mounted the horse she had taken from John Chisum's corral. She drew out her last strip of beef jerky and began to chew. It was tough, stringy, and pungent with the taste of mesquite smoke. But the morsel of food seemed to settle her stomach. She had just popped the last bite into her mouth when she noticed a horse and rider coming toward her on the trail just ahead.

For a moment she thought the sight might be an illusion, for horse and rider blended into the half-light of morning and the shadows of the trees in such a way as to make them seem like wraiths. But as she drew closer, the rider nudged his horse forward in her direction.

Squinting, she peered ahead. She felt wary suddenly. Her pulse began to pound in her neck and temples. There was a certain familiarity to the rider. Could it be Noah? She lifted a hand in greeting. But, no—this wasn't Noah. The man removed his hat and tipped his head.

"Mornin', señorita," he said as he approached.

Isobel's breath hung in her throat. "Jim Jackson."

"Most folks call me Snake."

She glanced to the side of the trail, hoping to spot a path of escape, but Snake was already drawing his six-shooter.

"Me and some of the boys just happened to be passin' Casey's Mill yesterday," Snake said, casually taking aim at her heart, "and one of the hands mentioned seein' you on the road. Mrs. Buchanan, he told me, ridin' all alone. That's when I come to realize that I hadn't quite finished the job I started on you the other day on that hillside. Seems yer kinda like a cat, huh? Got nine lives."

"Mr. Jackson, you can see I'm unarmed," Isobel said, keeping the tremble from her voice with effort. "I'm traveling to Lincoln to find Noah Buchanan. I have no further business with you."

"No business with me? What about this here packet of papers I been carryin' around for five years? Don't you want that business, señorita?" He slapped his saddlebag and gave her a wink. "Took it off yer papa, y'know. The day I shot him dead."

Isobel clenched her jaw but said nothing. Snake had ridden close enough now that she could see his yellow eyes set deep beneath the heavy brow. Purple light shone on his lantern jaw. His malevolent grin lacked only the flicker of a forked tongue to make the resemblance to his nickname complete.

"Now, don't deny it. You been chasin' me ever since you come to Lincoln County, señorita. First you seen me do ol' Tunstall in. Then you pieced together about me blowin' yer papa to kingdom come. And you been haulin' yer pretty little butt after me—all the way to Murphy's ranch, where you tried to shoot off my pecker. And then back to Lincoln where you and your Mexican-lovin' husband tried to shoot me down."

"*You* chased *us* from Lincoln," Isobel corrected.

"Aw, well, it don't really matter now. Point is, it's time for one of us to finish the game. And I reckon it had better be me."

"I don't want to challenge you anymore, Snake. I know you killed my father and John Tunstall. Nothing I can do to you will change that. So I renounce my claim. Take my family's land titles. Take our jewels. Just let me go freely to Lincoln."

"What's this? Has the little devil lost her fire?"

"Yes, I have. I'm through fighting. I'm going to pass you in peace and go on my way."

Flicking the reins, Isobel rode toward Snake. Their horses brushed on the narrow trail. She kept her eyes from his face and tried to will away the terrible memories of blood and death that assaulted her. Don Albert Matas. John Henry Tunstall. Dick Brewer. Sheriff Brady. Deputy Hindman. Frank Baker. William Morton. William McCloskey.

"Oh, señorita." Snake grabbed her arm, nearly jerking the wounded shoulder from its socket. As he pulled her backward on the saddle, he released the safety on his six-shooter. "I'm afraid we got unfinished business."

"Let me go, Snake!" she hissed.

"You really thought I was just gonna let you ride on by me?"

"I had hoped you would be man enough to holster your gun." She stared into the slitted eyes, seeing the gold streaks that mingled with pale brown. Her mouth felt dry as she tried to keep her gaze from his weapon. "I swear I no longer have a quarrel with you, Snake. Let me go."

Smiling slowly, he raised the gun to her head and jabbed it into her temple. "Yer dumber than I thought, señorita. Ya see, I got me a lot of killin' to do to make up fer the bunch of Mexicans that murdered my parents."

"I had nothing to do with the death of your parents," she gasped as cold steel pressed against her head. Pain wrenched through her shoulder where he pinned her against him. "I tell you, I want only . . . only peace."

"Somebody's gotta pay. Might as well be you."

With his last word Snake pulled the trigger. An instant before the blast, Isobel tilted her head and sank into her saddle. The bullet blew away Dick Brewer's hat and slammed into a tree. Both horses bolted at the noise, but Snake still gripped Isobel's arm. The animals fought against the confinement, turning in circles. Using her free hand, Isobel fumbled with the knife sheath tied to her saddle.

Snake muttered a curse. He righted his gun and took aim a second time. Isobel whipped the long-bladed knife across his arm. The six-shooter tumbled into the grass in a spray of blood.

"Damnation!" Snake yelled.

He lunged at Isobel and both riders tumbled to the ground. The air whooshed from Isobel's lungs. She rolled, trying to get away. Snake tangled her legs with his as he pulled his own knife from his belt.

"Now," he growled, climbing onto the writhing woman. "Now, we'll see."

Frantic, she jabbed his back just as he went for her throat. Her knife sank into flesh and struck bone. Snake bellowed and bolted upright with the pain. Then his knife flashed downward and buried in her arm, not an inch from the bullet wound.

"Stop!" she shrieked, twisting in pain. "Stop this madness!"

"I'll kill you first."

He pulled the knife from her arm and went for her throat a

second time. She squirmed and thrust. Her knife buried deep in his stomach. He gagged.

Barely able to breathe beneath his weight, she tried to jerk the weapon away but lost her grip on it. If only she could escape . . . now . . . while he was wounded. She tried to push out from under him.

He reared. The yellow eyes flashed with hatred. She knocked at the swinging steel in his hand. The blade glanced off her cheek. She screamed. Blood splattered from her face to his.

He grunted. "Bitch."

Blood seeped from the corner of his mouth and trickled onto his heavy jaw. Still he grappled with her. He caught a handful of her hair and twisted her head backward, grinding her scalp into the dirt. She could see nothing but trees. Her throat exposed to his blade, she waited for the final cut.

"Se'rita," he mumbled. As he slumped forward, his knife slid against her throat. The edge bit through her skin. Sliced her earlobe. Buried in the dirt beside her head.

"Snake!" She lay beneath him, listening as the last gurgle of breath left his chest. Panting, she shoved the dead weight of his body from hers. Holding her neck, she struggled to her knees. The scene of horror drew a muffled cry.

Snake Jackson lay on the ground, her knife buried in his stomach. Blood soaked his shirt and puddled on the road.

"I've killed him . . ." She whispered. "I've killed him after all."

She buried her face in her bloodied hands. Bile rose in her throat. She stumbled to the roadside and hung over a tree branch, retching with fear and revulsion. Tears streamed down her cheeks and dripped pink bloodstains in the grass. For a moment she could do nothing but lean against the tree and cry.

How had it all come to this? Once she had longed to end the life of Jim Jackson. But now . . . now that she had killed him . . .

"God," she breathed. "Dear God."

Moving back across the road, she crossed the pool of blood in which Snake lay. She straggled through the grass down to the river and filled her hands with water. Splashing her face, she saw her own blood mingle with Snake's as it clouded the stream. The skin on her neck burned where the knife blade had scraped it raw. Her earlobe was sliced nearly through.

It was her arm that, once again, had suffered most. She mopped the blood and stuffed the torn-away sleeve of her shirtwaist against the knife wound. Cradling her injured shoulder, she slumped into the sweet green grass, stretched out her legs, and shut her eyes.

She had no idea how long she lay, resting from the struggle. Though she knew she had knifed Snake Jackson in self-defense, it hardly mattered. She had taken a life. She had killed.

Covering her eyes with her arm, she wept bitter tears. Death was ugly, painful, senseless. She had imagined satisfaction, victory after her revenge was complete. Instead she felt only revulsion.

She had to find Noah and turn him away from the same path. She had to show him what she had learned. It was her only hope of atonement.

When Isobel had regained her composure and her shoulder seemed to have stopped bleeding, she rolled onto her knees. Ripping off a strip from the hem of her petticoat, she fashioned it into a sling.

As she took a final drink of water, she gazed down at the rippling stream. Tufts of green moss drifted in the shallows. Silver trout flashed as they turned through the sunlit waters. A white butterfly danced across the surface of the river. It lit on the yellow petals of a blue-weed flower and fanned its delicate wings.

Isobel sniffed. Struggling to her feet, she climbed to the road. At the trail's edge, the two horses grazed side by side. She lowered her eyes as she walked toward the prone body of her enemy.

Crouching, she drew the knife blade from Snake Jackson's stomach. His sightless yellow eyes stared into the sky. Shuddering, she touched each lid to press it closed. Flies buzzed. She crossed his hands over his chest. Then she walked to the horses.

For a moment she stood resting her forehead on her mount's neck. She knew what she must do, for she had battled for her lands with her own life. And she had won them at the cost of another's.

Moving around her horse, she unbuckled Snake's saddlebag and slipped her hand inside. Her fingers closed on a slender packet. Drawing it out, she saw her father's neat handwriting on the outside of the yellowed envelope.

"Spanish Land-Grant Titles," the words read in both English and Spanish, "the Possession of Maria Isobel Matas."

Bowing her head, Isobel held the packet to her breast. Land. She would be a landowner at last. But what good was all the land in the world without someone to share it? Isobel knew she held in her hand a possession that could draw the hand of any eligible man in New Mexico or Spain. She could have Don Guillermo or any other husband she chose.

Lifting her eyes to the mountains, she smiled. There was only one man she wanted. It was time to find him.

Chapter
20

When Isobel rode into Lincoln that night, Sheriff George W. Peppin met her on the road, his rifle drawn from its scabbard. The middle-aged man, known to many in town as "Dad" Peppin, scrutinized the young woman. As he took note of her blood-stained shirtwaist, her bandaged arm, her torn earlobe, and the thin line of blood across her neck, his eyes widened.

"Mrs. Buchanan? Is that you?"

Isobel tucked a wisp of her hair behind her ear, as if that might tidy her appearance. She cleared her throat, hoping the sheriff would put down his weapon. But when he didn't she spoke up.

"Do you know where my husband is, Sheriff? I've come to find him. It's an urgent matter."

"Noah Buchanan is holed up in Alexander McSween's house with some of the Regulators. Say . . . don't you know what's goin' on here in Lincoln, ma'am?"

"I know only one thing, sir. I have come for my husband."

"Well, you can't just come ridin' into town and—"

"Who's this?" Jimmie Dolan demanded from horseback as he emerged out of the darkness to join the sheriff. He wore a dark hat that seemed ill-perched on his mass of glossy waves. His darting black eyes took in the disheveled woman.

"It's Noah Buchanan's wife," Peppin answered.

"Mother of God, woman—you're covered in blood."

"Never mind my appearance, sir," Isobel said to the Irishman. "I am on my way to my husband."

"Buchanan is in a party with the other Regulators," Dolan spat. "They've tried to take over the town. Your husband's camped out with fourteen other hellions on the roof of Alexander McSween's house. They've knocked holes in the parapet and made the place a firing range."

Isobel glanced down the street, but the McSween house was too far to see in the darkness. "I'll go and fetch him, then."

"Like hell you will! My men will shoot him to the ground the minute he sets foot out of that house. This is war, Mrs. Buchanan. Twenty of McSween's men have occupied José Montaño's store. Nearly as many are settled in at Isaac Ellis's store."

"I'll go see Juan Patrón. He'll help me."

"That Mexican has ridden to Las Vegas like a banshee was after him. He means to save his skin if he can. Five of McSween's men are camped out at Patrón's house."

"If Mac has taken over the town, how do you propose to keep me from reaching my husband?" Isobel demanded.

"Because my men hold the *torreón*," Dolan shot back. "And I've got you." He gave Peppin a quick nod. "Take this woman to the Cisneros house, Sheriff. We'll hold her prisoner there. Maybe we can use her to bargain with."

"Prisoner!" Isobel exploded. "Listen, Mr. Dolan—"

"Take her away, Peppin."

Reluctantly the sheriff nudged Isobel with the end of his rifle. She clamped her mouth shut and began to ride down the street.

"Mr. Dolan," she called over her shoulder. "I have access to some of the finest lands in New Mexico. I took the title papers from Snake Jackson. If you'll set me free and allow my husband to leave, I'll willingly give them to you."

Dolan caught up with the sheriff and his prisoner. "Lands, eh? You say you took the title papers from Snake Jackson? Rattlesnake Jim Jackson?"

"How do you think I came to be covered in blood? The man nearly killed me."

"But you killed him instead?"

Isobel lowered her eyes. "You'll find his body on the main road to Roswell—at the joining of the Bonito and Hondo rivers."

"B'God, the woman's a banshee herself. Hand over those land titles," Dolan commanded, drawing his own gun.

"I don't have them with me, of course," she retorted. "You don't think I'm so foolish as to carry valuables into this murderous town, do you? I buried them. But if you'll set Noah free—"

"Ah, take her off m'hands, Peppin. I'll get the titles from her later. Can't have a banshee roamin' about town, can we?"

"Mr. Dolan, this woman is wounded," the sheriff said. "Don't you think I'd better take her over to Tunstall's store and let Doc Ealy have a look at her? He's a McSween man, but he's tried to stay out of the trouble. She'd be safe enough there."

"Any woman who could kill Snake Jackson and steal back those land titles he's been so proud of all these years can't be underestimated. Especially if she's tryin' to break out one of the Regulators. Let's let her husband and the rest of McSween's mob take a good look at my ace-in-the-hand. Take her to the Cisneros house, Peppin. And lock her up."

"Yes, sir."

The sheriff eyed Dolan as the little Irishman rode off into the night. He gave Isobel an apologetic shrug, then positioned his rifle in her direction once again.

"Will you send Dr. Ealy to tend me, Sheriff?" Isobel asked as they neared the tiny three-room adobe on the opposite side of the road from the McSween house. "Snake Jackson shot me in the shoulder, and before it had time to heal, he stabbed me there. My ear needs stitches, and my neck has been wounded. Please, sir . . . I must have a doctor. Send Taylor Ealy to me. He won't cause trouble. He's a missionary—a man of God."

"We'll see, Mrs. Buchanan. I'll do what I can for you."

Sheriff Peppin paraded Isobel past Alexander McSween's house, but it was so dark she could not be sure that Noah even saw her. The Cisneros family had fled Lincoln in haste, as had most of Lincoln's peaceable citizens. Dolan had taken over the Cisneros house, though it was too small to be used as a fortification. The sheriff led Isobel to the front bedroom, locked her inside, and stationed an armed guard at the entrance door.

From her position at the small curtained window, she could see the row of men lining the roof of the McSween house across the street. She tried to identify Noah among them, but there was not enough moonlight to make out anything clearly. For a long time she waited in hopes that Dr. Ealy would come—not so much to tend her wounds as to tell her the news of Lincoln and to reassure her that Noah was all right.

When no one came, she bathed her wounds in the washbasin and lay down across the double bed. Though she had not planned to rest deeply, the sun was well up when she was awakened by the sound of the door to her bedroom swinging wide.

"Breakfast, Mrs. Buchanan?" The young guard walked in with a loaf of fresh bread under one arm and a pot of hot coffee in his hand. His other hand rested lightly on the handle of his six-shooter. "Whoops, sorry to bust in on you like this. When I didn't hear nothin', I thought I'd better come take a looksee—make sure you didn't run off in the night, y'know. If you don't mind my sayin' so, ma'am, you shore don't look too perky this mornin'."

Isobel said nothing but slid out of bed as quickly as she could. She touched her hair and attempted to smooth the wrinkles from her shirtwaist while the guard set the bread and coffee on the dresser top.

"Say . . . did you really kill Rattlesnake Jim Jackson?" he asked finally, giving her a sideways glance. "That's the rumor goin' around, anyways."

"As I told Mr. Dolan, Snake's body is lying on the road that leads from John Chisum's ranch to Lincoln. And I don't wish to discuss this matter with you again."

The man nodded, as if he understood perfectly. "Didn't like Snake Jackson much myself, to tell you the truth. He was as ornery and mean as his name."

Isobel turned away, uncomfortable about speaking of the man whose life she had taken. "When will I be set free from this place?" she asked.

"Soon as things settle down. Early this mornin' McSween sent a message to our men sayin' they'd better leave the *torreón* double-quick. Mac claims he owns the *torreón* 'cause he bought the land there from Dolan a few years back to build a new church on. Our fellers have sent a letter to Colonel Dudley over at Fort Stanton askin' him to send soldiers to protect the *torreón*."

Isobel studied the young man, whose limp blond hair hung almost to his shoulders. His skinny face was lit by a pair of bright green eyes. When he smiled at her, she saw a set of widely spaced teeth scattered haphazardly across his gums.

"I reckon John Kinney, Buck Powell, Jesse Evans, and the others will hightail it up here from San Patricio when they hear about what McSween's gone and done in Lincoln," he added. "Dolan thinks his posse is gonna get here by this afternoon."

"And then?"

"A shootin' match, I'd guess." He backed toward the door, keeping his eyes on his prisoner. "I'll be outside if you need me. Just holler."

"What is your name, sir?"

"Ike Teeters. I come from down Seven Rivers way."

"You're in the Seven Rivers Gang?"

He chuckled, showing the row of uneven teeth. "Not hardly. My eyes don't see too good from a distance, ma'am. If the truth be known, my shootin's downright pitiful. But I can do guardin' work. I'm fine at that."

"Why don't you wear spectacles, Ike?"

He frowned. "Hmm. Never gave that notion any thought. Figured spectacles were fer old folks."

"Dr. Ealy wears them. He's quite a young man still."

"Sure enough? Well, I ain't got the money anyways. My family's poor folks, ma'am. Chisum pushed us off nearly all of our land. And he keeps us broke most of the time. It's all we can do to get by."

"John Chisum?"

"Sure. We're just small cattlemen down Seven Rivers way. We can't do nothin' against a powerful man like Chisum. Marion Turner, Milo Pearce, Sam Perry, the Beckwith brothers—most of 'em's good fellers. Law-abidin', hardworkin' men. Not like them outlaws John Kinney and Jesse Evans. But we Seven Rivers men joined up with Dolan to fight Chisum. We got to have help or we're gonna go under."

"But this fight is between Dolan and McSween. John Chisum isn't even in Lincoln County right now. And he never wears a gun. He's tried his best to stay out of the trouble."

"That's what *you* think." He tapped his temple. "We know better, us Seven Rivers folk."

Giving her a broad grin, he walked backward through the doorway. As he was shutting the door behind him, he poked his head through the gap. "I'll see if I can get you a doctor, Mrs. Buchanan. You look mighty puny to me. Mighty puny."

Instead of sending a contingent of soldiers from Fort Stanton, Colonel Dudley chose to send Dr. Appel. About mid-afternoon Ike Teeters knocked on Isobel's bedroom door, unlocked it, and escorted the post surgeon into the room.

She had been staring out the window, trying to spot Noah amidst the constantly rotating group of men who guarded the McSween house from the parapet. Then she saw the man who had performed the erroneous postmortem on John Tunstall's body. He was walking across the road toward the Cisneros house, and she quickly tried to think how she should handle him.

"Afternoon, Mrs. Buchanan," the doctor said, removing his hat as he stepped through the door. He was a truly handsome man, dashing in his double-breasted uniform with its rows of brass buttons. But his face—with its trimmed mustache, cleft chin, and bright blue eyes—revealed no emotion on seeing the blood-spattered woman.

"My name is Dr. Daniel Appel," he said by way of introduction. "I understand you were wounded yesterday morning."

Isobel glanced at the pile of red-stained cloths by her bed. "A knife wound. My shoulder."

"It looks as though your earlobe and neck received a laceration."

"Yes, sir."

"May I examine you?"

"I would prefer Dr. Ealy, sir. He and I are close acquaintances, and the knife wound is in a rather delicate location." She tried to blush but didn't succeed. The truth was, she wanted Dr. Ealy so she could talk to him about the situation in Lincoln.

Dr. Appel glanced at Ike. "I'm expected to report to Colonel Dudley at the fort. If the patient refuses to be examined, I'm afraid there's nothing I can—"

"But Dolan won't let Doc Ealy have a look at her," Ike interrupted.

"Ridiculous. Taylor Ealy is as good a doctor as Lincoln is going to get. Jimmie Dolan is taking this matter too far—especially where a woman is concerned." His eyes darted back to Isobel. "If you will allow me to perform the initial treatment, Mrs. Buchanan, I'll insist on Dr. Ealy for follow-up care."

Relief visible in her smile, Isobel nodded. "Yes, please. That will be fine."

The procedure took longer than Isobel had expected. Dr. Appel wanted to know all about her battle with Snake Jackson. She tried to be accurate, but the sight of Ike Teeters gaping in amazement at her exploit caused her to gloss over some of the more horrible details. After the surgeon had recorded the whole matter in his notebook, he sent Ike outside while he examined Isobel's shoulder and ear.

The stitching proved painful, though Dr. Appel showed himself both skilled and gentle. While he sutured the wounds, he briefly recounted his attempt to negotiate with Alexander McSween. Mac, Isobel learned, had no intention of backing down this time. He was tired of running for his life and hiding out in the woods. He meant to stand up to Jimmie Dolan, no matter what the cost. Dr. Appel was clearly disgusted with the lawyer's refusal to compromise.

When he finished sewing Isobel's wounds, the surgeon instructed her to rest. But before he could leave the room, she sat up in bed and caught the sleeve of his jacket.

"You're a reasonable man, sir," she whispered. "I want you to know that I came to Lincoln only to fetch my husband and return to our homestead. Jimmie Dolan has captured me and holds me here. I don't even know if my husband is all right. Please—can you help me?"

"Madam, by your own confession, you have taken a man's life. Sheriff Peppin has every right to hold you here until the matter can be resolved. As to your husband . . . Noah Buchanan is alive and well. He's at Alexander McSween's house, and I'm sure he intends to stay there until the hostilities have ended."

"Can you take him a message for me?" Isobel begged.

"I'm late to the fort as it is. I'm sorry, Mrs. Buchanan."

He spoke briefly with Ike Teeters just outside the doorway. Isobel tried to listen, but she could discern nothing. Finally her door was shut and locked.

She peered through the window to find that a swirling dust storm had blown up during her surgery. In the flying dirt she saw Dr. Appel ride out of town without pausing to return to the McSween house.

Minutes after the surgeon's departure, John Kinney, Buck Powell, and their posse rode into Lincoln. Isobel was still at her window when she saw one of their number fire his six-shooter into the air. The men reined their horses into the corral of the Wortley Hotel, a few hundred feet west of the McSween house. The moment the men dismounted, they began shooting at the enemy house, their bullets shattering shutter slats and gouging holes in the adobe outer walls.

Hearing the shots, fifteen McSween men poured out of the Montaño store and ran toward the house. As they passed the *torreón*, Dolan's men who were inside shouted for them to stop. They answered with a volley of gunfire.

The McSween force continued to race down the street. They bolted into the lawyer's house to join the other Regulators. The opposing gunmen showered the corral and hotel with bullets. Kinney and his men rushed for cover. For several minutes the gunfight raged.

Isobel, hidden behind the thick adobe wall of the Cisneros house, peeked out from the corner of the window. To her horror, she finally spotted Noah on Alexander McSween's roof. She could see Noah's black Stetson moving back and forth behind the parapet as he fired through the newly gouged holes. The wind was hellacious, dust flying so thick Isobel could not make out the mountains behind the houses on the other side of the street. Finally dust combined with the sunset to put an end to the shooting as darkness settled over Lincoln.

Creeping back to her bed, Isobel lay exhausted, breathing heavily from the sheer emotion of the day's events. Her shoulder throbbed, but somehow it was her earlobe that hurt the worst. Pain from the wound shot into her temple and down her neck. She bathed her injuries at the basin once again, then re-dressed her shoulder.

Ike Teeters knocked on the door as she was sliding into bed. "You doin' okay, Mrs. Buchanan?"

"Was anyone wounded in the shooting?"

"Nobody on our side. Don't know about McSween's bunch."

Isobel shut her eyes and rested her head on the pillow. "When will Dr. Ealy come, Ike?"

"I'll try to fetch him fer ya in the mornin'. But if the shootin' keeps up, could be hard to get him across the street."

"Thank you, Ike."

"G'night, Mrs. Buchanan. Sleep tight."

Isobel lay with her head turned so that her ear would not touch the pillow. It hardly mattered. She couldn't sleep, thinking about Noah and how she had been a part of the events that had led him into such peril. If only she could send him word. The McSween forces held the upper hand in Lincoln, and Noah could escape. He just had to.

It was almost dark the following day before Ike managed to slip Taylor Ealy across the street to the Cisneros house. The missionary doctor entered through the back door and hurried to Isobel's bedroom with his bag of medications and bandages.

"Susan's in a fit over you!" he exclaimed as he examined the sutured knife wounds. "She wanted to come with me, but I wouldn't let her. Dear heaven, what a fray. We thought we had everything going God's way here in Lincoln—Susan's school had twenty children, half of them Mexican and half American. Sabbath School met every Sunday morning at ten o'clock, and I preached at four in the afternoon. We had a roomful of people every week. Overflowing sometimes! We'd put two stoves into Tunstall's mercantile and fixed up the whole front of the store as our mission. I was gardening and tending to people's medical needs. Not one month ago Squire Green Wilson offered to sell me five acres of land in the middle of town to build a church. The superintendent of home mission work in Denver was sending us an organ, a dozen Testaments, another dozen Moody and Sankey number one hymnals—"

"Dr. Ealy," Isobel interrupted the flow, unable to contain her own need to speak. "Please . . . can you send a message to Noah for me? I must let him know that I want him to leave the McSween house and go home. Revenge is useless, futile. Oh, Dr. Ealy, please help me save Noah's life."

The doctor smiled and patted her hand. "Now, calm down. Mac's men have the advantage in Lincoln. Mary, Susan, and I have chosen to stay in Tunstall's store with our possessions. But we do know everything that's been going on in town these past few days. Mac has more than sixty fighters on his side. Dolan's posse numbers only forty. The only two places in town Dolan holds are his mercantile and the Wortley Hotel. Everything else is fortified with McSween men."

"Will it be a war, then?"

"Who can tell? Dolan keeps asking Fort Stanton for help, but Colonel Dudley is on strict orders from the War Department to stay out of civil matters. Still, Dolan does have some fierce men on his side. There's John Kinney and his gang. And there's Jesse Evans. He's out on bail in the Tunstall murder case, you know."

"What about the Seven Rivers men?"

"They're solidly behind Dolan. They hate John Chisum."

"Has he been so terrible to them? It's hard to imagine."

"God only knows in these matters, Isobel." He brushed aside her hair to take a look at her earlobe. "Chisum claims the Seven Rivers men regularly rustle cattle from his herds, and the Seven Rivers men claim Chisum stole their land and left them all on the brink of poverty. It's like everything in this war—there are two equally determined sides. The law holds with Dolan, but McSween has the greater force of men."

"And I'm held prisoner here in the midst of it all."

"I'll try to get word to Sheriff Peppin. If you're being held for the death of Jim Jackson, you deserve the chance to post bail. And if Dolan is keeping you here just as bait, it's illegal. By tomorrow we'll have you out of this—"

Gunfire ripped through the street. Dr. Ealy clamped his mouth shut. Shouting erupted. A horse whinnied.

Leaving Isobel prone on the bed, the doctor crept to the window. "Oh no!" he said in a loud whisper. "A black trooper from the fort has just ridden into town, and McSween's men are firing at him. Don't they see he's a soldier? He's in uniform, for heaven's sake."

Isobel rolled from the bed and crawled across the floor to join the doctor. As she lifted her head, she saw the cavalryman's horse rear and the soldier tumble to the ground. Recovering quickly, he mounted again and rode toward the Wortley Hotel as bullets churned up the ground behind him.

Ike Teeters burst into the bedroom. "Doc, you better get back to Tunstall's store. There's likely to be more shootin', and I'm only supposed to protect Mrs. Buchanan here."

Dr. Ealy glanced at Isobel as he made for the door. "I'll try to return. Keep the wounds clean."

"Take my message to Noah! Please!" She didn't know whether he heard or not, for the doors slammed behind him, and then the house fell silent.

So, too, did the town of Lincoln. But as Isobel crawled into bed, she knew that McSween's men had made a grave error in firing on the soldier. Colonel Dudley would be furious. The incident might just trigger the officer to send his troops to Lincoln in spite of the War Department's orders. If so, there was no doubt in Isobel's mind that Dudley would support Dolan against McSween.

Closing her eyes, she let out a breath. For the hundredth time that day she breathed a prayer for the safety of Noah Buchanan. She conjured up his vivid blue eyes, his bronze skin, his dark hair, his gentle hands. Dear God, she was responsible for one man's death. *Please, keep it from becoming two.*

The third day of the battle was July 17. Isobel learned this from Ike Teeters, who said he always kept track of such things. The day brought hostilities even more to a head in Lincoln Town. From her window refuge Isobel watched as

Dolan's men climbed across the hillsides south of town. She knew at once their goal—to pick off the McSween loyalists who held the rooftops of so many houses in town.

Once the firing began, it was directed back and forth between the McSween men on the rooftops and the Dolan men in the hills. Ike joined Isobel at the window, but as he could make out nothing but a blur from that distance, she was compelled to tell him what was happening.

"The Montaño store crowd is firing into the hills," she said. "Dolan's men are well protected, but I can see where they are by the smoke from their gunfire."

"How 'bout McSween's bunch? Any of 'em coming down from the rooftops?"

"Some." Isobel strained to see without lifting her head too far over the windowsill. She remembered Dick Brewer's death too vividly to make such an error. "The roof of Mac's house is almost empty. Thank goodness."

"Hey, I thought you were on Mac's side."

"I want the life of my husband to be preserved."

The guard nodded. "I got me a wife. A real good gal, and purty, too. Mexican."

"Children?"

"One on the way." He grinned, his gap-toothed smile as cheerful as anything Isobel had seen since arriving in Lincoln. "How 'bout you?"

Isobel pondered the unusual absence of her monthy time. She had attributed its disappearance to the tension of the days—riding across the countryside, being shot and then knifed. But she looked down at her stomach and gazed at the tiny mound.

"Not yet, Ike," she said softly. "But if God wills it, perhaps one day."

He nodded. "We reckon our first'll get borned come Christmastime. My way of thinkin' makes it a gal, but Juanita's hopin' fer a boy. So's he can help me run the cattle when he's all growed up. You want a boy or a gal, Mrs.—"

"Wait!" Isobel clamped her hand over Ike's arm. "Some of Dolan's men are coming out of hiding and riding down the hill. They must believe they've cleared the rooftops."

She watched as a pair of horses wove downward. Suddenly

from the Montaño store a shot rang out. One of the Dolan horsemen tumbled from his mount and fell to the ground. The other fled. Bullets zinged across the hillside, and the McSween rooftops filled with men once again.

"They've shot a Dolan man," Isobel cried. "McSween's men are keeping up the firing and won't let anyone near to tend him. Oh, someone should be allowed to go! I can see the poor man lying there in the heat of the sun. He's writhing in pain."

"Gut shot?"

"It looks that way."

"Bad luck there. Terrible way to go. Can you see who it is?"

Isobel shook her head. "I don't know the man."

She and Ike stayed at the window while the two sides blasted away at each other. Now and again Isobel thought she caught sight of Noah's hat, but for the most part he was keeping well beneath the edge of the parapet.

At some point in the late afternoon Dr. Appel returned to Lincoln. He and three other soldiers rode up into the hills to retrieve the wounded Dolan man. Despite the soldiers' uniforms, Alexander McSween's men kept up their fire. Both Ike and Isobel felt certain this second incident of shooting at U.S. soldiers would surely bring Colonel Dudley to town.

Late in the evening Isobel saw Dr. Ealy—in the company of two McSween men—slip out the back door of the Tunstall store. It was no time before a volley of shots from the direction of the *torreón* pinpointed their exit. Seconds later the good doctor could be seen racing back to the cover of the store.

No more bullets were fired that night, but early the next morning Ike woke Isobel with the news that Dr. Ealy and his entire family were marching straight down the middle of Lincoln Town's only road. Isobel rushed from her bed to see Taylor and Mary Ealy, each cradling a child as they strode through town.

"Where are they going?" she asked.

"Ben Ellis got shot in the neck yesterday," Ike said. "Least that's what I heard from one of Dolan's men who slipped by the house here early this mornin' to make sure I still had you penned up. Some fellers tried to sneak the doctor out to tend him, but our men in the *torreón* wouldn't let 'em past. I guess the Doc up and decided to just get on down to the Ellis place with his wife and children along so's nobody'd fire on him."

Isobel watched in horror while the small family she had grown to love walked down a street that only the day before had been crisscrossed with bullets. Silence reigned, and the Ealy family made it safely to the Ellis home.

In fact, the fourth day of Isobel's imprisonment remained mostly quiet. The shooting slowed, though no one but the Ealys dared to venture out into the street. Ike Teeters sat with Isobel most of the day. He told her all about his family; all about the town of Seven Rivers down on the Pecos; all about his dream of owning a big herd like John Chisum's. She finally had to turn him out when darkness fell.

As she bathed her wounds and crawled into bed, she turned over in her mind the possibility of escape. Though Ike had let down his guard—how could she bring herself to put him in a position of peril? If she escaped, Ike would be at Jimmie Dolan's mercy. And as much as she rued it, Isobel had come to care for the gap-toothed cowboy too much.

Nevertheless, she decided, if the shooting slowed the following day, she would beg Ike to convey her message across the street to Noah. She could wait no longer.

But dawn brought the pop of gunfire as the sniping began again. Isobel changed into one of the dresses Ike had found for her in the house—a simple gown of pale yellow cotton. To the rattle of bullets slamming into houses, she washed and combed her hair. Then she knocked on the door to her bedroom.

"Ike," she said through the thick wood. "I must speak with you."

He unlocked the door. "Yer lookin' spunky this mornin', Mrs. Buchanan. You gonna eat this breakfast I got for ya?"

She glanced at the usual loaf of bread and pot of coffee on the table outside her room. She knew it was more food than many of the people in town must have by now. Surely supplies were growing slim. Children would be hungry.

"I can't eat, Ike." She pushed her hands into the pockets of

the yellow dress. "I must go and see Noah. Will you escort me
across the street?"

"Aw, I can't do that, ma'am. It's against my orders from
Jimmie Dolan."

"Please, Ike! You saw that no one shot at Taylor Ealy because Mary and the children were along. We'd be safe. You
could take me to Mac's house for just a moment. Then after I
talked to Noah, you could bring me back here. Hold a gun on
me if you like. I won't run—I promise. Oh, Ike, if you love
your wife, you know how important this is to me! Please,
please take me."

Ike scratched at his scraggly locks. "It'd sure be risky business. Things is gettin' hot out there again this mornin'."

"We'll hold up a white pillowcase for a flag. Only let me
go—"

"What the hell is that?" At the sound of shouting and
horses' hooves, Ike interrupted Isobel's pleas and bolted to the
window. Isobel was at his side in a second.

"Soldiers!" she cried. "They've come from Fort Stanton.
Sheriff Peppin is riding with Colonel Dudley."

"Wahoo! That means we got the army on our side, Mrs.
Buchanan!" Ike did a little dance around the room. Isobel
might have used the moment to feel betrayed, but there would
have been little point. Clearly Ike was right, and the soldiers
had ridden into town on Dolan's behalf.

"Count 'em for me, would ya, Mrs. Buchanan?" the young
man asked.

"Colonel Dudley," she said. "Four officers. Eight . . . nine
. . . ten . . . eleven black cavalrymen. More than twenty white
infantrymen. And . . . *Dios mio*—guns!"

"Dudley's brung the howitzer!" Ike whooped as he
squinted to see. "She's a twelve pounder. And there's a rapid-
fire Gatling gun comin' along behind. Golly, Dolan's got this
battle licked now. Mac might as well give up."

He swung around, but Isobel had slumped onto her bed.
She buried her face in her hands. It was too late. Too late. The
soldiers had come to blow away Alexander McSween's forces. Among the men would be Noah Buchanan.

Chapter
❦ 21 ❦

Before Colonel Dudley and the soldiers had even settled in a camp, Isobel watched as several of Dolan's men ran to Alexander McSween's house and began to pour coal oil around the wooden windowframes.

"What do they mean to do?" she asked Ike, though she felt a terrible dread that she already knew.

"Reckon they're gonna try to burn out the McSween bunch."

"Burn them!" Isobel rose to her feet, but Ike pushed her down again out of bullet range.

"Won't do much good," he drawled. "The house is adobe. It ain't gonna burn worth a lick."

"But the windowframes. And the roof. Oh, Ike, you must take me across the street at once. I must save my husband."

"Calm yourself, now. Tell you what—I'll step outside and see if I can find out what's happenin' with the soldiers and all."

The moment Ike had gone, Isobel threw herself against the windowframe. But the stout wooden poles imbedded in the adobe refused to give. She ran to the door and tried the knob, but Ike had locked it. Frantic, she raced to the window again.

"Noah!" she screamed. "Noah Buchanan!"

When no heads appeared over the top of McSween's parapet, she took up a chair and began smashing it against the wood poles that barred her window. "Let me out, Jimmie Dolan!" she hollered. *"Asesino! Culebra! Yo grito como si me mataran. Diablo, que lleva su merecido!"*

"Hey, now!" Ike barged into the room. Isobel flew at him, fists pummeling as she tried to push past to the door. He grabbed her arms and hurled her backward. She stumbled and rolled to the floor, a heap of torn cotton dress and tangled hair.

"Now, what's all this, ma'am?" Ike said after he'd locked the door behind them. He bent over the sobbing woman and took her shoulders. "You know I can't let you get away, Mrs. Buchanan. I got my orders."

She shrugged away from the pain of his hand on her knife wound. "My husband is in that house! I must go there! I must—"

"You'd never get nowhere near McSween's place. Even if I did set you free."

Her heart breaking, Isobel struggled up from the floor and ran to the window. Clutching the bars, she peered outside.

"Soon as McSween's men saw Colonel Dudley hit town," Ike said softly, coming up beside her, "they hightailed it out of here. The Montaño store's empty. So is the Ellis place."

Isobel turned to him, her face swollen and streaked with tears. "Then Mac's force is almost gone!"

"He ain't got nobody left on his side but the men in his own house."

Isobel leaned her forehead against the cool whitewashed adobe. Noah was in Alexander McSween's house. Noah and so few others. How could they hope to hold out against such an army?

"Where is that colonel?" Isobel demanded. "I must speak to him. He's violating the laws by coming into town this way."

"He's setting up camp down the street. Everyone thinks he's gonna aim them guns at McSween's house. He already threatened to blow up Montaño's store. That's how come everybody ran off."

"An army colonel can't threaten citizens of the United

States, can he?" Growing angry now, she brushed the back of her hand across one cheek to dry her tears.

"Dudley may be a hard-drinkin' man, but he's got some smarts, too. He sent messages tellin' both McSween and Dolan that he's just here to protect women and children. But he also said if anyone fires on his soldiers, he's gonna blow 'em to kingdom come."

"But that means Dolan's men can fire at will on the McSween house. Yet, no one in the McSween's house can shoot back for fear of hitting a soldier. It's not fair."

" 'Course it ain't. But that's war for ya." Ike patted her arm. "Now settle down and let me bring in that breakfast. There ain't nothin' you can do, Mrs. Buchanan. Not a thing. Anyway . . . you won't be the first widow to come out of Lincoln County. Believe you me."

Sauntering away, he unlocked the door, slipped through, and relocked it from the outside. Isobel could hear him whistling as he heated up the breakfast coffee.

Isobel was given no opportunity to consider escape again. Shortly after noon Dolan's posse, under the command of Sheriff Peppin, filled the Cisneros house where she was staying— along with two other small houses to the south and west of the McSween home. It became clear that the men had completely circled Alexander McSween's house.

No one entered Isobel's room, but she could hear the men outside the locked bedroom door, talking with Ike and loading their rifles. They were laughing and joking, whooping over their sure victory against a band that once had outnumbered them.

Unable to rest despite the throbbing pain in her shoulder, Isobel drew a chair to the window. She could see some of the Seven Rivers men creeping toward the enemy McSween house. Covering her mouth with her fist, she watched as they pried the bullet-torn shutters from the adobe walls, smashed the glass windowpanes with their rifle butts, and began shouting across the stacks of adobe bricks that had been built up inside as a barricade.

"We got a warrant for the arrest of Alexander McSween!"

one of them called into the house. "Squire Wilson done signed it, so you ain't got no choice."

From inside the house Isobel heard a voice, but she could not make out the words. The Seven Rivers man called out to the listening Dolan posse, "McSween says he won't surrender. Says he's got warrants fer *our* arrest." He turned back to the window. "Hey, let us see them warrants, McSween!"

After considerably more shouting, the Seven Rivers men moved away from the house. Isobel knew that their action had been no more than a formality so they could claim to have attempted to serve the warrant on McSween before his death.

And she had no doubt that Alexander McSween must die. How many would die with him? Noah . . . Billy Bonney . . . Sue McSween? She had barely thought the name when out of the house marched Mrs. McSween herself. Head up and shoulders back, she strode down the suddenly silent street toward the *torreón*. For a moment Isobel took this as a good sign. If anyone could stand up to a U.S. colonel, it was Sue McSween with her sharp tongue and quick mind.

Yet the moment she was gone, Dolan's men swarmed the house across the street. They poured coal oil over the window's a second time and lit it. Suddenly a flame sprang up from the back of the house, which Isobel knew contained the kitchen. She watched in fear as the fire burned for some time. But as Ike had predicted, it did go out.

As Dolan's men began to move away from the house, Regulators began to fire from Tunstall's store. Thinking of Susan and the Ealys, Isobel held her breath while the firing erupted from both sides. At least someone on McSween's side was *outside* the smoldering house and able to defend it.

Just when Isobel thought the men in the house might be able to make a break, a second fire began to billow from the other side of the U-shaped house. This time a pillar of smoke rose as the fire began to crawl slowly from one room to the next.

The afternoon wore on, and Isobel sat helpless at her window. Her throat ached from choking back tears. Several times she was certain she saw Noah's form appear in a window, but he quickly sought cover. Smoke poured from the windows as hazy figures moved around inside.

Isobel murmured prayers while images of Noah Buchanan filtered through her mind. The evening he had lifted her onto his horse and carried her into the shadows of the pines. She could remember the smell of him . . . leather and sunshine and dust. She saw his clean-shaven face appearing over the tub in which she lay naked . . . the handsomest man she had ever seen . . . she had believed him an angel sent from heaven. And he was. The way he had held her, kissed her, loved her. His clear voice ringing through the valley with hymns. His strong hands laboring to build, milk, cook, wrestle cattle . . . and write stories.

Oh, Noah! If only she could change the past.

A deafening explosion shattered her memories. Glass windows from the burning house blew out. Isobel screamed. Suddenly she could hear men shouting outside the door to her bedroom. She darted across the room to listen.

"Naw, she's Buchanan's wife!" Ike's voice. "Leave her be, fellers."

"C'mon, Ike. Let's have a look at her. Ain't she the one sent Snake Jackson hoppin' over coals in hell?"

"Yeah, Ike! Let's take a gander at Buchanan's woman."

"Hell, boys, if I did that, ol' Dolan would skin me alive. He means to string her up for murder, don't ya know?"

"Murder? Hoo-wee!"

Isobel swallowed at the thick knot in her throat. Murder? But of course—what chance would she have to prove herself innocent? Dr. Appel had treated her wounds, and the surgeon had felt no compunction over lying about the condition of John Tunstall's corpse. He could make it look as though she had not acted out of self-defense but had simply stabbed Snake Jackson to death.

Feeling ill, she returned to the window. The explosion had come from somewhere inside Mac's house. Perhaps a gunpowder keg had caught fire. Now the house was raging with flames. As Isobel watched, Sue McSween marched down the street to her home and strode inside, seeming oblivious to the conflagration.

It was almost evening when Sue left the burning house and headed for John Tunstall's store, where Susan Gates and the

Ealys were staying. That did little good, for almost at once, the Dolan posse began to set fire to the mercantile.

Mary Ealy ran out of the store carrying the two children and set them on the road. Taylor followed with a stack of Bibles in his arms. Susan raced from the building with her textbooks in tow and a collection of slates under one arm.

"Susan!" Isobel cried, pounding on the window's pole. "Susan, please!"

But now a wagon had rolled to the front of Tunstall's mercantile. Driven by soldiers, it was soon loaded with the Ealys' possessions. The Ealys and Susan climbed on board, Susan clutching one of the little girls in her arms, and the wagon rolled away.

"Susan!" Isobel screamed her friend's name one last time, but the petite red-haired schoolteacher had evidently seen too much. White-faced, she stared blankly ahead, her large gray eyes fixed on nothing.

The wagon made its final trip from the Tunstall store as darkness fell over the valley. It carried Sue McSween's organ, more of Dr. Ealy's books, and a large sack of flour. By this time flames had eaten through the entire McSween house but for one small section at the back. Though the night was moonless, the raging fire lit the mountains on both sides of town. Shooting increased until all Isobel could hear was the crack of gunfire and the roar of the flames.

She hung against the windowframe, not caring whether she died by a random shot or not. It was impossible to imagine how anyone could still be alive inside the burning house. Then Isobel suddenly saw figures running from the back adobe wall. Gunfire intensified. A silhouetted man crumpled to the ground.

For a moment the shooting stopped. Isobel ran to her door to see if she could hear what was being said by the men in the next room.

"McSween said he'd surrender," someone shouted. "Look, Bob Beckwith is goin' in after him."

Racing back to the window, Isobel tried to make out what was happening. She heard a voice cry out from the yard of the burning house. It must have been that of Alexander McSween. "I shall never surrender!" the man roared.

At his words all hell broke loose. Bullets flew. Bodies tumbled to the ground. Rifles blazed wildly. Dolan's men poured out of the Cisneros house, leaving Isobel completely alone. She saw more men—the Regulators who had tried to save their friends in McSween's house—jump from the windows of the Tunstall store. Dogs barked. The flames leapt higher.

Sounds of victory erupted from the McSween courtyard as Jimmie Dolan's men began to leap and shout and fire their rifles in jubilation. Isobel sank onto her chair, watching the devilish dance around the fire.

"McSween's dead!" someone shouted as he ran past her window, a jug of whisky in his hand. "McSween's dead, McSween's dead!"

"How many killed?" another man cried from the portal of the Tunstall store.

"Got 'em all. All the Regulators are dead!"

"Six dead in the courtyard! Naw, five. All shot dead. McSween's one of 'em!"

"Yahoo! We got 'em all. Every last one of them damned outlaws!"

Isobel covered her face with her hands and began to cry. Noah . . . beloved Noah. *Dear God, let him rest in peace.*

Chapter
❧ *22* ❧

Isobel slumped in her chair, her arms folded on the wide windowsill and her head resting on them. The acrid tang of smoke filled her nostrils. Shots continued as they had most of the night. Someone had broken into Tunstall's store, and men were still carrying away the looted goods. Isobel could hear them laughing as they drank whisky and shouted about their victory.

Sniffing, she shut her eyes. She had not slept all night, though now the first purple light of dawn was beginning to streak the sky. How could she sleep? How could she ever go on? But of course it wouldn't be long before Jimmie Dolan remembered her. She would face her own death soon. Somehow that hardly seemed to matter.

Memories of Spain and the rich pasture of Catalonia drifted across her mind. Horses cantering over green hills. White cliffs. A crashing blue sea. Grapes. White sheep.

And then she saw New Mexico. Blue sky arching heavenward. Fragrant piñon trees. Gurgling streams. Yuccas covered with thick white blossoms. Spiny cacti garlanded with pink blooms.

She imagined she was bending to pick one of those cactus

flowers. Leaning forward, her hair fell over her shoulders. She straightened and placed the blossom in a pair of strong, sun-weathered hands. "Noah," she whispered. "Noah."

"Isobel . . ." The voice came from somewhere outside herself. She tried to lift her head to see his face, but the wound in her ear hurt too much.

"Noah?"

"Isobel . . ." She heard her name again. Or was it just the wind whispering through the junipers? "Isobel . . ."

A warm hand covered her injured shoulder. She jumped. The chair tumbled backward to the floor as she struggled to her feet. And there he was . . . the tall, dark angel of her dreams. Noah Buchanan.

"Didn't mean to scare you, darlin'," he said, "but we don't have much time. Got to get out of this place while Ike's keeping watch."

Isobel blinked. "Noah . . ."

"Me, Billy, Jim French, Tom O'Folliard, and a couple of others made it out of McSween's house in the dark just before the shooting got really hot. I'm not really sure who's alive and who isn't because I took off in this direction to get you. I didn't even know you were in Lincoln till I heard you screaming at Susan this afternoon." He stopped and rubbed his hand over his forehead. "Mac got killed, you know. Dolan's men shot him dead. I saw the whole thing."

"Noah . . ."

It was the only word Isobel could seem to force out of her mouth. He grinned and tucked his arm around her. "C'mon, darlin'. Ike won't be able to steer those drunkards away from the house much longer. Let's head out."

As though her dream had taken on a measure of reality, Isobel felt Noah lift her into his arms and carry her from the room that had been her prison for five days. She tilted her head to see Ike Teeters standing in the doorway.

"Good luck, Mrs. Buchanan," he said, giving her a jaunty wave. "You're fine company, y'know? Easy to talk to. Say . . . send me a letter when that first little one gets borned. Juanita can read it to me. She knows her ABCs real good."

For the first time in many hours the trace of a smile drifted across Isobel's lips. "Thank you, Ike. I hope Jimmie Dolan won't harm you. He'll be looking for me to hang me—"

"Hang you? Hell, I just made that up. Didn't want those drunk fellers to get their hands on ya, is all. Dolan probably forgot he even had you. I shore ain't gonna remind him." He gave her a gap-toothed grin. "Well, so long. Guess it's time for me to go join the boys for a celebration."

As Ike stepped out the front door of the Cisneros house, Noah carried Isobel out the back. The black stallion was waiting, and Noah settled his wife against his chest before spurring the horse away from the scene of murder, bloodshed, and mayhem.

They rode through the back hills, staying clear of the road as the morning light drifted through the trees. When they had reached a clearing safely away from the danger, Noah reined the horse and turned Isobel toward him.

"Ike told me Snake tore into you," he whispered.

She gazed into eyes the color of the New Mexico sky. "I killed him, Noah. But I was wrong to do it, even though I was fighting for my life. It's not my place to take a life. Revenge is not the way."

For a long time he mused on the gray smoke that marred the sky over Lincoln Town. "You know, the minute I figured out it was you yelling at Susan Gates through the window of that house across the street, all the bluster went out of me. I just wanted to get to you—to protect you. The drive for vengeance seemed downright empty compared with the notion of spending a lifetime with my Spanish spitfire."

He bent and kissed her lips, a soft brushing of mouths that quickened into an urgent searching. His arms tightened around her, seeking solace for all those empty days.

"Oh, Noah, I was sure you had been burned alive or shot," she murmured into the skin of his neck. "I thought I had lost you forever."

"I couldn't let that happen, darlin'. I love you too much."

A gentle smile tilted her lips. "And I love you, Noah Buchanan."

"Good," he said, giving her a hug. "Love's about all we have because I don't intend to take you anywhere near Lincoln County ever again. I'm going to write John Chisum and cancel the sale of the land. We'll go north somewhere and build ourselves a life. I can run cattle for someone up there. We'll get us a little place—it may not be much—but it'll be ours and it'll be clean and safe. Isobel, I'd like to give you children. I'd like to provide for you and protect you—"

"And write stories for me?" With the barest hint of a giggle, she drew out the New York letter she had transferred to the pocket of the yellow dress she now wore. " 'Sunset at Coyote Canyon' is to be published, Noah. And the magazine wants more of your stories. I'll type the second one you wrote, shall I? I'll use my Remington. And perhaps we'll live on the lands I won back from Snake Jackson. Beautiful, rich pasturelands just north of Santa Fe. Green country with mountains filled with turquoise and silver . . ."

But Noah heard nothing. His mouth moved to cover Isobel's, his arms enfolding the woman with whom he would share a lifetime in this land of enchantment.

Epilogue

For my readers who are as interested in the historical portrayal of the Lincoln County War as in the love story of Noah and Isobel Buchanan, I offer this final note.

BILLY BONNEY (alias Billy the Kid)—Escaped from the burning McSween house with several other Regulators just minutes before Alexander McSween was shot. Lived for three more years, during which he engaged in more killings and daring getaways. Shot to death on the night of July 13, 1881, by Sheriff Pat Garrett, a former friend. Billy was about twenty-one years old.

JIMMIE DOLAN—Financially ruined, he brought himself back to power and wealth through an advantageous marriage and several shrewd business moves. Took over the Tunstall Mercantile in Lincoln and the Tunstall ranch on the Rio Feliz. Later served as county treasurer and territorial senator. Died a natural death on February 26, 1898, at age fifty.

SUSAN GATES—Moved to Zuni, New Mexico, with Dr. Taylor Ealy and his family. Taught school to the Indians there. Married José Perea, a young Presbyterian minister. Later moved with him to Jemez and then to Corrales, New Mexico, where she became the mother of a son.

TAYLOR AND MARY EALY—Served as missionaries in Zuni, New Mexico, from 1878 to 1881. Returned to Pennsylvania, where Dr. Ealy began a medical practice and a profitable baby powder company. More about the Ealy family can be read in *Missionaries, Outlaws, and Indians*, edited and annotated by Norman J. Bender.

JOHN CHISUM—Returned to Lincoln County after the war. Built a new home, the "Long House," at South Spring River Ranch. Developed a malignant tumor on his neck. Went to Kansas City and Arkansas for treatment but died in Eureka Springs on December 20, 1884. Buried in Paris, Texas. Read more about John Chisum in *My Girlhood Among Outlaws* by Lily Klasner.

JUAN PATRÓN—Moved his family to Puerto de Luna, New Mexico, after the Lincoln County War. Murdered there by hired assassin Mitch Maney on April 9, 1884. Patrón was twenty-nine years old. Maney's case never went to trial.

SUSAN McSWEEN—Started her own ranching venture in Three Rivers, an area distant from Lincoln. Remarried in 1884. Obtained a divorce in 1891. Became wealthy through skilled management of her vast lands and 8,000 head of cattle. Considered "a woman of genius." Died in 1931 at age eighty-six.

These fine books, among others, provide a well-rounded view of the history of the Lincoln County War:

Violence in Lincoln County, 1869–1881, William A. Keleher
Pat Garrett: The Story of a Western Lawman, Leon C. Metz
Maurice G. Fulton's History of the Lincoln County War, Robert N. Mullin, ed.
John Henry Tunstall, Frederick W. Nolan
Billy the Kid: A Handbook, Jon Tuska

Billy the Kid: A Short and Violent Life, Robert M. Utley

High Noon in Lincoln: Violence on the Western Frontier, Robert M. Utley

Merchants, Guns & Money: The Story of Lincoln County and Its Wars, John P. Wilson

Author's Note

In writing *Outlaw Heart* I traced the actual historical events of the Lincoln County War in New Mexico. Except for the fictional participation of Isobel Matas, Noah Buchanan, and Rattlesnake Jim Jackson the remainder of the characters and the sequence of happenings are as accurate as I was able to uncover them in my research. Although any errors are my own responsibility, I owe my thanks for research assistance and inspiration to Tim Palmer, Terry Koenig, Lynn Koenig, Lowell Nosker, Bob Hart and the Lincoln County Heritage Trust, Jeremy and Cleis Jordan of Casa de Patrón, Father John Elmer, Sylvia Johnson, Nita Harrell, and Sue Breisch Johnson.

My appreciation goes to my agent, Patricia Teal, for her enthusiastic support.

Most of all, I wish to thank my editor, Judith Stern, who believed in this book for so many years, and who had the fortitude and the vision to see it into print.

I would welcome hearing from readers. Write to me care of the Publicity Dept., The Berkley Publishing Group, 200 Madison Avenue, New York, NY 10016.

If you enjoyed OUTLAW HEART
by Catherine Palmer, you'll want to look
for a new *Diamond Wildflower Romance*
every month . . .

SUMMER ROSE

Shane never knew the fires of longing
blazed so fiercely. Cassandra never dreamed
that temptation burned so deeply within her.
Amid the lush hills of Texas, they abandoned
all reason and followed a rare and
unbridled desire to the heart of rapture—
and discovered a passion that would bind
them together.

Turn the page for an exciting preview
of the newest
Diamond Wildflower Romance,
SUMMER ROSE
by Bonnie K. Winn
Available now from Diamond Books.

Approaching cautiously, Shane Lancer wondered if the innocent-seeming wagon was an ambush. Memories of Indian wars that had plagued the land assaulted him while his horse's ears pricked forward, its flared nostrils twitching. The horse had definitely picked up a scent. Either another beast or a human. With each step forward, Shane expected an assault. But no shots rang out. Silently he slid from the dapple-gray horse, unsheathing the rifle from its scabbard and checking the low-slung holster strapped to his leg.

It was hard to say who was more surprised when three scared-looking faces peered from around the side of the wagon. The raven-haired younger woman tried to shove a teen-age boy behind her, but he took a defensive stance in front of her. The red-haired woman smoothed capable hands over her calico skirt, but her face had paled considerably, causing her freckles to stand out in the hollows of her unlined face.

The dark-haired woman stepped aside, refusing to hide behind the boy. Her hands shook, but nonetheless she faced Shane bravely, holding a derringer tightly in those same shaking fingers. The red-haired woman swung her gaze between her friend's ridiculous weapon and Shane's long rifle.

Shane bit back a snort of contempt as the delicate woman still challenged him with that bit of useless metal. He looked her up and down, his compelling green eyes narrowing during the inspection. What was a beautiful creature like her doing out in the brush? he wondered.

She held the pistol out a bit as though expecting him to back off. He advanced even closer.

"If you have honorable intentions, sir, ambush would hardly be on your mind." The woman's voice shook only slightly, he noticed. Sure sounded like a priss, though.

"The hell it wouldn't. Only a fool would come out here by himself and not expect trouble." He gazed around the wagon, seeing only their furniture and supplies scattered on the ground. No one was in sight. But that didn't mean someone wasn't hidden somewhere close by. Perhaps in the ungainly wagon. "You mean to tell me you three are out here alone?"

The older of the two women answered. "I'm afraid so."

"Millicent!" The voice of the woman holding the gun filled with distress. Shane noticed her finger slipping toward the trigger of the pistol. While he didn't think much of her sissy weapon, he didn't want to test its merit on his hide.

"Well, you tell me what we're going to do out here without some help, Cassie. I believe this gentleman will rescue us."

Cassie emitted an unladylike snort of disbelief while she inched the derringer higher.

"We left the wagon train a few days back and we're heading southwest," Millicent explained after a moment.

Shane watched in amusement as Cassie sent the red-haired Millicent a look filled with warning. It was apparent she thought he was a ruthless bandito. He didn't mind baiting them. Especially the one with the flashing violet eyes and midnight-colored hair. But he didn't want to push her into actually taking a shot at him.

"So, what's the trouble, ladies?" He nodded at the dark-haired boy, who stared with guarded curiosity, his deep blue eyes resting on Shane's low-slung holster. At closer inspection the boy appeared to be around twelve or thirteen years old. They sure as hell were an odd trio.

Millicent pushed past Cassie and led Shane toward the rear of the wagon. "We believe the wheel's broken." Cassie kept the derringer trained on Shane as he moved along beside Millicent, who continued speaking. "I'm Millicent Groden. This is my friend Cassandra and her brother, Andrew Da—"

Shane interrupted. "You know, I might be tempted to fix the wheel, but not if you keep that gun pointed at my back." Shane turned around quickly, deftly taking the gun out of the surprised woman's hands before she could react. Holding Cassie's small hand a moment longer than necessary, he palmed the small gun.

"Silly little thing," he remarked. Glancing at Cassie's scared face, he continued, "But it could go off and hurt somebody. And the way you had it pointed, that somebody would probably have been me."

Cassie jerked her hand from his grasp, glaring when he

smiled easily. Shane leaned into the wagon and put the derringer up out of reach, noting her embarrassment at being so easily outmaneuvered. Silently she watched him turn back to the wheel.

Pushing his hat up on his forehead, Shane squatted down to inspect the damage. "Wheel's not all that's broken. Your axle's busted too."

He swung around as Cassie made a moue of disappointment. "You can fix it, can't you?"

Didn't expect much, did she. He pulled off his Stetson and scratched his shaggy head of chestnut hair.

"No, ma'am. I don't generally carry an extra axle in my saddlebags." She looked ready to puff up again. "But I can get my buckboard and take your stuff to town. We're only a couple of hours from there."

She seemed to wrestle with an answer, and he wondered if it was that hard for her to come up with a simple thank you. 'Course he hadn't done much to gain her confidence. Maybe he'd been on the trail too long—seemed his manners had deserted him. Hell, he hadn't even introduced himself.

"Where you headin'?" he asked, noting their wagon had been packed to overflowing before they'd unloaded it.

"To my uncle's ranch," Cassie finally replied.

Puzzled, he stared at her. He knew all the ranches around. If anyone was expecting an Easterner to show up, the news would have been all over the range by now.

"Who's your uncle?"

"Luke Dalton."

The corner of his mouth, which had turned upward a fraction, tightened abruptly.

"Dalton . . .?" he repeated almost inaudibly.

"Yes," Cassie replied. "You probably knew him. He died not too long ago. His place—"

"I know the place. Are you here to sell the land?"

"Why, no. We're going to try ranching," Cassie replied uncertainly. "Mister . . .?"

"Lancer. Shane Lancer."

Cassie's mouth opened in what seemed to be shock.

At least she'd reacted to his name. So, this was Dalton's niece who'd written back and told him to take his offer to the devil. He had an urge to leave her to that very fate. Would he never be free of the curse of the Daltons?

Shane unhooked a canteen from his pack and tossed it to the boy. "I'll send my buckboard. I expect you'll be all right till then." He had to leave before his temper blew. Mounting the horse, Shane dug his heels into the stallion and galloped away across the changing countryside.

Shane wondered what had possessed the Dalton woman to refuse his offer to buy her out. Why would she travel thousands of miles with only another woman and a young boy as companions?

Shane felt the knot in his craw grow. What was it about the Daltons that made them want to deny the natural order of things? This land had been settled and tamed by Lancers. But did that stop the Daltons from thinking they belonged here? Hell, no. They reminded him of a dog gnawing on a month-old bone, still hoping for a morsel.

Shane couldn't believe she was related to Luke Dalton. But a lifetime of hate would never be forgotten. Or forgiven. The deathbed promise he'd made to his father rang in Shane's head with unending clarity. He would get the Dalton land back for his father no matter what he had to do. He'd been the head of his family for the better part of his thirty-four years, far too long to let the sight of a pretty woman sway him from protecting the interests of the Lazy H.

Straightening in his saddle, Shane followed the line of the mesa that started sloping upward toward his own land. He planned to make sure no more Daltons desecrated his land, and certainly not at the whim of a mere woman, even if she did have eyes the color of ransomed jewels . . .

Cassie remembered the countless nights she'd lain awake trying to decide whether or not to accept her uncle's legacy. Night after night she'd told herself the reasons why she shouldn't give up her teaching job to pursue a wild dream. Each night had been spent listening to her neighbors quarrel through paper-thin walls. Coupling that with the disturbing sounds of crime from the streets below, Cassie was convinced they had to leave the slums.

Since their father's death, she and Andrew had been forced to move to a dreary tenement in a dismal section of Boston. It was all she could afford after the solicitor had absconded with their inheritance, but she'd always envisioned life where home was more than a cramped one-room flat. A life where fear didn't rule. She wanted so much more for Andrew than she could provide on her meager wages, so the inheritance from Uncle Luke had seemed like a godsend.

Now there was no turning back, no job to return to. She had escaped the suffocating life they'd led since her father's death, and nothing would make her give up this chance to make a new start . . .

Cassie felt an unexpected surge of camaraderie with Shane after sharing the miracle of a calf's birth. What a complex man he was, she thought, studying his face as he hunkered down by the newborn animal. She'd have thought a man who owned half the territory wouldn't be bothered by the plight of one of his thousands of cattle.

Because of her help Shane called a silent truce for the moment, letting his bitterness slip aside as he dropped lightly onto the grass at her side. There was plenty of time later to resurrect the past.

Having retrieved the canteen, Shane poured a generous amount of water in his hands and over his arms, washing away the afterbirth. Without asking permission, he picked up her hands, trickled water over them, and gently rubbed them clean with his own.

"What brings you out here?" he questioned.

Cassie purposely kept her eyes on the tottering calf, watching as the mother tenderly licked her new baby.

"Looking for my sheep," she explained briefly, trying to still the sudden breathlessness she felt at his touch.

Releasing her hands, Shane reached out to pull up a blade of weathered grass. Feeling suddenly bereft at the loss of his touch, she tucked her hands at her sides.

"Best I can remember, your uncle always had several dogs helping him, and even then he could have used another," Shane commented, sticking the blade of grass between his teeth and stretching his legs out. "Dogs keep the strays rounded up."

Cassie watched his long legs unfold as her heartbeat irrationally accelerated. His nearness unnerved her now that their shared task was completed. It was hard to remember that she needed to keep him at a distance for more than one reason. She felt her breath catch when he fastened his green eyes on hers.

He plucked another blade of grass, and Cassie tried not to stare as he pushed it past his mustache-covered lip.

Pulling her eyes away from his mouth, she tried to remember what he'd said. Oh, yes, the dogs. She answered shortly, "One of Uncle Luke's dogs died with him—went off the ledge at the same time. Manuelo kept old Pal alive—guess he was grieving pretty bad. I hate to take Pal back now because he's finally getting used to Manuelo, and I do have the other three dogs Manuelo's been taking care of. For now, I'll make do with them. And me."

"And you," he repeated softly as her stomach flip-flopped.

She studied the now dangling blade of grass that was carelessly tucked into the corner of his mouth. He eased the blade to the center of his firm lips. She swallowed, jerking her eyes away.

To her dismay, her gaze landed on his darkening green eyes. She couldn't control the sensations in her stomach that were creeping higher, threatening to cut off her breath. He'd pushed his Stetson back, revealing warm chestnut hair that shone in the sunlight. Cassie nibbled on her lower lip, staring at him.

Unaware of the beguiling picture she made, sitting in the meadow in her rolled-up trousers, hatless with her ebony tresses blowing gently in the breeze, she wondered if he sensed the unwilling attraction she was battling to overcome. The calf bawled, tottering about on unsteady legs. Cassie laughed in delight.

"I'm kind of looking forward to my new lambs now."

But Shane didn't seem to hear. She listened distractedly as her own laughter floated away on the wind. Gazing into her delicately carved face, Shane felt a sharp pang of regret that this vulnerable-looking woman was related to the man he'd sworn to avenge. He knew she had unwittingly stepped into a fight that had dominated a generation and torn apart a community. But he also knew he could not let past promises go unfulfilled.

One thing had set him on his heels: a woman who would peel off her stockings in the middle of a meadow just to help a cow. As though they shared a moment suspended out of time—out of reach with the past—he grasped her face in his hands.

As his lips captured hers, Cassie thought inanely that the lines near his eyes were even more fascinating up close than they'd been at a distance. The warm fullness of his lips, coupled with the incredible teasing of his mustache, launched Cassie into a world of sensation she wondered if she'd forgotten or had never really known.

It seemed perfectly natural to melt against the solidity of his body. As Shane gently grasped the long tresses of hair that flowed about her shoulders, Cassie felt a tingling response ricochet through her body. When his other hand massaged the tender flesh of her neck and exposed throat, Cassie felt her own fire build.

As the kiss deepened, Cassie shivered at the feelings his touch created. At the first thrust of his tongue, Cassie felt momentary alarm, but she quickly discarded it in the persistent rush of emotion that followed.

And, if possible, she entered even closer into his embrace. His tongue washed over hers, seeking, finding. Each thrust sent a bolt of liquid desire. Feeling his tongue stroking the recesses of her mouth, she weakened, feeling the heat searing a path through her body. One hand rested of its own accord on the thick expanse of corded muscle on his shoulder. The other wound itself through the thick locks of his shaggy chestnut hair.

When Shane pressed even closer, she felt the unfamiliar hardness of his male body. Gulping, she swallowed the ache that filled her throat and traveled downward at an alarming rate. An unexpected tingle between her thighs ignited as he ground himself even closer. Heavy dregs of honeylike warmth weighted down her limbs.

When Cassie thought she'd die of the exquisite agony he was causing, he pulled away abruptly. She searched his eyes for the reason and saw a blaze of desire tinged with undisguised regret. Then his eyes hardened into the flinty coals she'd remembered from the day before.

Cassie flushed hotly. What must he think of her? That she was a frustrated old maid ready to literally throw herself at the first available man?

"Cassie, you don't belong here. Most women would see that and sell out."

Unaware of the demons chasing him, Cassie flinched at his words. The warmth in her limbs was replaced by a slow chilling wash of reality. Their kiss had meant nothing. He was still trying to run her off—and she could never let herself slip and forget it.

Shakily she rose to her feet, unable to banish her own regret. Her emotion-filled voice was as soft as the breeze that whispered about them.

"You're right, but then I'm not most women."

Diamond Wildflower Romance

A breathtaking new line of spectacular novels set in the untamed frontier of the American West. Every month, Diamond Wildflower brings you new adventures where passionate men and women dare to embrace their boldest dreams. Finally, romances that capture the very spirit and passion of the wild frontier.

___*SUMMER ROSE* by Bonnie K. Winn
1-55773-734-7/$4.99
___*OUTLAW HEART* by Catherine Palmer
1-55773-735-5/$4.99
___*FRONTIER BRIDE* by Ann Carberry
1-55773-753-3/$4.99 (August 1992)
___*CAPTIVE ANGEL* by Elaine Crawford
1-55773-735-5/$4.99 (September 1992)

411

In the tradition of <u>Clan of the Cave Bear</u>, a remarkable story of one woman's quest in a world of untouched splendor...

National bestselling author
Lynn Armistead McKee

WOMAN OF THE MISTS

Among the tropical lands of America before Columbus, a proud people thrived. In this lush land, Teeka was awakening to the pleasures of love. In the eyes of Auro, the village shaman's son, young Teeka saw hope and desire, and a dream of discovering the mysteries of the heart. Until a rival tribe invaded their land, and a forceful warrior took Teeka as his bounty. He freed her heart to a fierce passion—and fulfilled the promise of love that lived within her soul...

___1-55773-520-4/$4.95

TOUCHES THE STARS

Among the tribes of the ancient everglades, no one was more powerful than the shaman. Born under a shooting star, Mi-sa was the shaman's daughter and inheritor of his magical gifts. She forged her own destiny of love and courage, despite the fear and hatred felt by her people. Her gift of vision could forever change the fate of a blossoming new world.

___1-55773-752-5/$5.50

352